A Biblical Epic

Kingdoms™

Scions of Josiah

Scions of Josiah
Copyright © 2007 by Lamp Post, Inc.

Requests for information should be addressed to:

Zondervan, *Grand Rapids, Michigan* 49530

Library of Congress Cataloging-in-Publication Data

Avery, Ben, 1974-
    Scions of Josiah / story by Ben Avery; art by Harold Edge.
        p. cm. -- (Kingdoms: a biblical epic; bk. 2)
        ISBN-13: 978-0-310-71354-8 (softcover)
        ISBN-10: 0-310-71354-4 (softcover)
        1. Graphic novels. I. Edge, Harold. II. Title.
        PN6727.A945S35 2007
        741.5'973--dc22

                                                              2007003149

This book published in conjunction with Lamp Post, Inc.; 8367 Lemon Avenue, La Mesa, CA 91941

Series Editor: Bud Rogers
Editor: Brett Burner
Managing Editor: Bruce Nuffer
Managing Art Director: Sarah Molegraaf

Printed in the United States of America

07 08 09 10 11 12 • 8 7 6 5 4 3 2 1

A Biblical Epic

Kingdoms™

Scions of Josiah

Series Editor: Bud Rogers
Story by Ben Avery
Art by Harold Edge and Mat Broome

ZONDERVAN®

LAMP POST

ZONDERVAN.com/
AUTHORTRACKER
follow your favorite authors

PROLOGUE
"The Manner of a King"

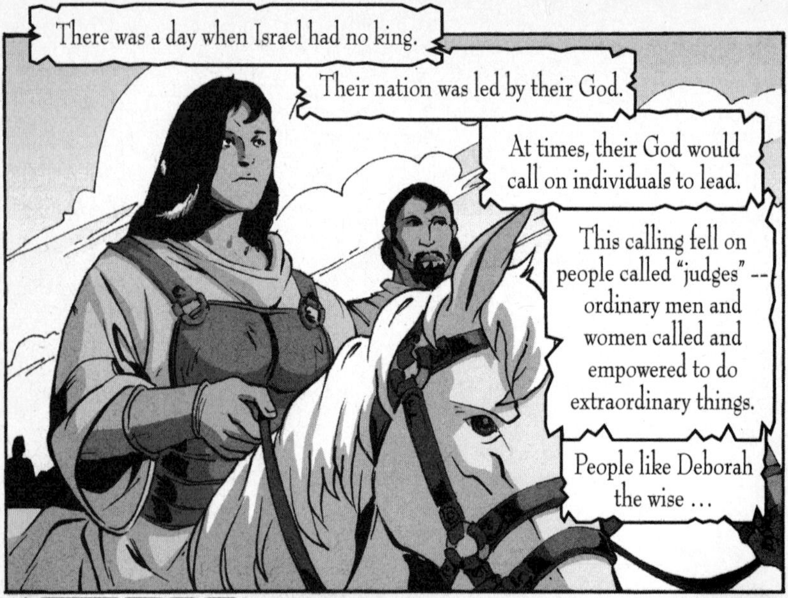
There was a day when Israel had no king.
Their nation was led by their God.
At times, their God would call on individuals to lead.
This calling fell on people called "judges" -- ordinary men and women called and empowered to do extraordinary things.
People like Deborah the wise ...

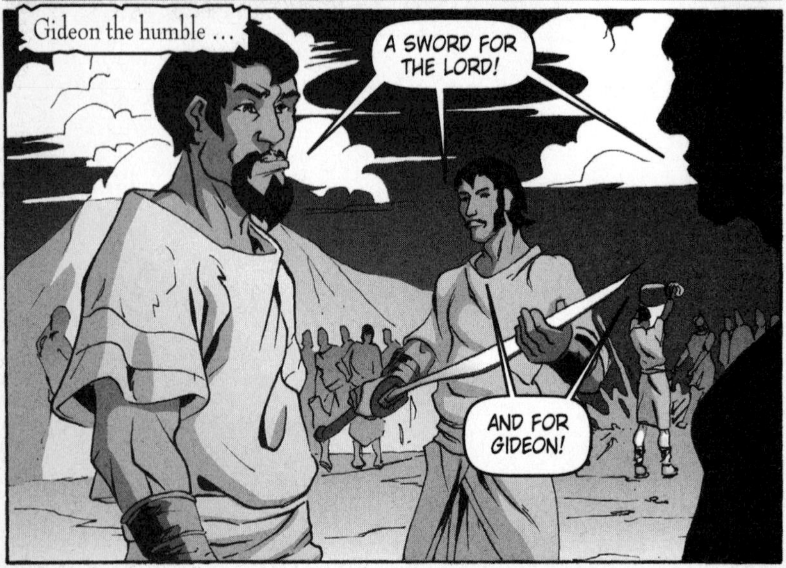
Gideon the humble ...
A SWORD FOR THE LORD!
AND FOR GIDEON!

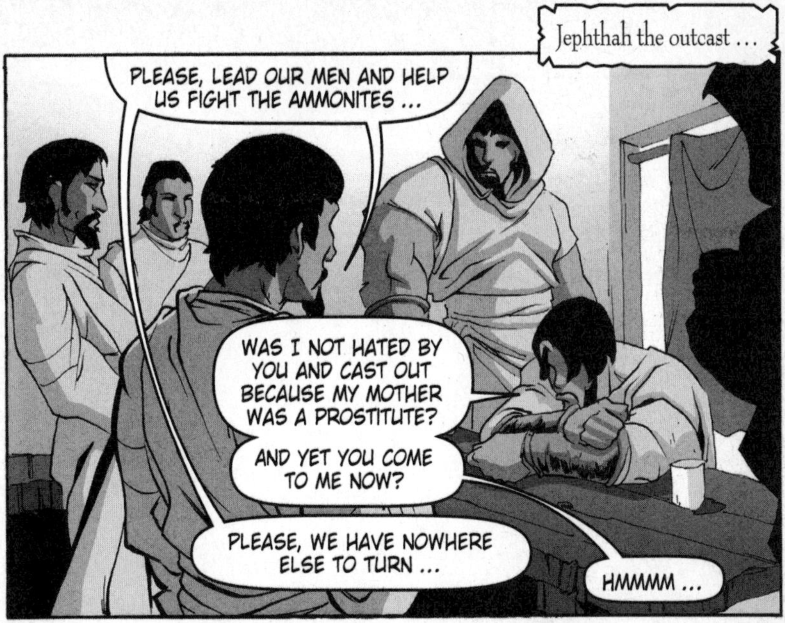
Jephthah the outcast ...
PLEASE, LEAD OUR MEN AND HELP US FIGHT THE AMMONITES ...
WAS I NOT HATED BY YOU AND CAST OUT BECAUSE MY MOTHER WAS A PROSTITUTE?
AND YET YOU COME TO ME NOW?
PLEASE, WE HAVE NOWHERE ELSE TO TURN ...
HMMMM ...

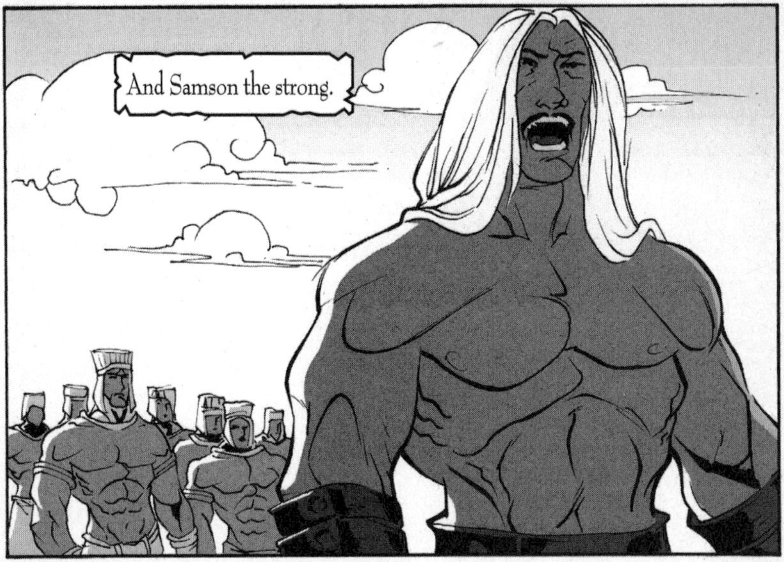
And Samson the strong.

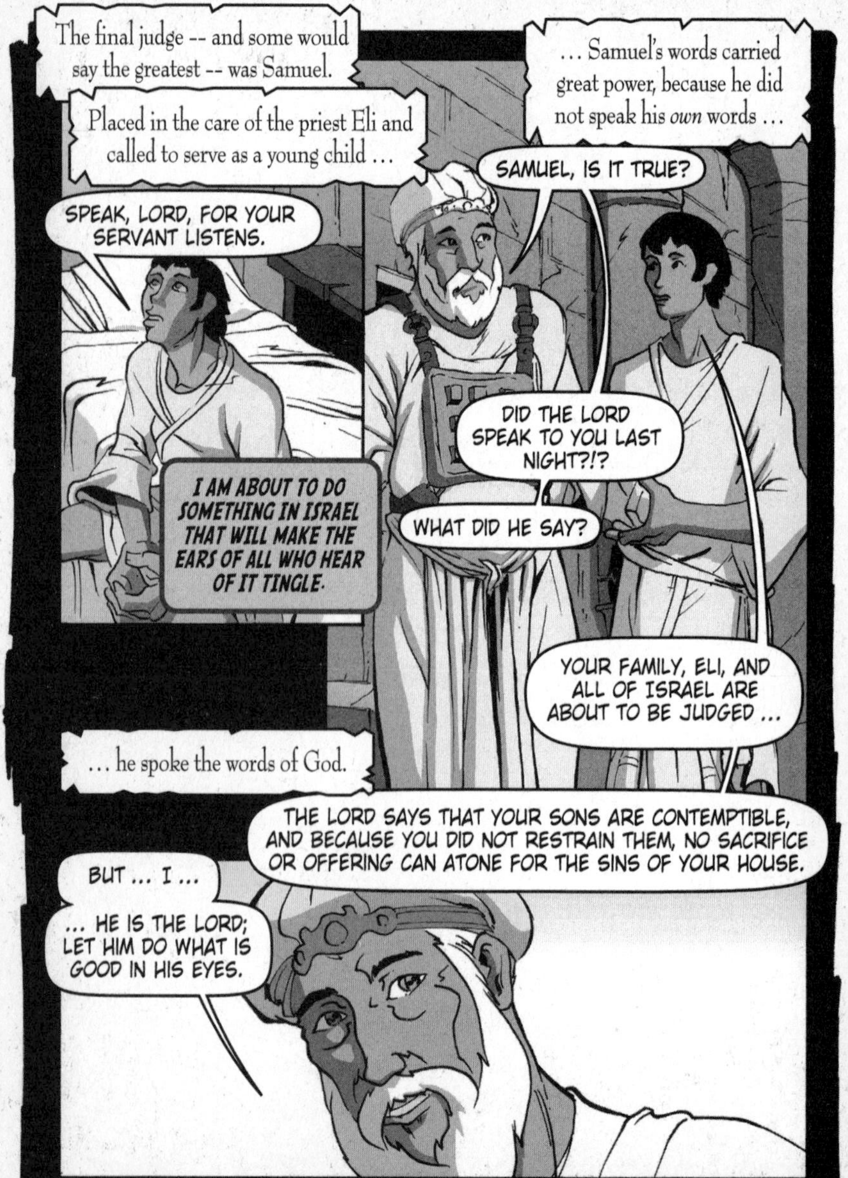
The final judge -- and some would say the greatest -- was Samuel.
Placed in the care of the priest Eli and called to serve as a young child ...
SPEAK, LORD, FOR YOUR SERVANT LISTENS.
I AM ABOUT TO DO SOMETHING IN ISRAEL THAT WILL MAKE THE EARS OF ALL WHO HEAR OF IT TINGLE.
... Samuel's words carried great power, because he did not speak his *own* words ...
SAMUEL, IS IT TRUE?
DID THE LORD SPEAK TO YOU LAST NIGHT?!?
WHAT DID HE SAY?
YOUR FAMILY, ELI, AND ALL OF ISRAEL ARE ABOUT TO BE JUDGED ...
... he spoke the words of God.
THE LORD SAYS THAT YOUR SONS ARE CONTEMPTIBLE, AND BECAUSE YOU DID NOT RESTRAIN THEM, NO SACRIFICE OR OFFERING CAN ATONE FOR THE SINS OF YOUR HOUSE.
BUT ... I ...
... HE IS THE LORD; LET HIM DO WHAT IS GOOD IN HIS EYES.

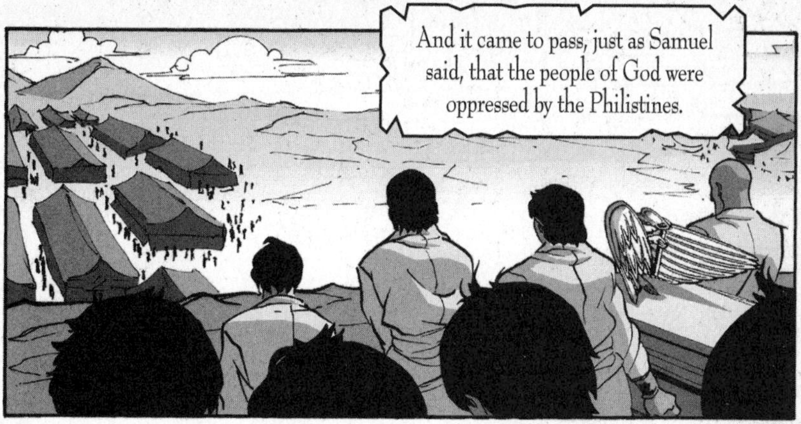
And it came to pass, just as Samuel said, that the people of God were oppressed by the Philistines.

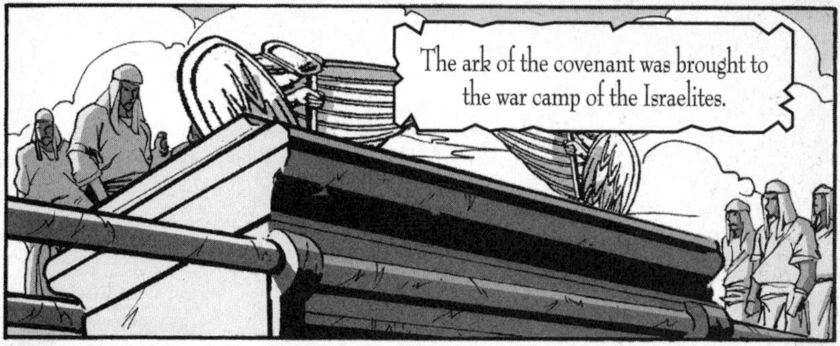
The ark of the covenant was brought to the war camp of the Israelites.

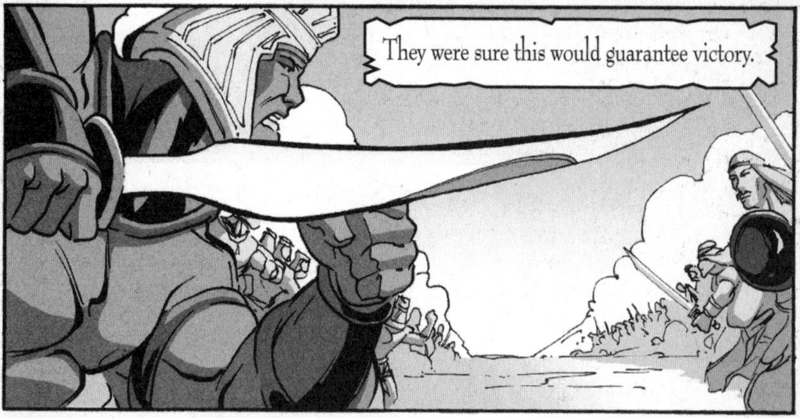
They were sure this would guarantee victory.

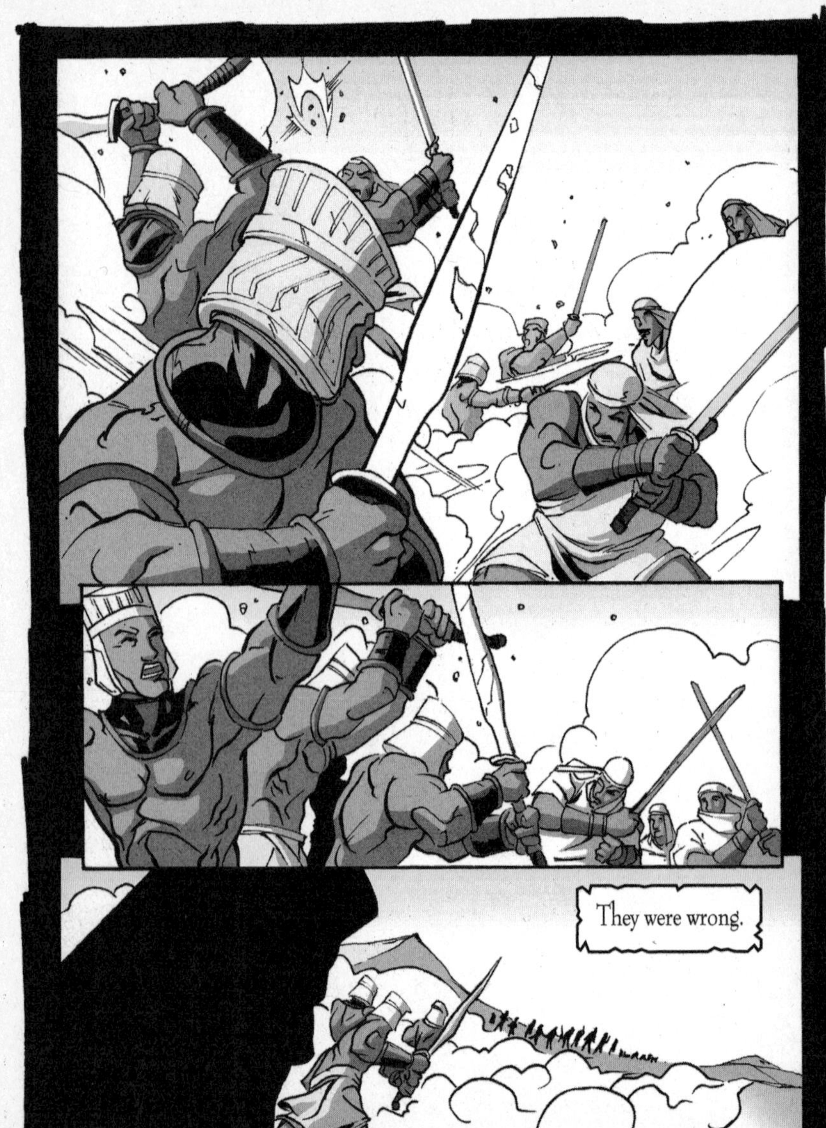
They were wrong.

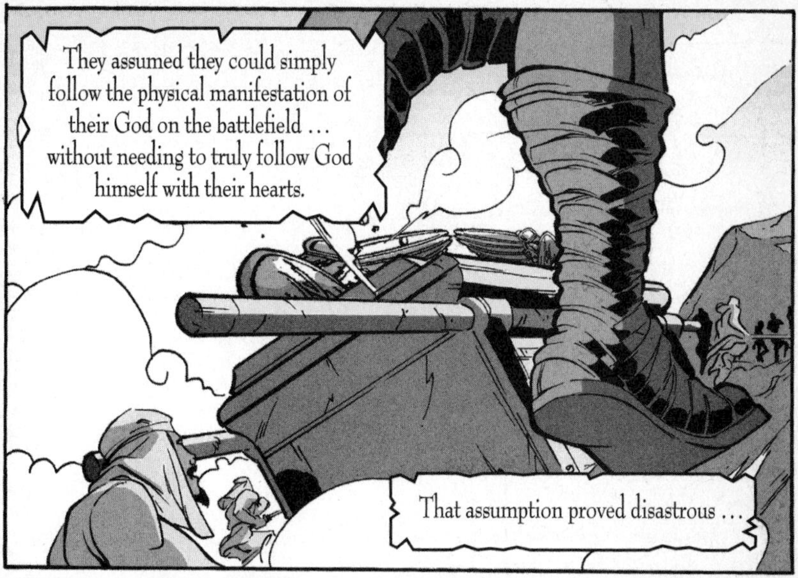
They assumed they could simply follow the physical manifestation of their God on the battlefield … without needing to truly follow God himself with their hearts.
That assumption proved disastrous …

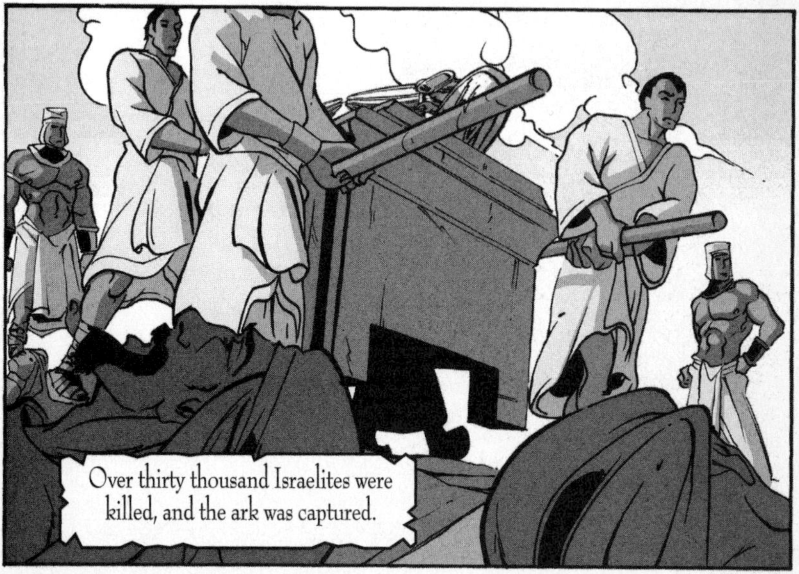
Over thirty thousand Israelites were killed, and the ark was captured.

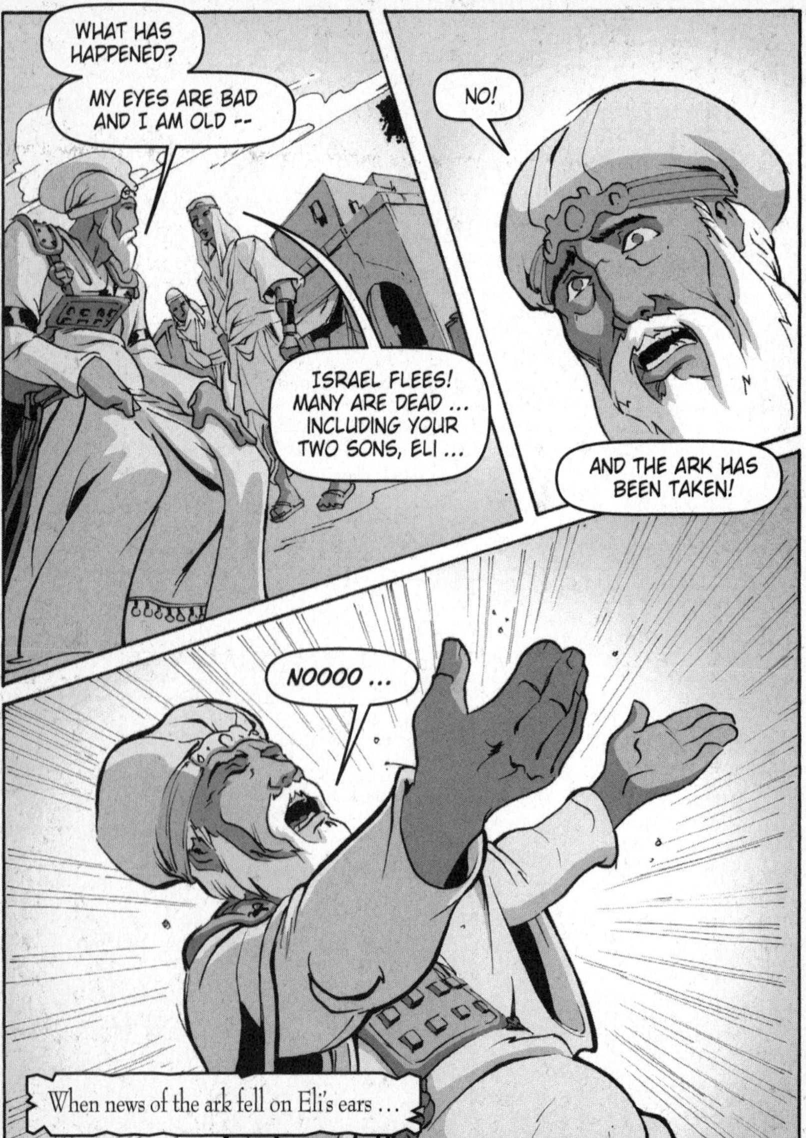
WHAT HAS HAPPENED?
MY EYES ARE BAD AND I AM OLD --
ISRAEL FLEES! MANY ARE DEAD ... INCLUDING YOUR TWO SONS, ELI ...
NO!
AND THE ARK HAS BEEN TAKEN!
NOOOO ...
When news of the ark fell on Eli's ears ...

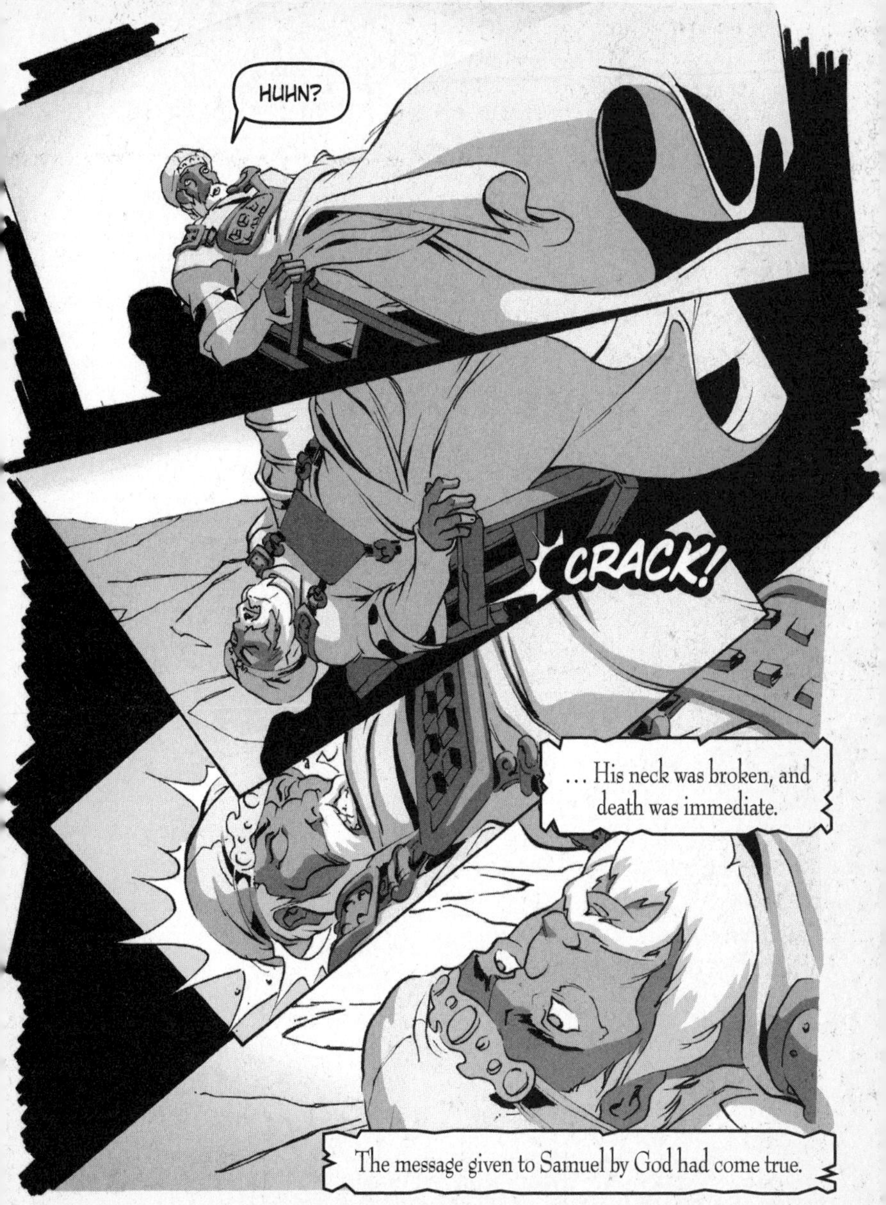
HUHN?
CRACK!
... His neck was broken, and death was immediate.
The message given to Samuel by God had come true.

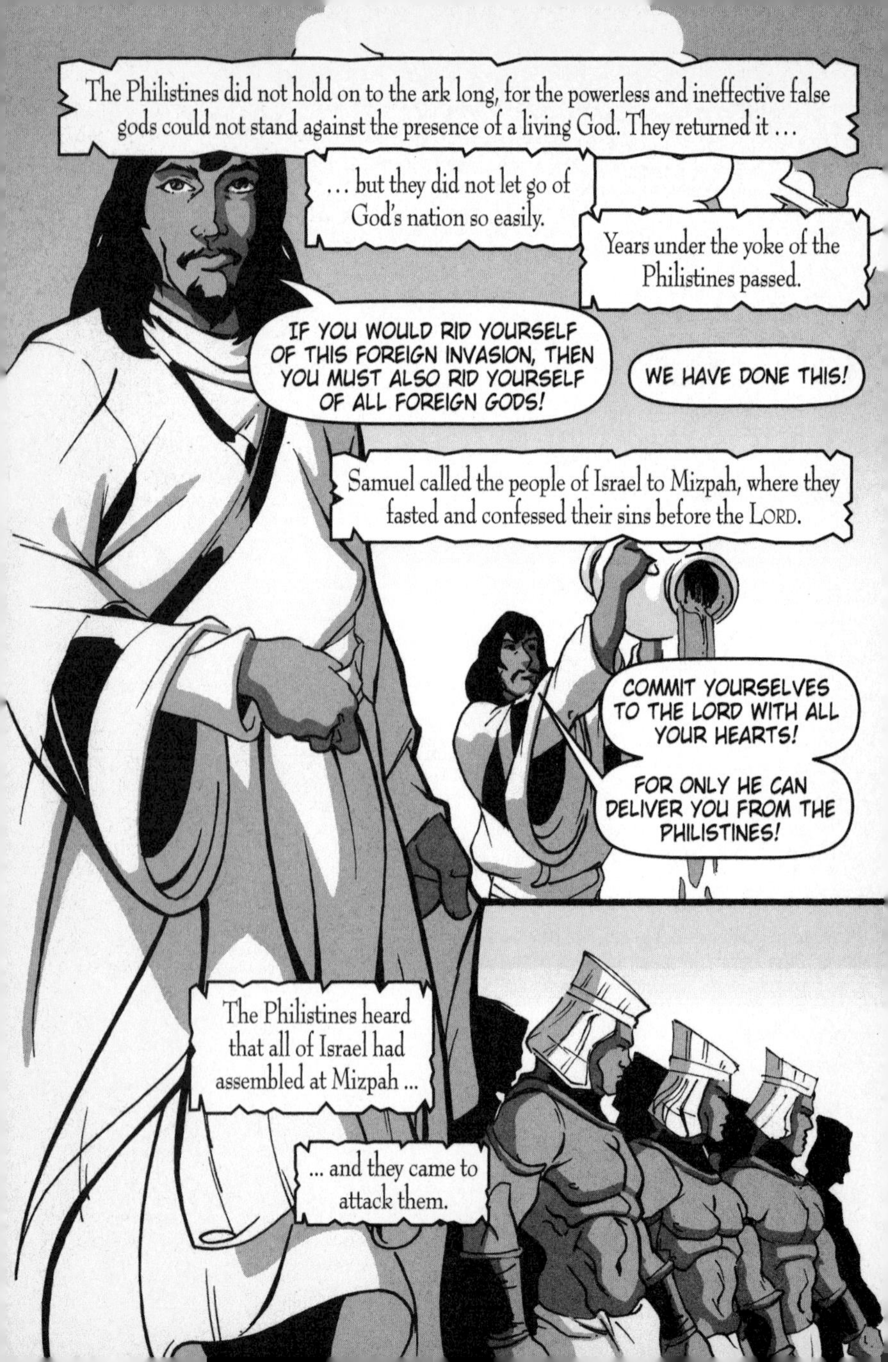

The Philistines did not hold on to the ark long, for the powerless and ineffective false gods could not stand against the presence of a living God. They returned it …
… but they did not let go of God's nation so easily.
Years under the yoke of the Philistines passed.
IF YOU WOULD RID YOURSELF OF THIS FOREIGN INVASION, THEN YOU MUST ALSO RID YOURSELF OF ALL FOREIGN GODS!
WE HAVE DONE THIS!
Samuel called the people of Israel to Mizpah, where they fasted and confessed their sins before the LORD.
COMMIT YOURSELVES TO THE LORD WITH ALL YOUR HEARTS!
FOR ONLY HE CAN DELIVER YOU FROM THE PHILISTINES!
The Philistines heard that all of Israel had assembled at Mizpah ...
... and they came to attack them.

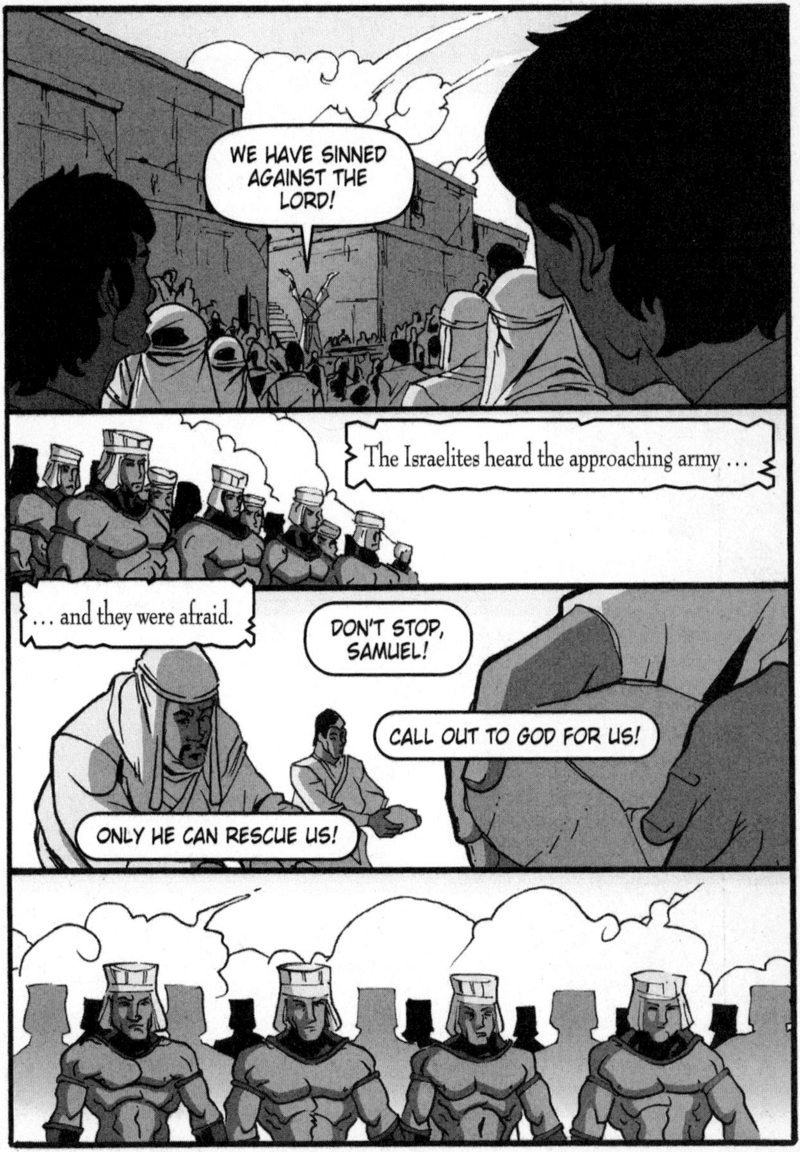
WE HAVE SINNED AGAINST THE LORD!
The Israelites heard the approaching army …
… and they were afraid.
DON'T STOP, SAMUEL!
CALL OUT TO GOD FOR US!
ONLY HE CAN RESCUE US!

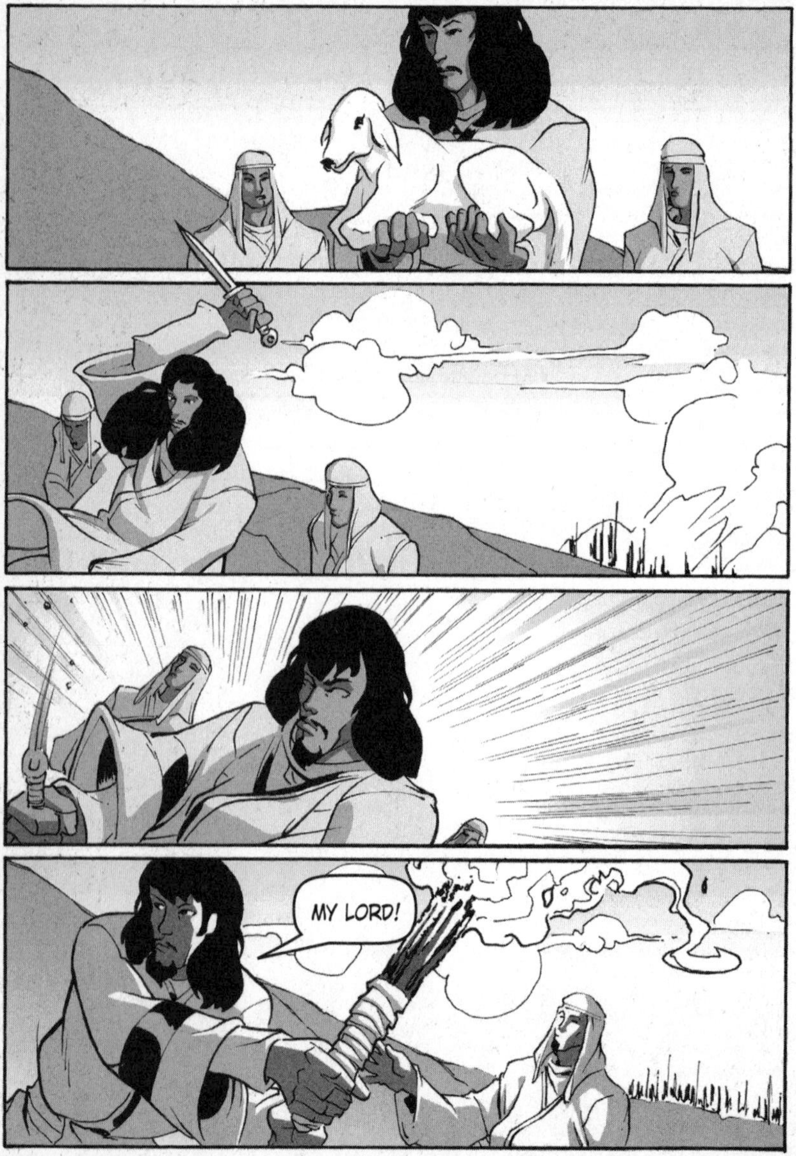
MY LORD!

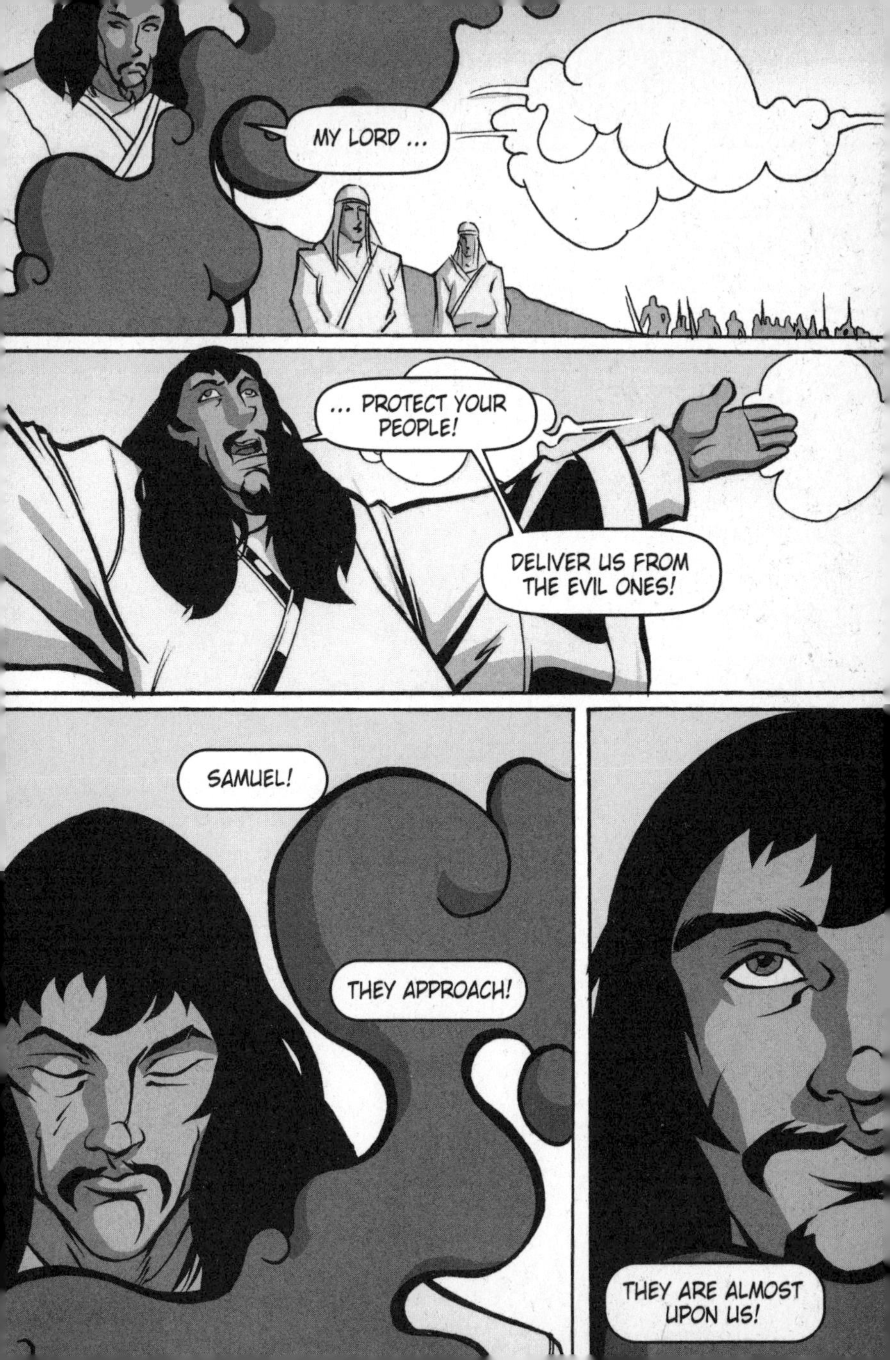
MY LORD ...
... PROTECT YOUR PEOPLE!
DELIVER US FROM THE EVIL ONES!
SAMUEL!
THEY APPROACH!
THEY ARE ALMOST UPON US!

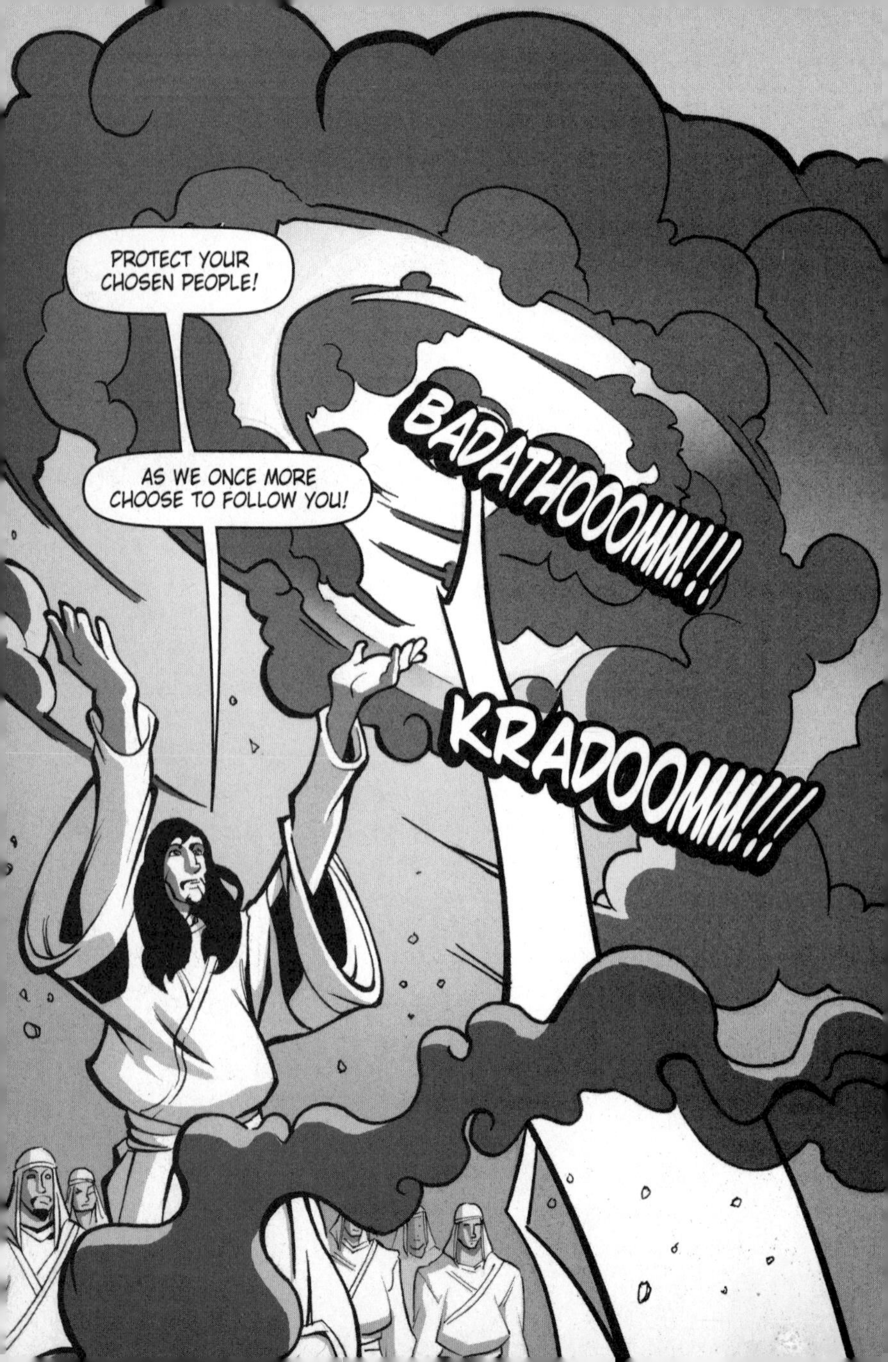
PROTECT YOUR CHOSEN PEOPLE!
AS WE ONCE MORE CHOOSE TO FOLLOW YOU!
BADATHOOOMM!!!
KRADOOMM!!!

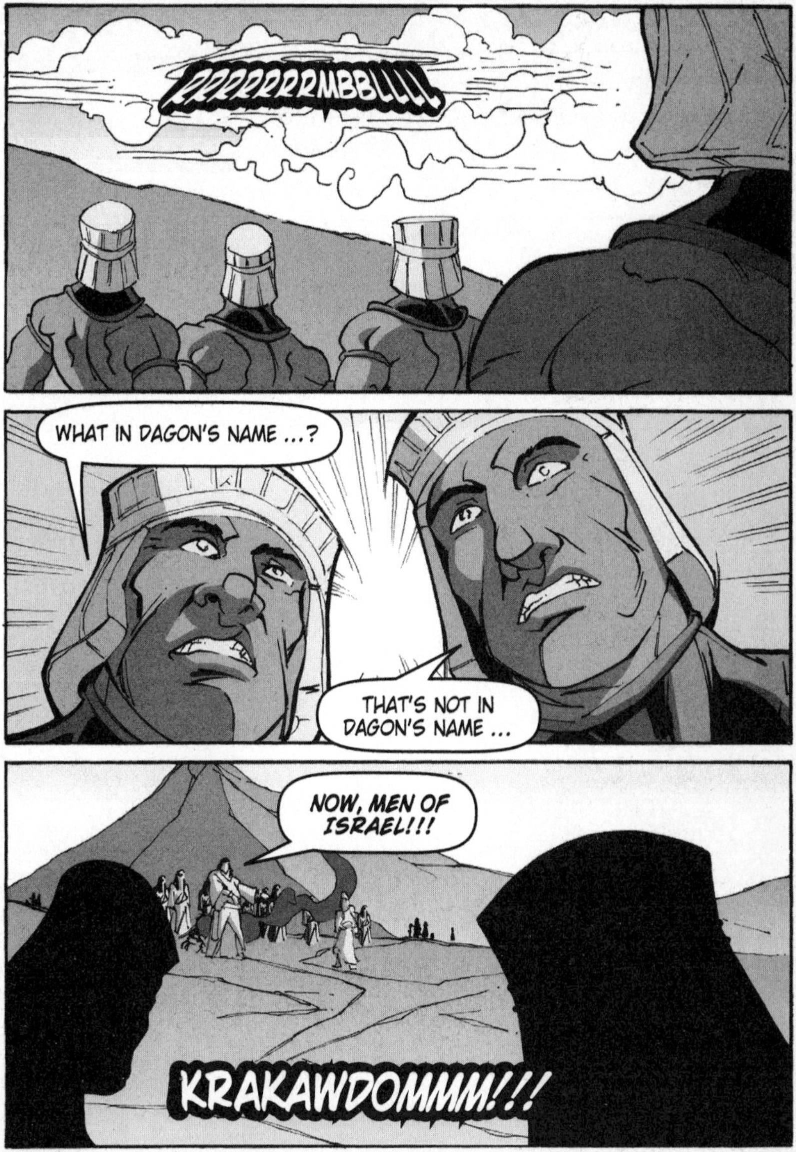
RRRRRRRRMBBLLLLL
WHAT IN DAGON'S NAME ...?
THAT'S NOT IN DAGON'S NAME ...
NOW, MEN OF ISRAEL!!!
KRAKAWDOMMM!!!

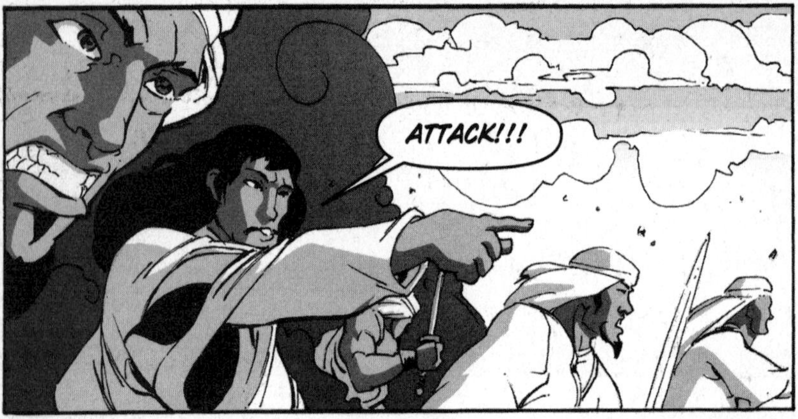
ATTACK!!!

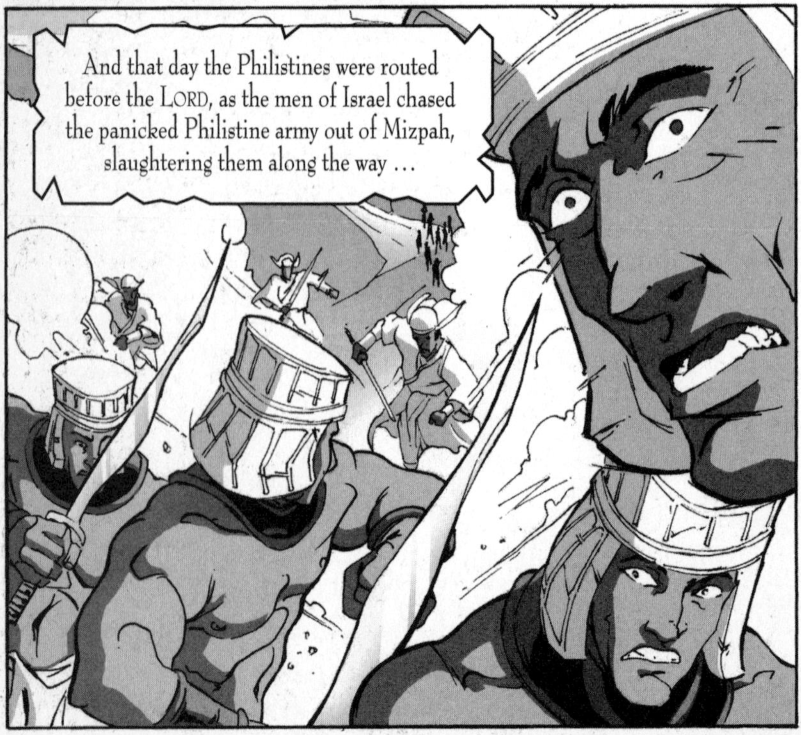
And that day the Philistines were routed before the LORD, as the men of Israel chased the panicked Philistine army out of Mizpah, slaughtering them along the way …

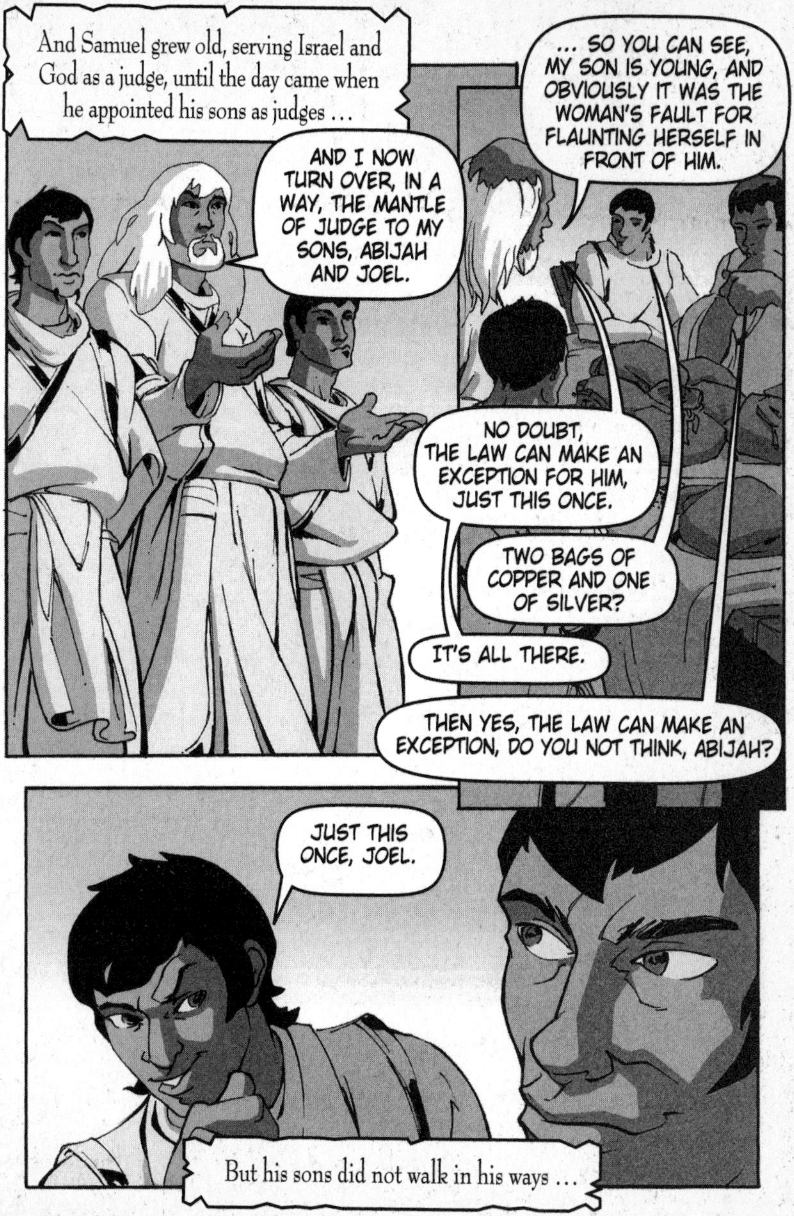
And Samuel grew old, serving Israel and God as a judge, until the day came when he appointed his sons as judges …
AND I NOW TURN OVER, IN A WAY, THE MANTLE OF JUDGE TO MY SONS, ABIJAH AND JOEL.
… SO YOU CAN SEE, MY SON IS YOUNG, AND OBVIOUSLY IT WAS THE WOMAN'S FAULT FOR FLAUNTING HERSELF IN FRONT OF HIM.
NO DOUBT, THE LAW CAN MAKE AN EXCEPTION FOR HIM, JUST THIS ONCE.
TWO BAGS OF COPPER AND ONE OF SILVER?
IT'S ALL THERE.
THEN YES, THE LAW CAN MAKE AN EXCEPTION, DO YOU NOT THINK, ABIJAH?
JUST THIS ONCE, JOEL.
But his sons did not walk in his ways …

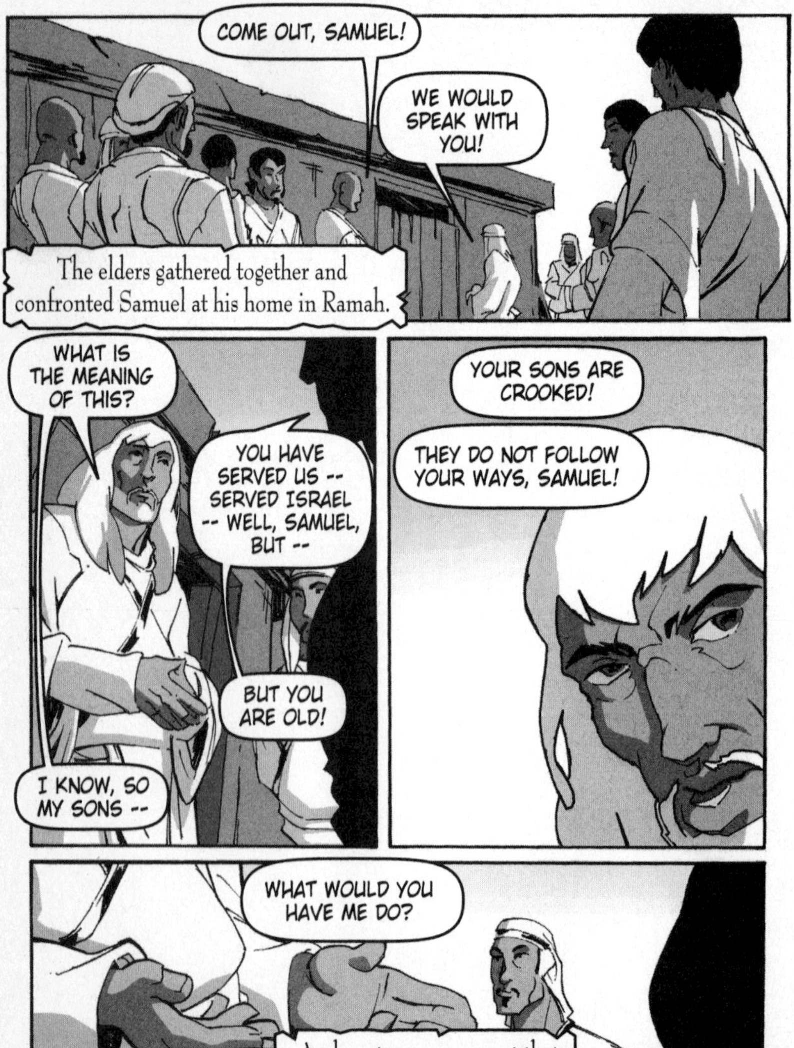
COME OUT, SAMUEL!
WE WOULD SPEAK WITH YOU!
The elders gathered together and confronted Samuel at his home in Ramah.
WHAT IS THE MEANING OF THIS?
YOU HAVE SERVED US -- SERVED ISRAEL -- WELL, SAMUEL, BUT --
BUT YOU ARE OLD!
I KNOW, SO MY SONS --
YOUR SONS ARE CROOKED!
THEY DO NOT FOLLOW YOUR WAYS, SAMUEL!
WHAT WOULD YOU HAVE ME DO?
And next came a request that would change all of Israel ...
... forever.

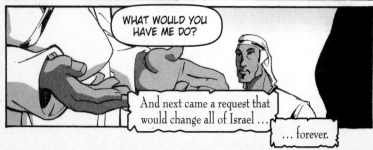

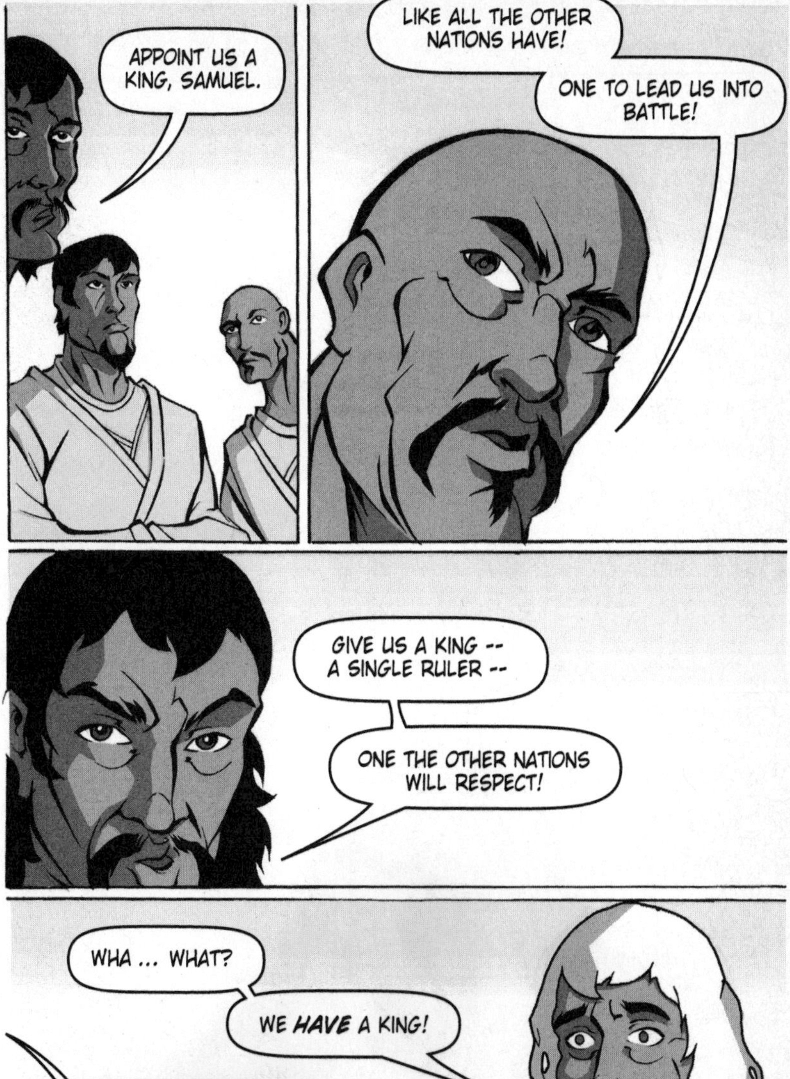

APPOINT US A KING, SAMUEL.
LIKE ALL THE OTHER NATIONS HAVE!
ONE TO LEAD US INTO BATTLE!
GIVE US A KING -- A SINGLE RULER --
ONE THE OTHER NATIONS WILL RESPECT!
WHA ... WHAT?
WE HAVE A KING!
WE WANT SOMEONE WITH A FACE THE OTHER RULERS AND KINGS CAN SEE AND HEAR!!!

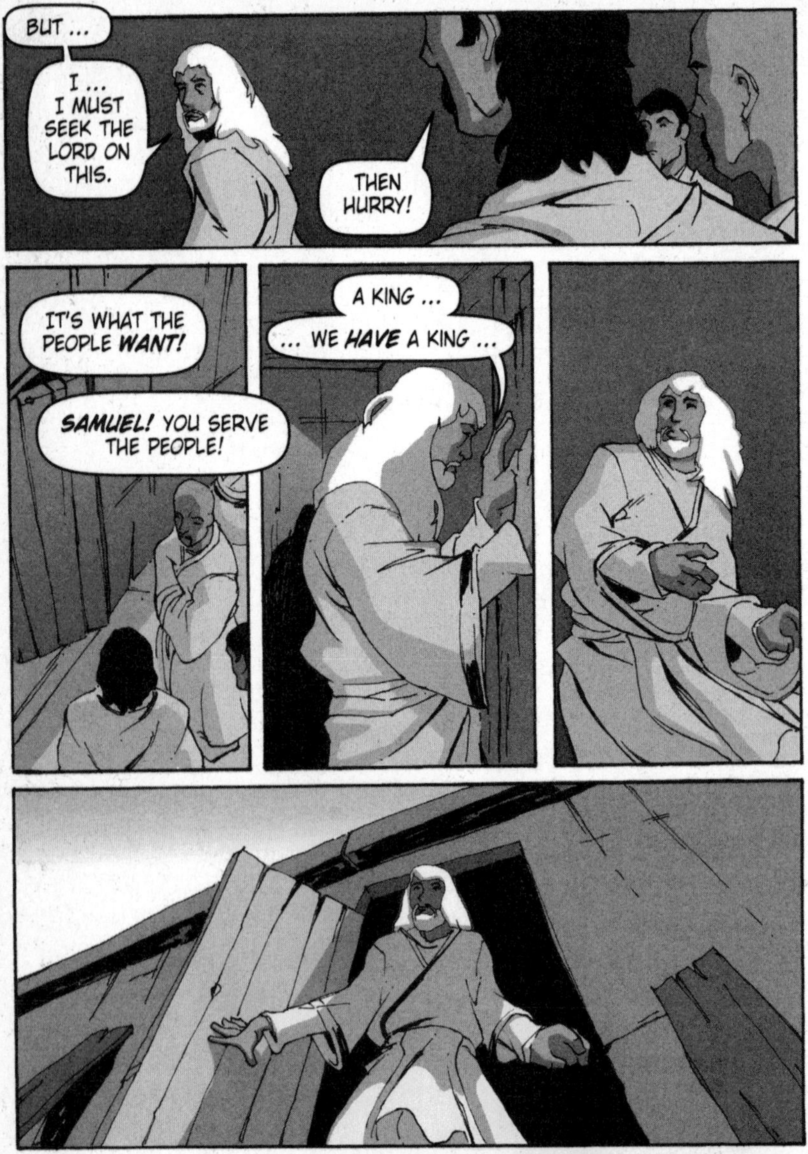
BUT ...
I ... I MUST SEEK THE LORD ON THIS.
THEN HURRY!
IT'S WHAT THE PEOPLE WANT!
SAMUEL! YOU SERVE THE PEOPLE!
A KING ...
... WE HAVE A KING ...

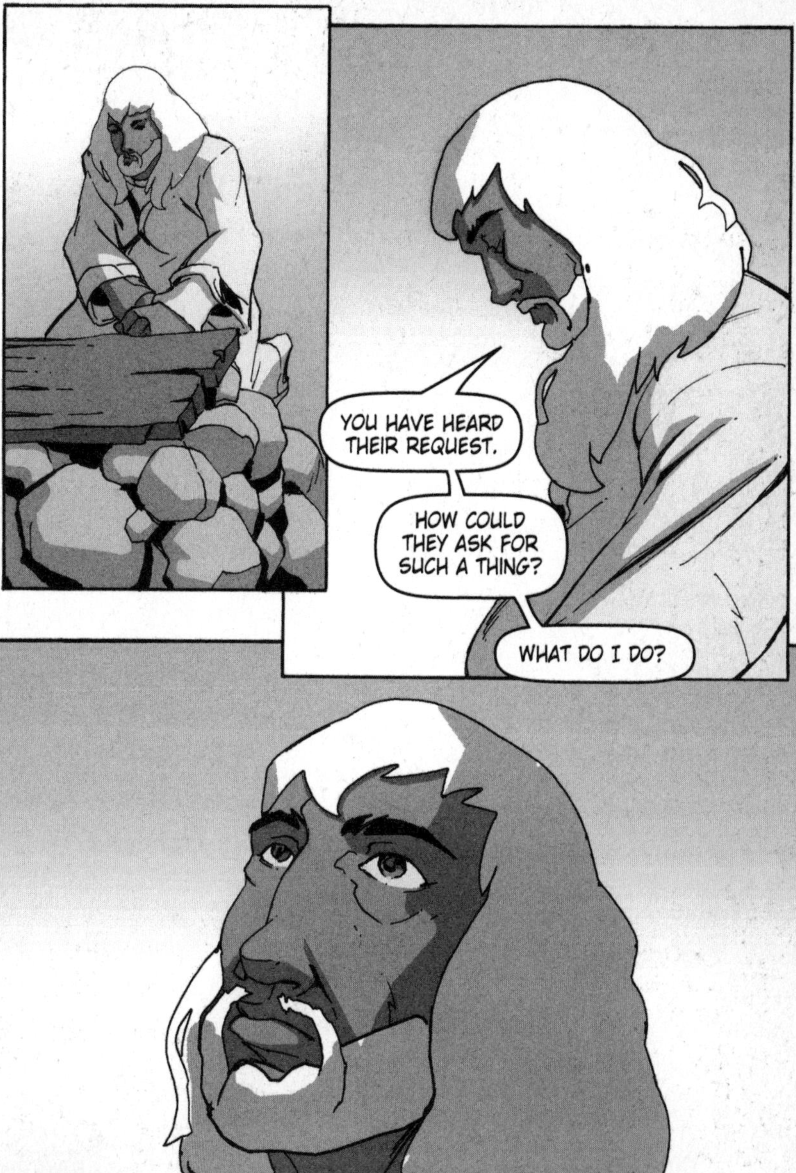
YOU HAVE HEARD THEIR REQUEST.
HOW COULD THEY ASK FOR SUCH A THING?
WHAT DO I DO?

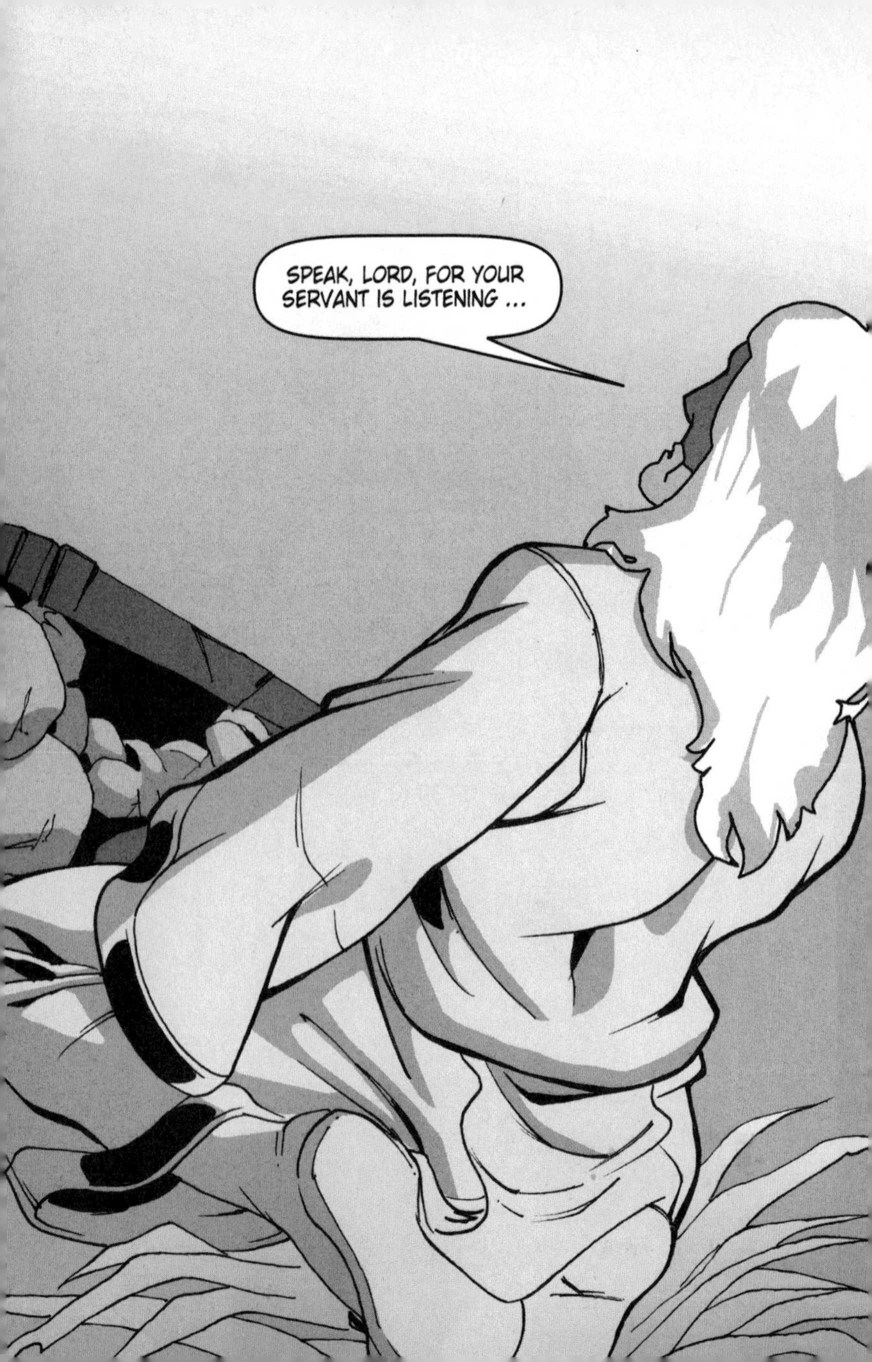
SPEAK, LORD, FOR YOUR SERVANT IS LISTENING ...

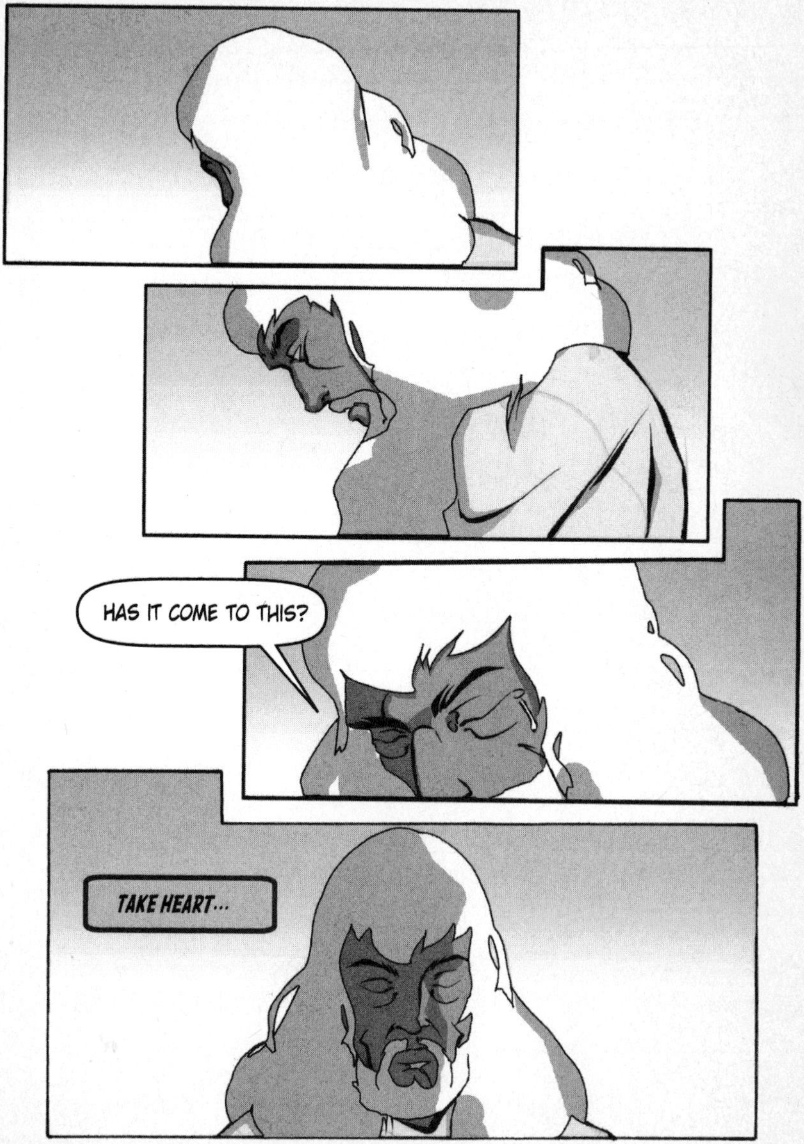
HAS IT COME TO THIS?
TAKE HEART...

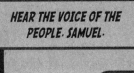
HEAR THE VOICE OF THE PEOPLE, SAMUEL.

THEY HAVE NOT REJECTED YOU: THEY HAVE REJECTED ME AS THEIR KING.

AS THEY HAVE DONE SINCE THE DAY I BROUGHT THEM OUT OF EGYPT UP UNTIL THIS DAY. AS THEY HAVE FORSAKEN ME FOR OTHER GODS DURING THAT TIME, SO THEY ARE DOING NOW WITH YOU.

SO HEAR THEIR VOICE.

BUT WARN THEM SOLEMNLY, TAKING CARE TO MAKE SURE THEY KNOW THE MANNER OF THE KING THAT SHALL REIGN OVER THEM.

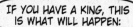

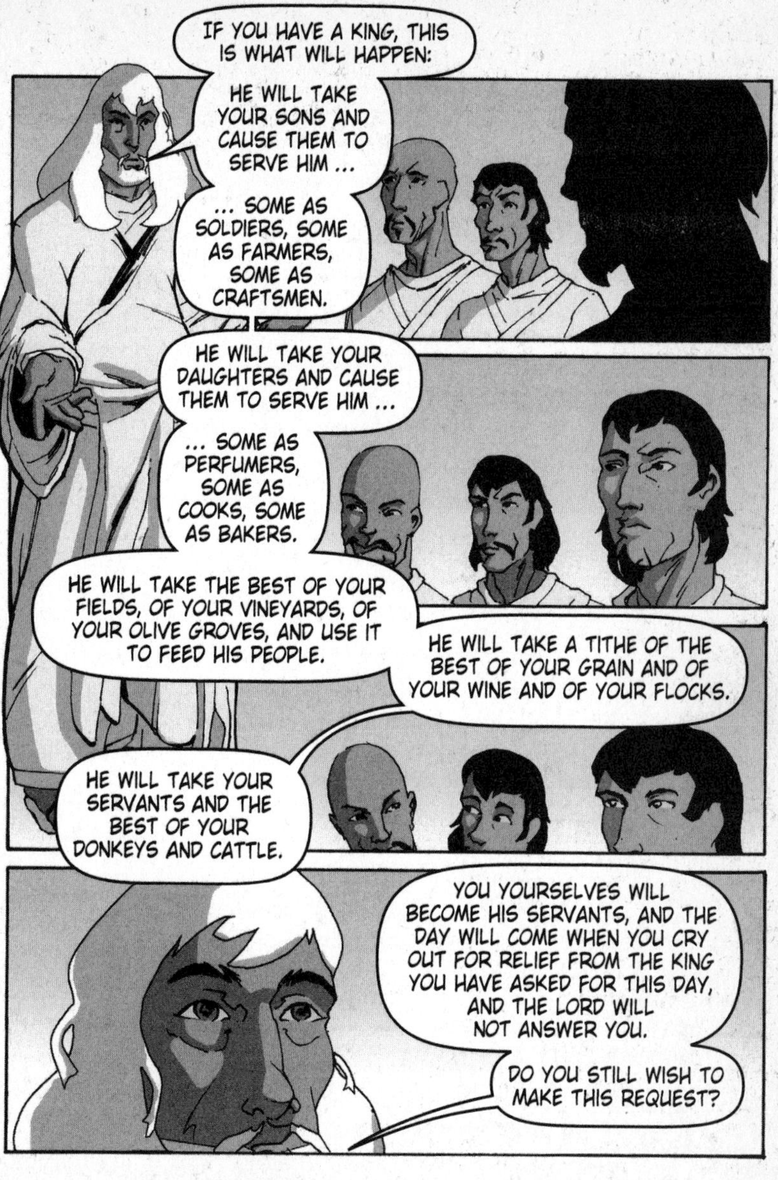

IF YOU HAVE A KING, THIS IS WHAT WILL HAPPEN:

HE WILL TAKE YOUR SONS AND CAUSE THEM TO SERVE HIM ...

... SOME AS SOLDIERS, SOME AS FARMERS, SOME AS CRAFTSMEN.

HE WILL TAKE YOUR DAUGHTERS AND CAUSE THEM TO SERVE HIM ...

... SOME AS PERFUMERS, SOME AS COOKS, SOME AS BAKERS.

HE WILL TAKE THE BEST OF YOUR FIELDS, OF YOUR VINEYARDS, OF YOUR OLIVE GROVES, AND USE IT TO FEED HIS PEOPLE.

HE WILL TAKE A TITHE OF THE BEST OF YOUR GRAIN AND OF YOUR WINE AND OF YOUR FLOCKS.

HE WILL TAKE YOUR SERVANTS AND THE BEST OF YOUR DONKEYS AND CATTLE.

YOU YOURSELVES WILL BECOME HIS SERVANTS, AND THE DAY WILL COME WHEN YOU CRY OUT FOR RELIEF FROM THE KING YOU HAVE ASKED FOR THIS DAY, AND THE LORD WILL NOT ANSWER YOU.

DO YOU STILL WISH TO MAKE THIS REQUEST?

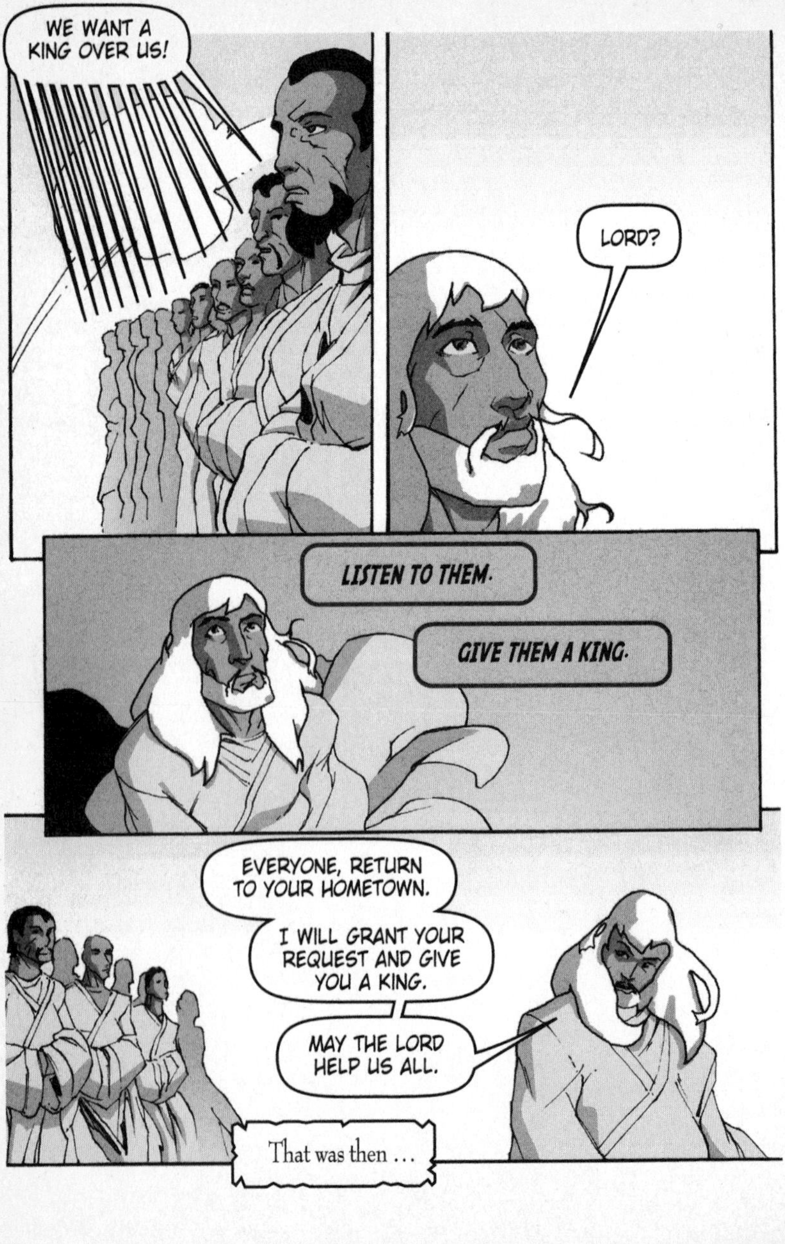
WE WANT A KING OVER US!
LORD?
LISTEN TO THEM.
GIVE THEM A KING.
EVERYONE, RETURN TO YOUR HOMETOWN.
I WILL GRANT YOUR REQUEST AND GIVE YOU A KING.
MAY THE LORD HELP US ALL.
That was then …

CHAPTER ONE
"The Fool"

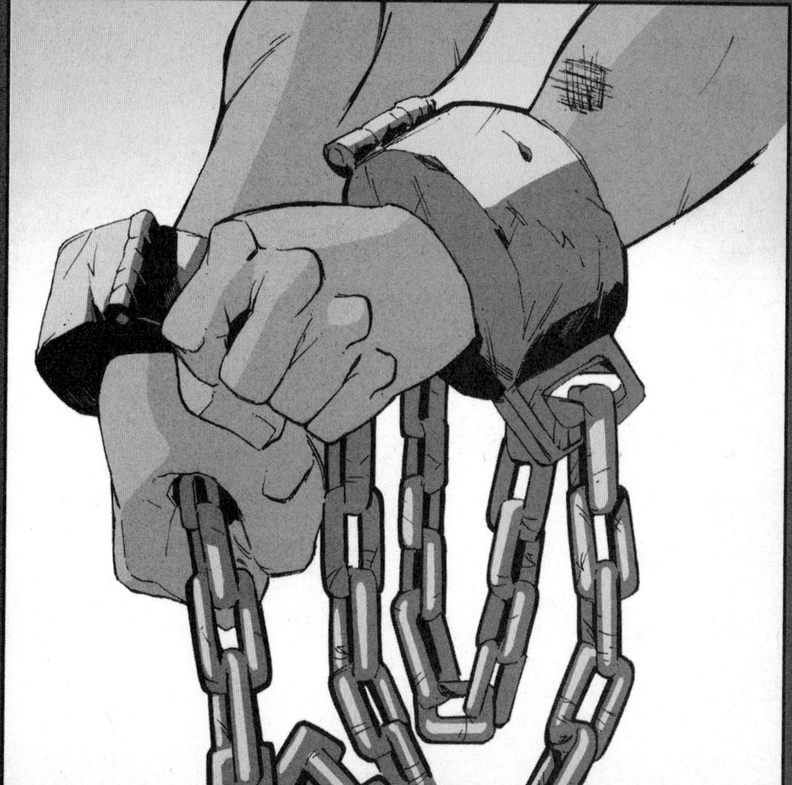

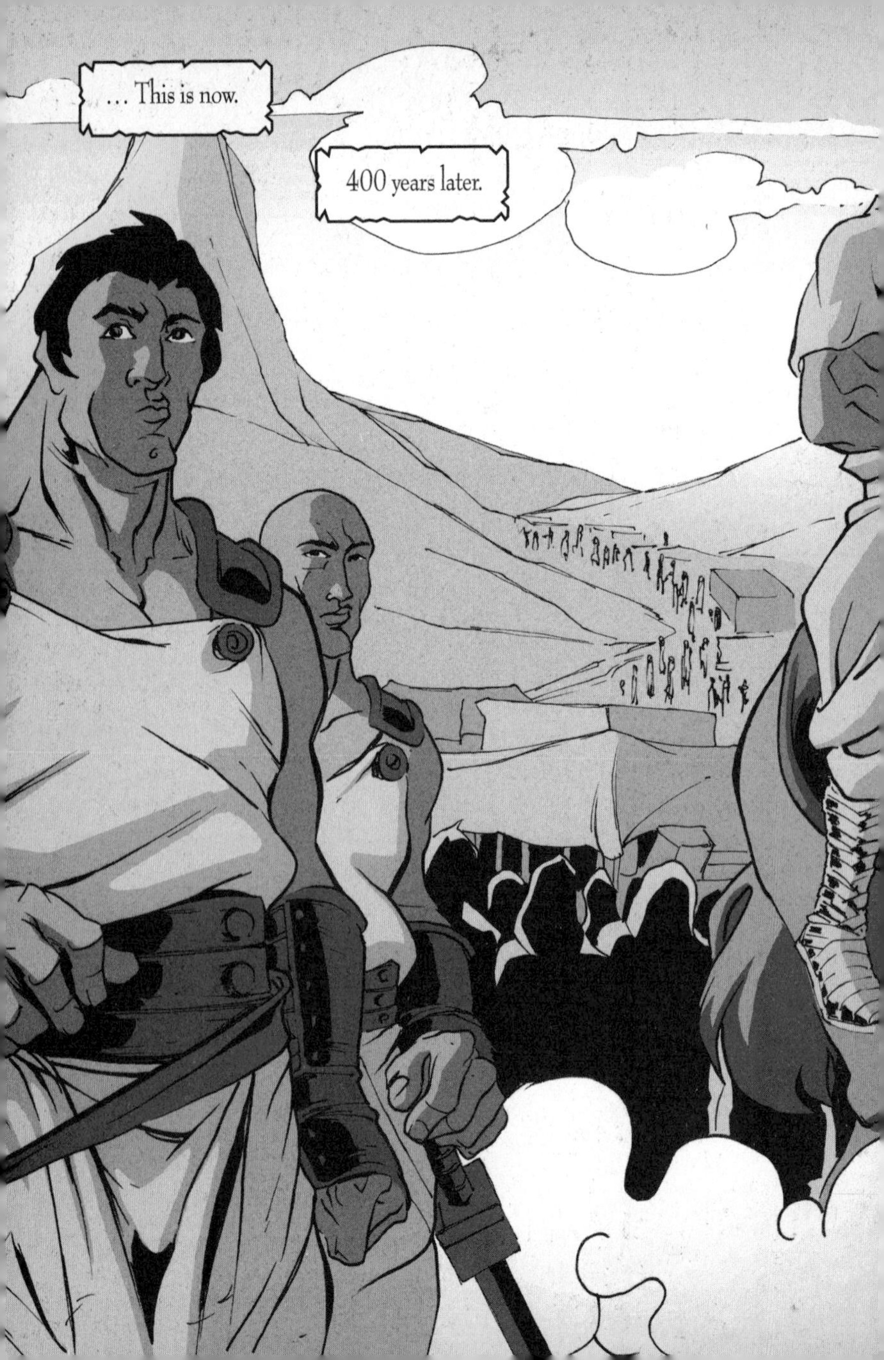
... This is now.
400 years later.

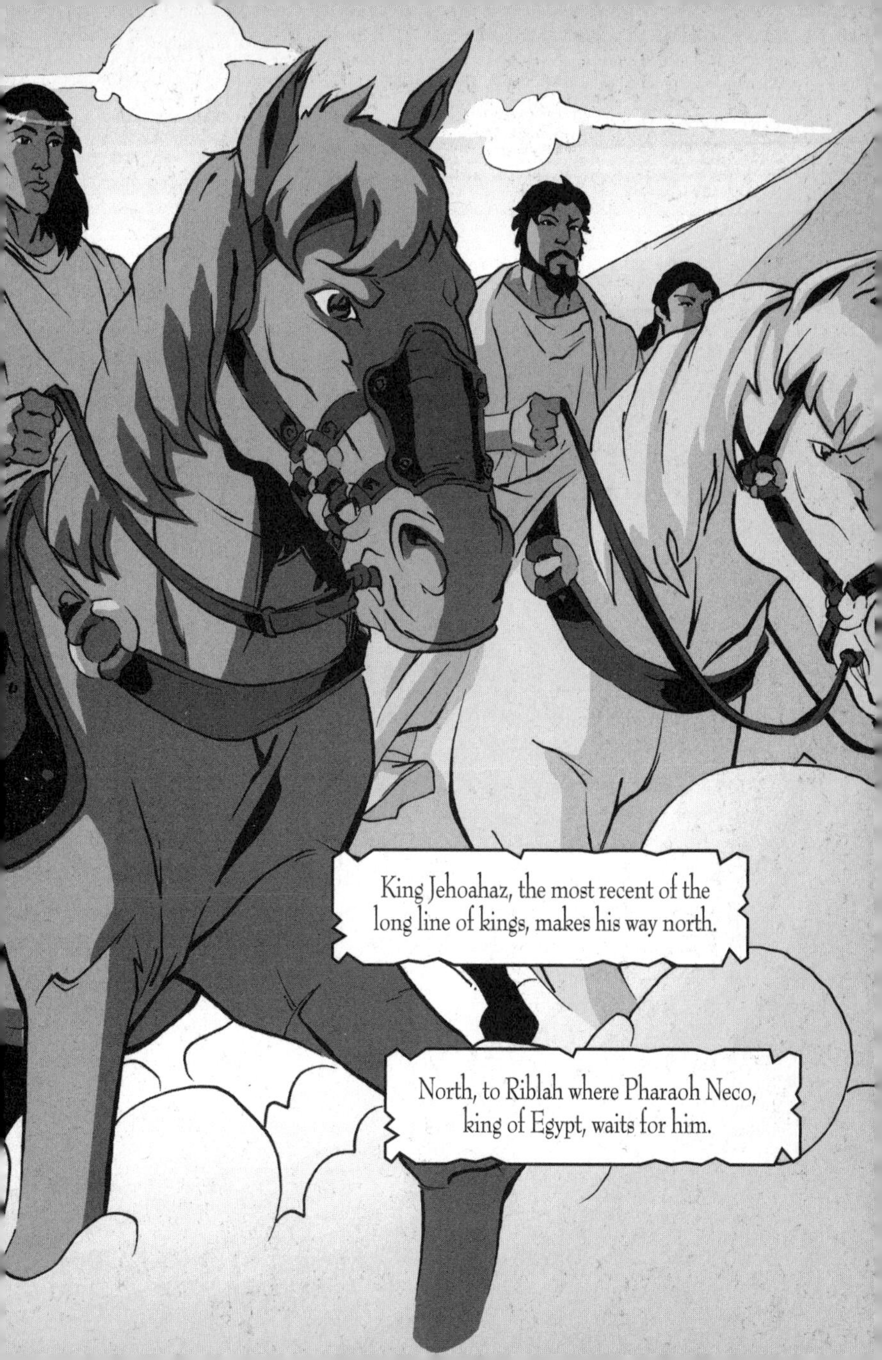
King Jehoahaz, the most recent of the long line of kings, makes his way north.
North, to Riblah where Pharaoh Neco, king of Egypt, waits for him.

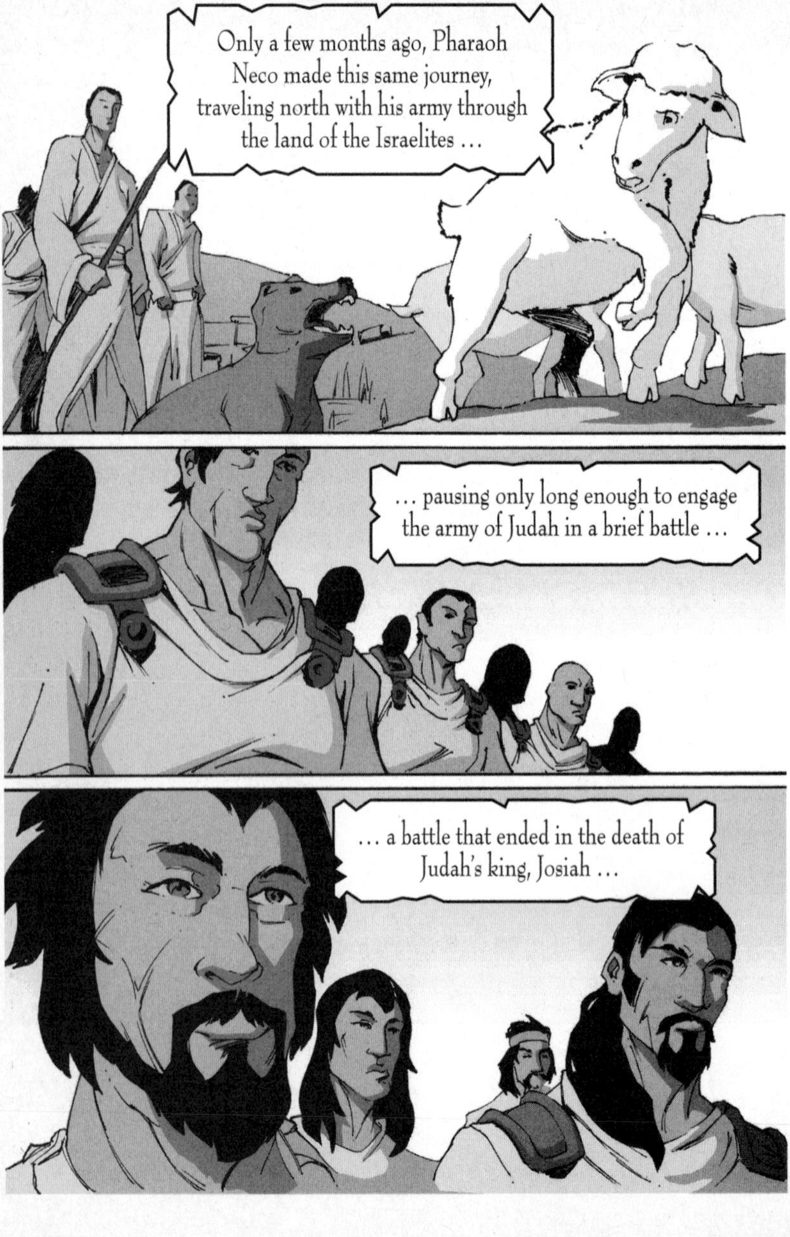
Only a few months ago, Pharaoh Neco made this same journey, traveling north with his army through the land of the Israelites …
… pausing only long enough to engage the army of Judah in a brief battle …
… a battle that ended in the death of Judah's king, Josiah …

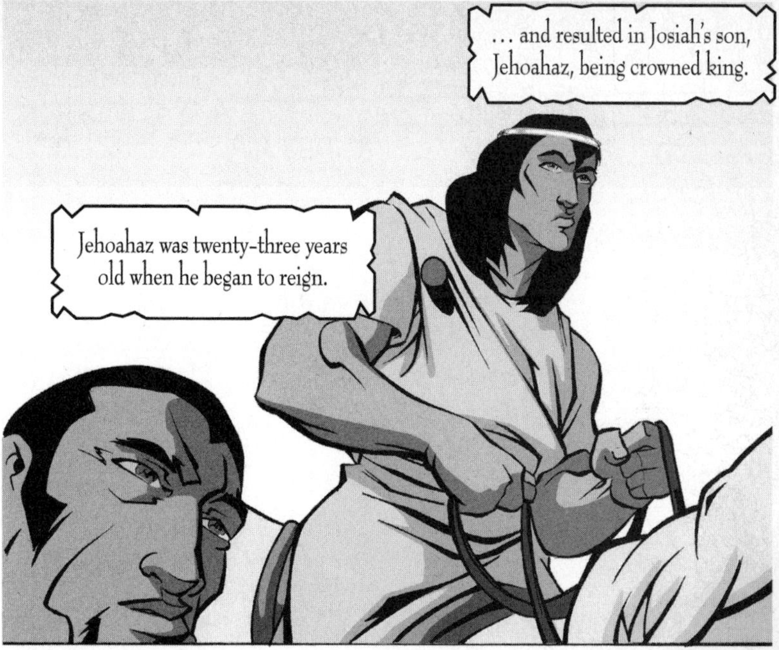
… and resulted in Josiah's son, Jehoahaz, being crowned king.
Jehoahaz was twenty-three years old when he began to reign.

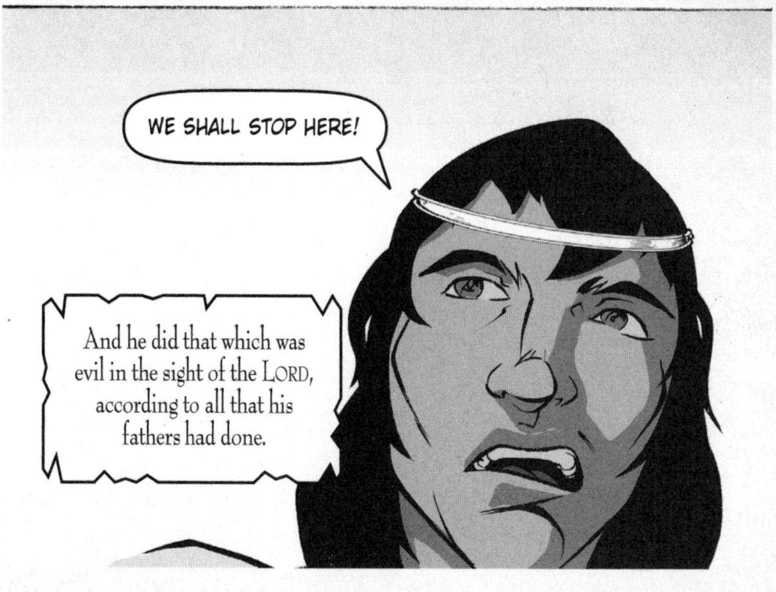
WE SHALL STOP HERE!
And he did that which was evil in the sight of the LORD, according to all that his fathers had done.

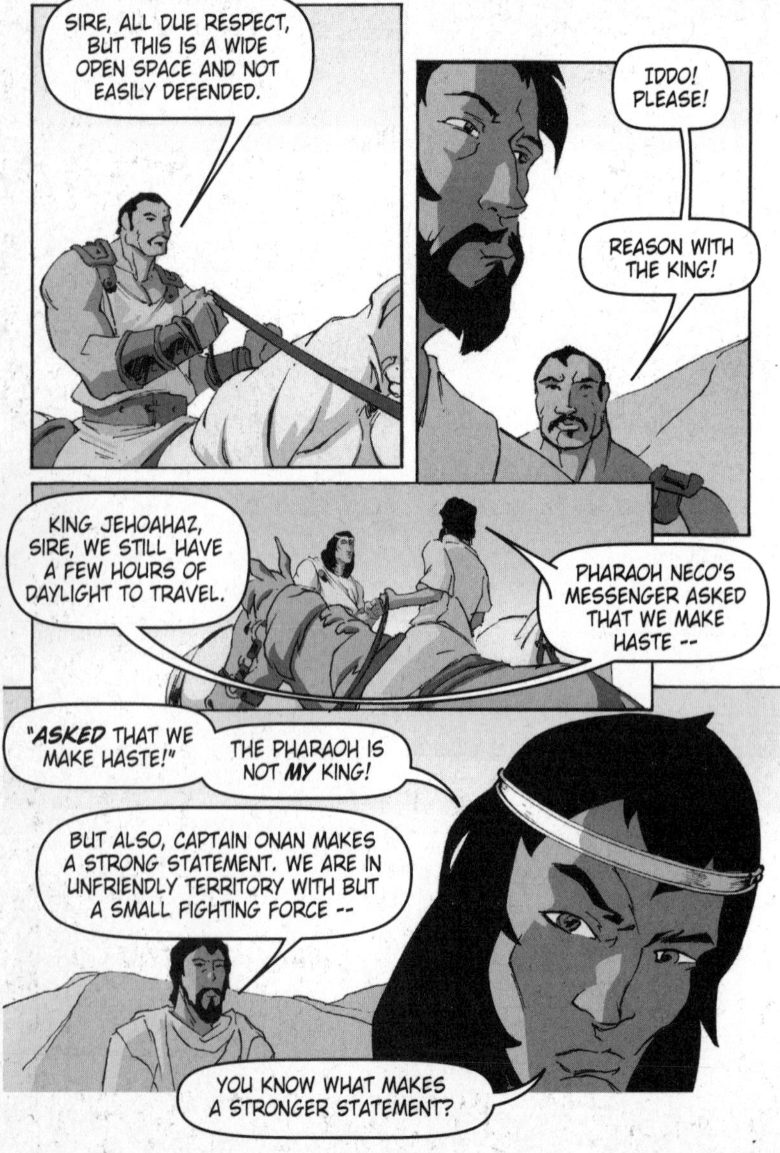
SIRE, ALL DUE RESPECT, BUT THIS IS A WIDE OPEN SPACE AND NOT EASILY DEFENDED.
IDDO! PLEASE!
REASON WITH THE KING!
KING JEHOAHAZ, SIRE, WE STILL HAVE A FEW HOURS OF DAYLIGHT TO TRAVEL.
PHARAOH NECO'S MESSENGER ASKED THAT WE MAKE HASTE --
"ASKED THAT WE MAKE HASTE!"
THE PHARAOH IS NOT MY KING!
BUT ALSO, CAPTAIN ONAN MAKES A STRONG STATEMENT. WE ARE IN UNFRIENDLY TERRITORY WITH BUT A SMALL FIGHTING FORCE --
YOU KNOW WHAT MAKES A STRONGER STATEMENT?

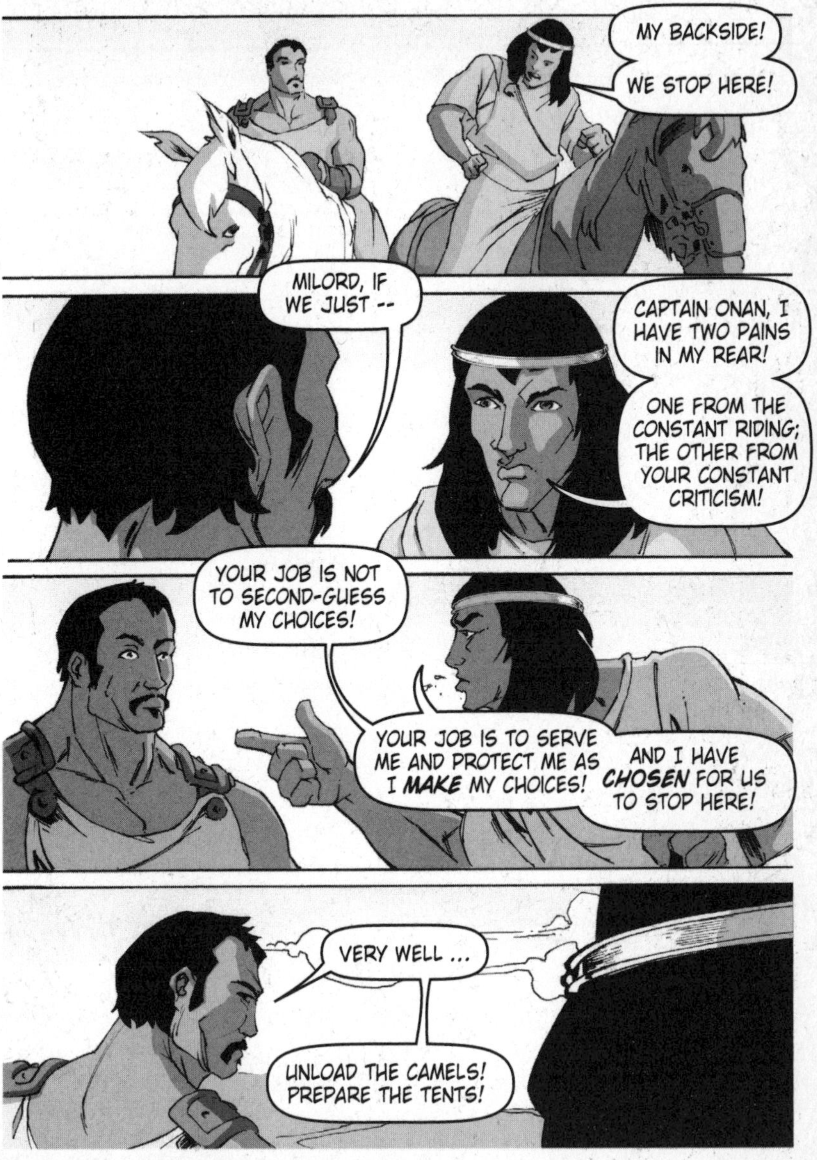
MY BACKSIDE!
WE STOP HERE!
MILORD, IF WE JUST --
CAPTAIN ONAN, I HAVE TWO PAINS IN MY REAR!
ONE FROM THE CONSTANT RIDING; THE OTHER FROM YOUR CONSTANT CRITICISM!
YOUR JOB IS NOT TO SECOND-GUESS MY CHOICES!
YOUR JOB IS TO SERVE ME AND PROTECT ME AS I ***MAKE*** MY CHOICES!
AND I HAVE ***CHOSEN*** FOR US TO STOP HERE!
VERY WELL ...
UNLOAD THE CAMELS! PREPARE THE TENTS!

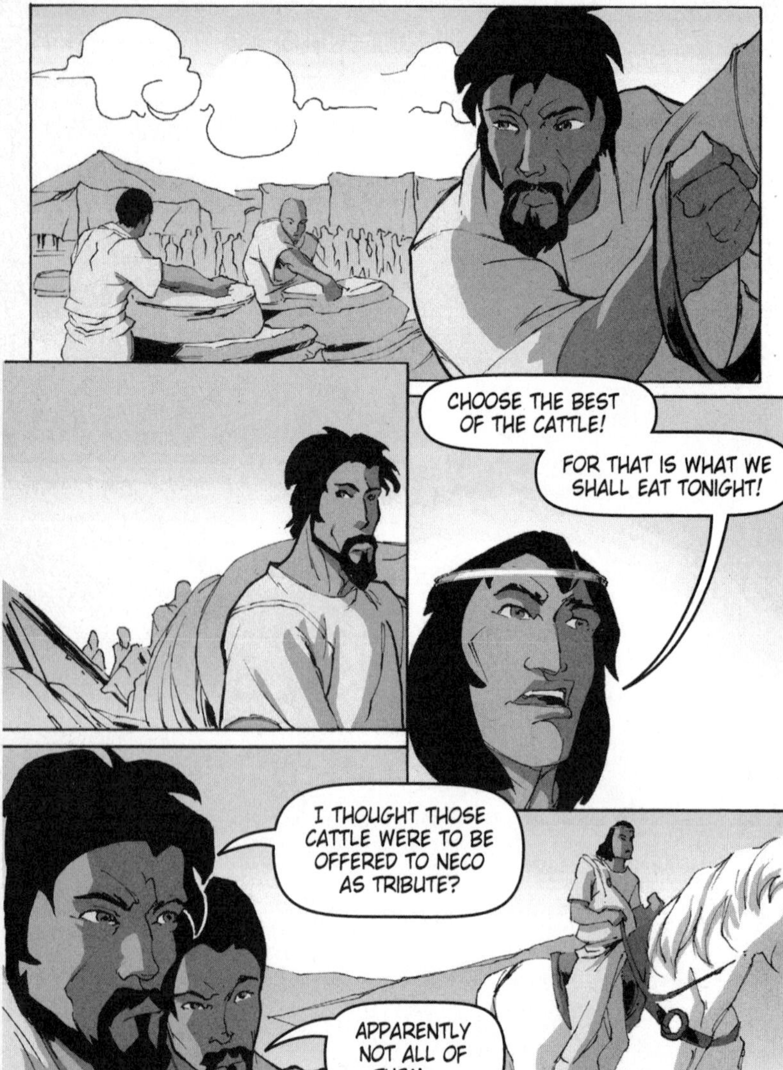
CHOOSE THE BEST OF THE CATTLE!
FOR THAT IS WHAT WE SHALL EAT TONIGHT!
I THOUGHT THOSE CATTLE WERE TO BE OFFERED TO NECO AS TRIBUTE?
APPARENTLY NOT ALL OF THEM ...

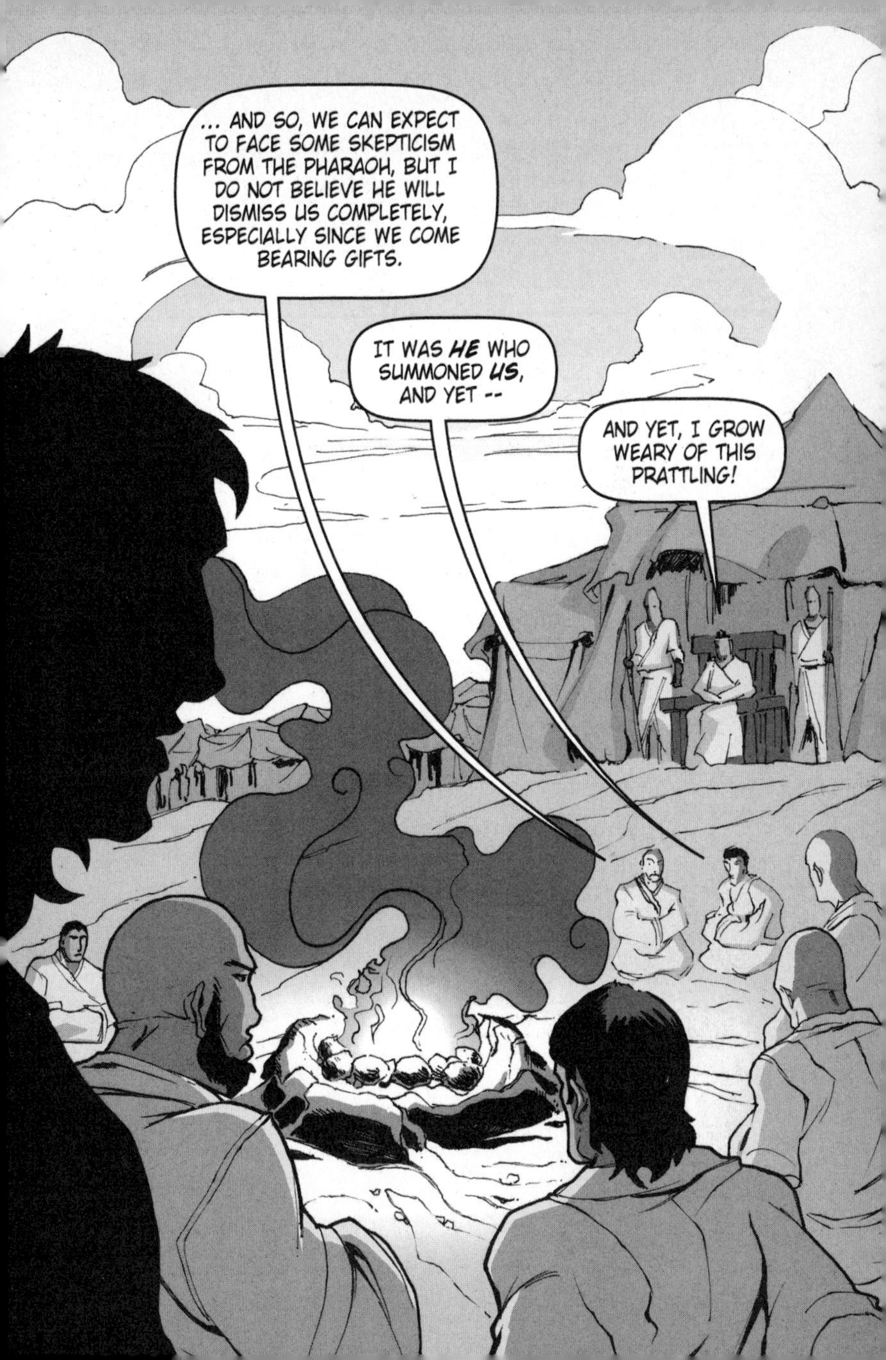
... AND SO, WE CAN EXPECT TO FACE SOME SKEPTICISM FROM THE PHARAOH, BUT I DO NOT BELIEVE HE WILL DISMISS US COMPLETELY, ESPECIALLY SINCE WE COME BEARING GIFTS.
IT WAS ***HE*** WHO SUMMONED ***US***, AND YET --
AND YET, I GROW WEARY OF THIS PRATTLING!

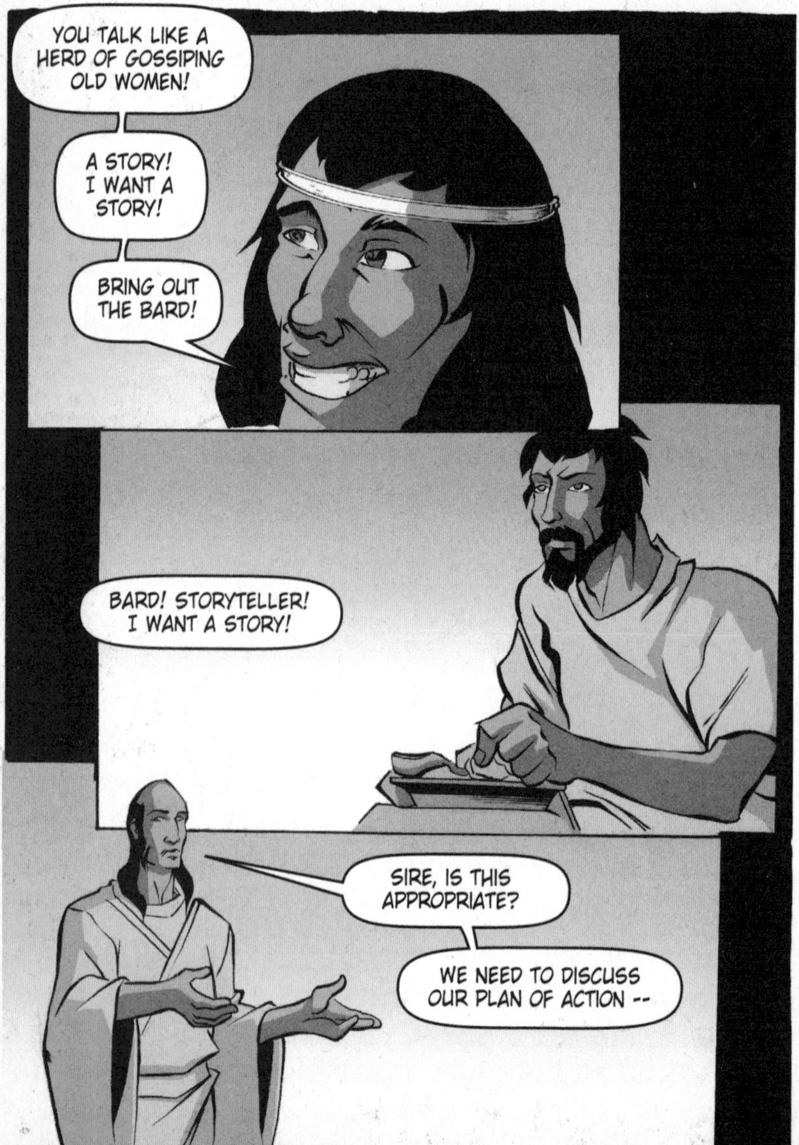
YOU TALK LIKE A HERD OF GOSSIPING OLD WOMEN!
A STORY! I WANT A STORY!
BRING OUT THE BARD!
BARD! STORYTELLER! I WANT A STORY!
SIRE, IS THIS APPROPRIATE?
WE NEED TO DISCUSS OUR PLAN OF ACTION --

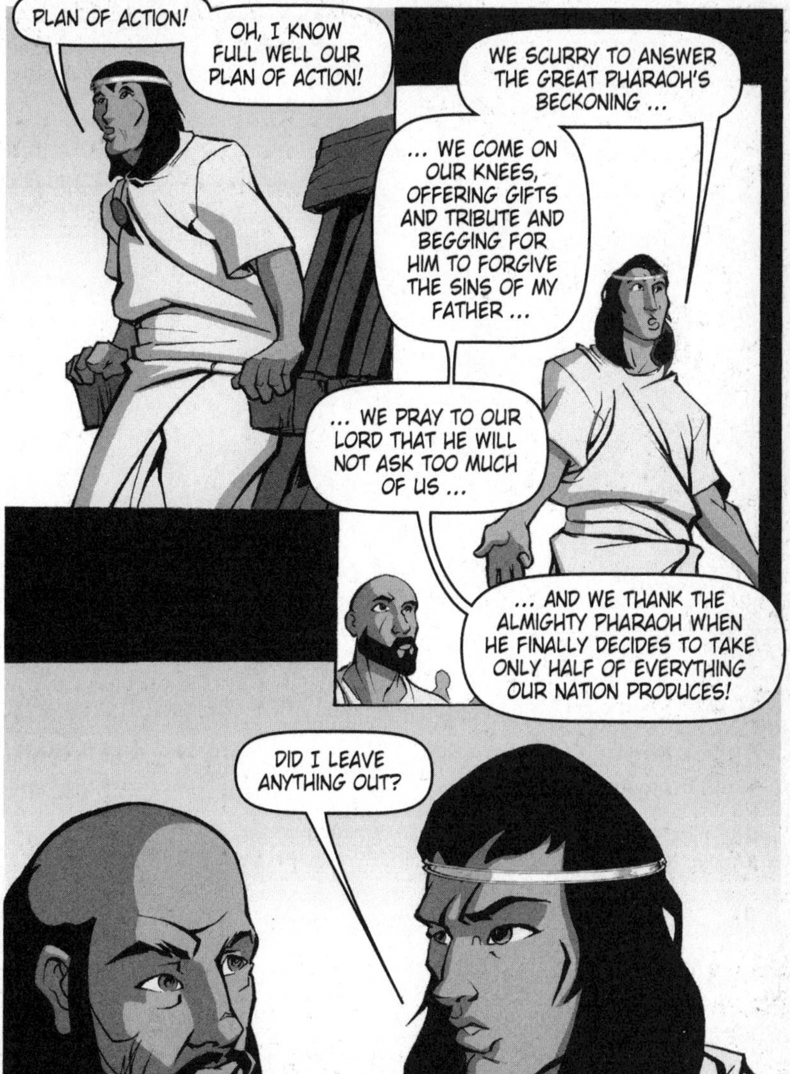
PLAN OF ACTION!
OH, I KNOW FULL WELL OUR PLAN OF ACTION!
WE SCURRY TO ANSWER THE GREAT PHARAOH'S BECKONING ...
... WE COME ON OUR KNEES, OFFERING GIFTS AND TRIBUTE AND BEGGING FOR HIM TO FORGIVE THE SINS OF MY FATHER ...
... WE PRAY TO OUR LORD THAT HE WILL NOT ASK TOO MUCH OF US ...
... AND WE THANK THE ALMIGHTY PHARAOH WHEN HE FINALLY DECIDES TO TAKE ONLY HALF OF EVERYTHING OUR NATION PRODUCES!
DID I LEAVE ANYTHING OUT?

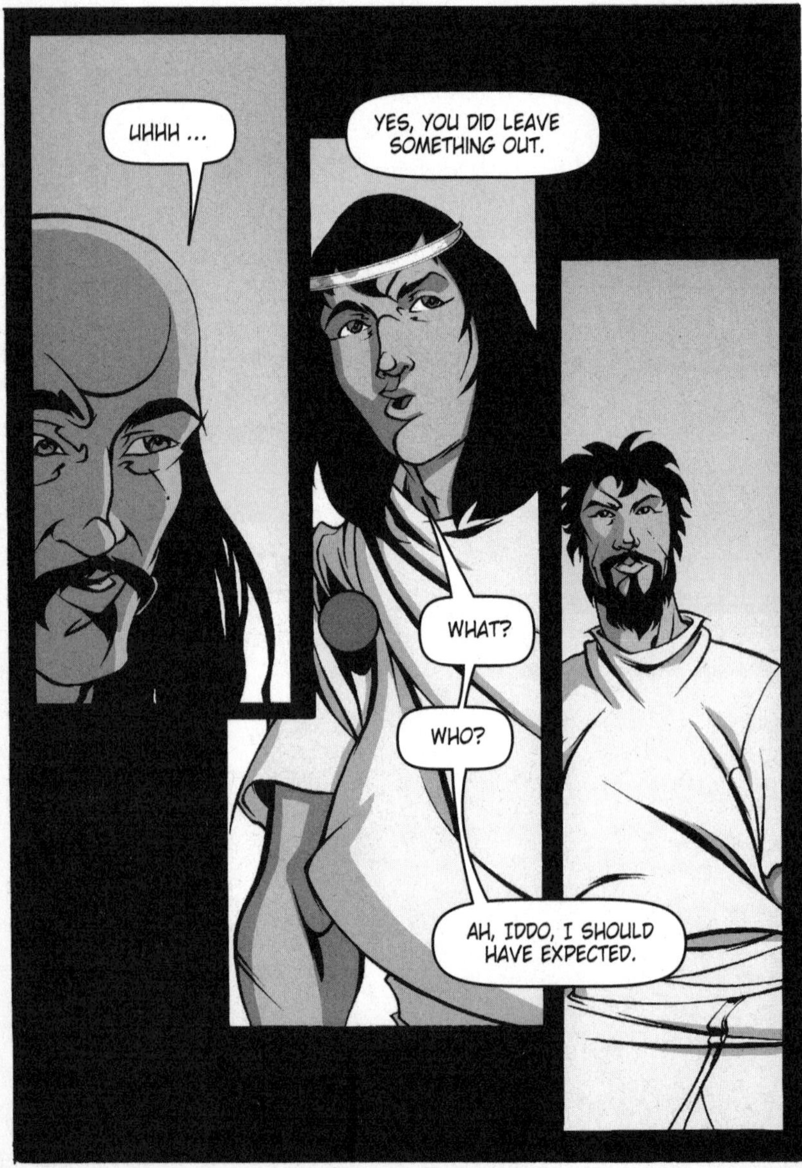
UHHH ...
YES, YOU DID LEAVE SOMETHING OUT.
WHAT?
WHO?
AH, IDDO, I SHOULD HAVE EXPECTED.

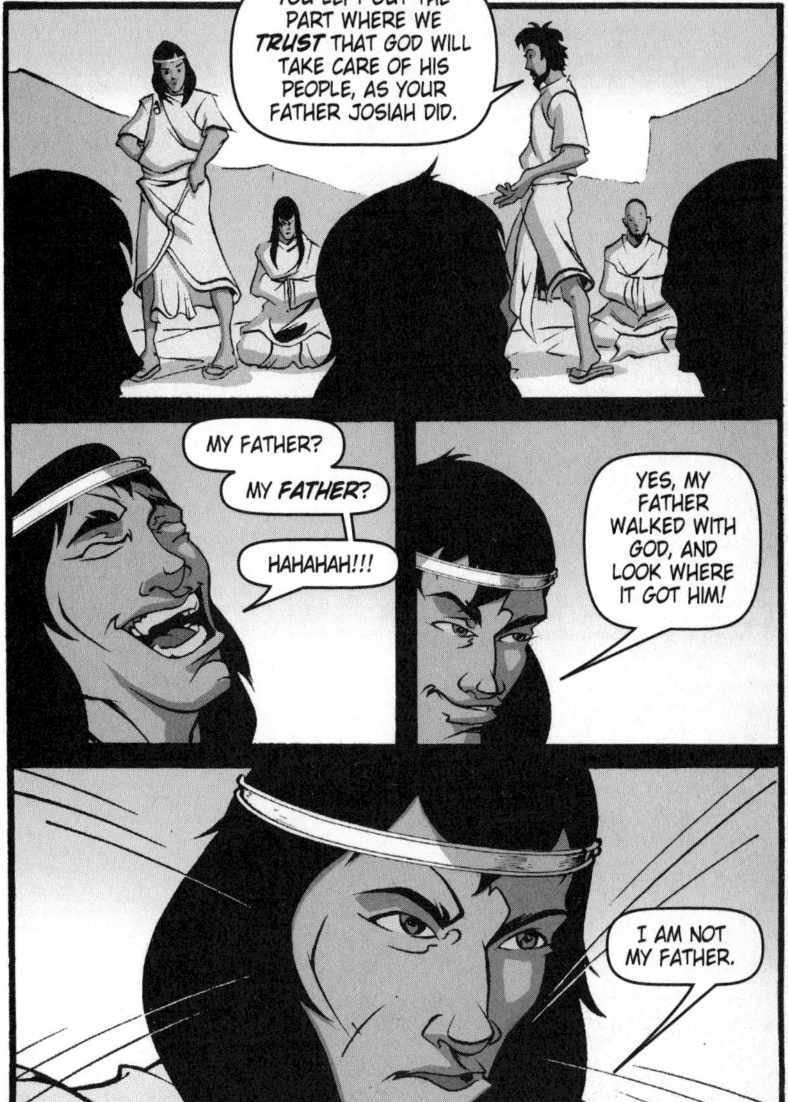
YOU LEFT OUT THE PART WHERE WE *TRUST* THAT GOD WILL TAKE CARE OF HIS PEOPLE, AS YOUR FATHER JOSIAH DID.
MY FATHER?
MY *FATHER*?
HAHAHAH!!!
YES, MY FATHER WALKED WITH GOD, AND LOOK WHERE IT GOT HIM!
I AM NOT MY FATHER.

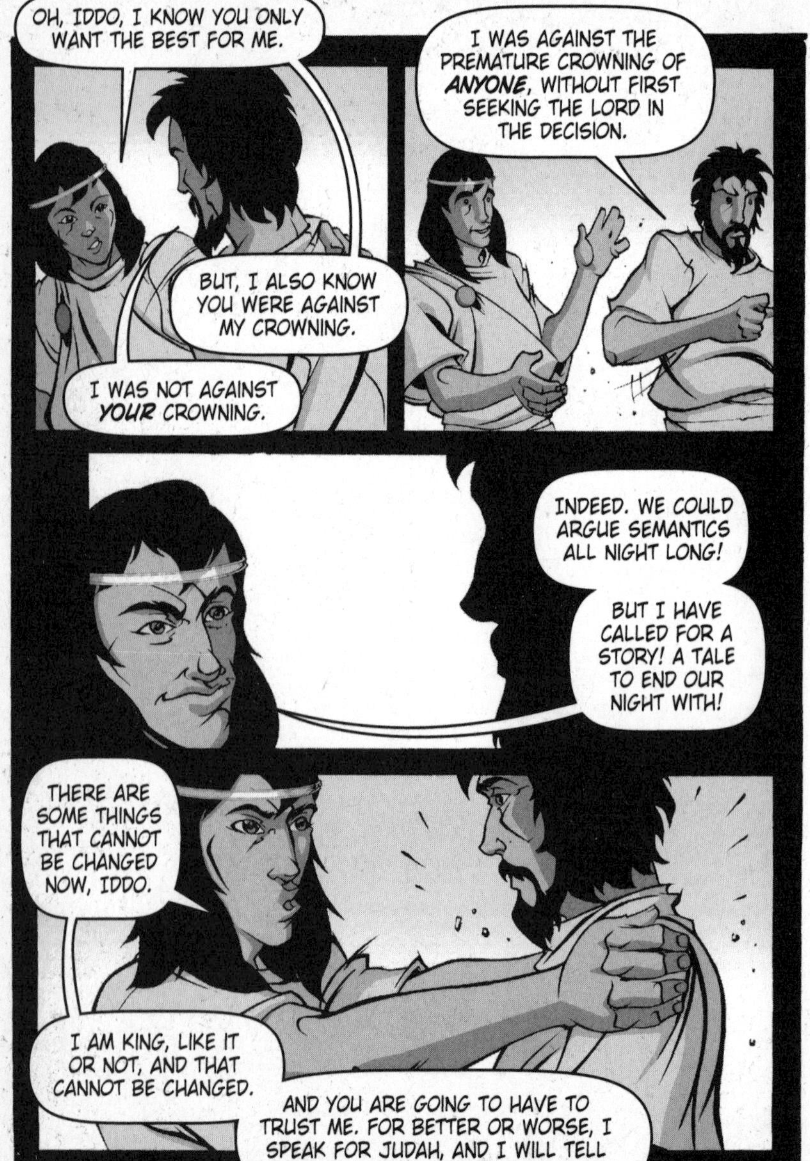
OH, IDDO, I KNOW YOU ONLY WANT THE BEST FOR ME.
BUT, I ALSO KNOW YOU WERE AGAINST MY CROWNING.
I WAS NOT AGAINST *YOUR* CROWNING.
I WAS AGAINST THE PREMATURE CROWNING OF *ANYONE*, WITHOUT FIRST SEEKING THE LORD IN THE DECISION.
INDEED. WE COULD ARGUE SEMANTICS ALL NIGHT LONG!
BUT I HAVE CALLED FOR A STORY! A TALE TO END OUR NIGHT WITH!
THERE ARE SOME THINGS THAT CANNOT BE CHANGED NOW, IDDO.
I AM KING, LIKE IT OR NOT, AND THAT CANNOT BE CHANGED.
AND YOU ARE GOING TO HAVE TO TRUST ME. FOR BETTER OR WORSE, I SPEAK FOR JUDAH, AND I WILL TELL PHARAOH WHAT NEEDS TO BE SAID.

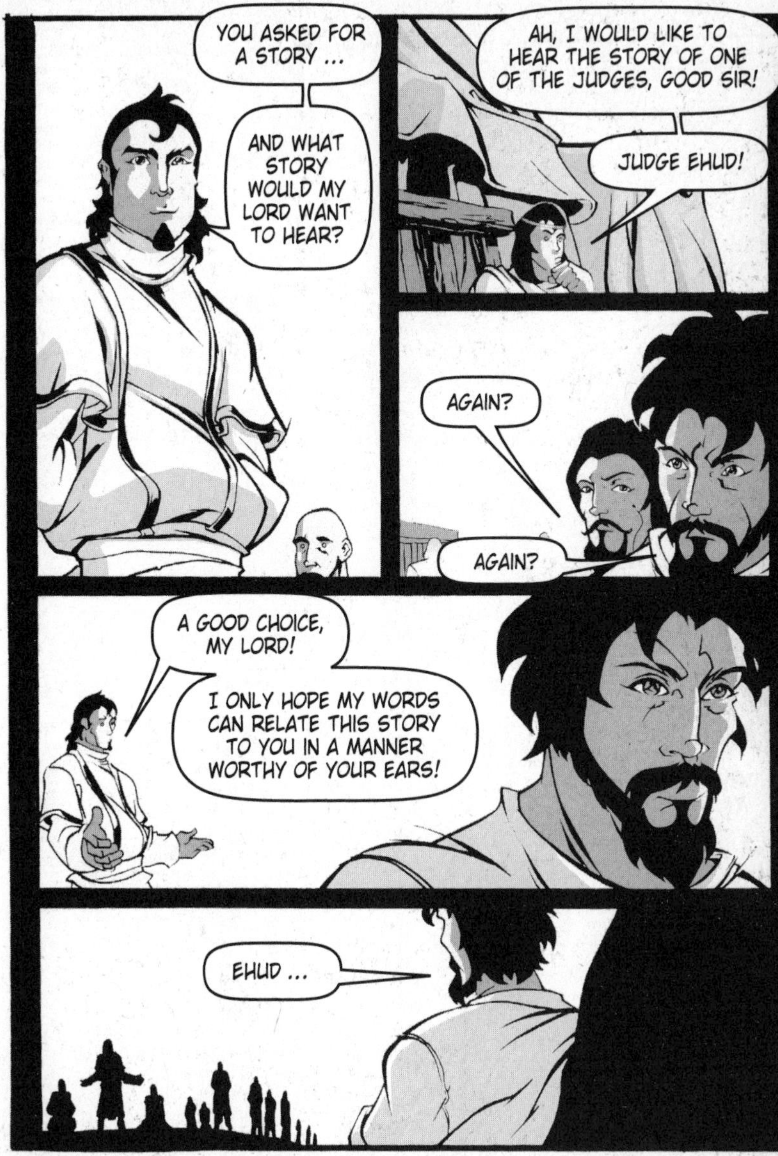
YOU ASKED FOR A STORY ...
AND WHAT STORY WOULD MY LORD WANT TO HEAR?
AH, I WOULD LIKE TO HEAR THE STORY OF ONE OF THE JUDGES, GOOD SIR!
JUDGE EHUD!
AGAIN?
AGAIN?
A GOOD CHOICE, MY LORD!
I ONLY HOPE MY WORDS CAN RELATE THIS STORY TO YOU IN A MANNER WORTHY OF YOUR EARS!
EHUD ...

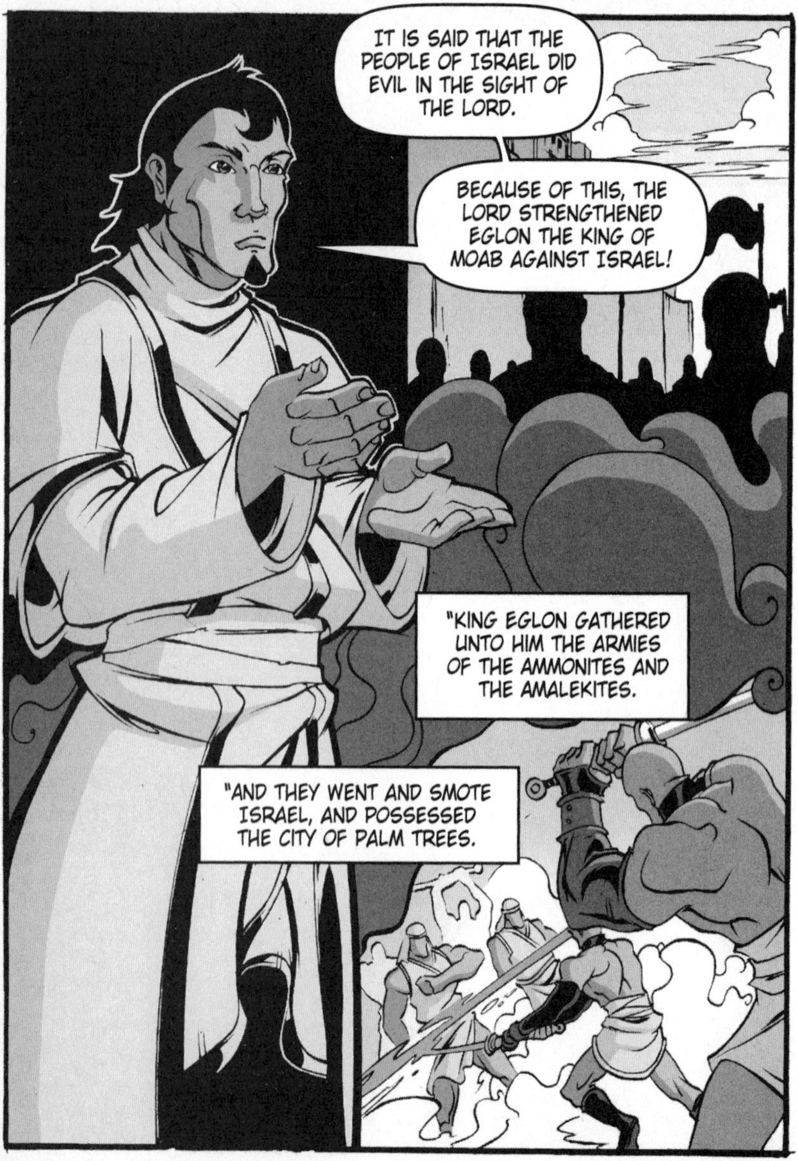
IT IS SAID THAT THE PEOPLE OF ISRAEL DID EVIL IN THE SIGHT OF THE LORD.
BECAUSE OF THIS, THE LORD STRENGTHENED EGLON THE KING OF MOAB AGAINST ISRAEL!
"KING EGLON GATHERED UNTO HIM THE ARMIES OF THE AMMONITES AND THE AMALEKITES.
"AND THEY WENT AND SMOTE ISRAEL, AND POSSESSED THE CITY OF PALM TREES.

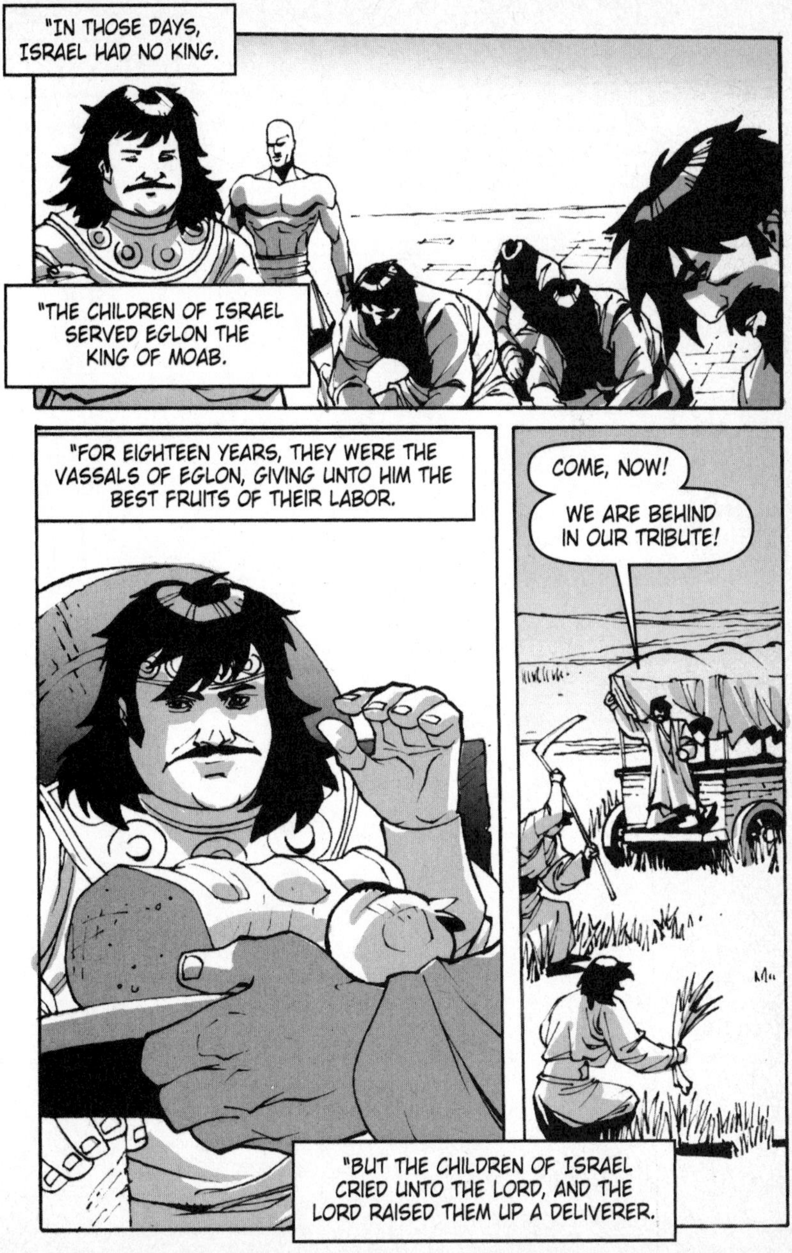
"IN THOSE DAYS, ISRAEL HAD NO KING.
"THE CHILDREN OF ISRAEL SERVED EGLON THE KING OF MOAB.
"FOR EIGHTEEN YEARS, THEY WERE THE VASSALS OF EGLON, GIVING UNTO HIM THE BEST FRUITS OF THEIR LABOR.
COME, NOW!
WE ARE BEHIND IN OUR TRIBUTE!
"BUT THE CHILDREN OF ISRAEL CRIED UNTO THE LORD, AND THE LORD RAISED THEM UP A DELIVERER.

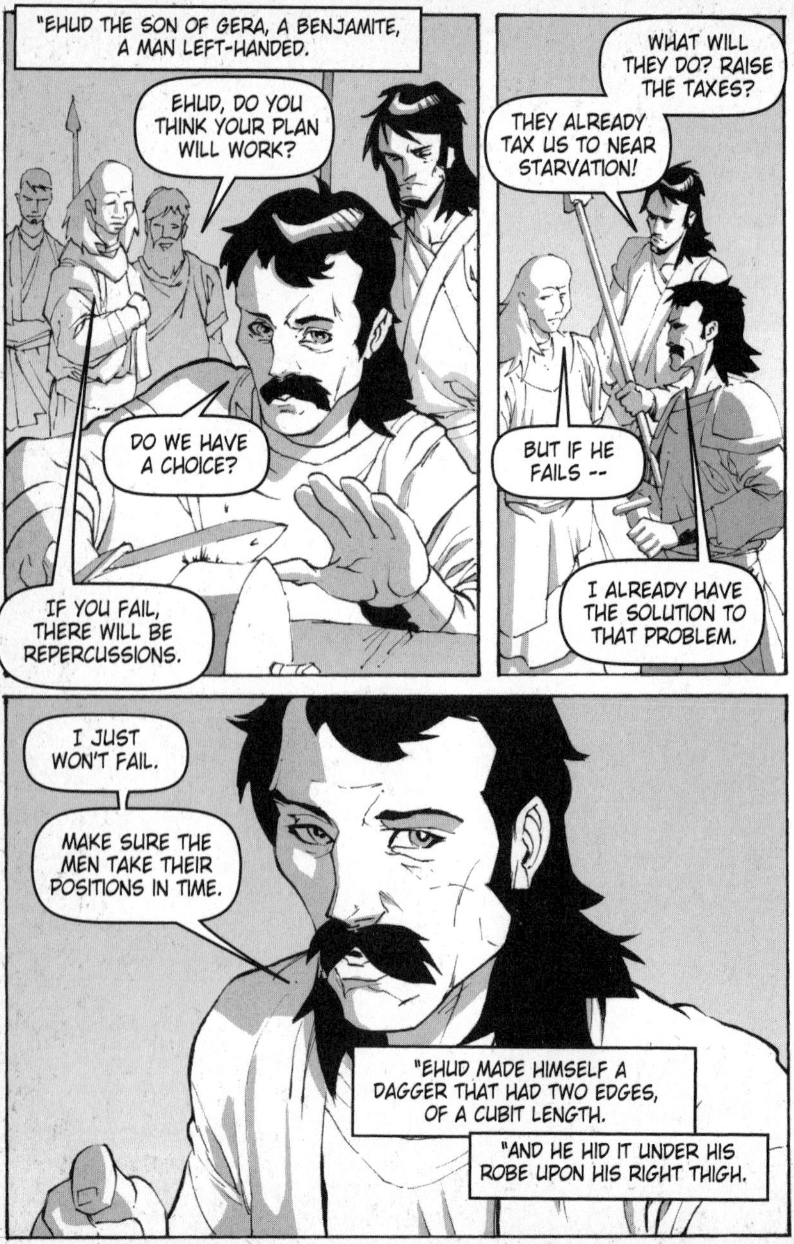
"EHUD THE SON OF GERA, A BENJAMITE, A MAN LEFT-HANDED.
EHUD, DO YOU THINK YOUR PLAN WILL WORK?
DO WE HAVE A CHOICE?
IF YOU FAIL, THERE WILL BE REPERCUSSIONS.
WHAT WILL THEY DO? RAISE THE TAXES?
THEY ALREADY TAX US TO NEAR STARVATION!
BUT IF HE FAILS --
I ALREADY HAVE THE SOLUTION TO THAT PROBLEM.
I JUST WON'T FAIL.
MAKE SURE THE MEN TAKE THEIR POSITIONS IN TIME.
"EHUD MADE HIMSELF A DAGGER THAT HAD TWO EDGES, OF A CUBIT LENGTH.
"AND HE HID IT UNDER HIS ROBE UPON HIS RIGHT THIGH.

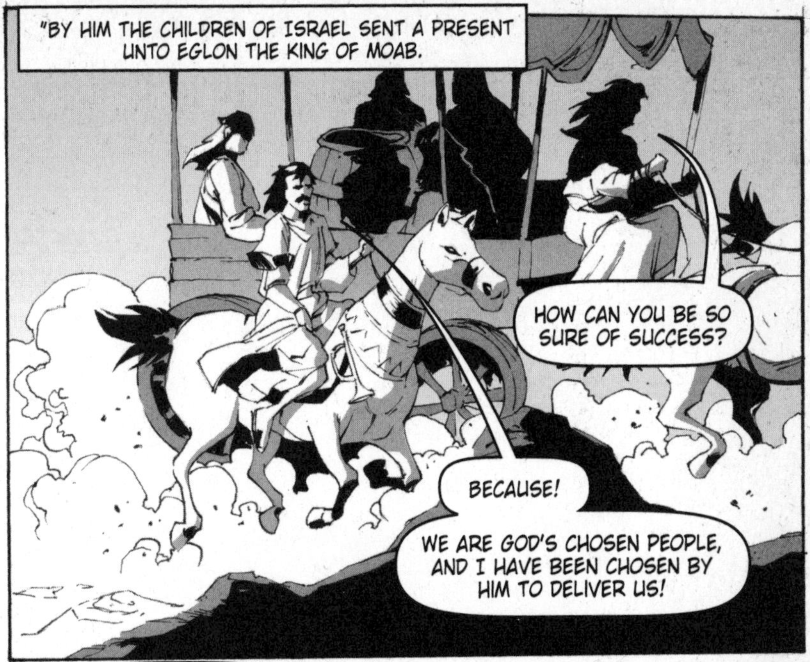
"BY HIM THE CHILDREN OF ISRAEL SENT A PRESENT UNTO EGLON THE KING OF MOAB.
HOW CAN YOU BE SO SURE OF SUCCESS?
BECAUSE!
WE ARE GOD'S CHOSEN PEOPLE, AND I HAVE BEEN CHOSEN BY HIM TO DELIVER US!

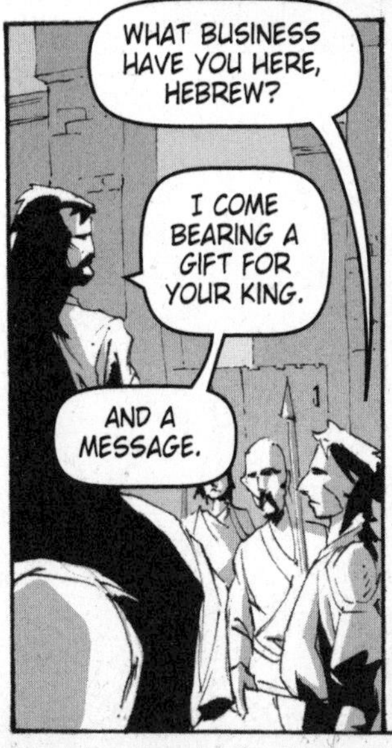
WHAT BUSINESS HAVE YOU HERE, HEBREW?
I COME BEARING A GIFT FOR YOUR KING.
AND A MESSAGE.

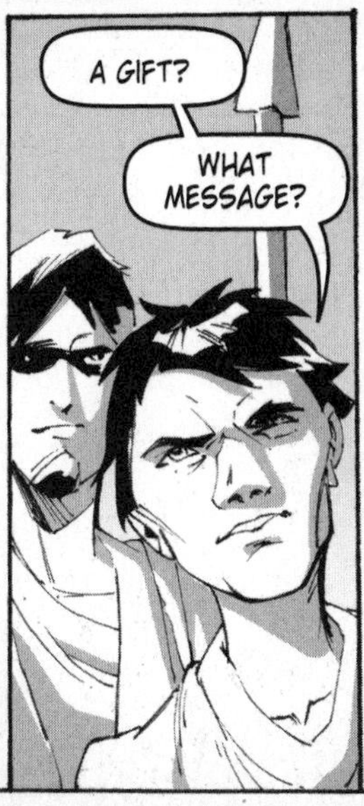
A GIFT?
WHAT MESSAGE?

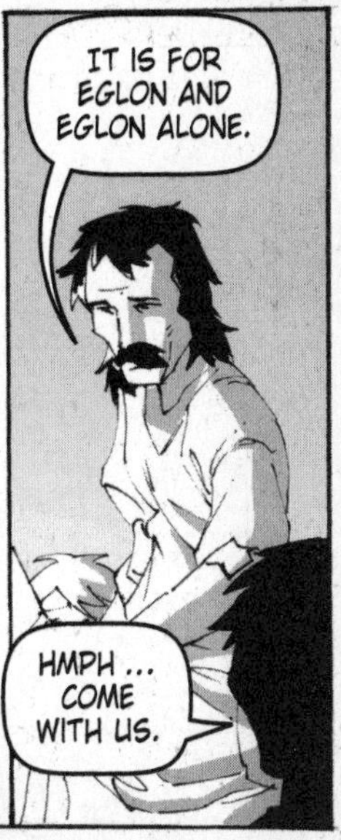
IT IS FOR EGLON AND EGLON ALONE.
HMPH ... COME WITH US.

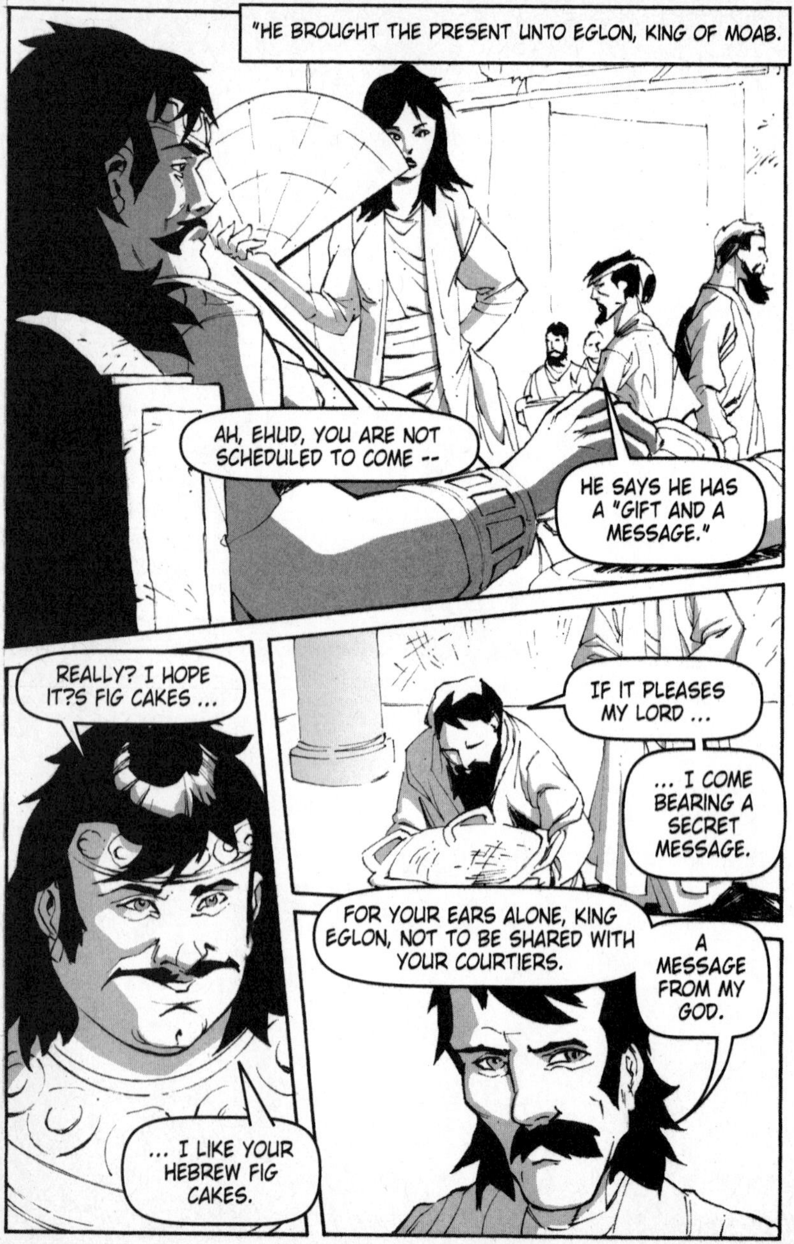
"HE BROUGHT THE PRESENT UNTO EGLON, KING OF MOAB.
AH, EHUD, YOU ARE NOT SCHEDULED TO COME --
HE SAYS HE HAS A "GIFT AND A MESSAGE."
REALLY? I HOPE IT?S FIG CAKES ...
... I LIKE YOUR HEBREW FIG CAKES.
IF IT PLEASES MY LORD ...
... I COME BEARING A SECRET MESSAGE.
FOR YOUR EARS ALONE, KING EGLON, NOT TO BE SHARED WITH YOUR COURTIERS.
A MESSAGE FROM MY GOD.

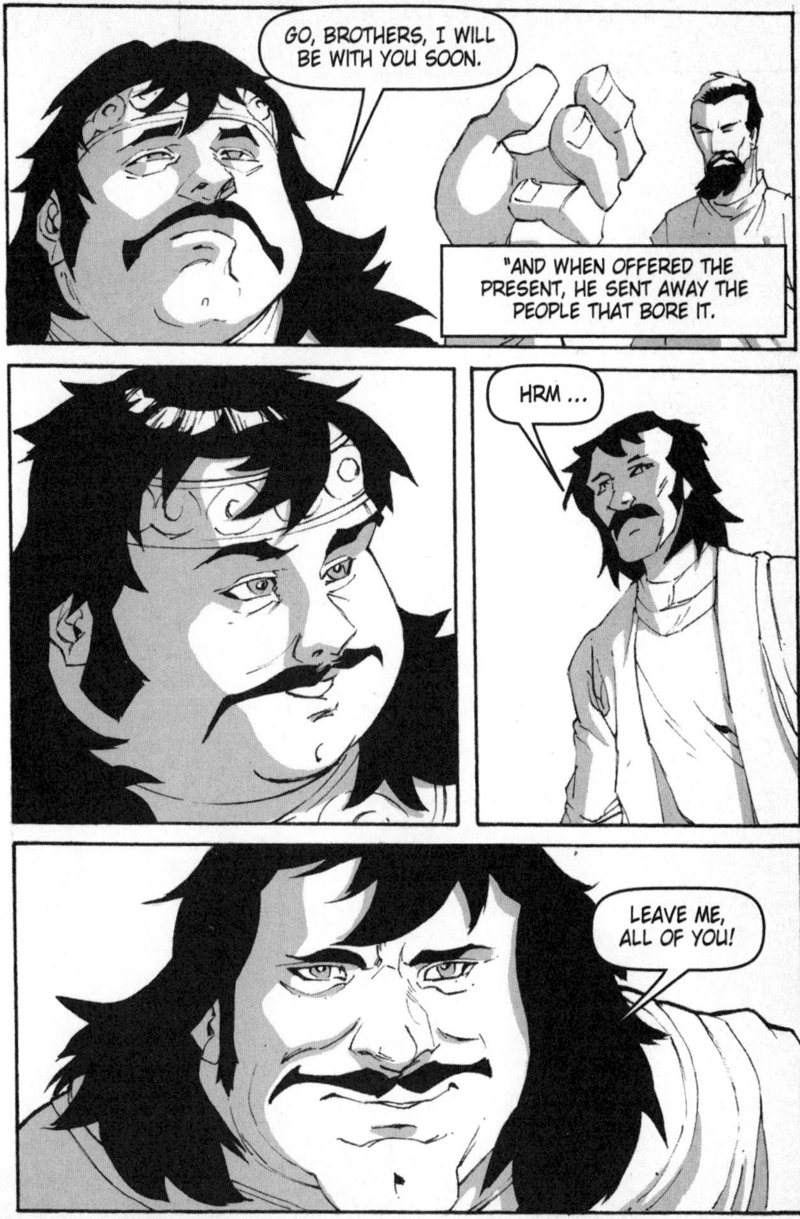
GO, BROTHERS, I WILL BE WITH YOU SOON.
"AND WHEN OFFERED THE PRESENT, HE SENT AWAY THE PEOPLE THAT BORE IT.
HRM ...
LEAVE ME, ALL OF YOU!

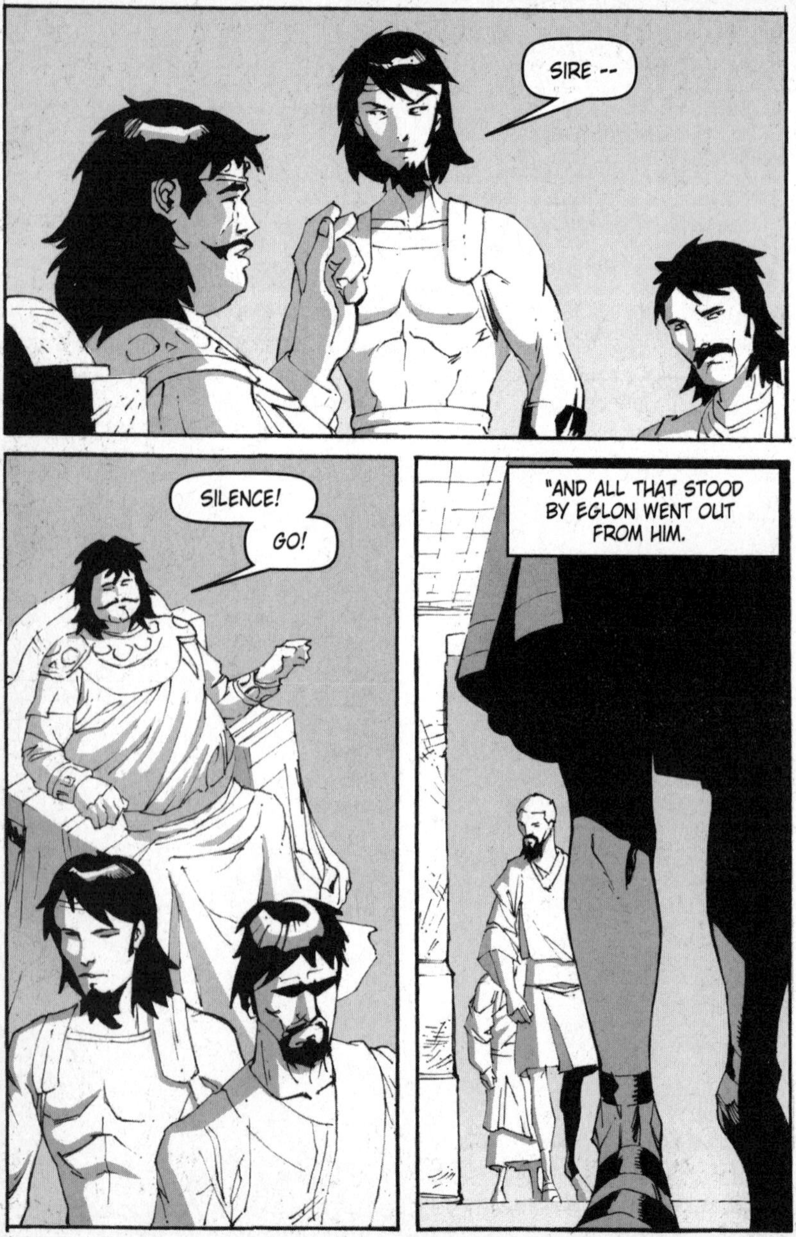
SIRE --
SILENCE!
GO!
"AND ALL THAT STOOD BY EGLON WENT OUT FROM HIM.

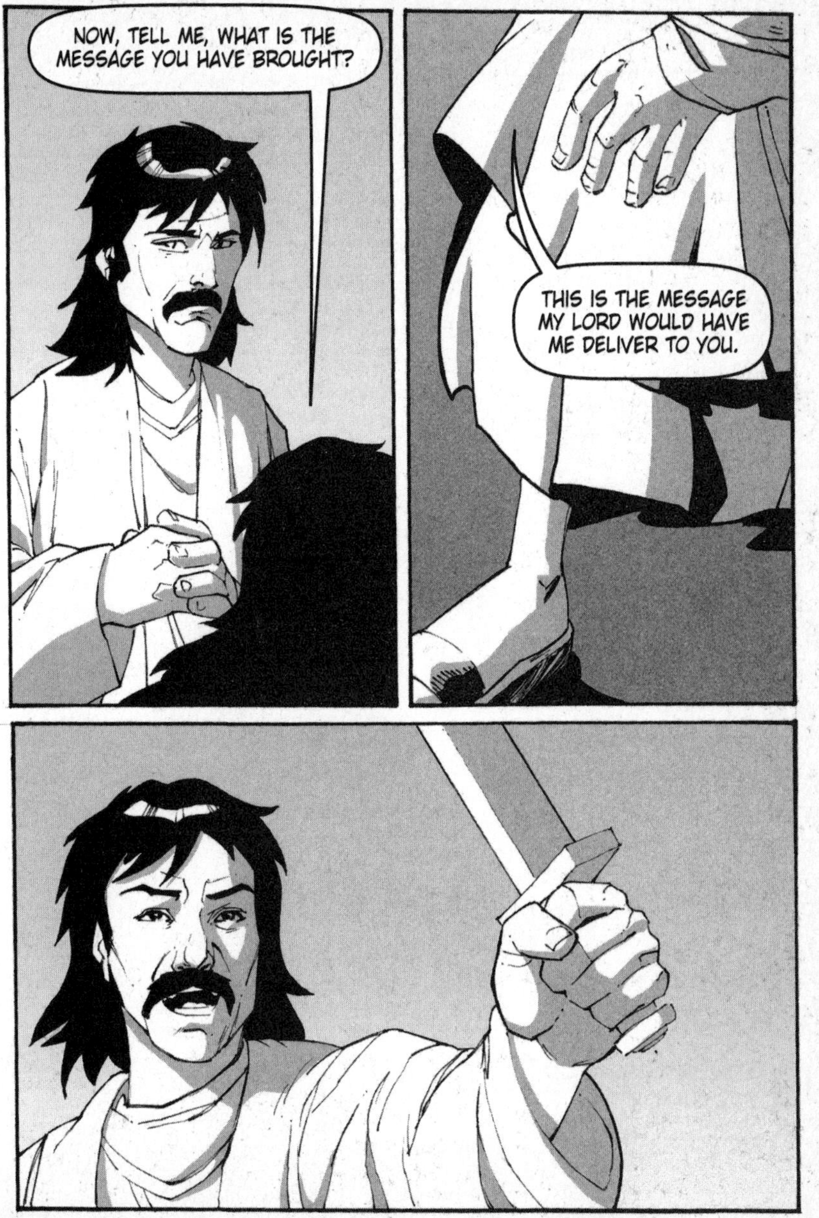
NOW, TELL ME, WHAT IS THE MESSAGE YOU HAVE BROUGHT?
THIS IS THE MESSAGE MY LORD WOULD HAVE ME DELIVER TO YOU.

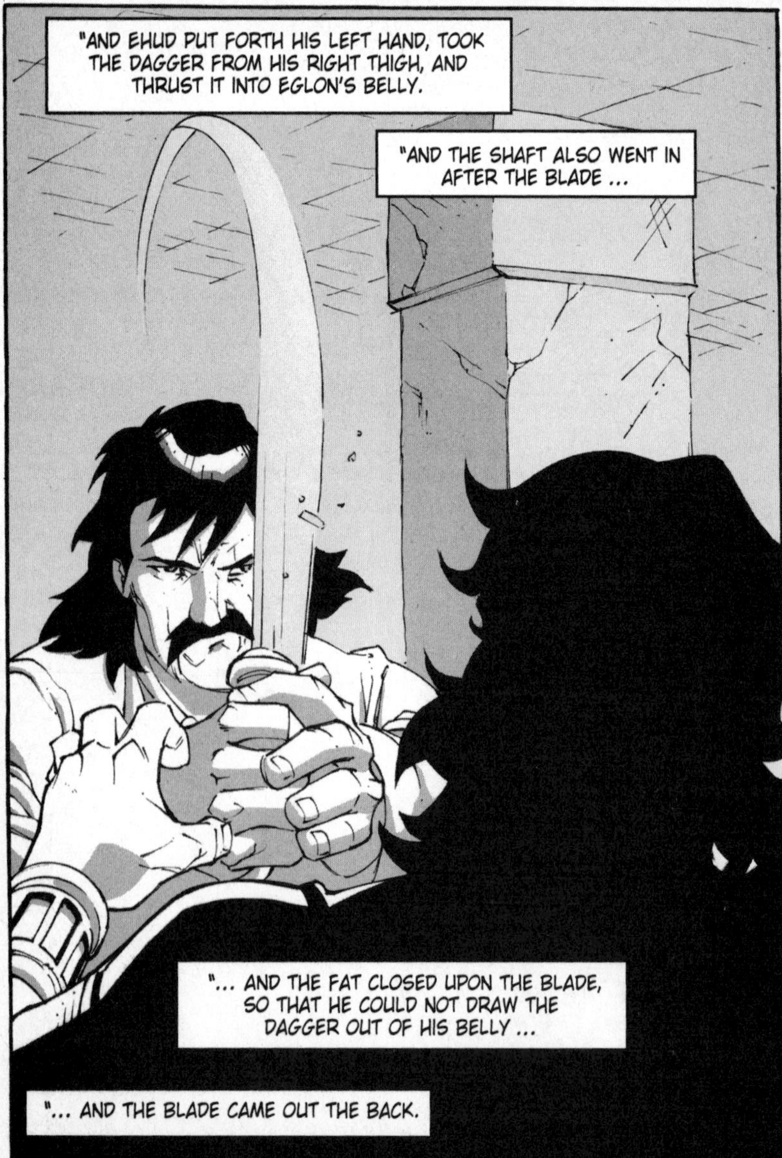
"AND EHUD PUT FORTH HIS LEFT HAND, TOOK THE DAGGER FROM HIS RIGHT THIGH, AND THRUST IT INTO EGLON'S BELLY.
"AND THE SHAFT ALSO WENT IN AFTER THE BLADE ...
"... AND THE FAT CLOSED UPON THE BLADE, SO THAT HE COULD NOT DRAW THE DAGGER OUT OF HIS BELLY ...
"... AND THE BLADE CAME OUT THE BACK.

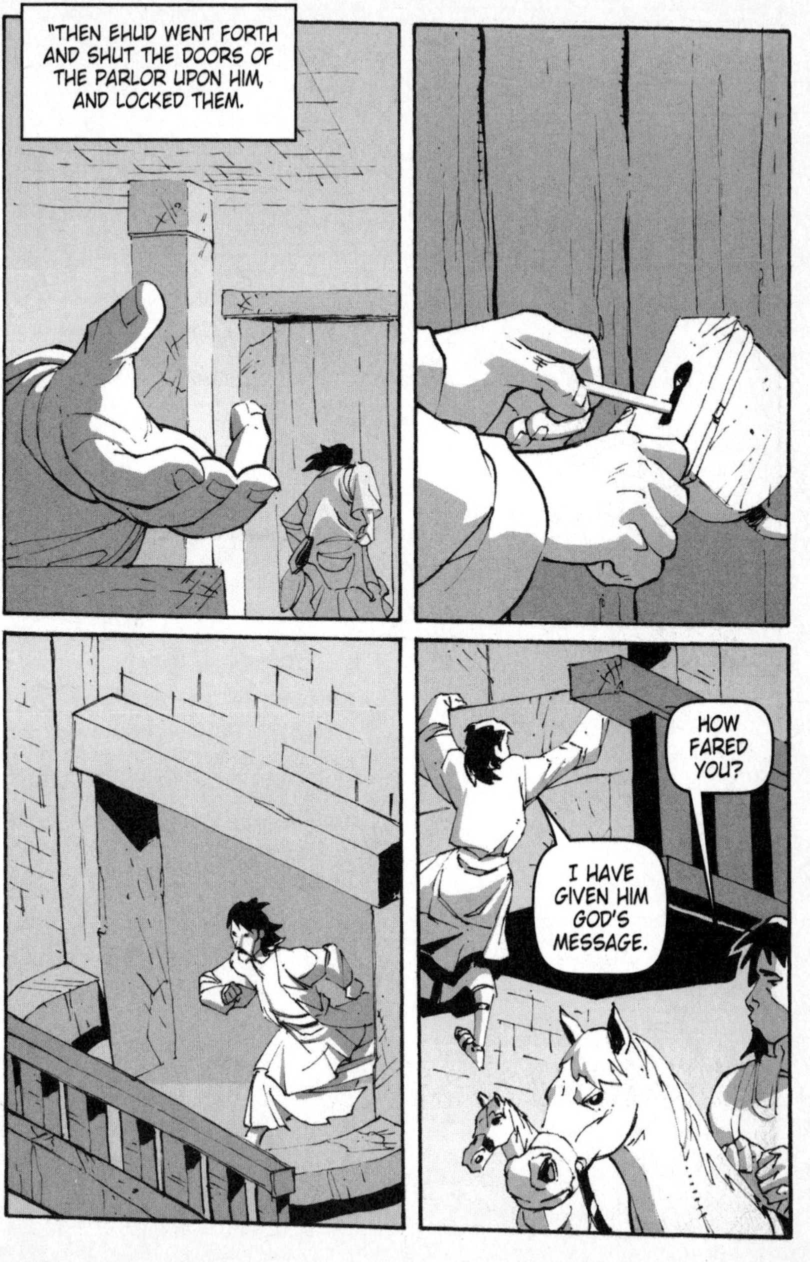
"THEN EHUD WENT FORTH AND SHUT THE DOORS OF THE PARLOR UPON HIM, AND LOCKED THEM.
HOW FARED YOU?
I HAVE GIVEN HIM GOD'S MESSAGE.

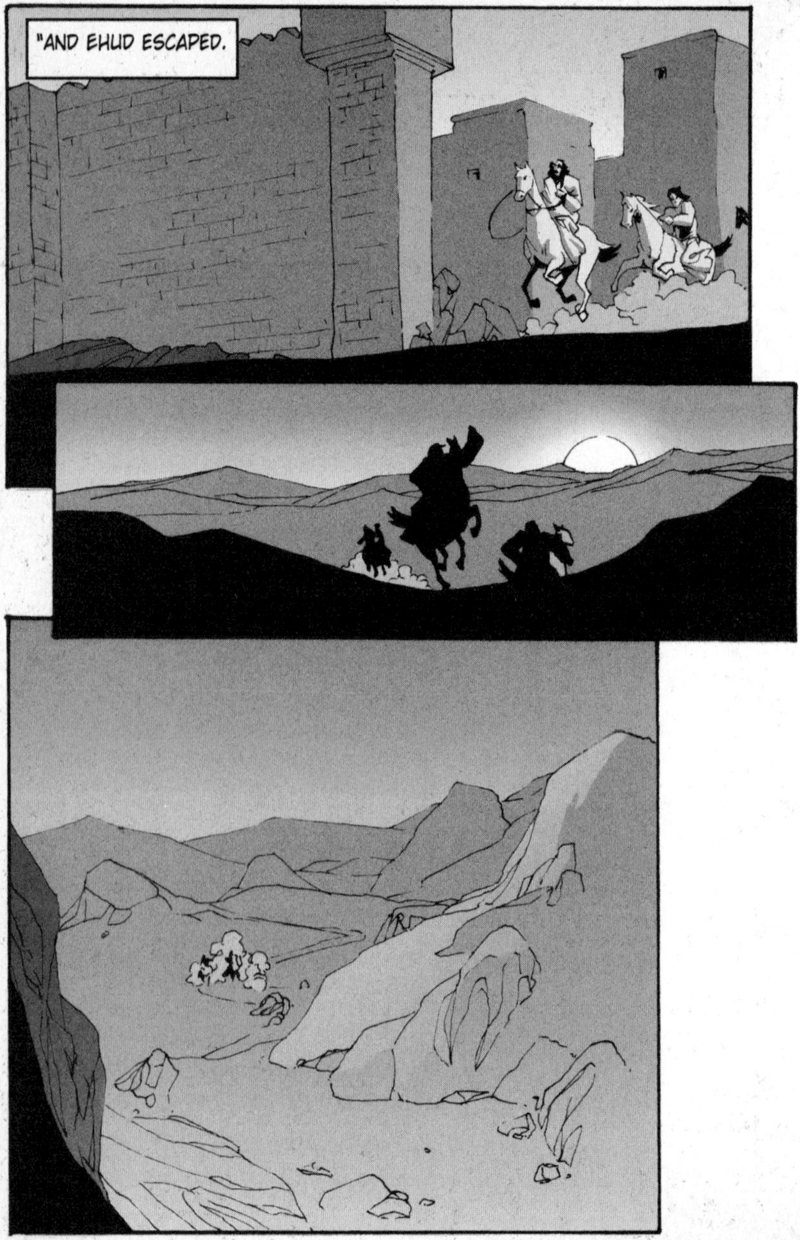
"AND EHUD ESCAPED.

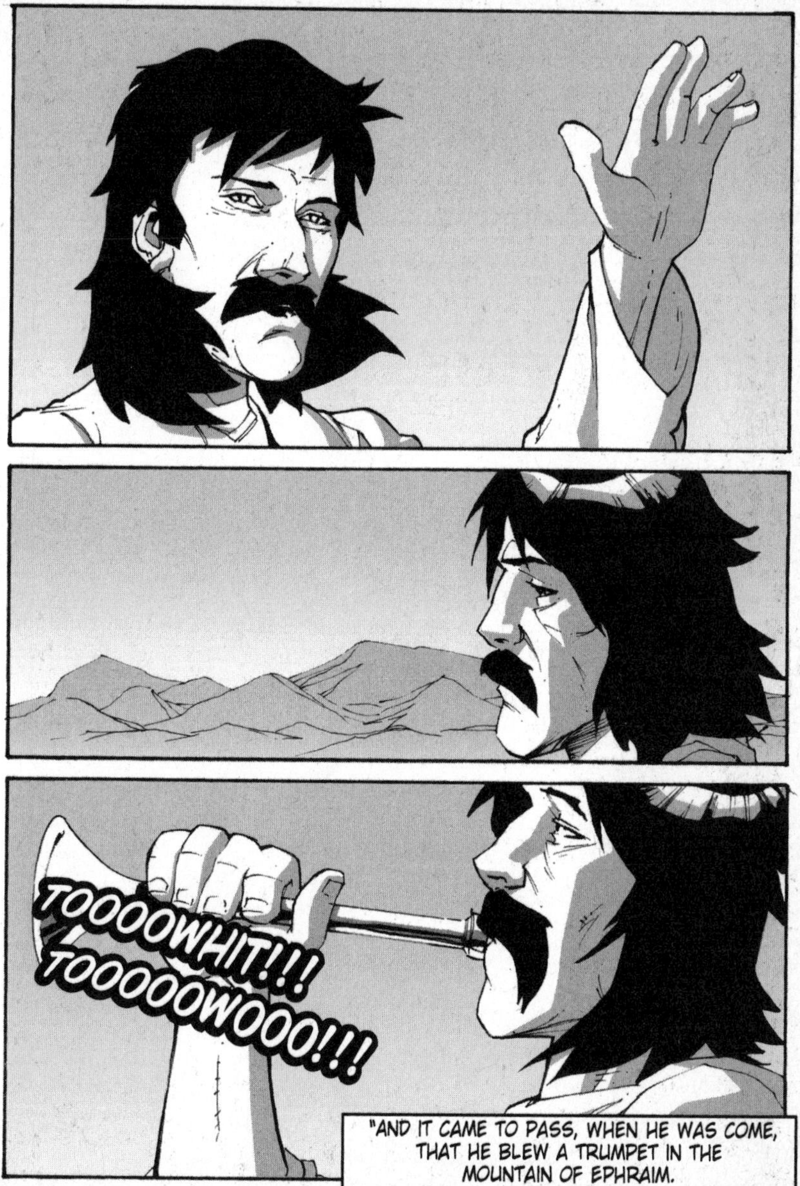
TOOOOWHIT!!!
TOOOOOWOOO!!!
"AND IT CAME TO PASS, WHEN HE WAS COME, THAT HE BLEW A TRUMPET IN THE MOUNTAIN OF EPHRAIM.

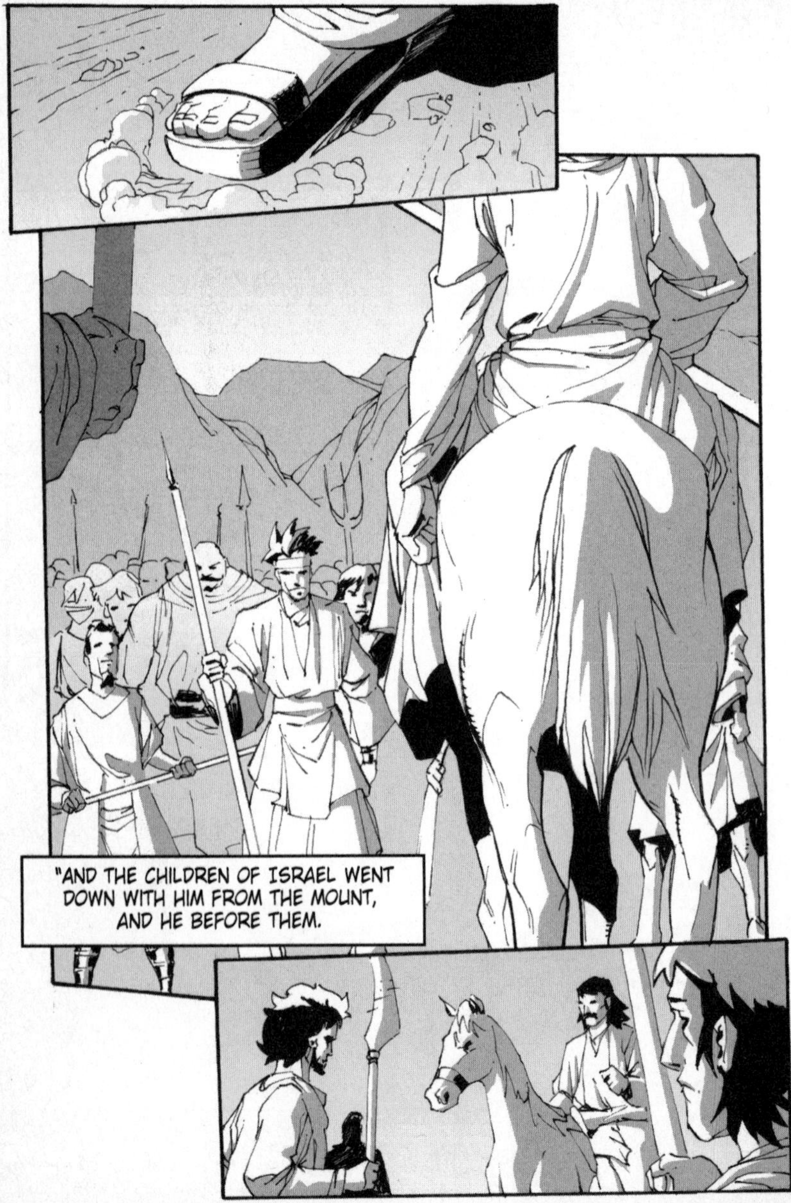
"AND THE CHILDREN OF ISRAEL WENT DOWN WITH HIM FROM THE MOUNT, AND HE BEFORE THEM.

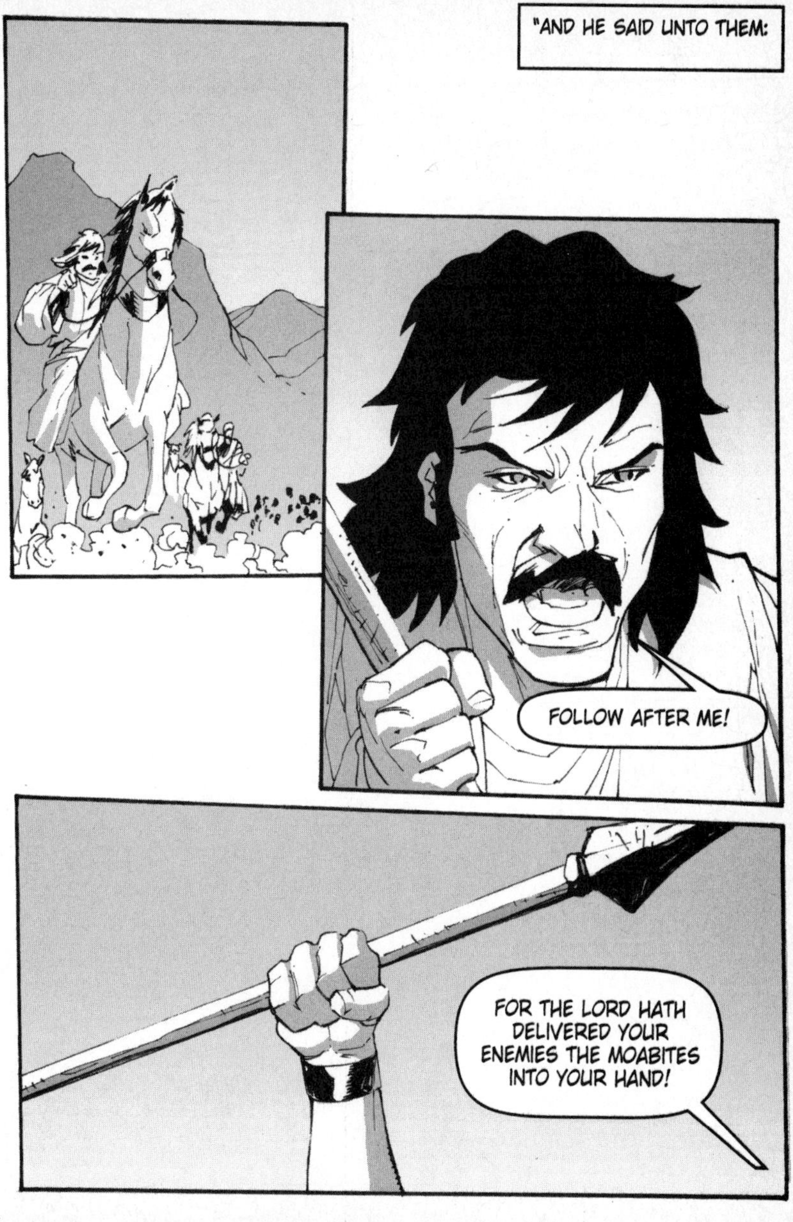
"AND HE SAID UNTO THEM:
FOLLOW AFTER ME!
FOR THE LORD HATH DELIVERED YOUR ENEMIES THE MOABITES INTO YOUR HAND!

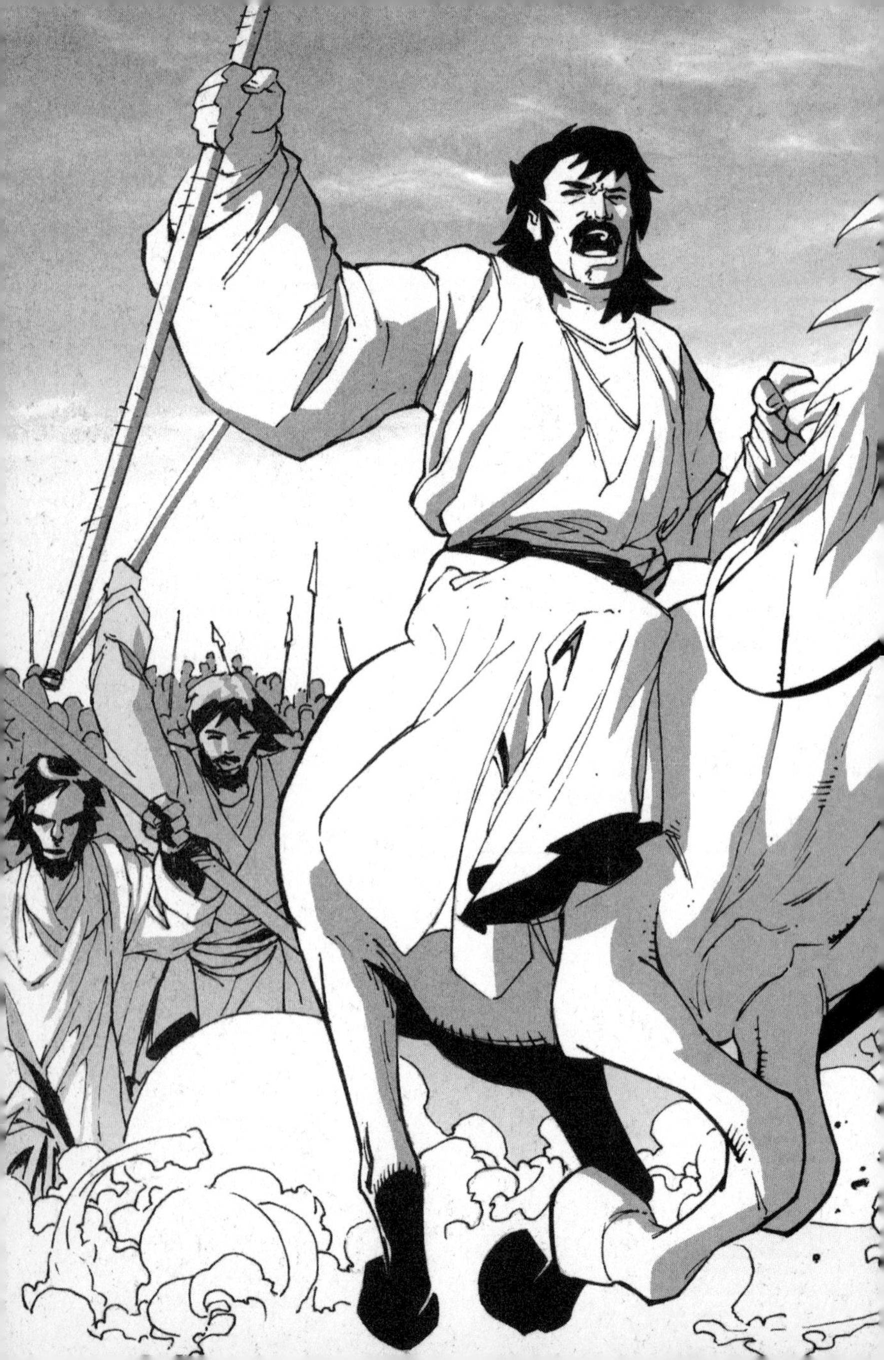

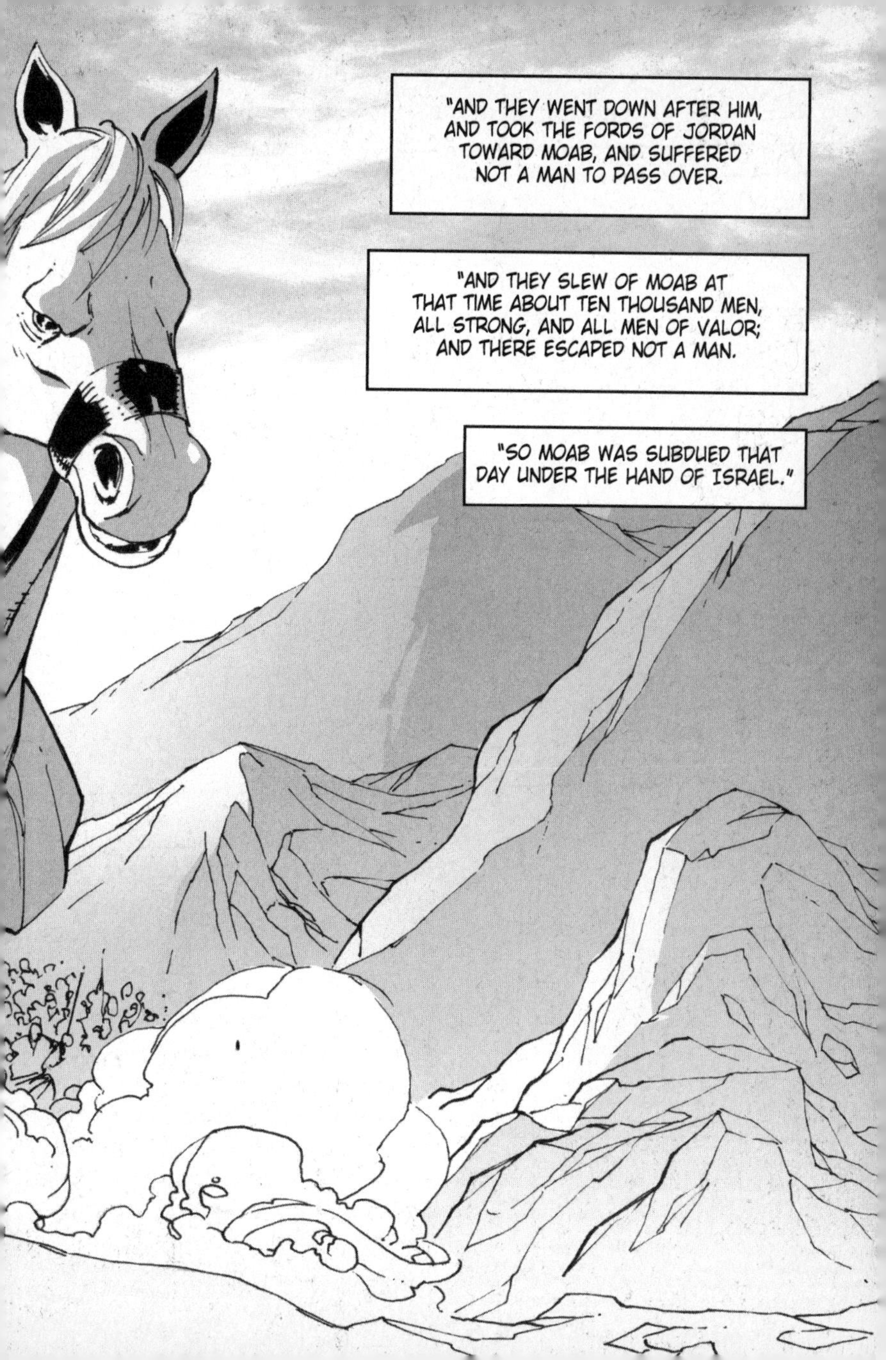
"AND THEY WENT DOWN AFTER HIM, AND TOOK THE FORDS OF JORDAN TOWARD MOAB, AND SUFFERED NOT A MAN TO PASS OVER.
"AND THEY SLEW OF MOAB AT THAT TIME ABOUT TEN THOUSAND MEN, ALL STRONG, AND ALL MEN OF VALOR; AND THERE ESCAPED NOT A MAN.
"SO MOAB WAS SUBDUED THAT DAY UNDER THE HAND OF ISRAEL."

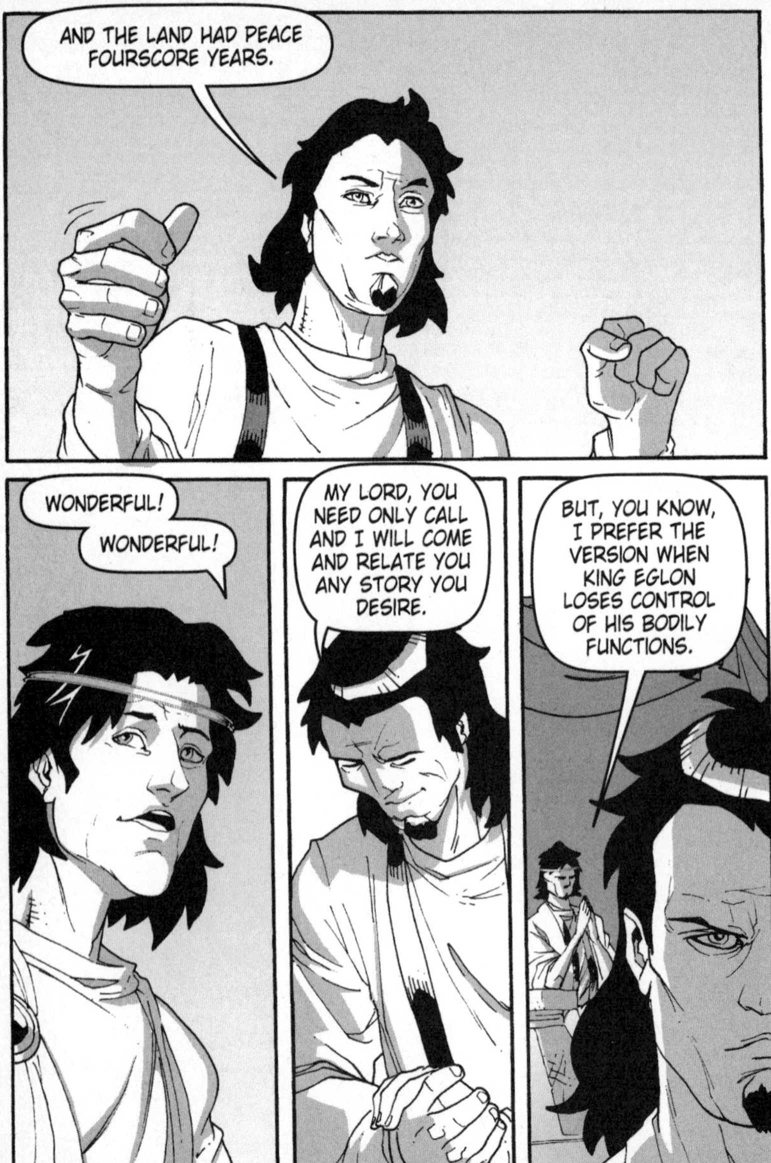
AND THE LAND HAD PEACE FOURSCORE YEARS.
WONDERFUL!
WONDERFUL!
MY LORD, YOU NEED ONLY CALL AND I WILL COME AND RELATE YOU ANY STORY YOU DESIRE.
BUT, YOU KNOW, I PREFER THE VERSION WHEN KING EGLON LOSES CONTROL OF HIS BODILY FUNCTIONS.

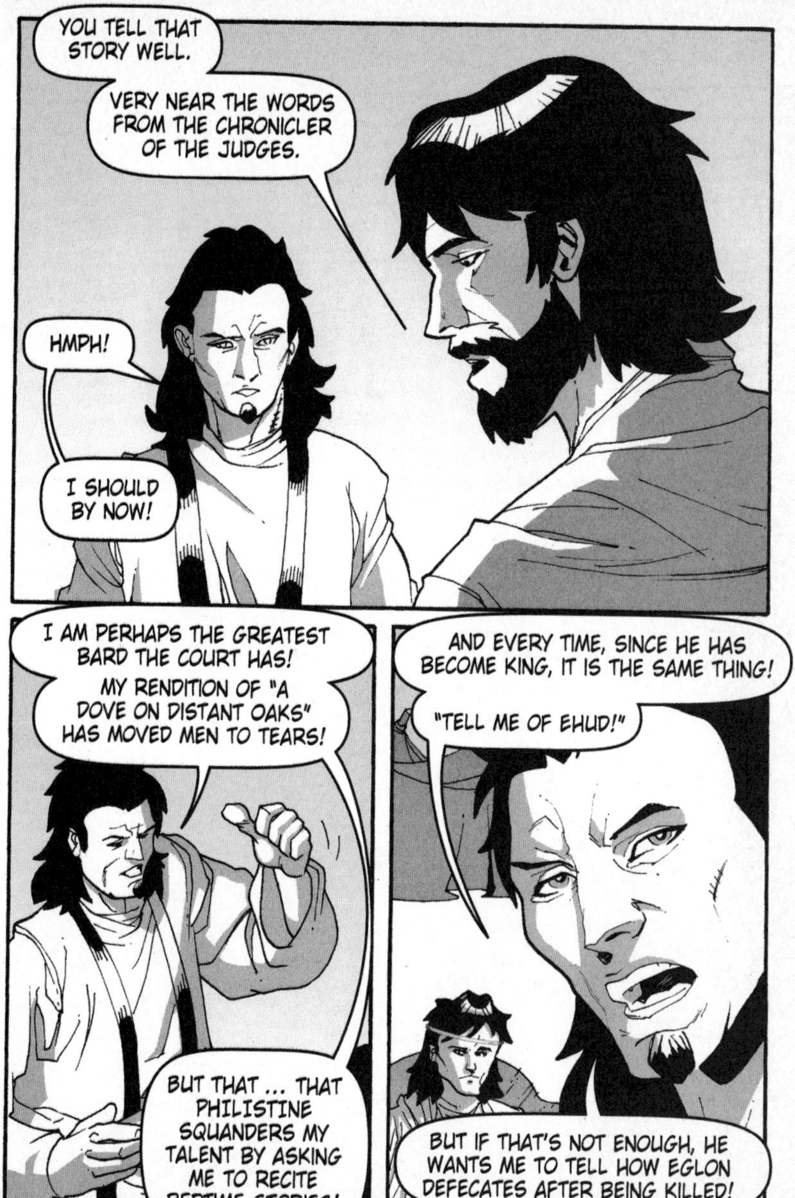
YOU TELL THAT STORY WELL.
VERY NEAR THE WORDS FROM THE CHRONICLER OF THE JUDGES.
HMPH!
I SHOULD BY NOW!
I AM PERHAPS THE GREATEST BARD THE COURT HAS!
MY RENDITION OF "A DOVE ON DISTANT OAKS" HAS MOVED MEN TO TEARS!
BUT THAT ... THAT PHILISTINE SQUANDERS MY TALENT BY ASKING ME TO RECITE BEDTIME STORIES!
AND EVERY TIME, SINCE HE HAS BECOME KING, IT IS THE SAME THING!
"TELL ME OF EHUD!"
BUT IF THAT'S NOT ENOUGH, HE WANTS ME TO TELL HOW EGLON DEFECATES AFTER BEING KILLED!
I AM A BARD, NOT A COURT JESTER!

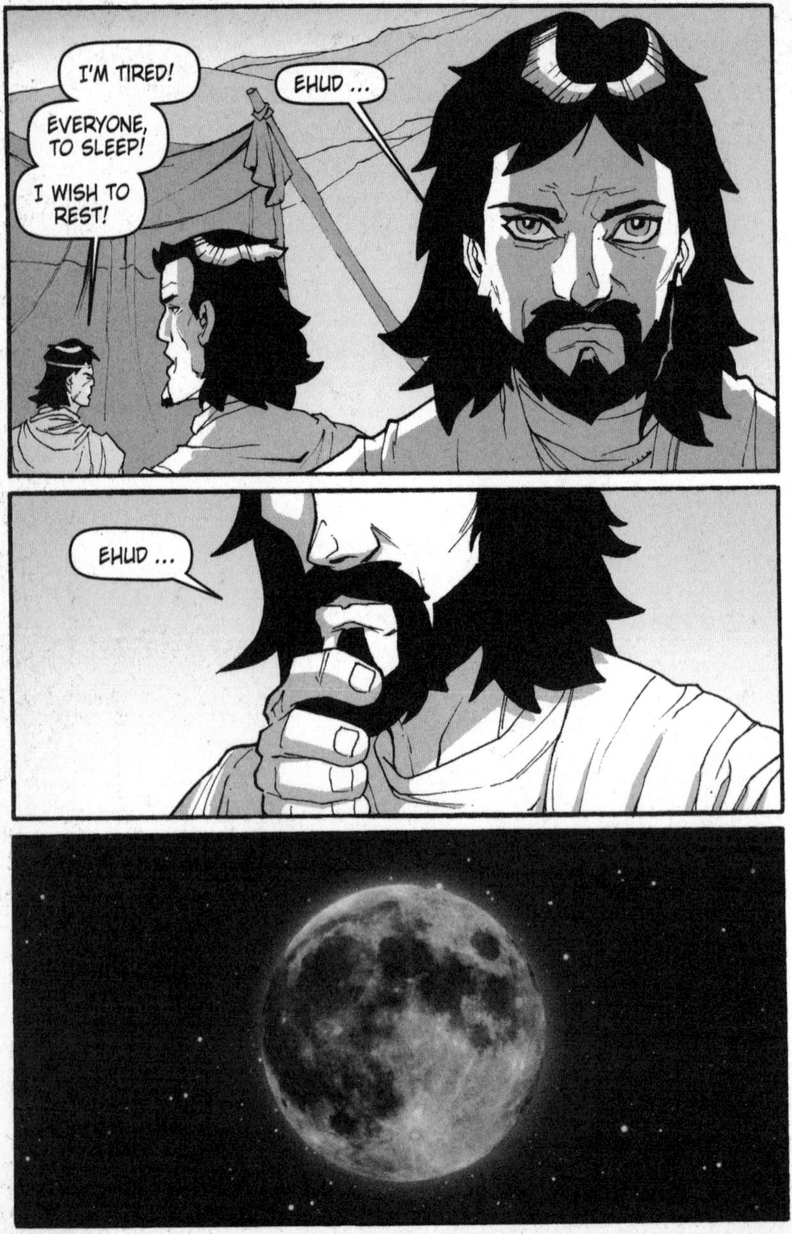
I'M TIRED!
EVERYONE, TO SLEEP!
I WISH TO REST!
EHUD ...
EHUD ...

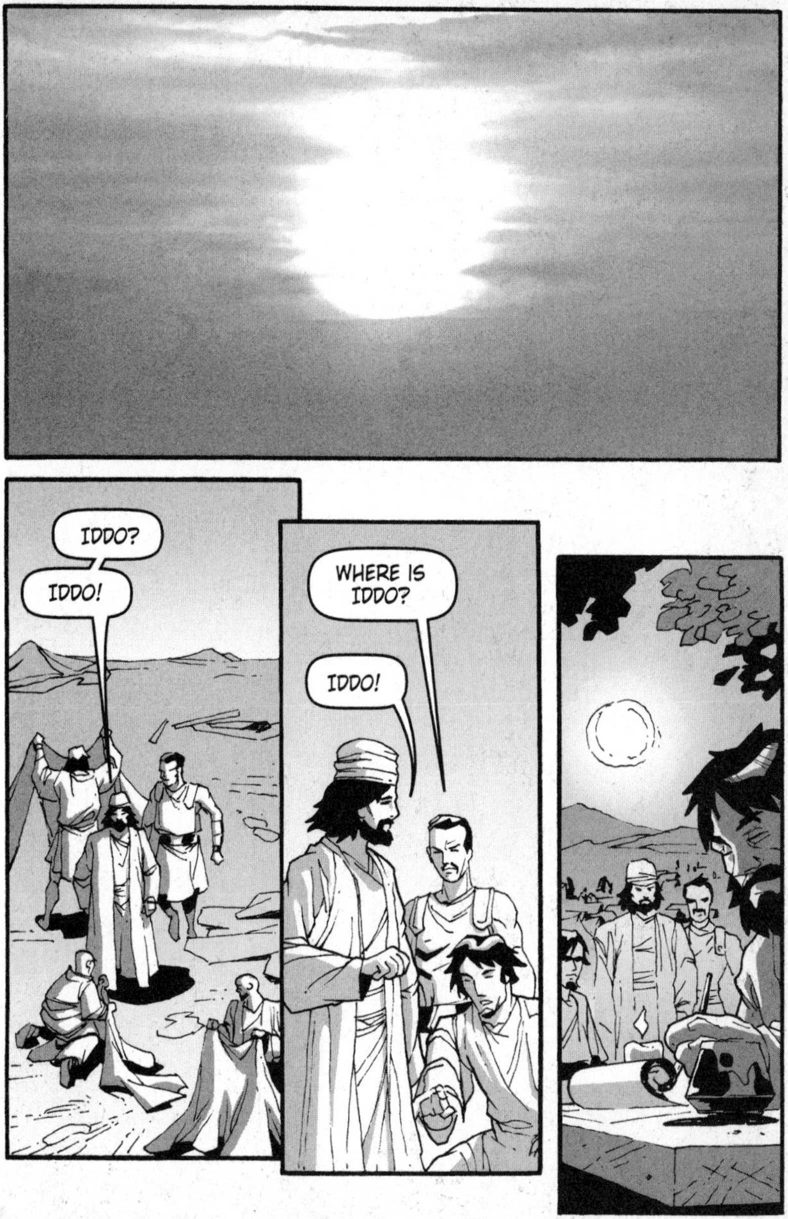
IDDO?
IDDO!
WHERE IS IDDO?
IDDO!

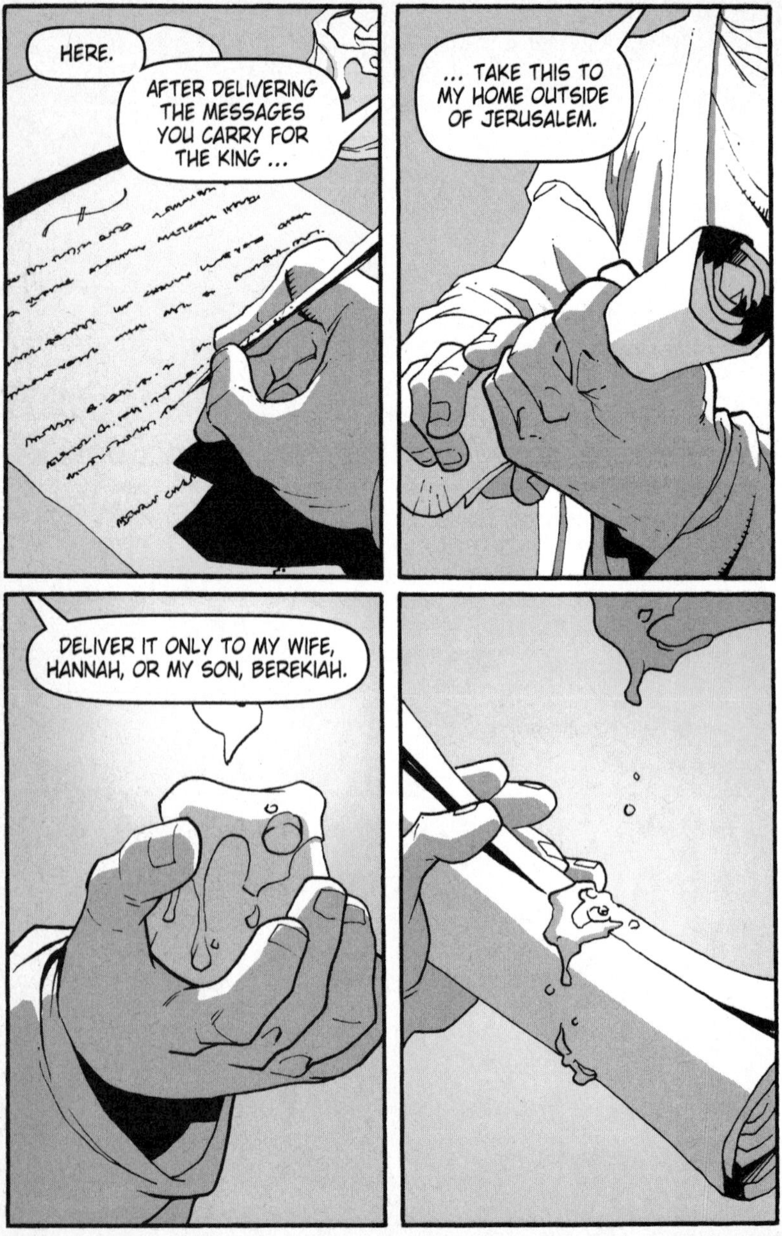
HERE.
AFTER DELIVERING THE MESSAGES YOU CARRY FOR THE KING ...
... TAKE THIS TO MY HOME OUTSIDE OF JERUSALEM.
DELIVER IT ONLY TO MY WIFE, HANNAH, OR MY SON, BEREKIAH.

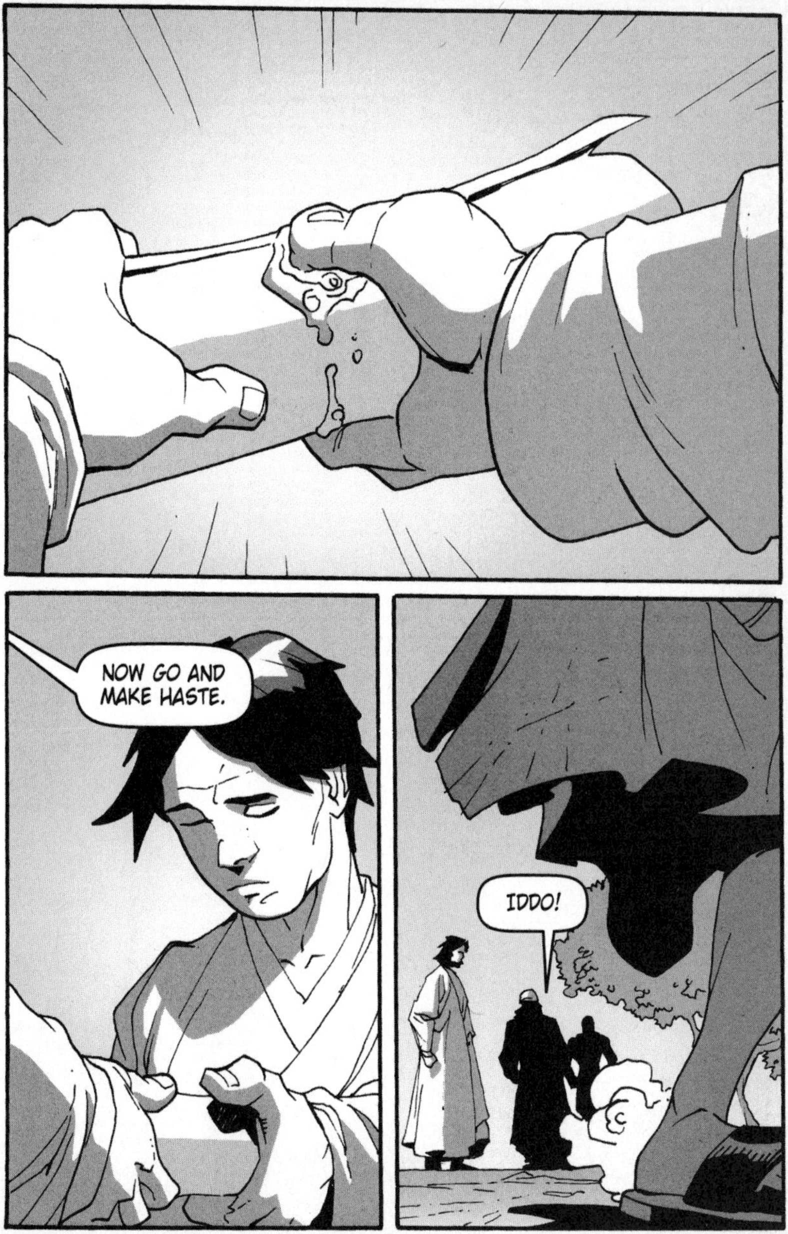
NOW GO AND MAKE HASTE.
IDDO!

GENTLEMEN ...

IDDO, WE HAVE A PROBLEM.

KING JEHOAHAZ HAS NOT STIRRED FROM HIS BED THIS MORNING ...

OH NO ... IS HE --

YES, HE'S ALIVE ... THAT'S NOT THE PROBLEM.

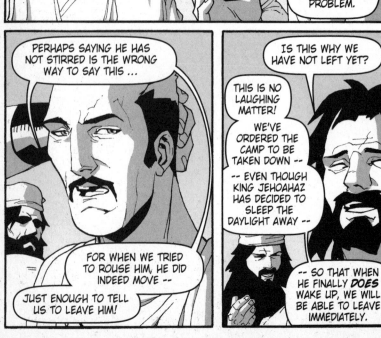

PERHAPS SAYING HE HAS NOT STIRRED IS THE WRONG WAY TO SAY THIS ...

FOR WHEN WE TRIED TO ROUSE HIM, HE DID INDEED MOVE --

JUST ENOUGH TO TELL US TO LEAVE HIM!

IS THIS WHY WE HAVE NOT LEFT YET?

THIS IS NO LAUGHING MATTER!

WE'VE ORDERED THE CAMP TO BE TAKEN DOWN --

-- EVEN THOUGH KING JEHOAHAZ HAS DECIDED TO SLEEP THE DAYLIGHT AWAY --

-- SO THAT WHEN HE FINALLY *DOES* WAKE UP, WE WILL BE ABLE TO LEAVE IMMEDIATELY.

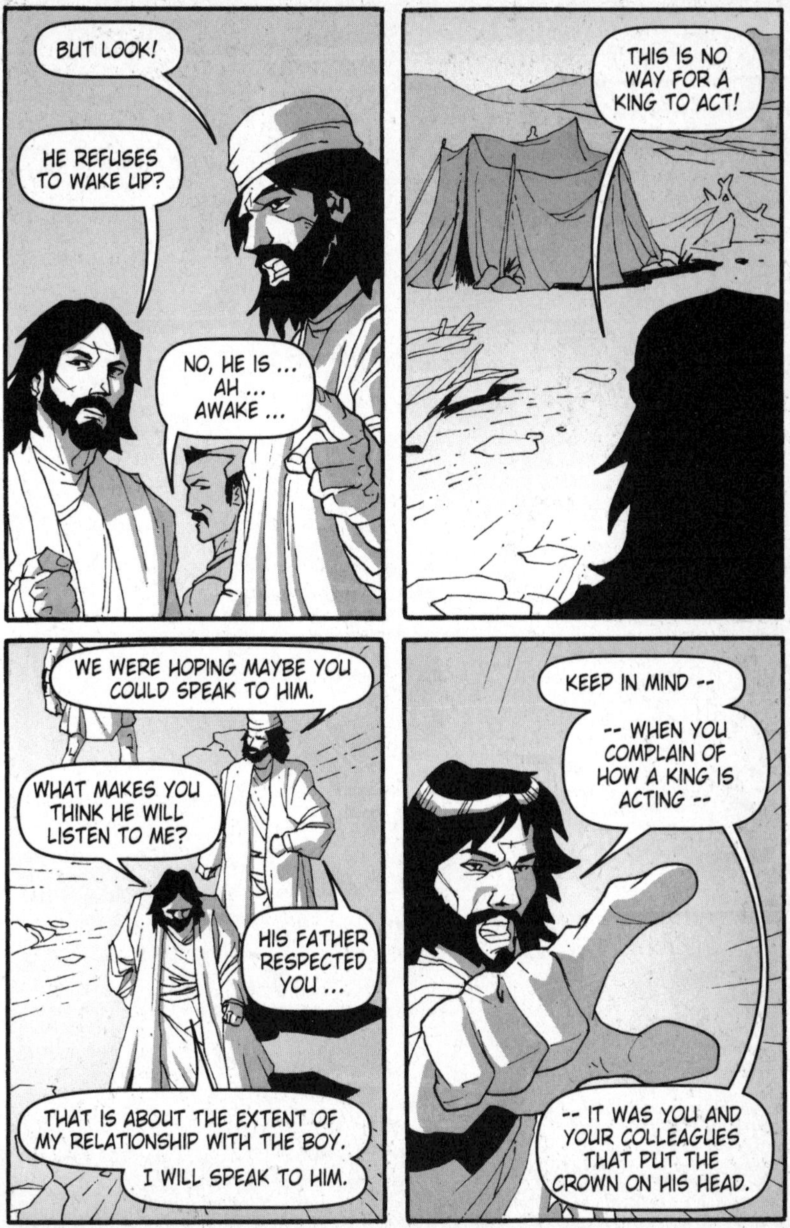
BUT LOOK!
HE REFUSES TO WAKE UP?
NO, HE IS ... AH ... AWAKE ...
THIS IS NO WAY FOR A KING TO ACT!
WE WERE HOPING MAYBE YOU COULD SPEAK TO HIM.
WHAT MAKES YOU THINK HE WILL LISTEN TO ME?
HIS FATHER RESPECTED YOU ...
THAT IS ABOUT THE EXTENT OF MY RELATIONSHIP WITH THE BOY.
I WILL SPEAK TO HIM.
KEEP IN MIND --
-- WHEN YOU COMPLAIN OF HOW A KING IS ACTING --
-- IT WAS YOU AND YOUR COLLEAGUES THAT PUT THE CROWN ON HIS HEAD.

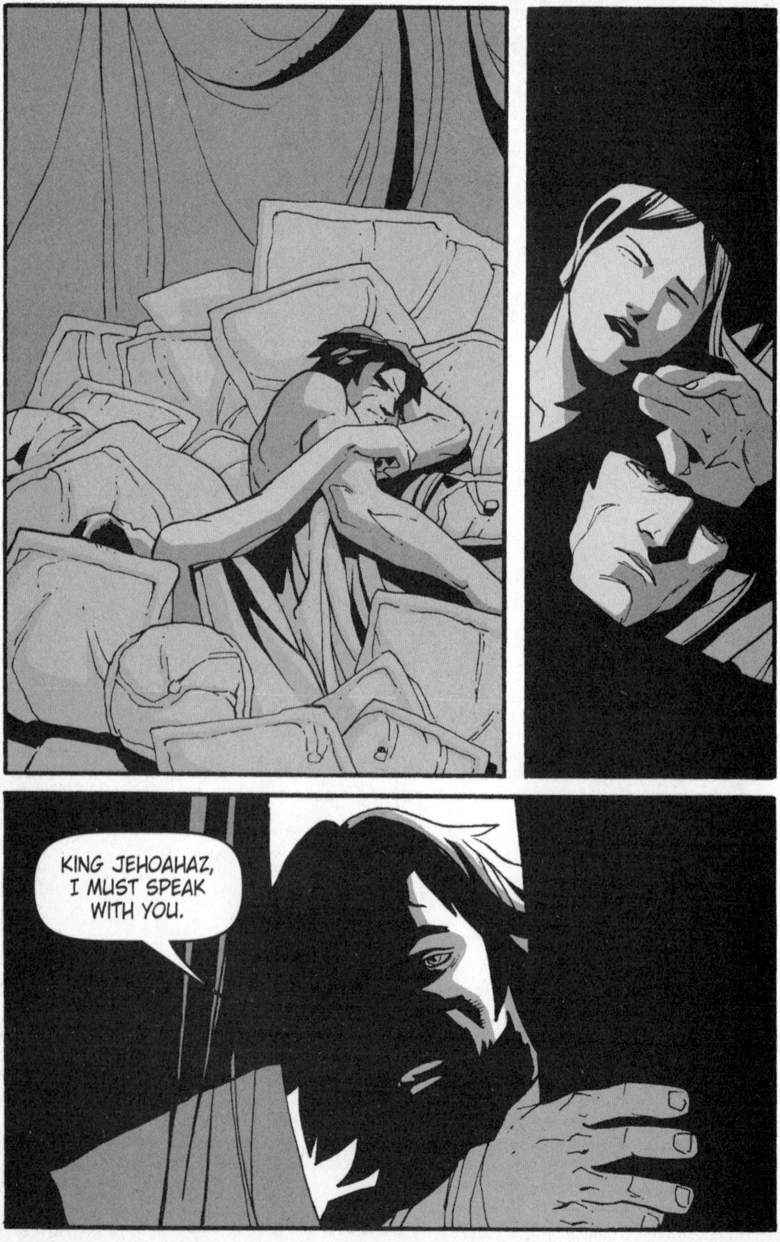
KING JEHOAHAZ, I MUST SPEAK WITH YOU.

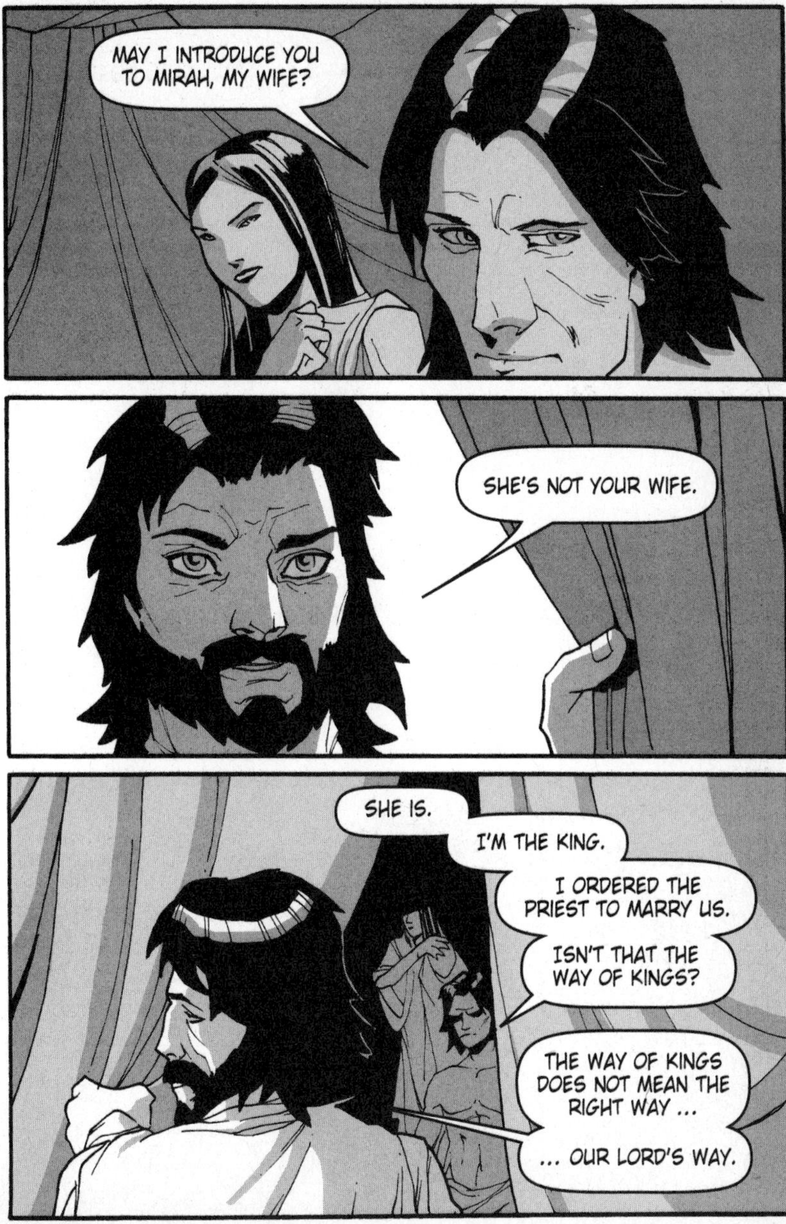
MAY I INTRODUCE YOU TO MIRAH, MY WIFE?
SHE'S NOT YOUR WIFE.
SHE IS.
I'M THE KING.
I ORDERED THE PRIEST TO MARRY US.
ISN'T THAT THE WAY OF KINGS?
THE WAY OF KINGS DOES NOT MEAN THE RIGHT WAY ...
... OUR LORD'S WAY.

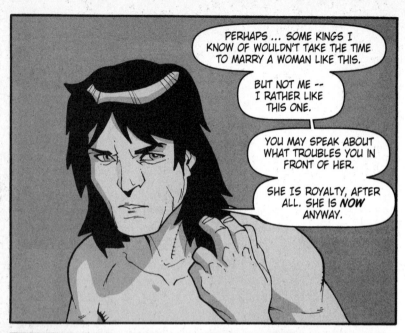

PERHAPS ... SOME KINGS I KNOW OF WOULDN'T TAKE THE TIME TO MARRY A WOMAN LIKE THIS.

BUT NOT ME -- I RATHER LIKE THIS ONE.

YOU MAY SPEAK ABOUT WHAT TROUBLES YOU IN FRONT OF HER.

SHE IS ROYALTY, AFTER ALL. SHE IS *NOW* ANYWAY.

YOU *KNOW* WHAT "TROUBLES" ME!

NOW, NOW, IDDO.

SHE'S MERELY PRAYING THAT THE GODS WOULD GRANT US A SON!

ATTENDANTS!!!

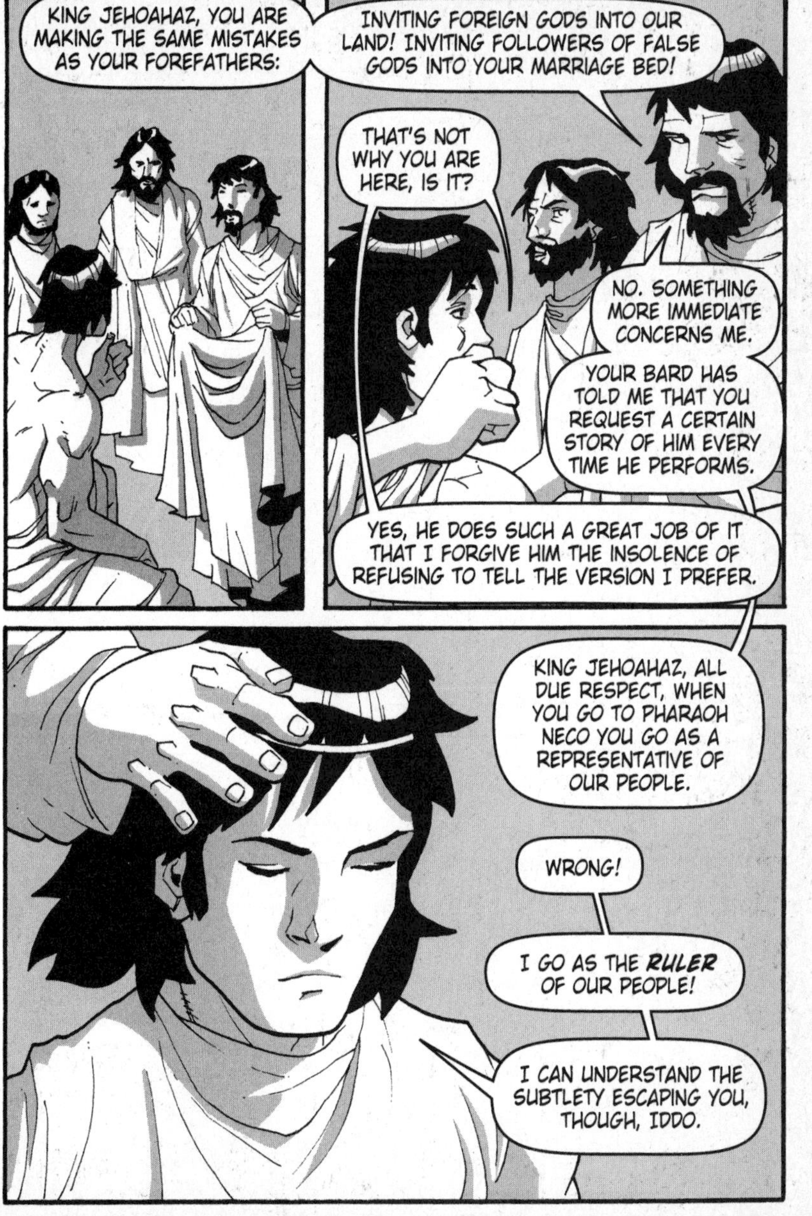
KING JEHOAHAZ, YOU ARE MAKING THE SAME MISTAKES AS YOUR FOREFATHERS:
INVITING FOREIGN GODS INTO OUR LAND! INVITING FOLLOWERS OF FALSE GODS INTO YOUR MARRIAGE BED!
THAT'S NOT WHY YOU ARE HERE, IS IT?
NO. SOMETHING MORE IMMEDIATE CONCERNS ME.
YOUR BARD HAS TOLD ME THAT YOU REQUEST A CERTAIN STORY OF HIM EVERY TIME HE PERFORMS.
YES, HE DOES SUCH A GREAT JOB OF IT THAT I FORGIVE HIM THE INSOLENCE OF REFUSING TO TELL THE VERSION I PREFER.
KING JEHOAHAZ, ALL DUE RESPECT, WHEN YOU GO TO PHARAOH NECO YOU GO AS A REPRESENTATIVE OF OUR PEOPLE.
WRONG!
I GO AS THE ***RULER*** OF OUR PEOPLE!
I CAN UNDERSTAND THE SUBTLETY ESCAPING YOU, THOUGH, IDDO.

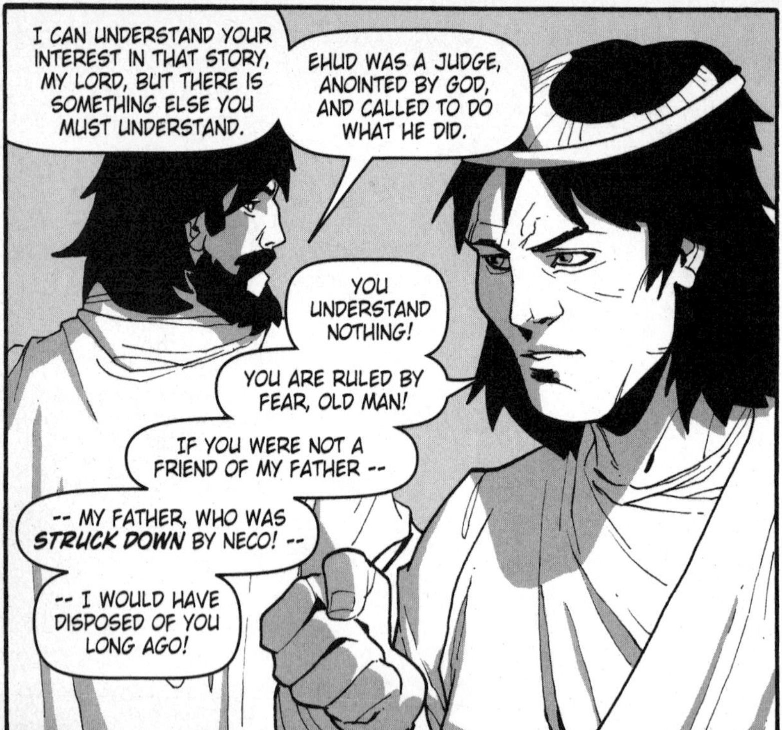
I CAN UNDERSTAND YOUR INTEREST IN THAT STORY, MY LORD, BUT THERE IS SOMETHING ELSE YOU MUST UNDERSTAND.
EHUD WAS A JUDGE, ANOINTED BY GOD, AND CALLED TO DO WHAT HE DID.
YOU UNDERSTAND NOTHING!
YOU ARE RULED BY FEAR, OLD MAN!
IF YOU WERE NOT A FRIEND OF MY FATHER --
-- MY FATHER, WHO WAS ***STRUCK DOWN*** BY NECO! --
-- I WOULD HAVE DISPOSED OF YOU LONG AGO!

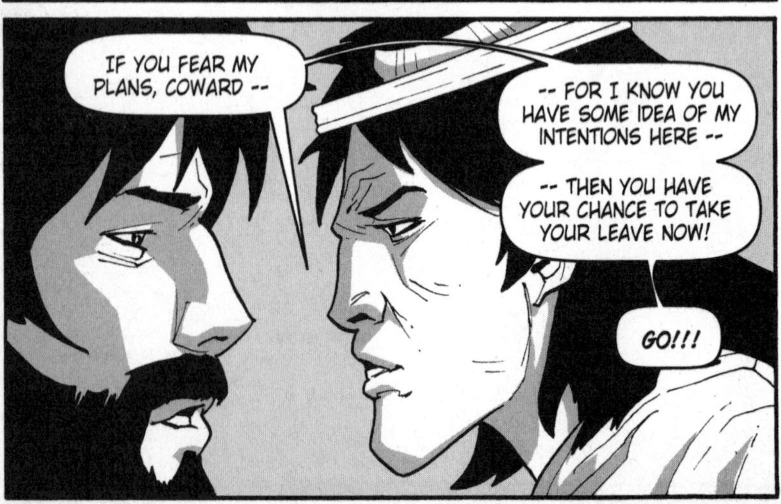
IF YOU FEAR MY PLANS, COWARD --
-- FOR I KNOW YOU HAVE SOME IDEA OF MY INTENTIONS HERE --
-- THEN YOU HAVE YOUR CHANCE TO TAKE YOUR LEAVE NOW!
GO!!!

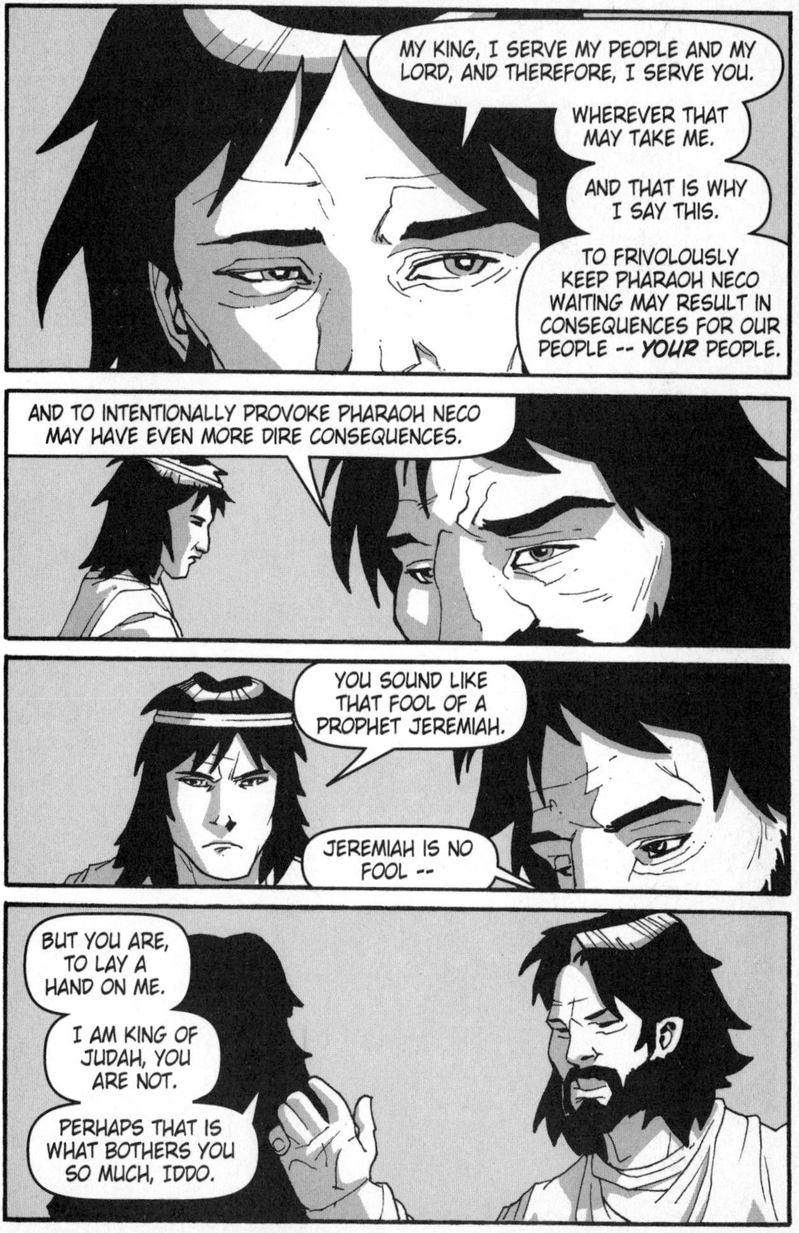
MY KING, I SERVE MY PEOPLE AND MY LORD, AND THEREFORE, I SERVE YOU.
WHEREVER THAT MAY TAKE ME.
AND THAT IS WHY I SAY THIS.
TO FRIVOLOUSLY KEEP PHARAOH NECO WAITING MAY RESULT IN CONSEQUENCES FOR OUR PEOPLE -- *YOUR* PEOPLE.
AND TO INTENTIONALLY PROVOKE PHARAOH NECO MAY HAVE EVEN MORE DIRE CONSEQUENCES.
YOU SOUND LIKE THAT FOOL OF A PROPHET JEREMIAH.
JEREMIAH IS NO FOOL --
BUT YOU ARE, TO LAY A HAND ON ME.
I AM KING OF JUDAH, YOU ARE NOT.
PERHAPS THAT IS WHAT BOTHERS YOU SO MUCH, IDDO.

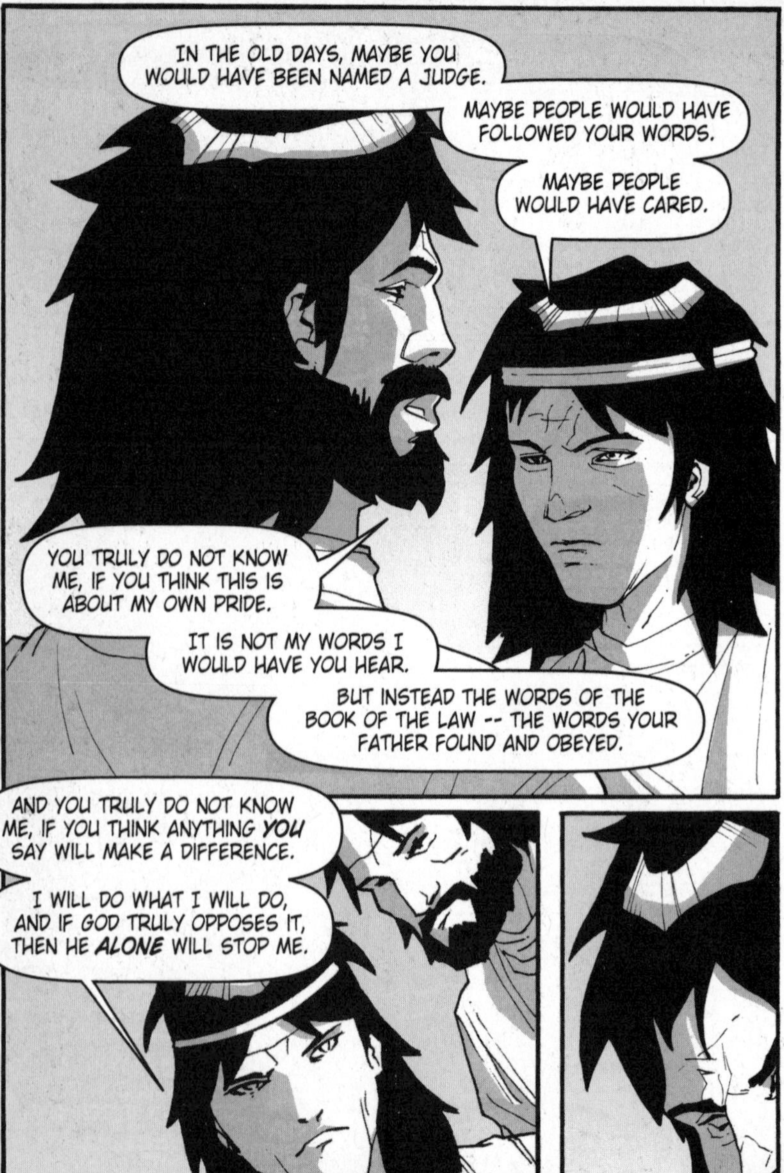
IN THE OLD DAYS, MAYBE YOU WOULD HAVE BEEN NAMED A JUDGE.
MAYBE PEOPLE WOULD HAVE FOLLOWED YOUR WORDS.
MAYBE PEOPLE WOULD HAVE CARED.
YOU TRULY DO NOT KNOW ME, IF YOU THINK THIS IS ABOUT MY OWN PRIDE.
IT IS NOT MY WORDS I WOULD HAVE YOU HEAR.
BUT INSTEAD THE WORDS OF THE BOOK OF THE LAW -- THE WORDS YOUR FATHER FOUND AND OBEYED.
AND YOU TRULY DO NOT KNOW ME, IF YOU THINK ANYTHING *YOU* SAY WILL MAKE A DIFFERENCE.
I WILL DO WHAT I WILL DO, AND IF GOD TRULY OPPOSES IT, THEN HE *ALONE* WILL STOP ME.

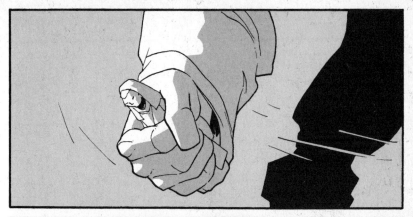

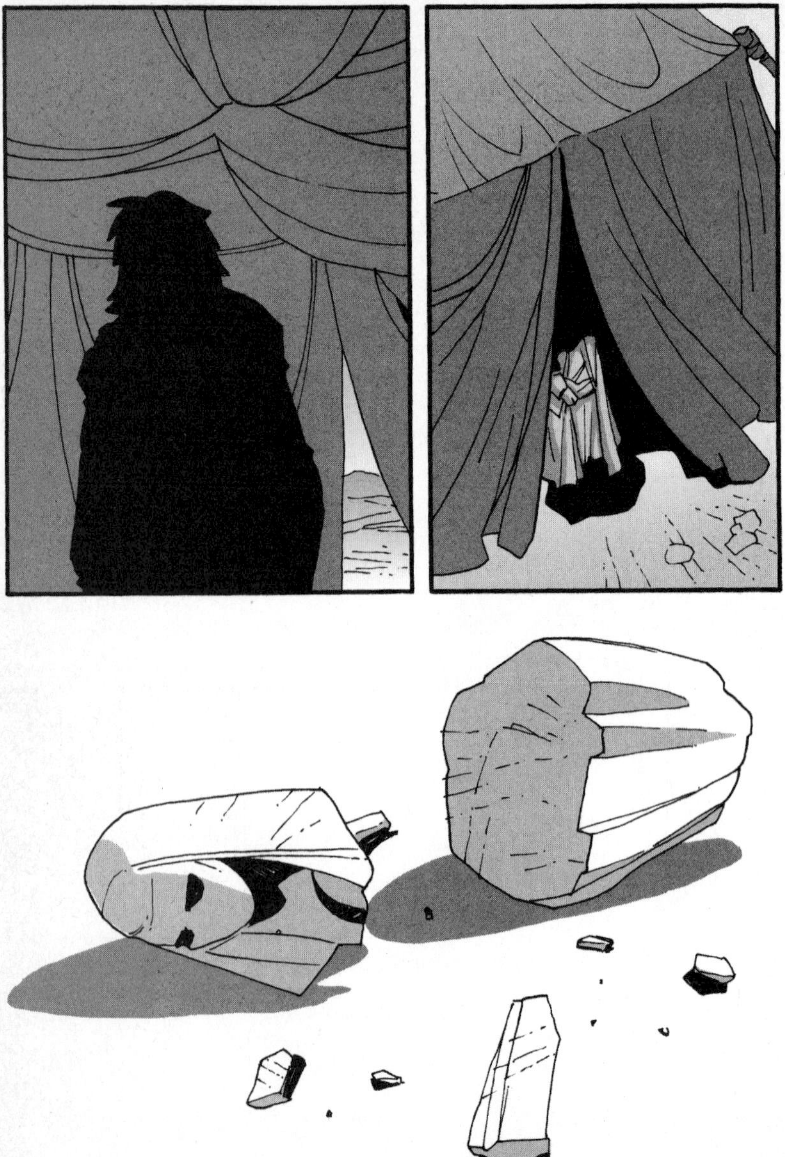

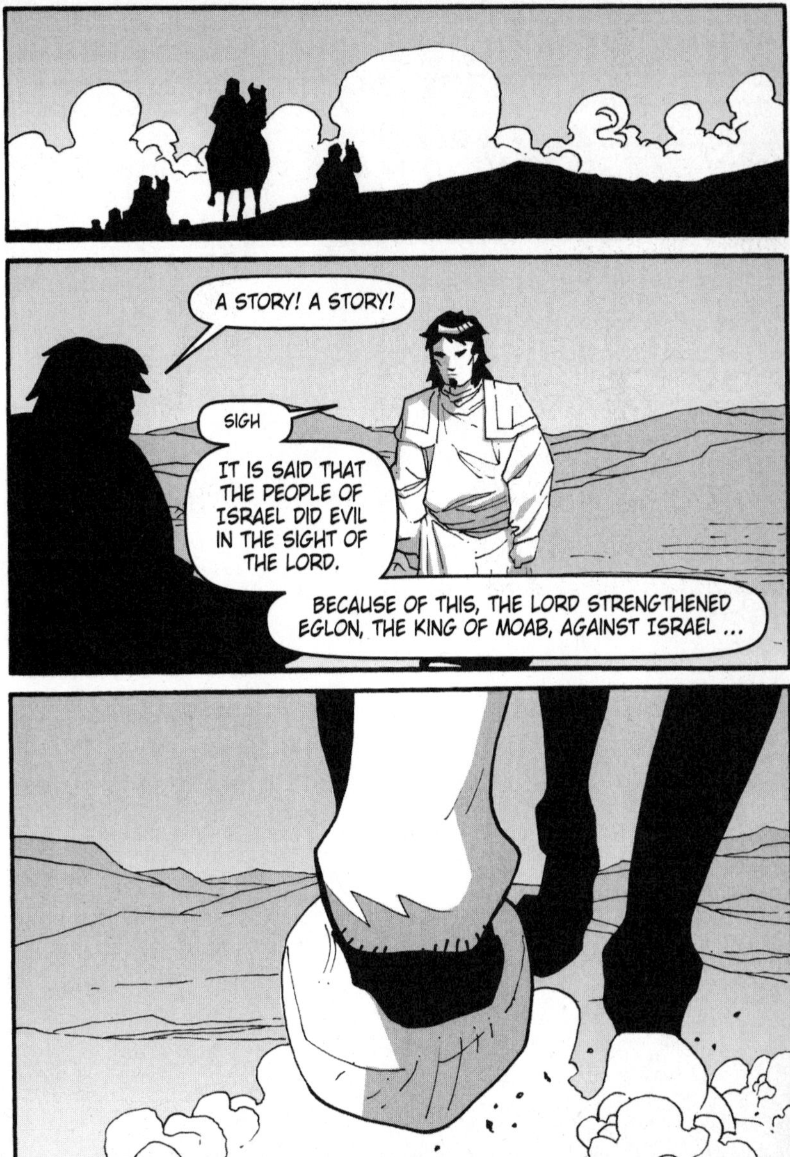
A STORY! A STORY!
SIGH
IT IS SAID THAT THE PEOPLE OF ISRAEL DID EVIL IN THE SIGHT OF THE LORD.
BECAUSE OF THIS, THE LORD STRENGTHENED EGLON, THE KING OF MOAB, AGAINST ISRAEL ...

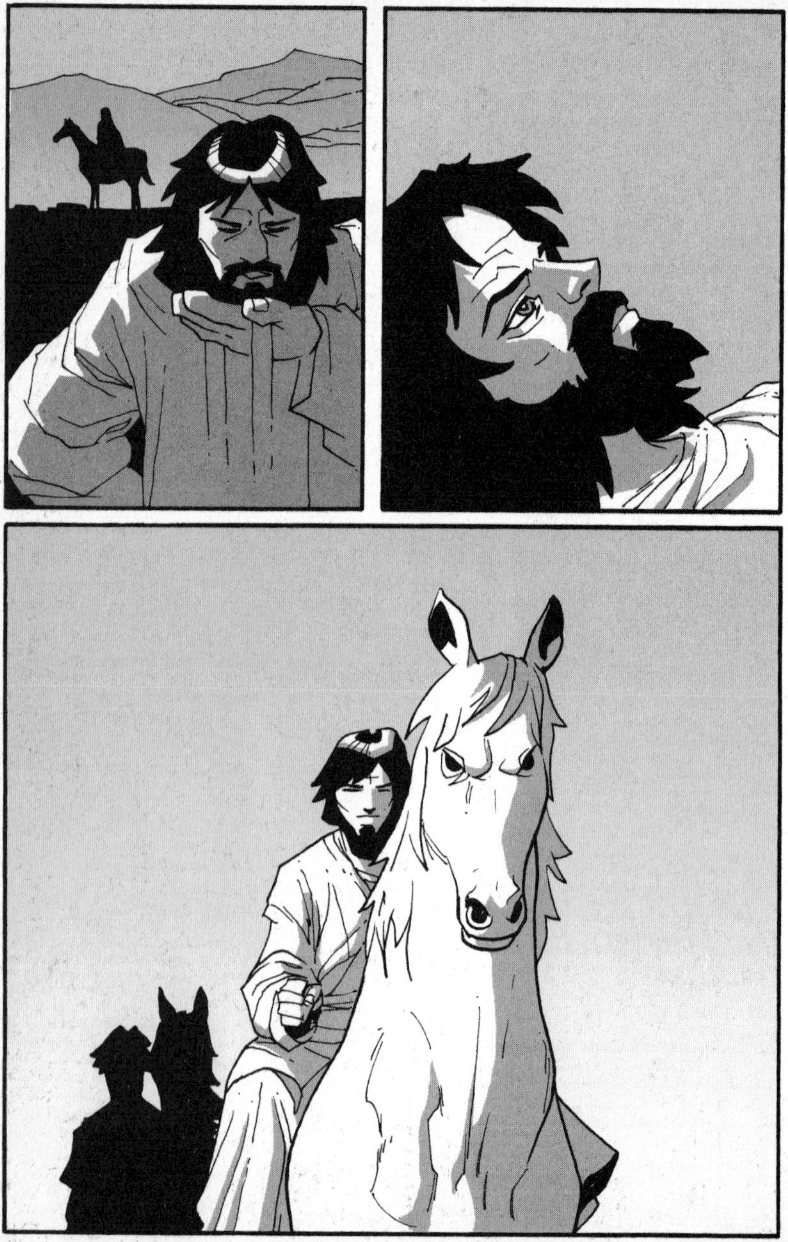

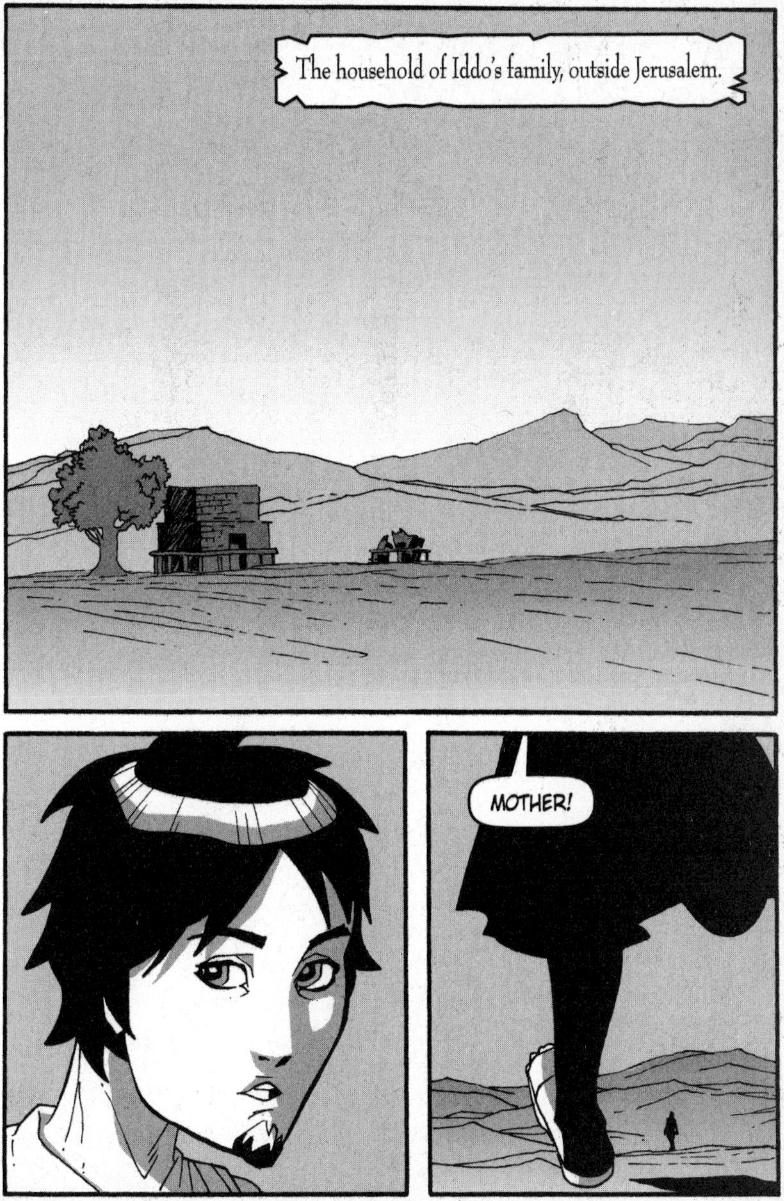
The household of Iddo's family, outside Jerusalem.
MOTHER!

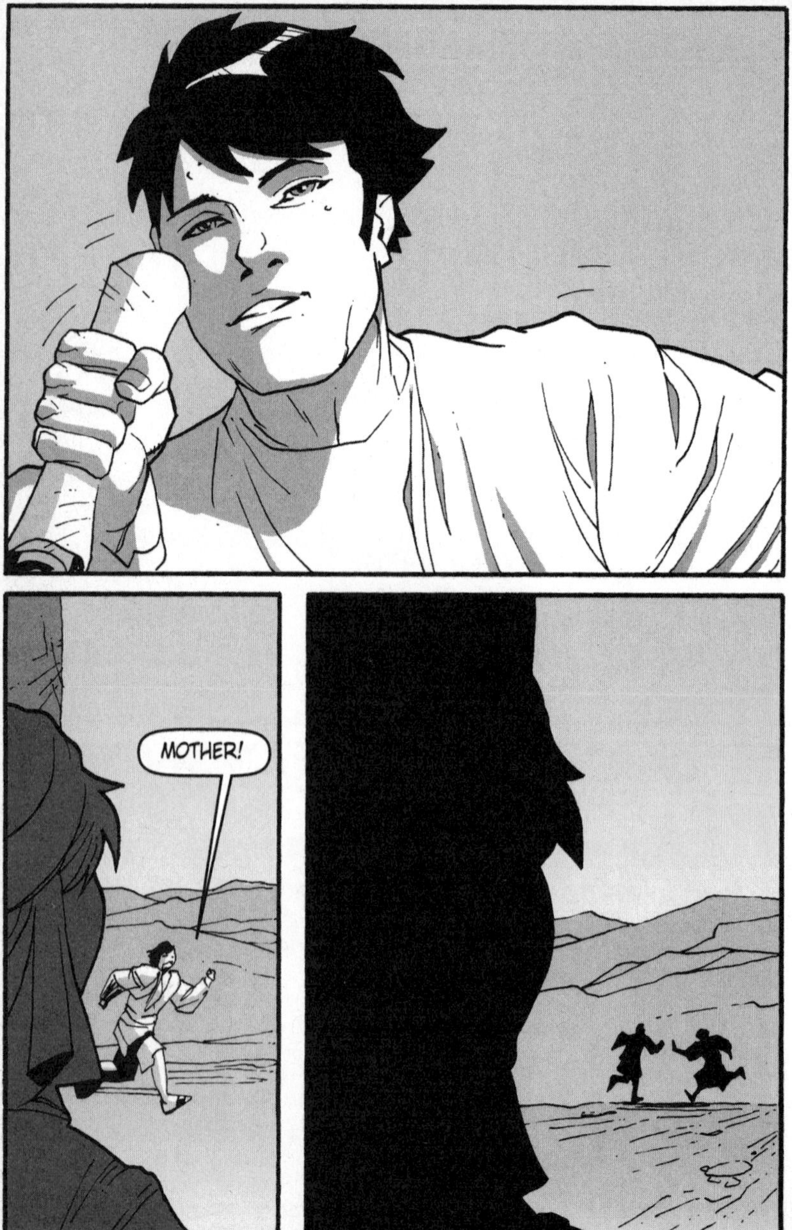
MOTHER!

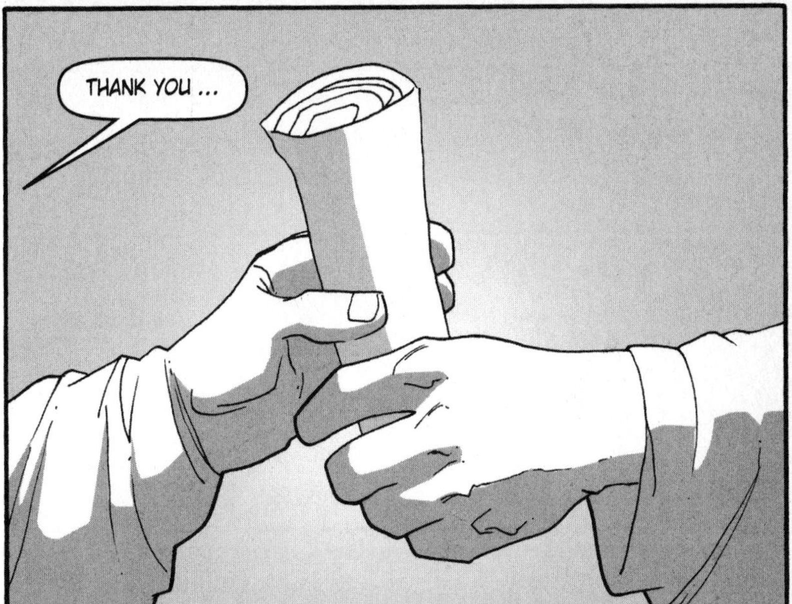
THANK YOU ...

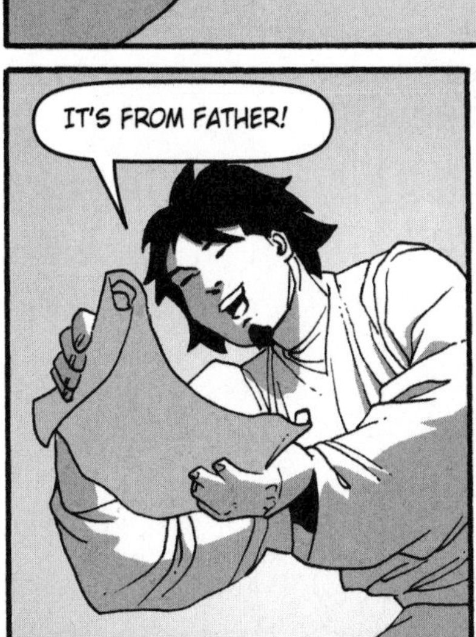
IT'S FROM FATHER!

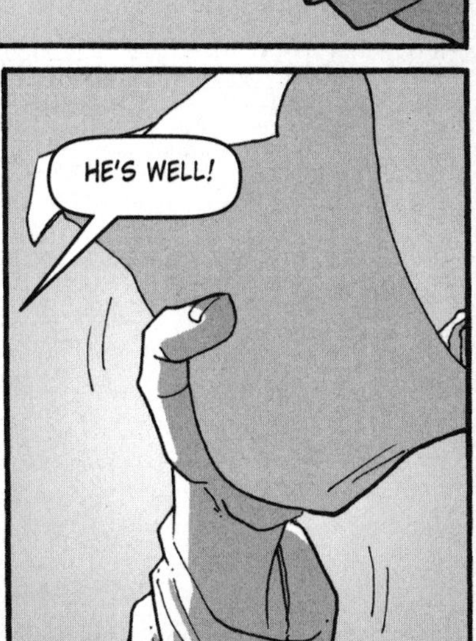
HE'S WELL!

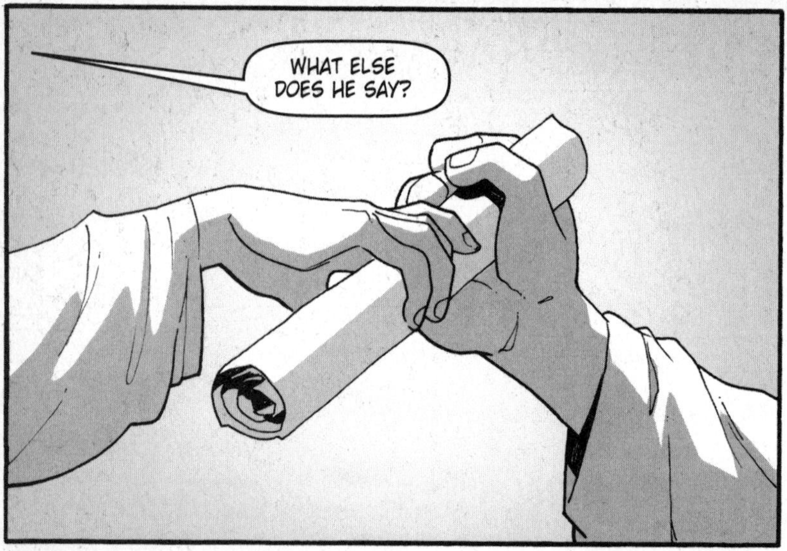
WHAT ELSE DOES HE SAY?
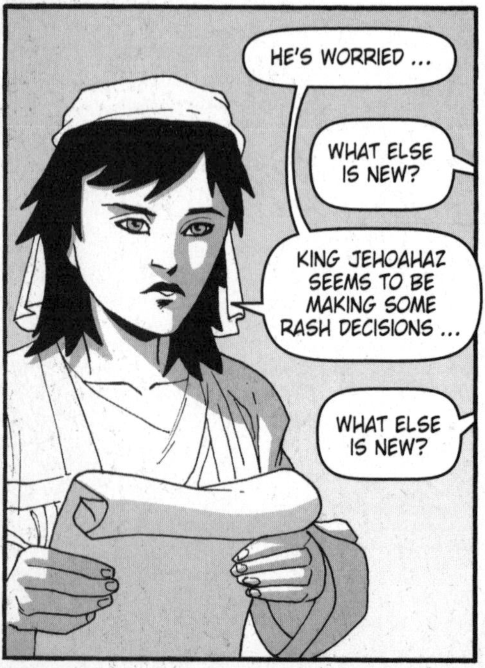
HE'S WORRIED ...
WHAT ELSE IS NEW?
KING JEHOAHAZ SEEMS TO BE MAKING SOME RASH DECISIONS ...
WHAT ELSE IS NEW?
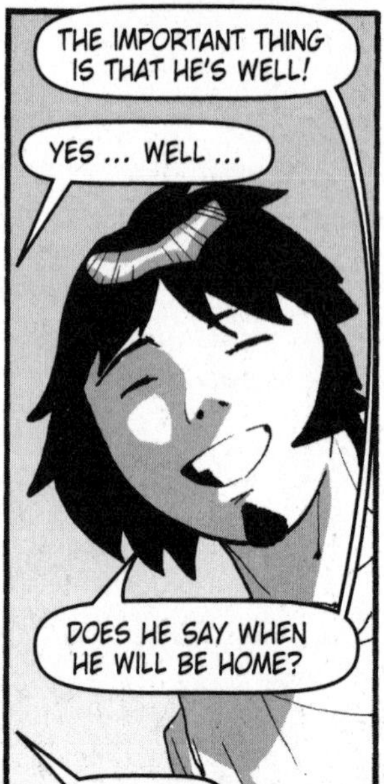
THE IMPORTANT THING IS THAT HE'S WELL!
YES ... WELL ...
DOES HE SAY WHEN HE WILL BE HOME?
NO, SON.

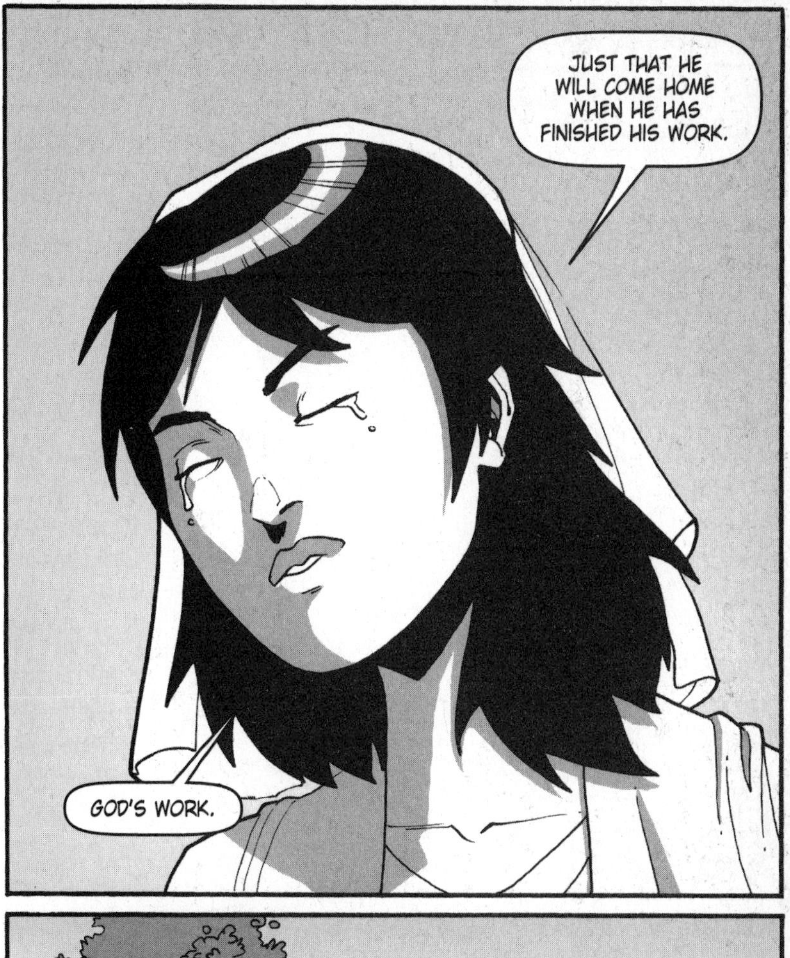
JUST THAT HE WILL COME HOME WHEN HE HAS FINISHED HIS WORK.
GOD'S WORK.
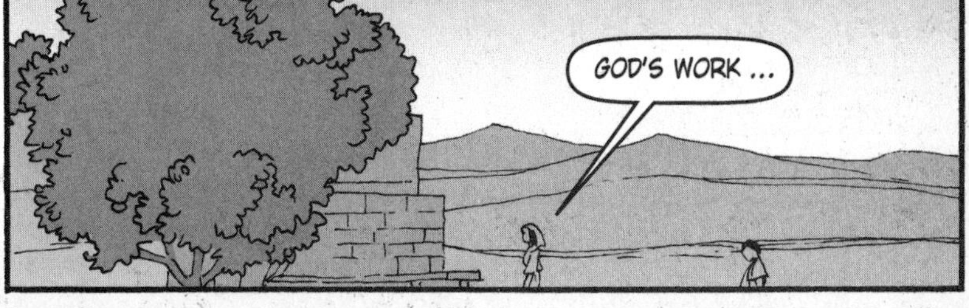
GOD'S WORK ...

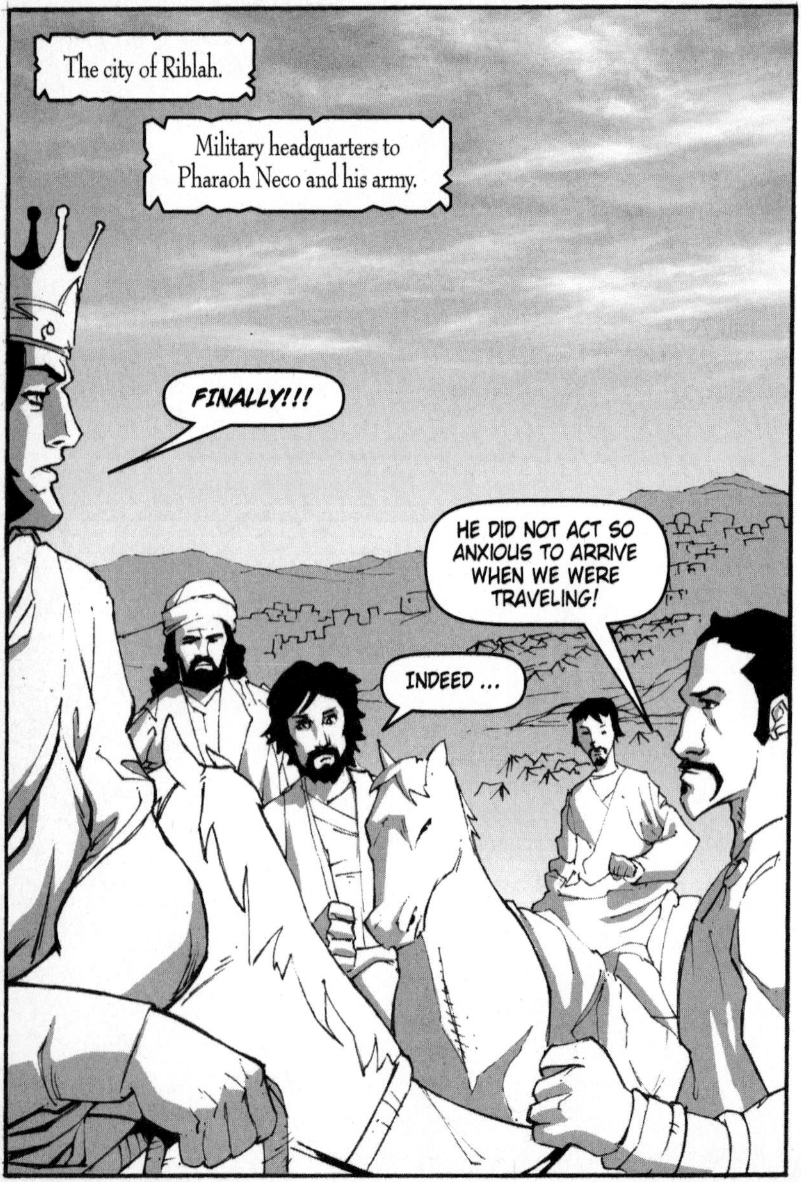
The city of Riblah.
Military headquarters to Pharaoh Neco and his army.
FINALLY!!!
INDEED ...
HE DID NOT ACT SO ANXIOUS TO ARRIVE WHEN WE WERE TRAVELING!

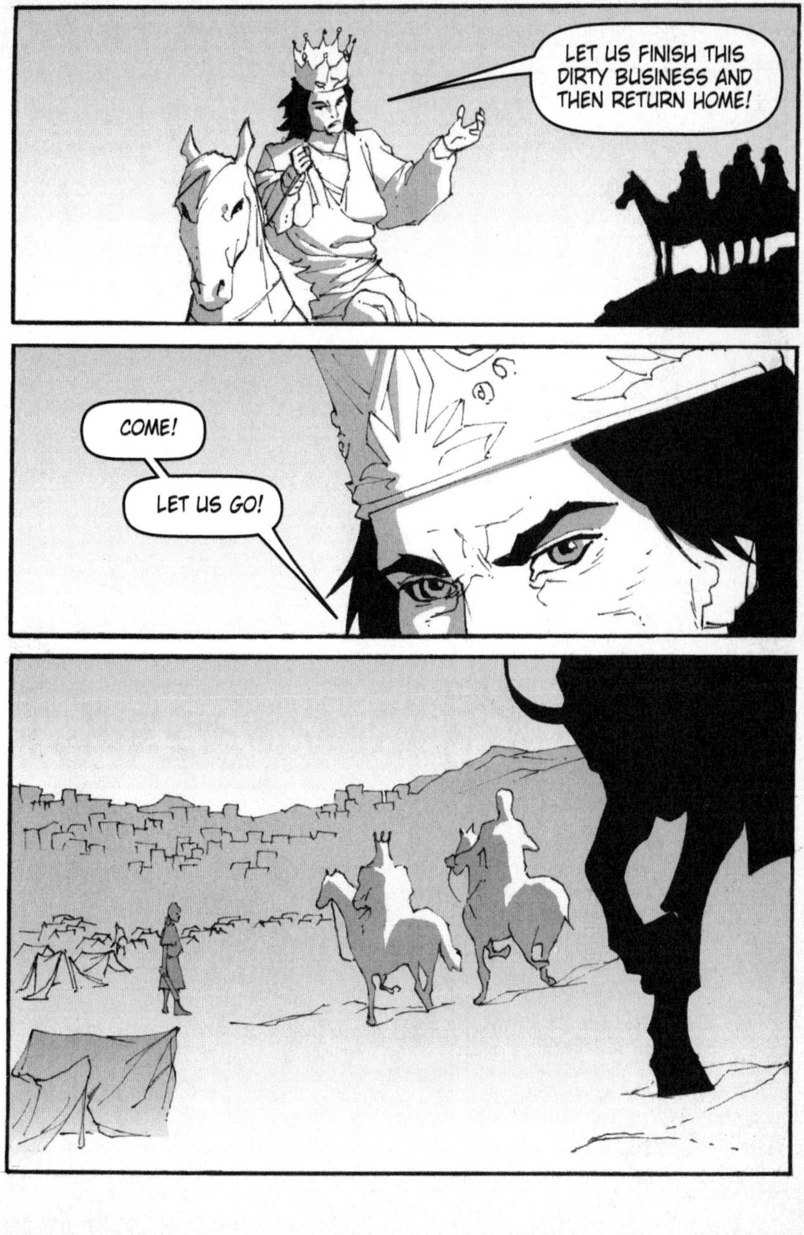
LET US FINISH THIS DIRTY BUSINESS AND THEN RETURN HOME!
COME!
LET US GO!

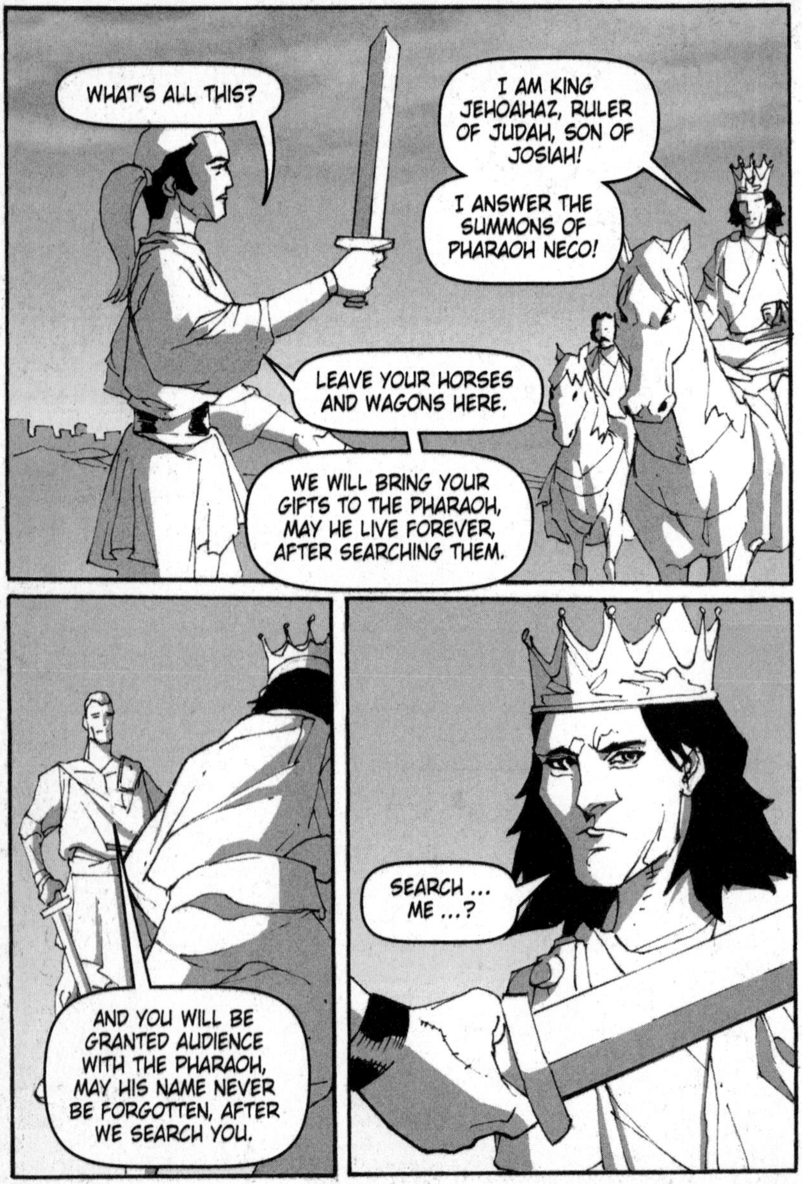
WHAT'S ALL THIS?
I AM KING JEHOAHAZ, RULER OF JUDAH, SON OF JOSIAH!
I ANSWER THE SUMMONS OF PHARAOH NECO!
LEAVE YOUR HORSES AND WAGONS HERE.
WE WILL BRING YOUR GIFTS TO THE PHARAOH, MAY HE LIVE FOREVER, AFTER SEARCHING THEM.
AND YOU WILL BE GRANTED AUDIENCE WITH THE PHARAOH, MAY HIS NAME NEVER BE FORGOTTEN, AFTER WE SEARCH YOU.
SEARCH ... ME ...?

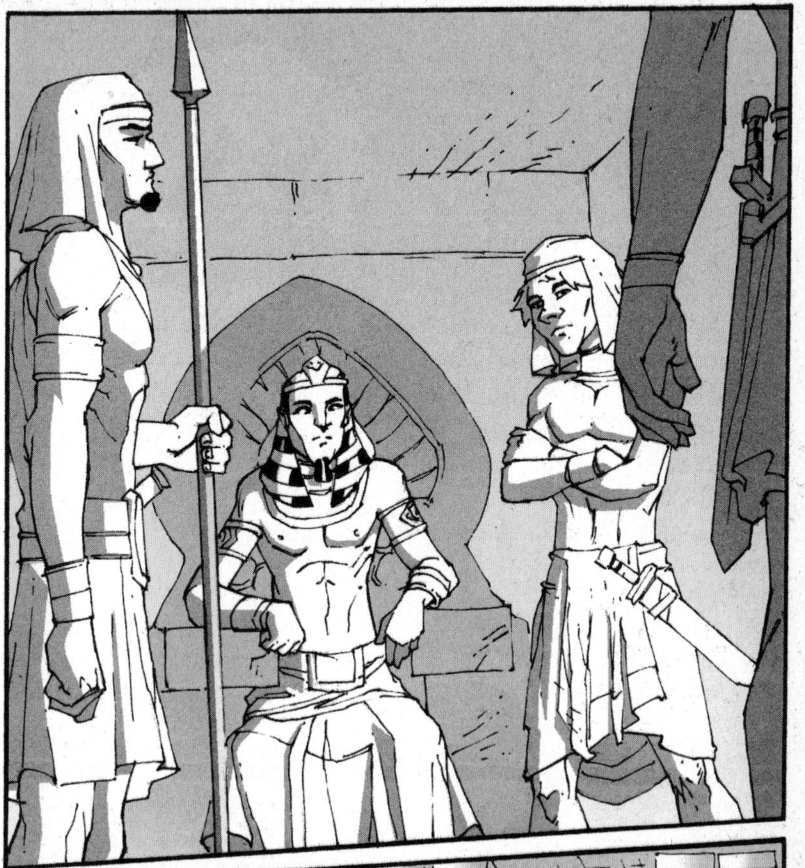

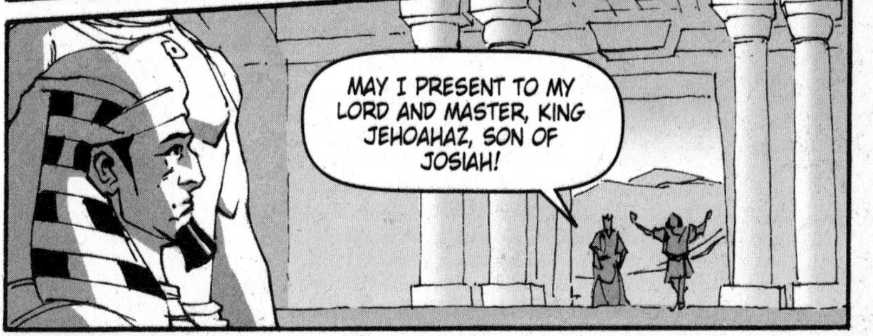
MAY I PRESENT TO MY LORD AND MASTER, KING JEHOAHAZ, SON OF JOSIAH!

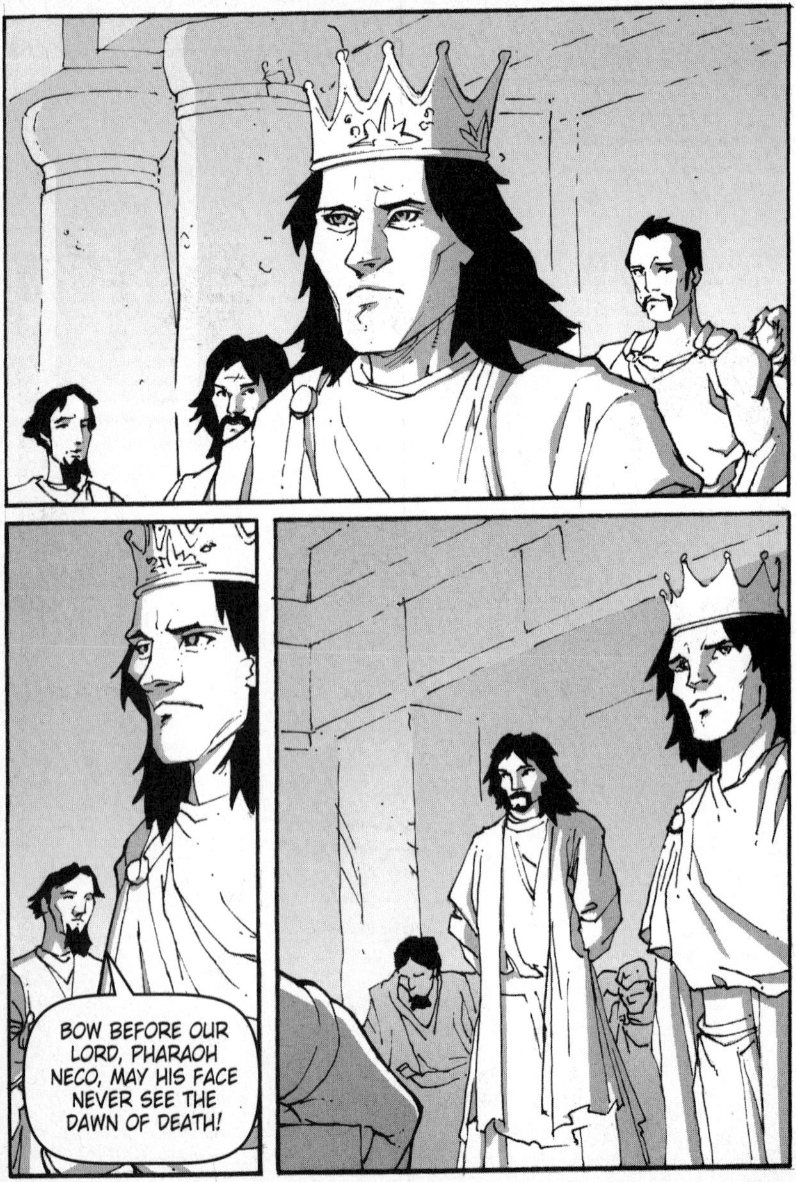
BOW BEFORE OUR LORD, PHARAOH NECO, MAY HIS FACE NEVER SEE THE DAWN OF DEATH!

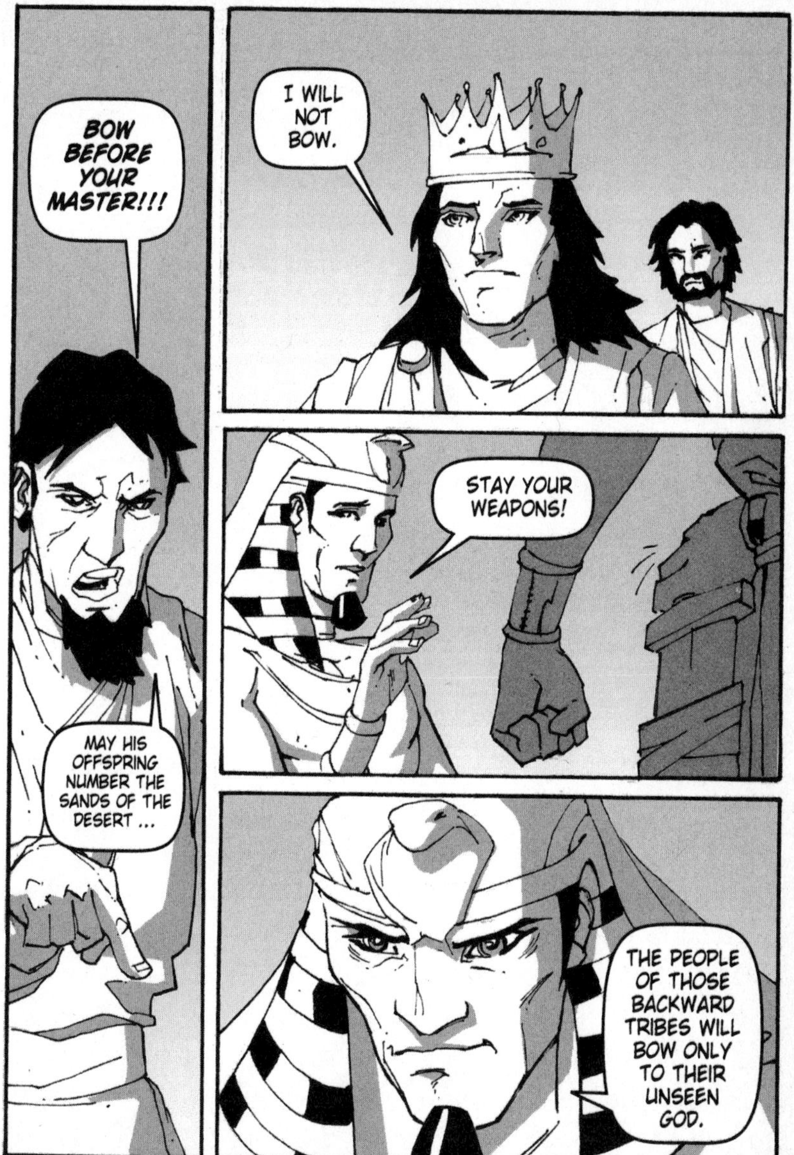
BOW BEFORE YOUR MASTER!!!
MAY HIS OFFSPRING NUMBER THE SANDS OF THE DESERT ...
I WILL NOT BOW.
STAY YOUR WEAPONS!
THE PEOPLE OF THOSE BACKWARD TRIBES WILL BOW ONLY TO THEIR UNSEEN GOD.

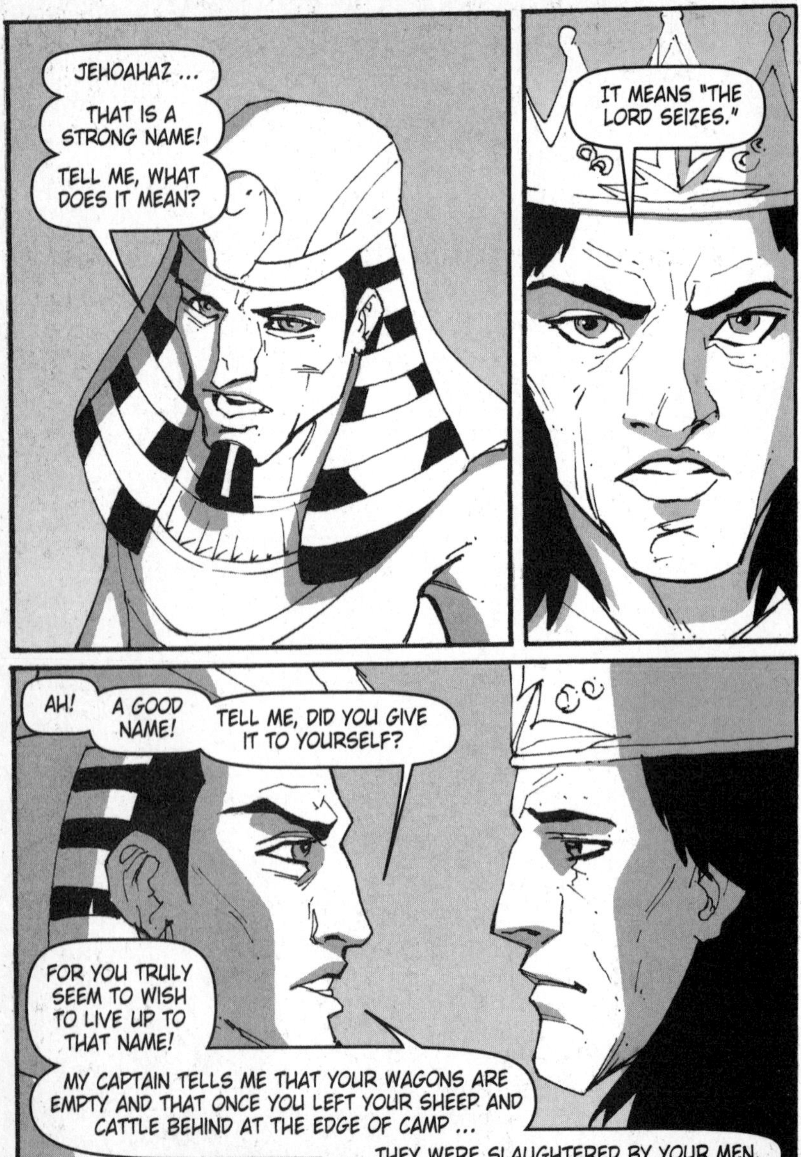
JEHOAHAZ ...
THAT IS A STRONG NAME!
TELL ME, WHAT DOES IT MEAN?
IT MEANS "THE LORD SEIZES."
AH!
A GOOD NAME!
TELL ME, DID YOU GIVE IT TO YOURSELF?
FOR YOU TRULY SEEM TO WISH TO LIVE UP TO THAT NAME!
MY CAPTAIN TELLS ME THAT YOUR WAGONS ARE EMPTY AND THAT ONCE YOU LEFT YOUR SHEEP AND CATTLE BEHIND AT THE EDGE OF CAMP ...
... THEY WERE SLAUGHTERED BY YOUR MEN.

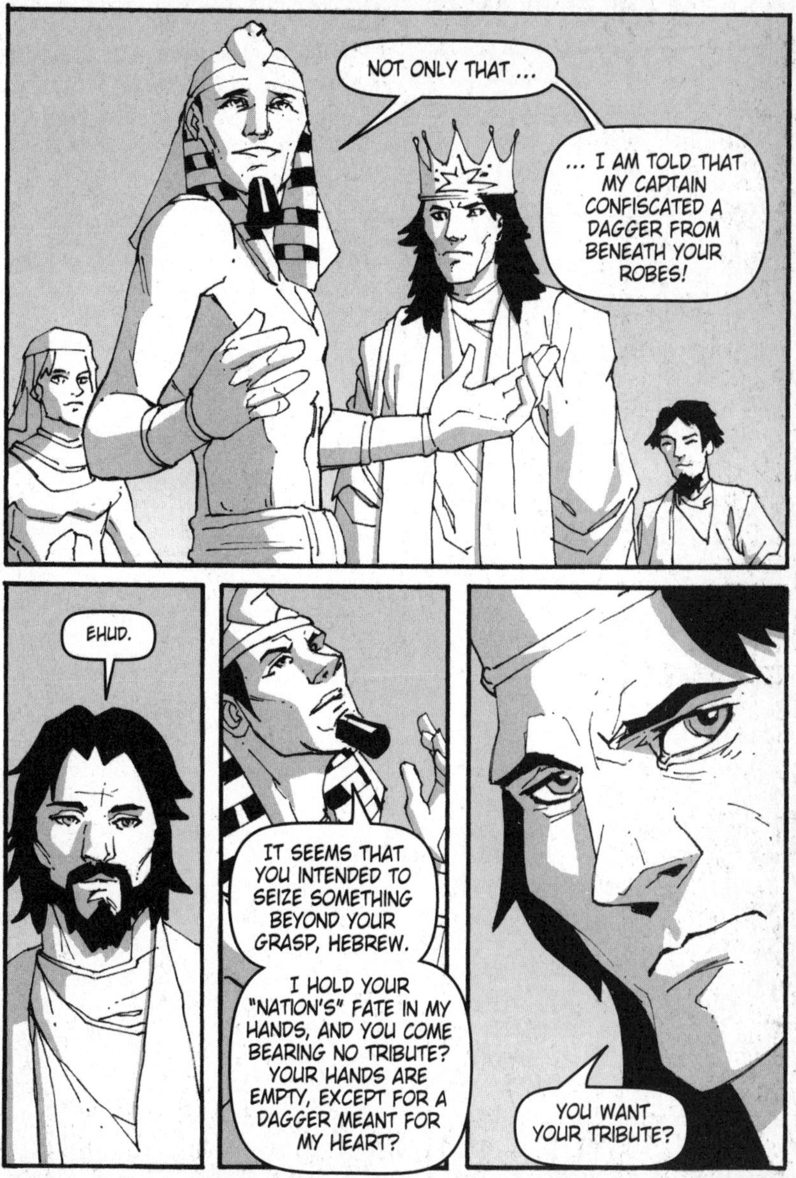
NOT ONLY THAT ...
... I AM TOLD THAT MY CAPTAIN CONFISCATED A DAGGER FROM BENEATH YOUR ROBES!
EHUD.
IT SEEMS THAT YOU INTENDED TO SEIZE SOMETHING BEYOND YOUR GRASP, HEBREW.
I HOLD YOUR "NATION'S" FATE IN MY HANDS, AND YOU COME BEARING NO TRIBUTE? YOUR HANDS ARE EMPTY, EXCEPT FOR A DAGGER MEANT FOR MY HEART?
YOU WANT YOUR TRIBUTE?

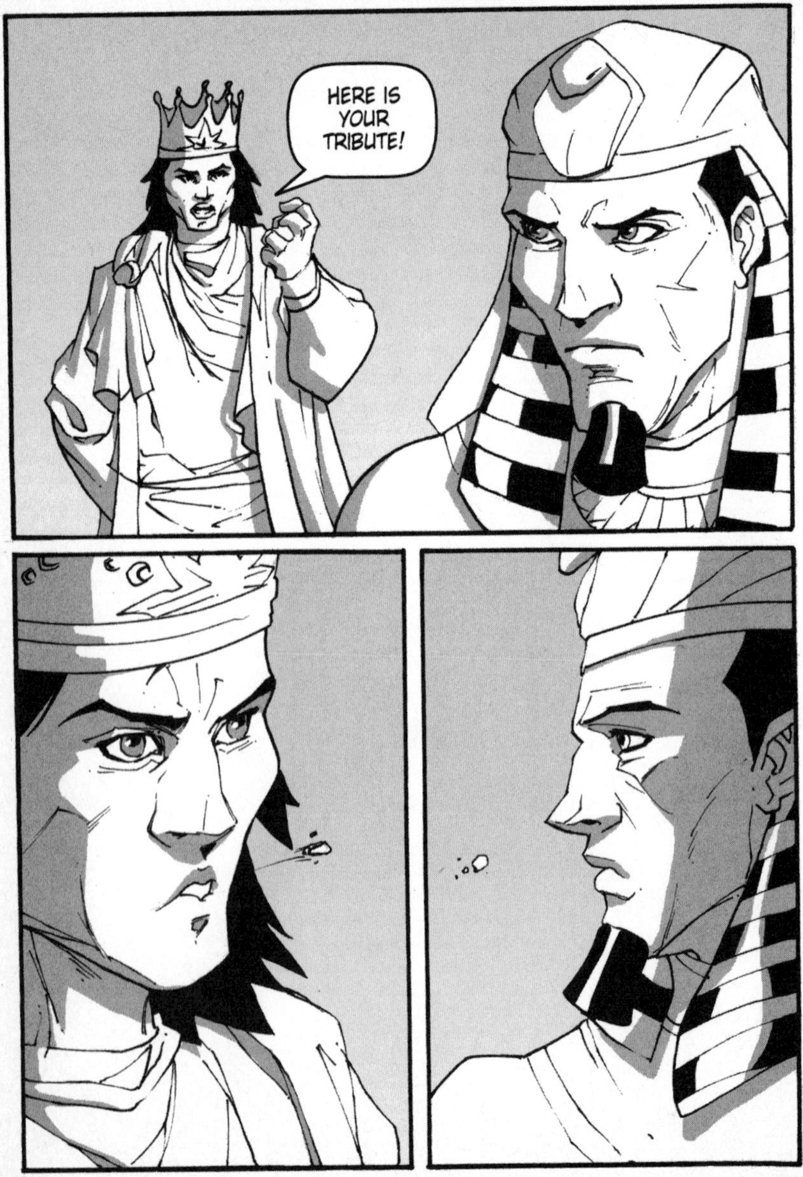
HERE IS YOUR TRIBUTE!

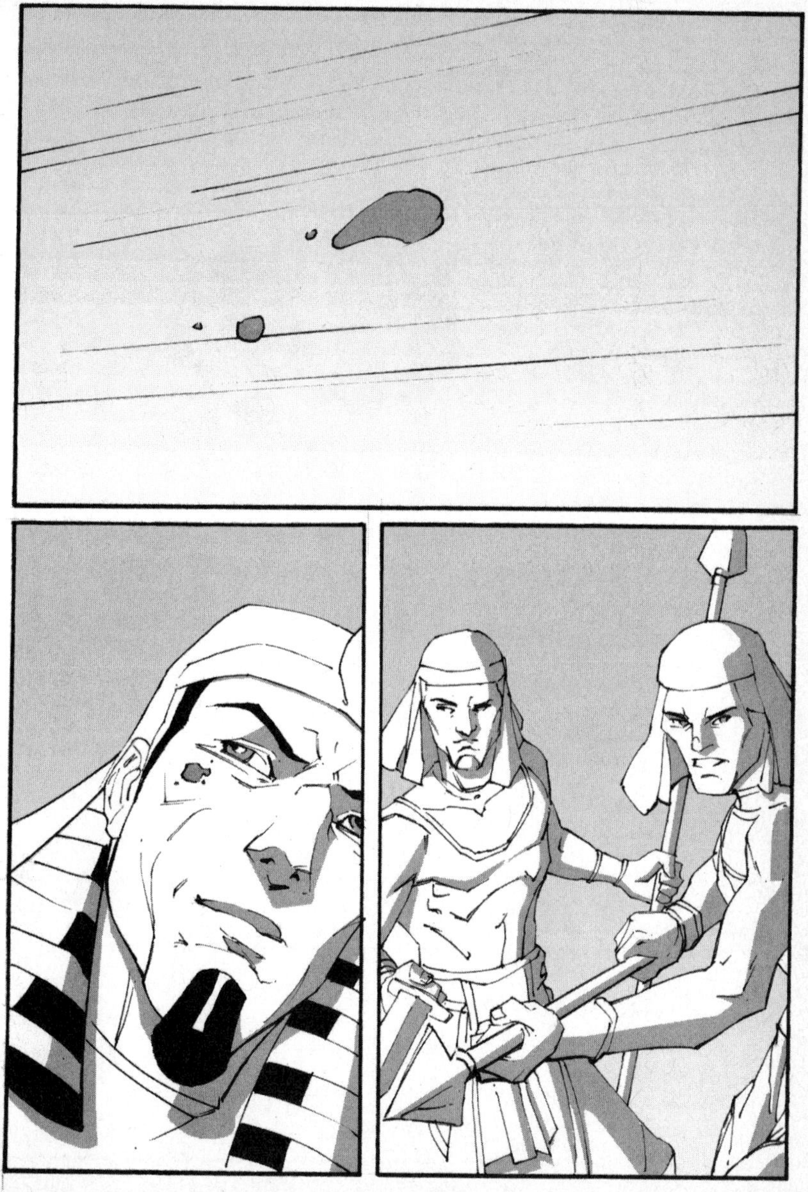

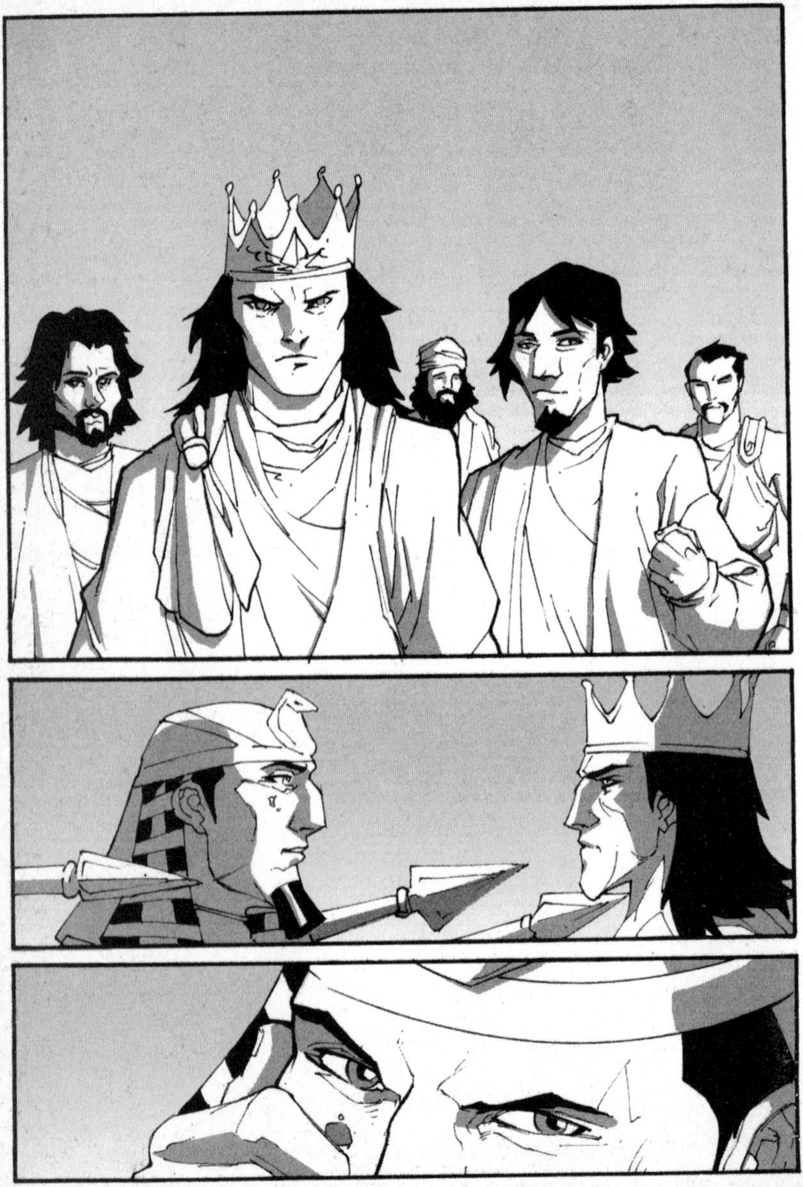

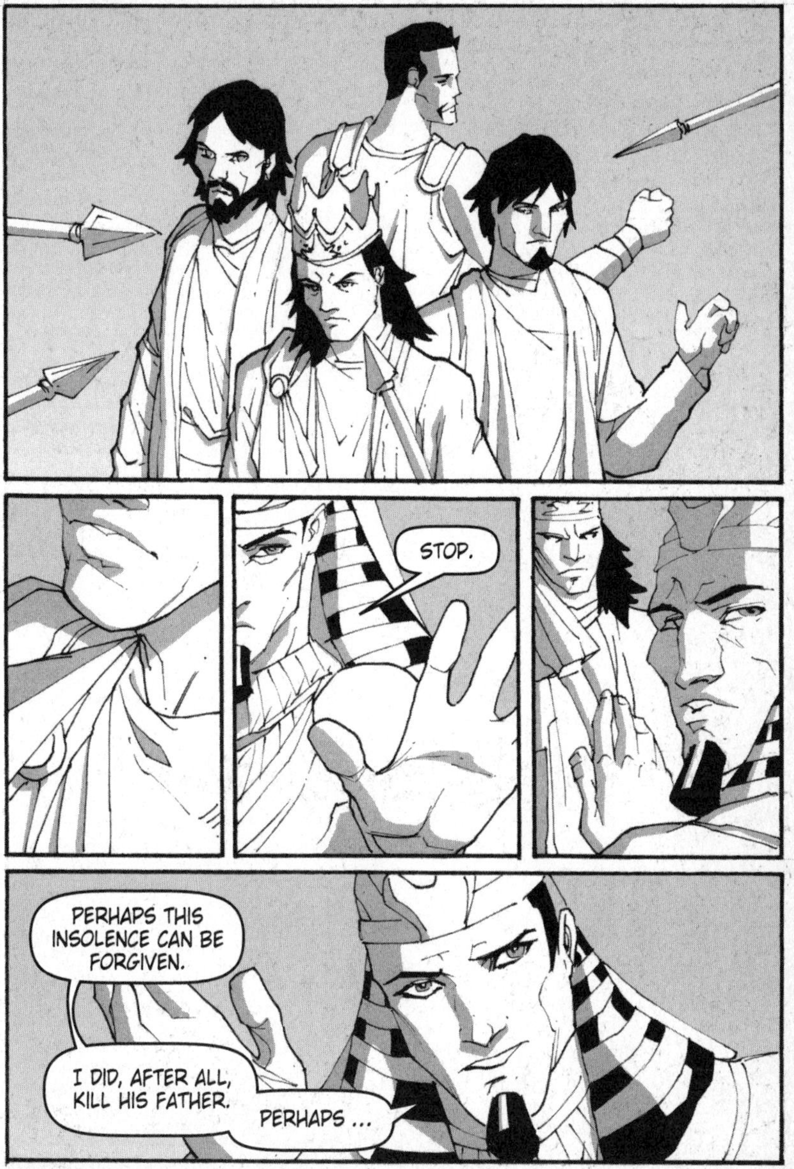
STOP.
PERHAPS THIS INSOLENCE CAN BE FORGIVEN.
I DID, AFTER ALL, KILL HIS FATHER.
PERHAPS ...

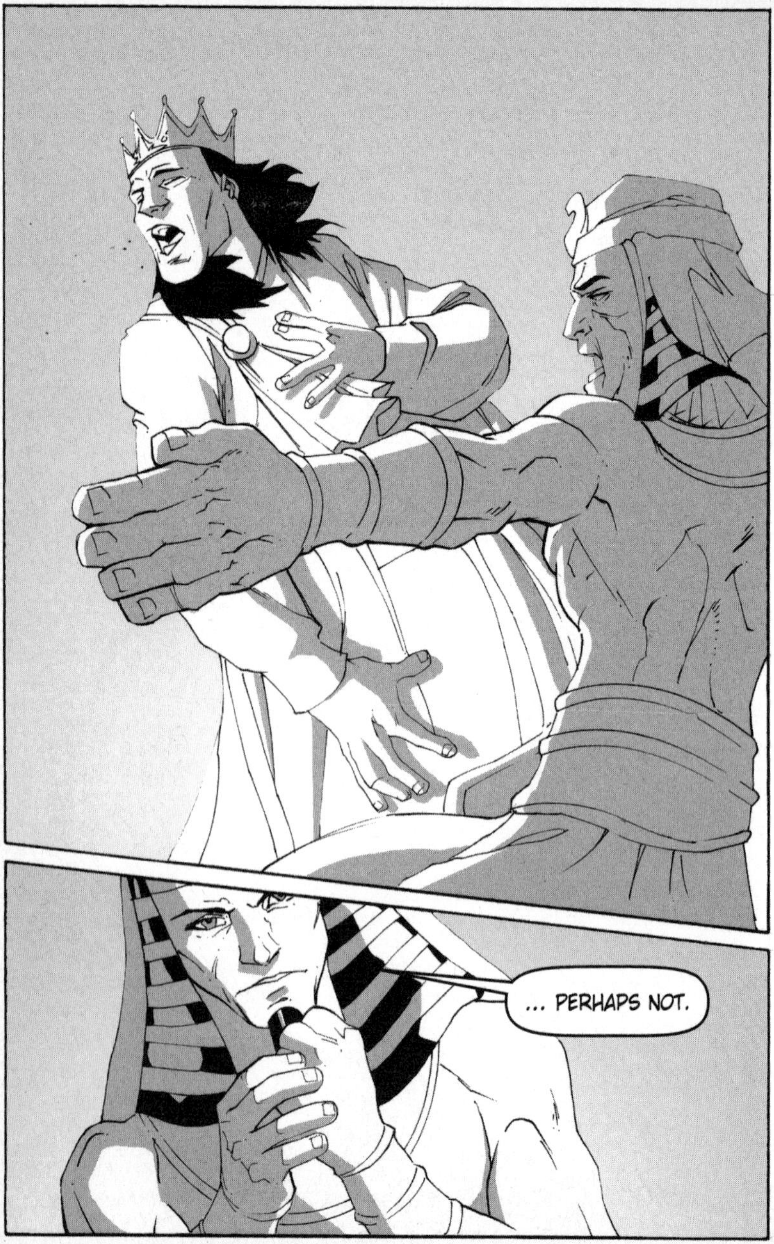
... PERHAPS NOT.

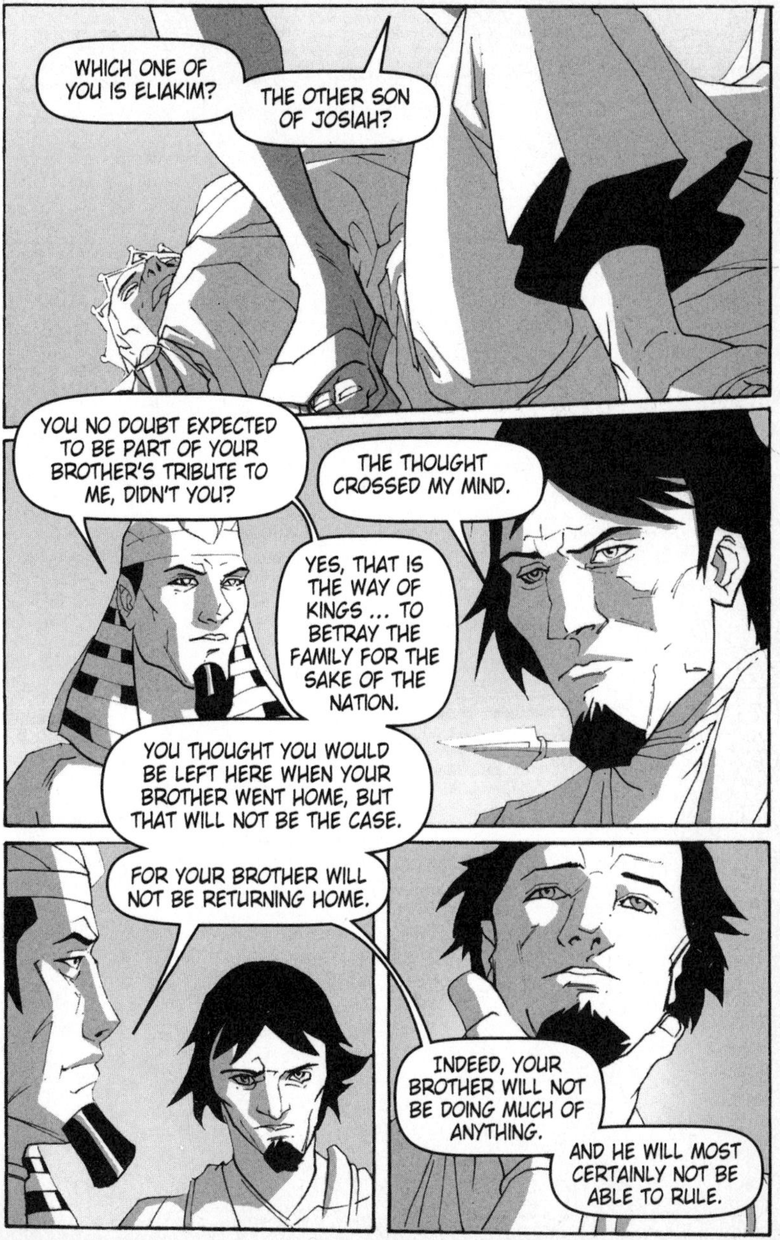
WHICH ONE OF YOU IS ELIAKIM?
THE OTHER SON OF JOSIAH?
YOU NO DOUBT EXPECTED TO BE PART OF YOUR BROTHER'S TRIBUTE TO ME, DIDN'T YOU?
THE THOUGHT CROSSED MY MIND.
YES, THAT IS THE WAY OF KINGS ... TO BETRAY THE FAMILY FOR THE SAKE OF THE NATION.
YOU THOUGHT YOU WOULD BE LEFT HERE WHEN YOUR BROTHER WENT HOME, BUT THAT WILL NOT BE THE CASE.
FOR YOUR BROTHER WILL NOT BE RETURNING HOME.
INDEED, YOUR BROTHER WILL NOT BE DOING MUCH OF ANYTHING.
AND HE WILL MOST CERTAINLY NOT BE ABLE TO RULE.

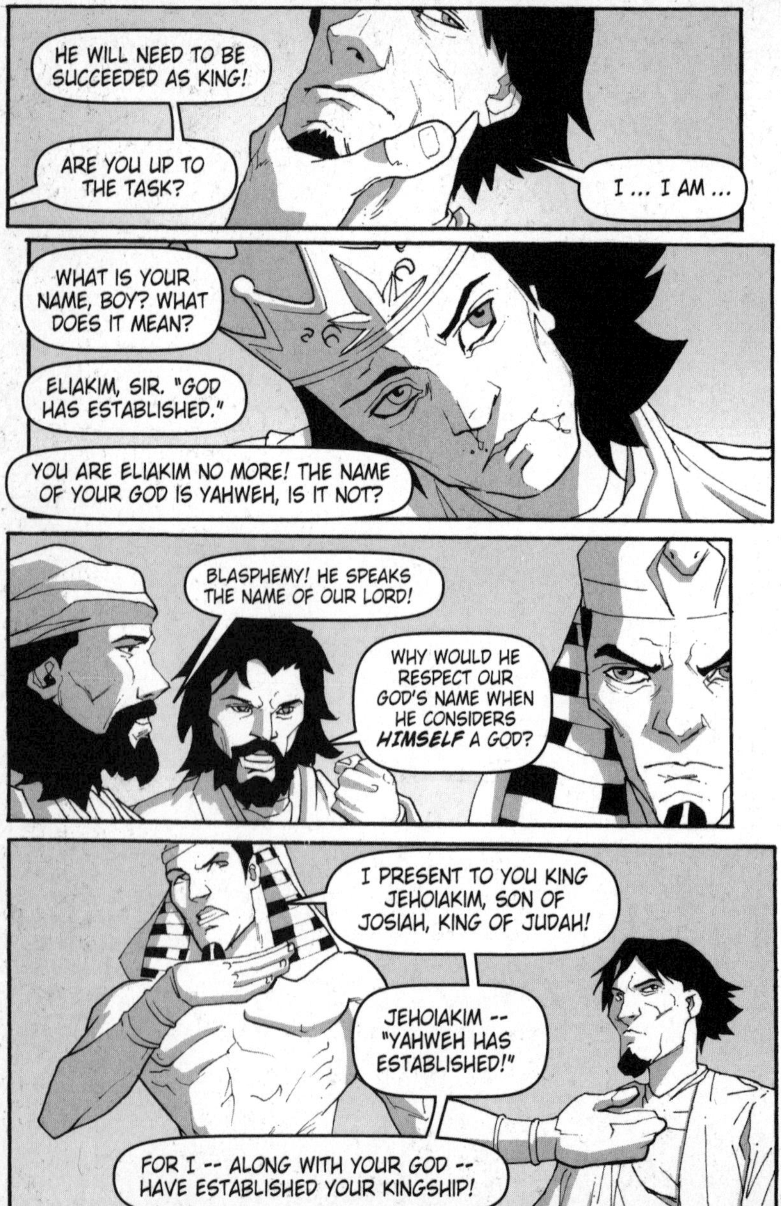
HE WILL NEED TO BE SUCCEEDED AS KING!
ARE YOU UP TO THE TASK?
I ... I AM ...
WHAT IS YOUR NAME, BOY? WHAT DOES IT MEAN?
ELIAKIM, SIR. "GOD HAS ESTABLISHED."
YOU ARE ELIAKIM NO MORE! THE NAME OF YOUR GOD IS YAHWEH, IS IT NOT?
BLASPHEMY! HE SPEAKS THE NAME OF OUR LORD!
WHY WOULD HE RESPECT OUR GOD'S NAME WHEN HE CONSIDERS ***HIMSELF*** A GOD?
I PRESENT TO YOU KING JEHOIAKIM, SON OF JOSIAH, KING OF JUDAH!
JEHOIAKIM -- "YAHWEH HAS ESTABLISHED!"
FOR I -- ALONG WITH YOUR GOD -- HAVE ESTABLISHED YOUR KINGSHIP!

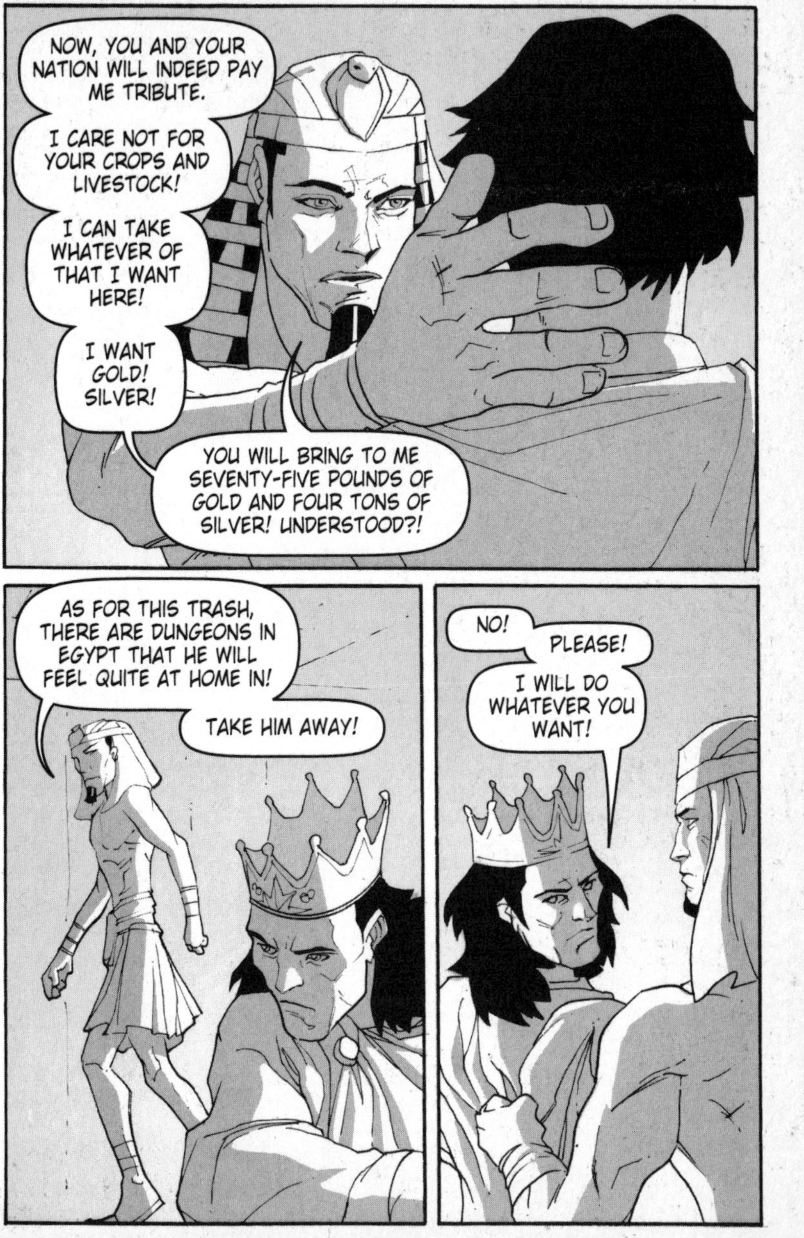
NOW, YOU AND YOUR NATION WILL INDEED PAY ME TRIBUTE.
I CARE NOT FOR YOUR CROPS AND LIVESTOCK!
I CAN TAKE WHATEVER OF THAT I WANT HERE!
I WANT GOLD! SILVER!
YOU WILL BRING TO ME SEVENTY-FIVE POUNDS OF GOLD AND FOUR TONS OF SILVER! UNDERSTOOD?!
AS FOR THIS TRASH, THERE ARE DUNGEONS IN EGYPT THAT HE WILL FEEL QUITE AT HOME IN!
TAKE HIM AWAY!
NO!
PLEASE!
I WILL DO WHATEVER YOU WANT!

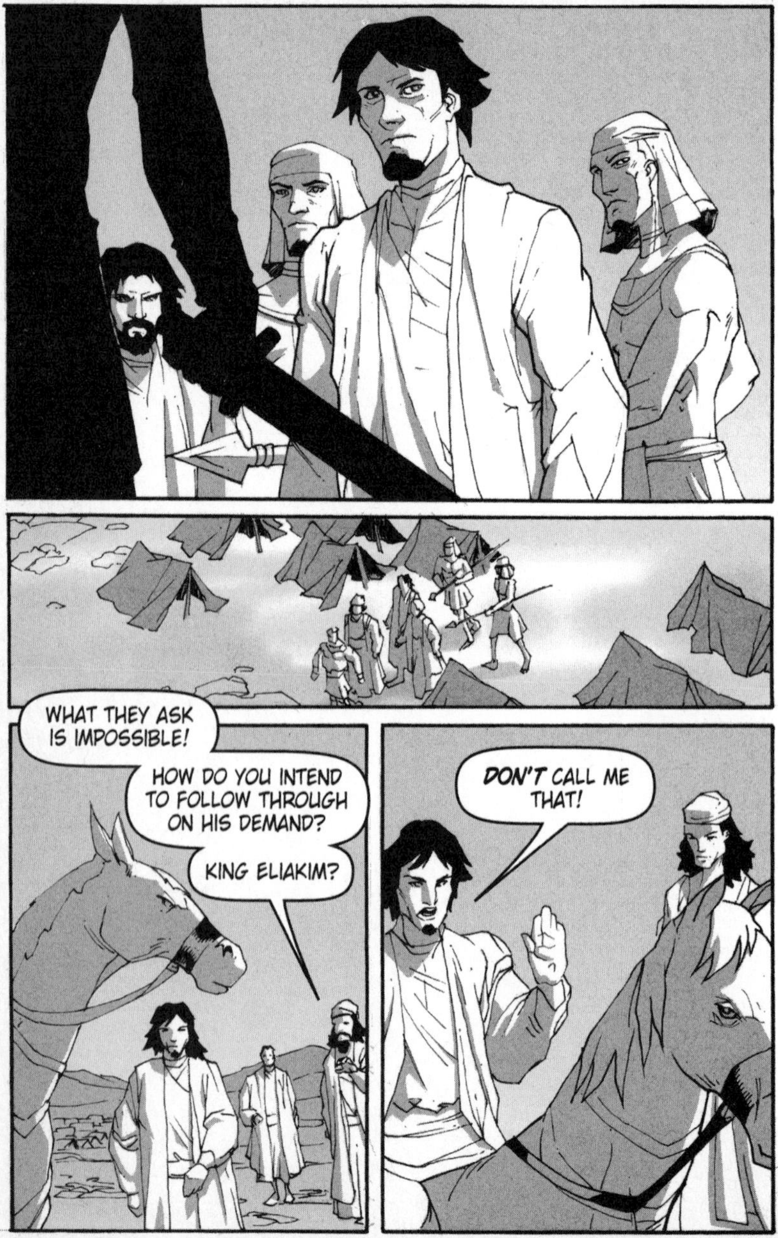
WHAT THEY ASK IS IMPOSSIBLE!
HOW DO YOU INTEND TO FOLLOW THROUGH ON HIS DEMAND?
KING ELIAKIM?
DON'T CALL ME THAT!

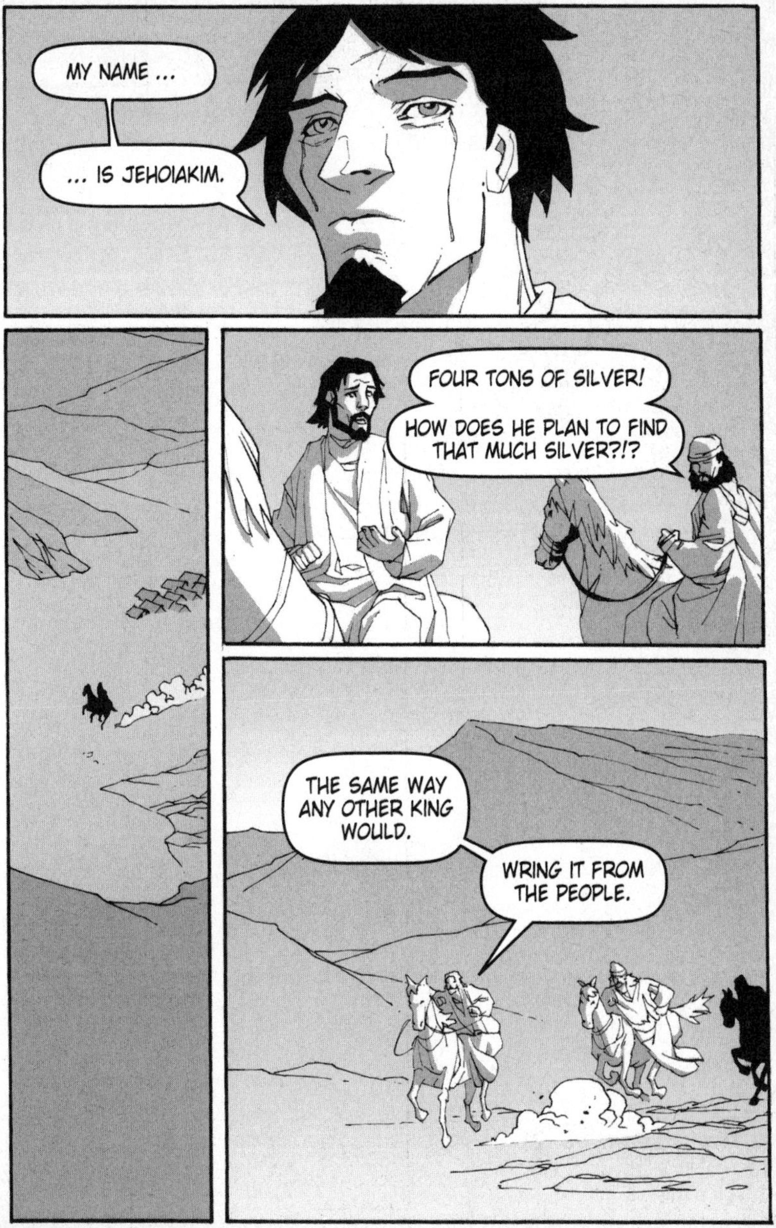
MY NAME ...
... IS JEHOIAKIM.
FOUR TONS OF SILVER!
HOW DOES HE PLAN TO FIND THAT MUCH SILVER?!?
THE SAME WAY ANY OTHER KING WOULD.
WRING IT FROM THE PEOPLE.

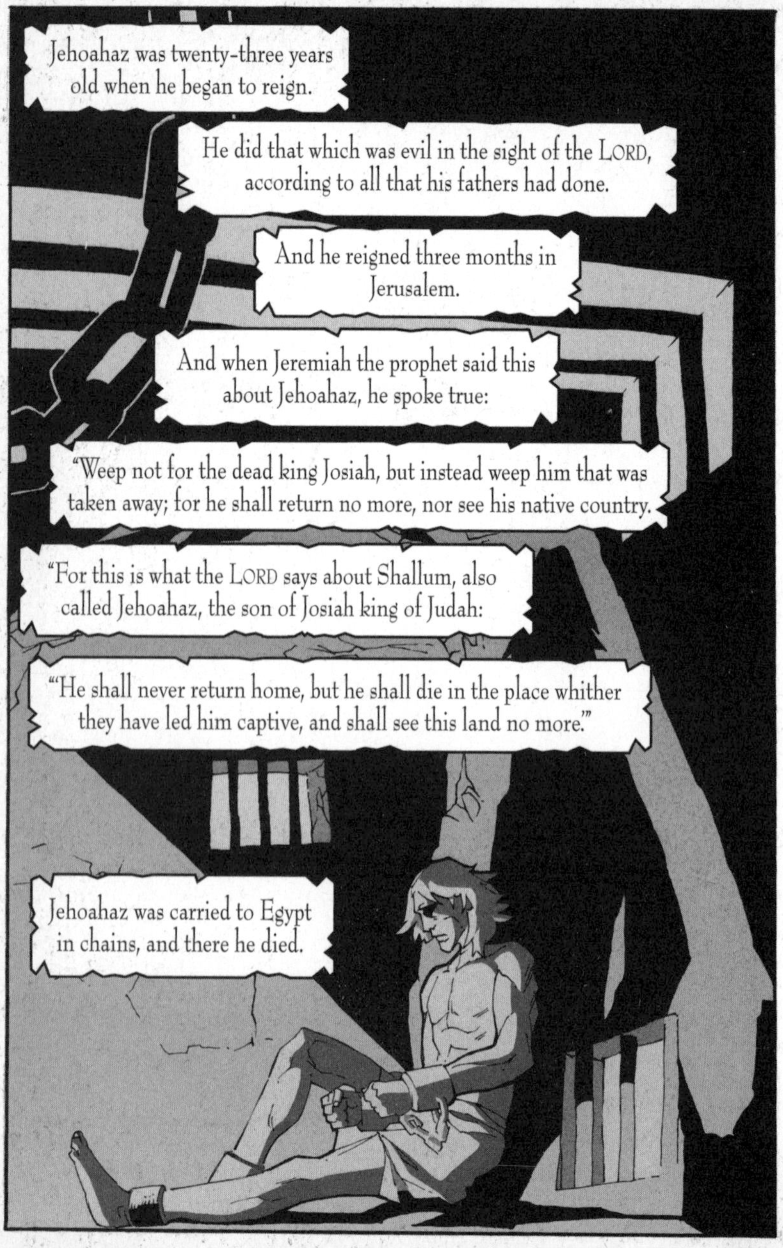
Jehoahaz was twenty-three years old when he began to reign.
He did that which was evil in the sight of the LORD, according to all that his fathers had done.
And he reigned three months in Jerusalem.
And when Jeremiah the prophet said this about Jehoahaz, he spoke true:
"Weep not for the dead king Josiah, but instead weep him that was taken away; for he shall return no more, nor see his native country.
"For this is what the LORD says about Shallum, also called Jehoahaz, the son of Josiah king of Judah:
"'He shall never return home, but he shall die in the place whither they have led him captive, and shall see this land no more.'"
Jehoahaz was carried to Egypt in chains, and there he died.

CHAPTER TWO
"The Coward"

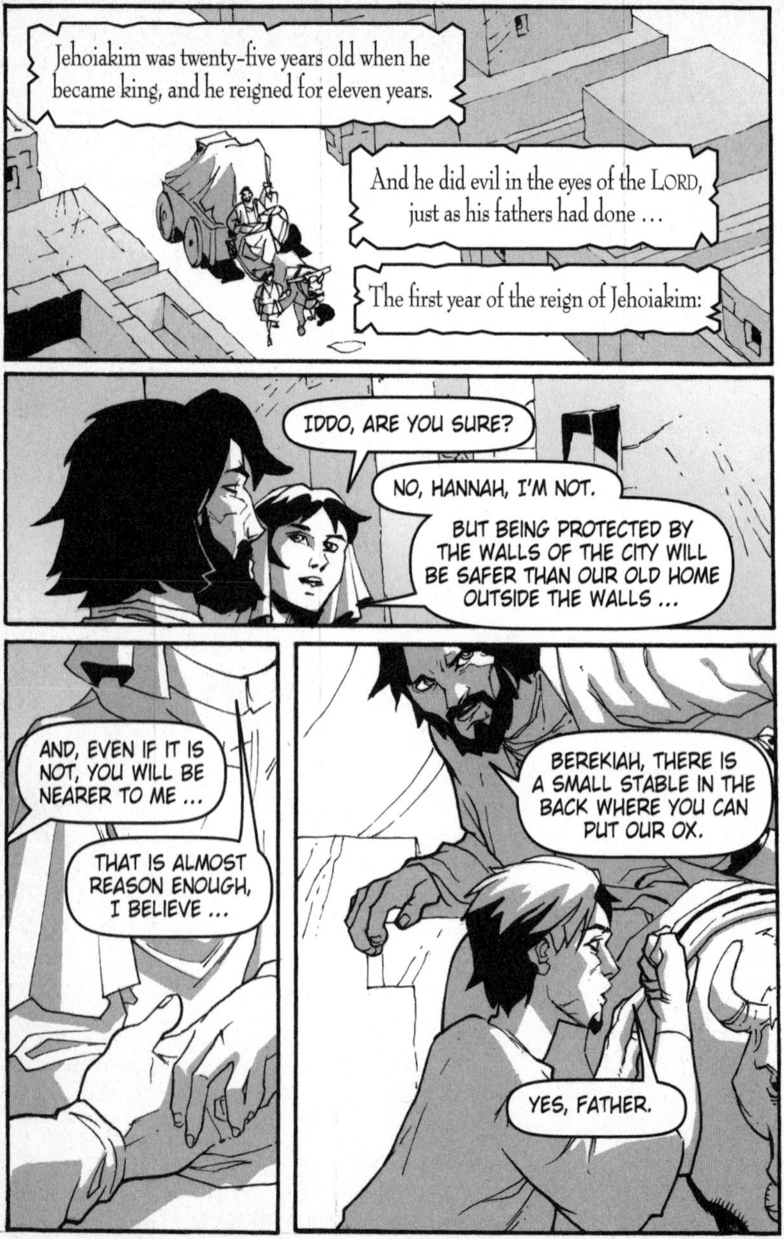
Jehoiakim was twenty-five years old when he became king, and he reigned for eleven years.
And he did evil in the eyes of the LORD, just as his fathers had done …
The first year of the reign of Jehoiakim:
IDDO, ARE YOU SURE?
NO, HANNAH, I'M NOT.
BUT BEING PROTECTED BY THE WALLS OF THE CITY WILL BE SAFER THAN OUR OLD HOME OUTSIDE THE WALLS …
AND, EVEN IF IT IS NOT, YOU WILL BE NEARER TO ME …
THAT IS ALMOST REASON ENOUGH, I BELIEVE …
BEREKIAH, THERE IS A SMALL STABLE IN THE BACK WHERE YOU CAN PUT OUR OX.
YES, FATHER.

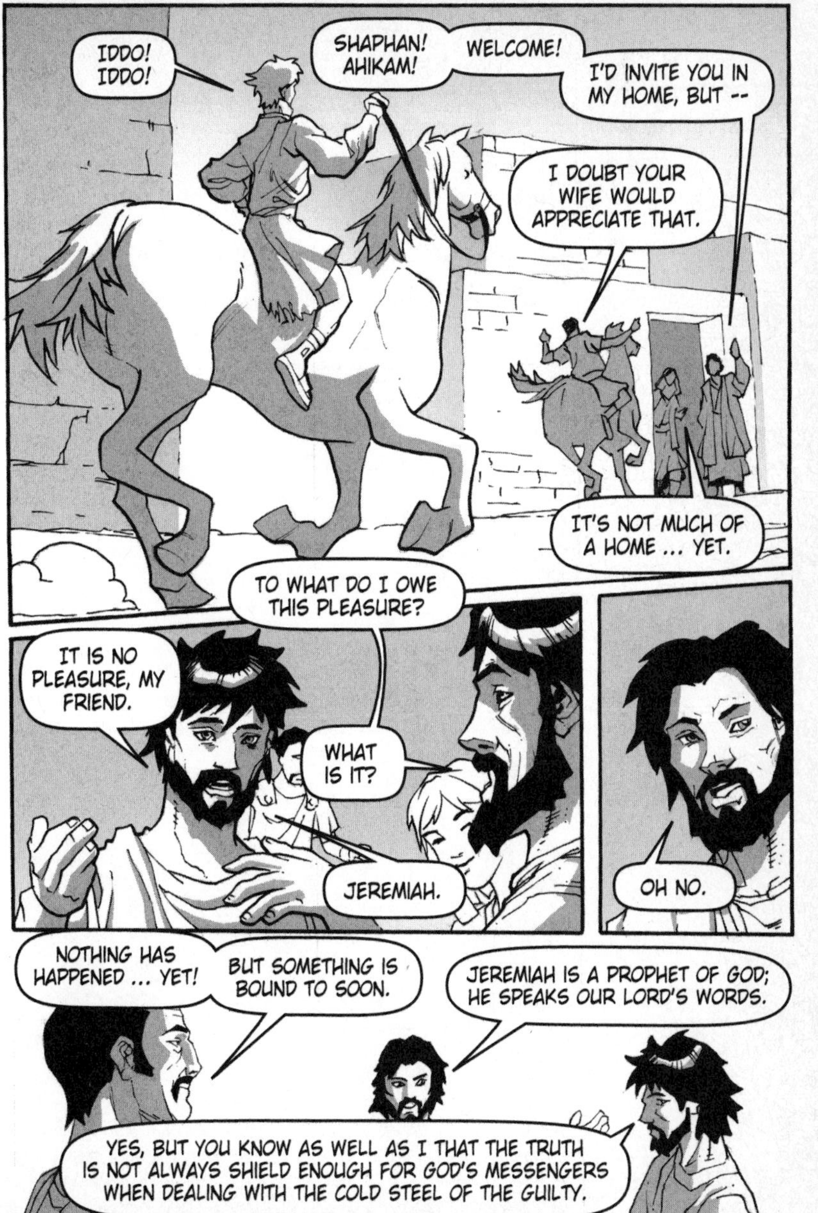
IDDO! IDDO!
SHAPHAN! AHIKAM!
WELCOME!
I'D INVITE YOU IN MY HOME, BUT --
I DOUBT YOUR WIFE WOULD APPRECIATE THAT.
IT'S NOT MUCH OF A HOME ... YET.
TO WHAT DO I OWE THIS PLEASURE?
IT IS NO PLEASURE, MY FRIEND.
WHAT IS IT?
JEREMIAH.
OH NO.
NOTHING HAS HAPPENED ... YET!
BUT SOMETHING IS BOUND TO SOON.
JEREMIAH IS A PROPHET OF GOD; HE SPEAKS OUR LORD'S WORDS.
YES, BUT YOU KNOW AS WELL AS I THAT THE TRUTH IS NOT ALWAYS SHIELD ENOUGH FOR GOD'S MESSENGERS WHEN DEALING WITH THE COLD STEEL OF THE GUILTY.

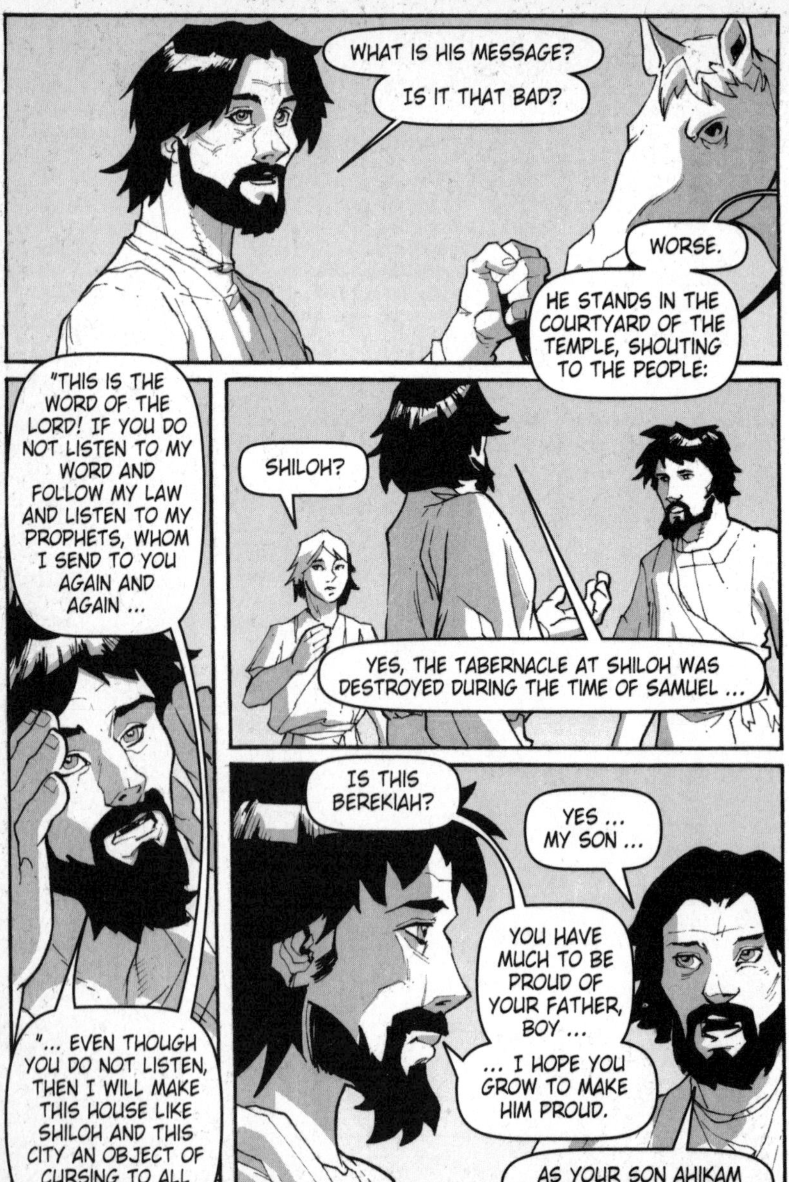
WHAT IS HIS MESSAGE?
IS IT THAT BAD?
WORSE.
HE STANDS IN THE COURTYARD OF THE TEMPLE, SHOUTING TO THE PEOPLE:
"THIS IS THE WORD OF THE LORD! IF YOU DO NOT LISTEN TO MY WORD AND FOLLOW MY LAW AND LISTEN TO MY PROPHETS, WHOM I SEND TO YOU AGAIN AND AGAIN ...
"... EVEN THOUGH YOU DO NOT LISTEN, THEN I WILL MAKE THIS HOUSE LIKE SHILOH AND THIS CITY AN OBJECT OF CURSING TO ALL NATIONS!"
SHILOH?
YES, THE TABERNACLE AT SHILOH WAS DESTROYED DURING THE TIME OF SAMUEL ...
IS THIS BEREKIAH?
YES ... MY SON ...
YOU HAVE MUCH TO BE PROUD OF YOUR FATHER, BOY ...
... I HOPE YOU GROW TO MAKE HIM PROUD.
AS YOUR SON AHIKAM HAS MADE YOU PROUD.

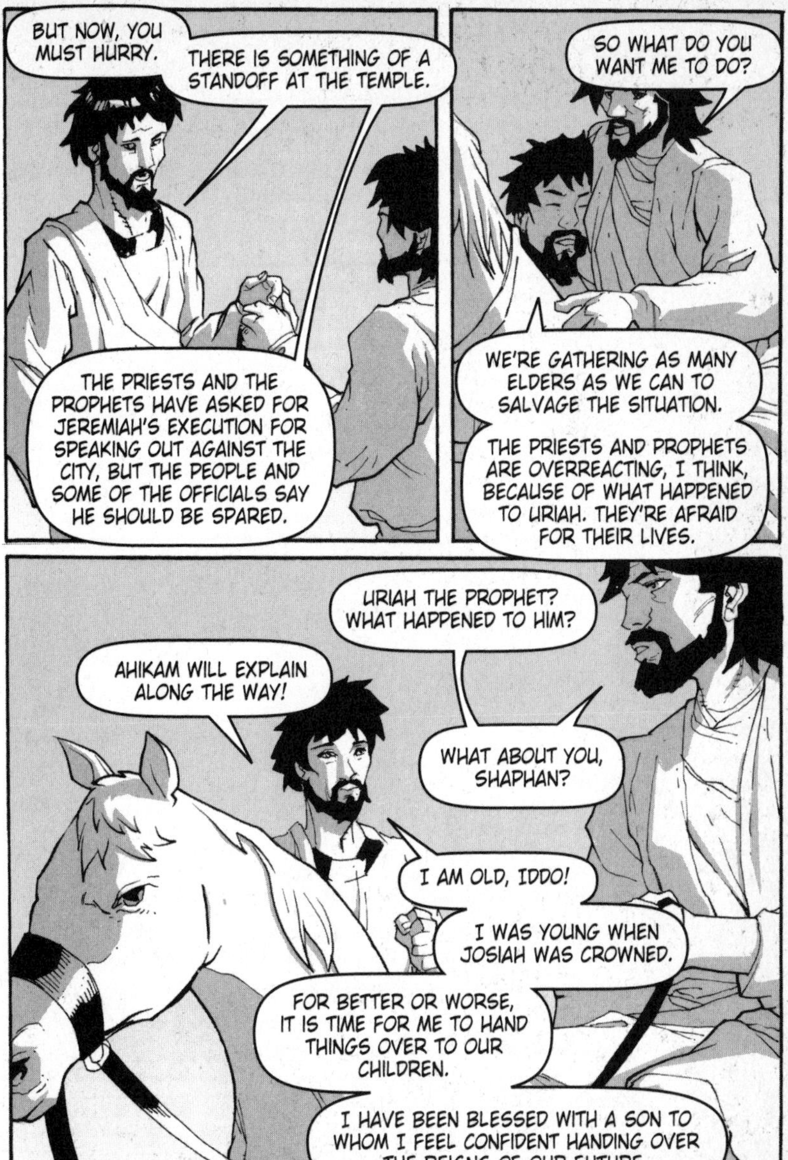
BUT NOW, YOU MUST HURRY.
THERE IS SOMETHING OF A STANDOFF AT THE TEMPLE.
THE PRIESTS AND THE PROPHETS HAVE ASKED FOR JEREMIAH'S EXECUTION FOR SPEAKING OUT AGAINST THE CITY, BUT THE PEOPLE AND SOME OF THE OFFICIALS SAY HE SHOULD BE SPARED.
SO WHAT DO YOU WANT ME TO DO?
WE'RE GATHERING AS MANY ELDERS AS WE CAN TO SALVAGE THE SITUATION.
THE PRIESTS AND PROPHETS ARE OVERREACTING, I THINK, BECAUSE OF WHAT HAPPENED TO URIAH. THEY'RE AFRAID FOR THEIR LIVES.
URIAH THE PROPHET? WHAT HAPPENED TO HIM?
AHIKAM WILL EXPLAIN ALONG THE WAY!
WHAT ABOUT YOU, SHAPHAN?
I AM OLD, IDDO!
I WAS YOUNG WHEN JOSIAH WAS CROWNED.
FOR BETTER OR WORSE, IT IS TIME FOR ME TO HAND THINGS OVER TO OUR CHILDREN.
I HAVE BEEN BLESSED WITH A SON TO WHOM I FEEL CONFIDENT HANDING OVER THE REIGNS OF OUR FUTURE.

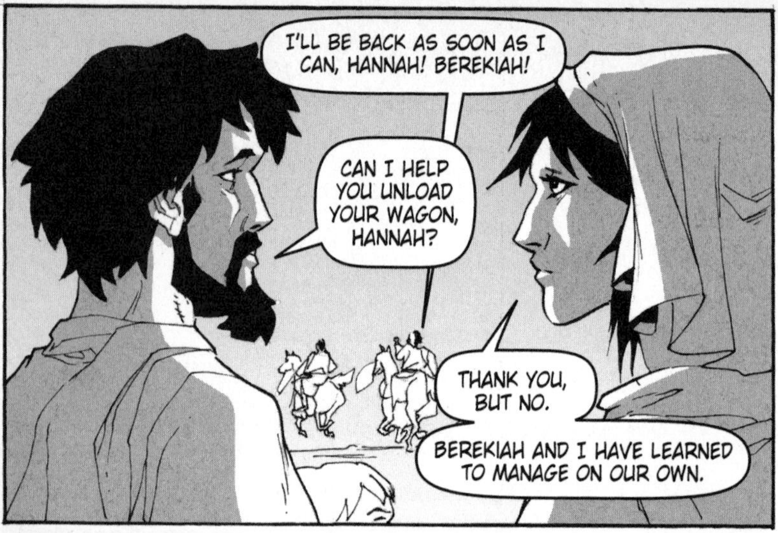
I'LL BE BACK AS SOON AS I CAN, HANNAH! BEREKIAH!
CAN I HELP YOU UNLOAD YOUR WAGON, HANNAH?
THANK YOU, BUT NO.
BEREKIAH AND I HAVE LEARNED TO MANAGE ON OUR OWN.

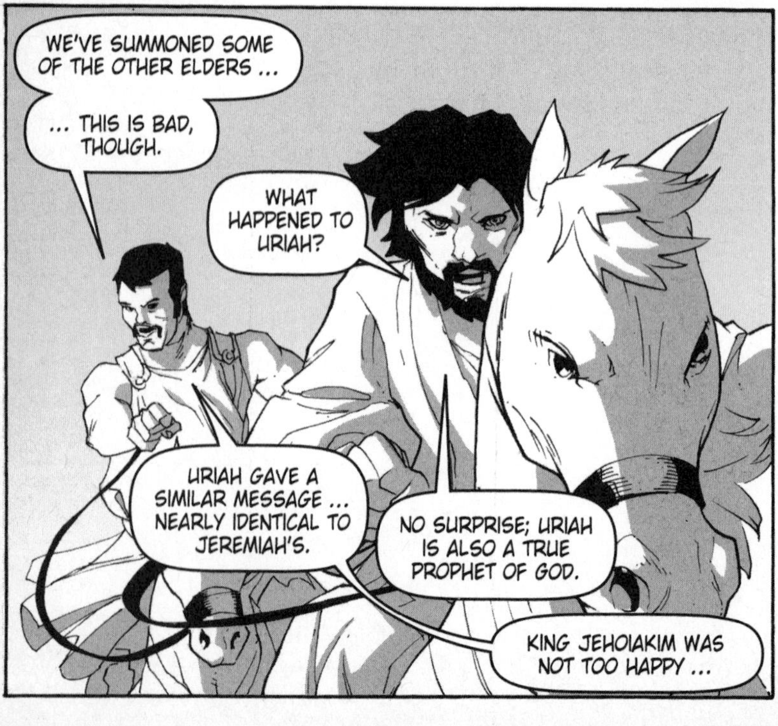
WE'VE SUMMONED SOME OF THE OTHER ELDERS ...
... THIS IS BAD, THOUGH.
WHAT HAPPENED TO URIAH?
URIAH GAVE A SIMILAR MESSAGE ... NEARLY IDENTICAL TO JEREMIAH'S.
NO SURPRISE; URIAH IS ALSO A TRUE PROPHET OF GOD.
KING JEHOIAKIM WAS NOT TOO HAPPY ...

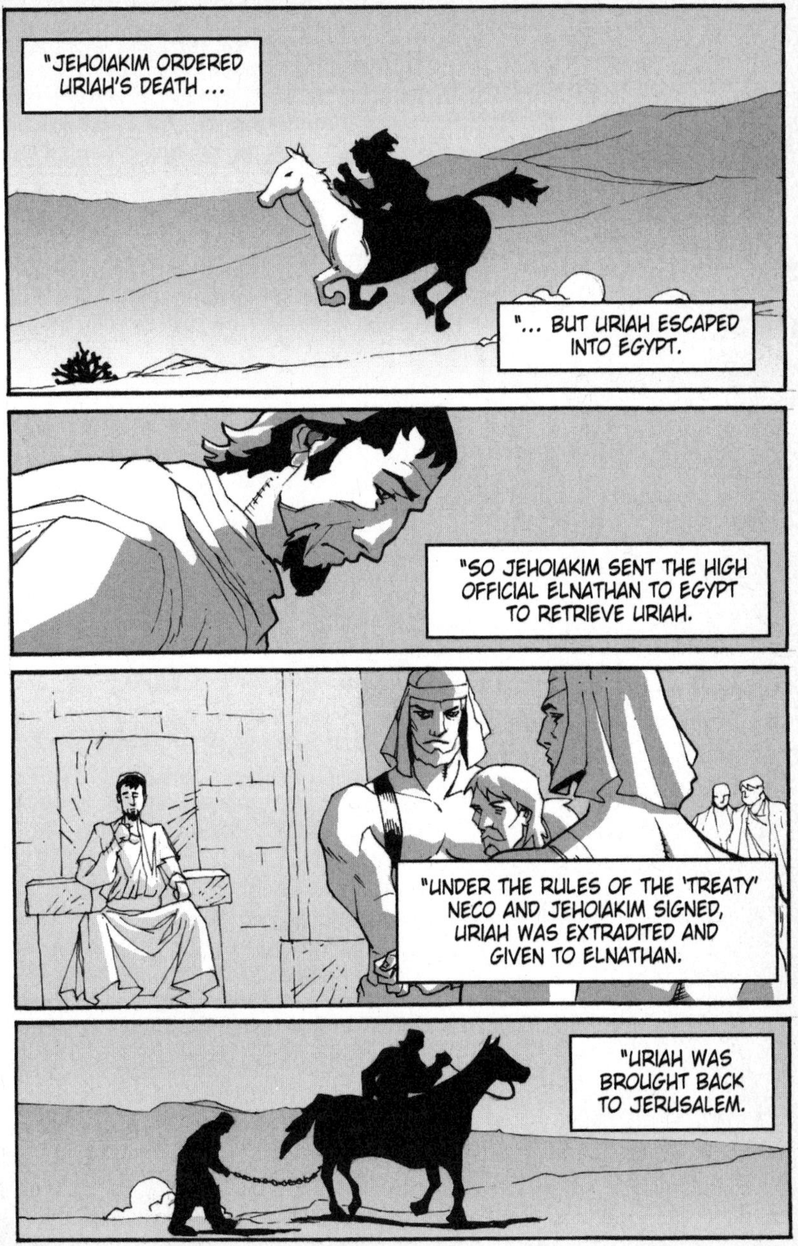
"JEHOIAKIM ORDERED URIAH'S DEATH ...
"... BUT URIAH ESCAPED INTO EGYPT.
"SO JEHOIAKIM SENT THE HIGH OFFICIAL ELNATHAN TO EGYPT TO RETRIEVE URIAH.
"UNDER THE RULES OF THE 'TREATY' NECO AND JEHOIAKIM SIGNED, URIAH WAS EXTRADITED AND GIVEN TO ELNATHAN.
"URIAH WAS BROUGHT BACK TO JERUSALEM.

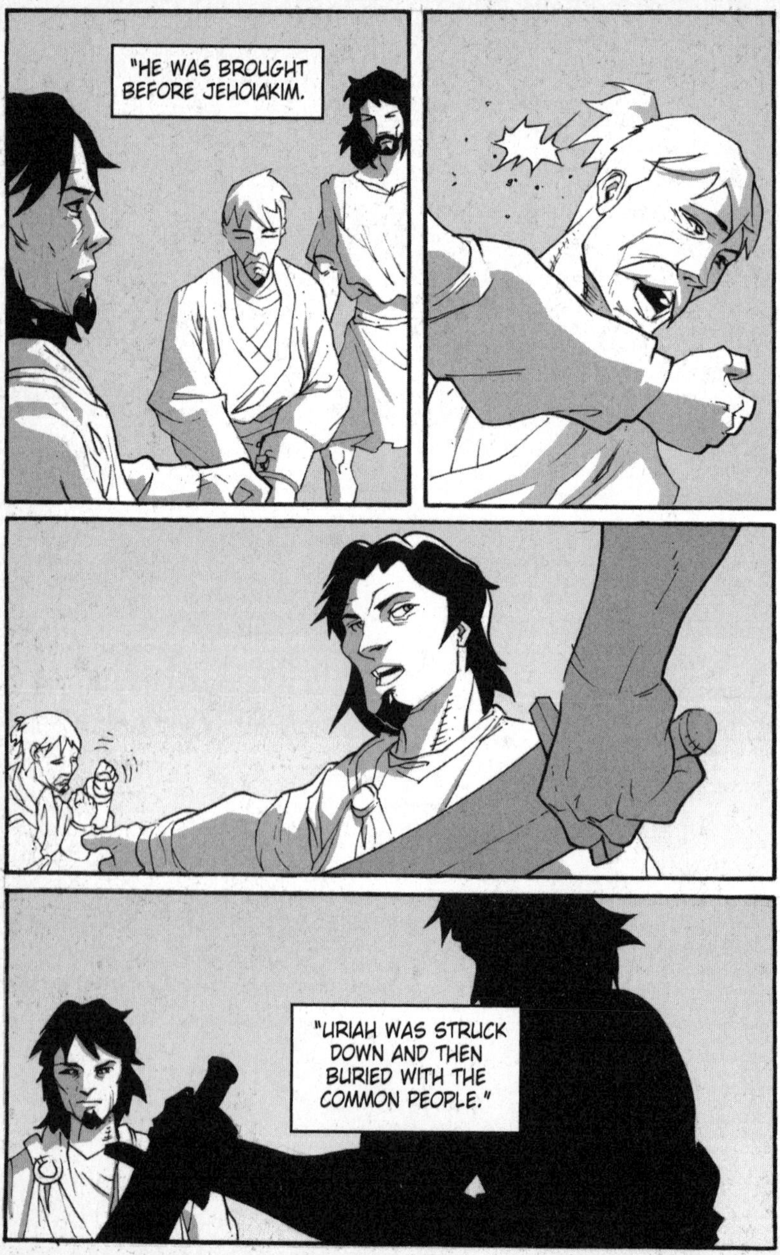
"HE WAS BROUGHT BEFORE JEHOIAKIM.
"URIAH WAS STRUCK DOWN AND THEN BURIED WITH THE COMMON PEOPLE."

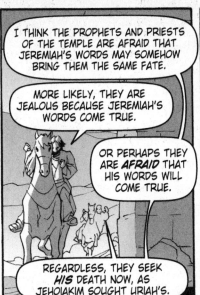

I THINK THE PROPHETS AND PRIESTS OF THE TEMPLE ARE AFRAID THAT JEREMIAH'S WORDS MAY SOMEHOW BRING THEM THE SAME FATE.

MORE LIKELY, THEY ARE JEALOUS BECAUSE JEREMIAH'S WORDS COME TRUE.

OR PERHAPS THEY ARE *AFRAID* THAT HIS WORDS WILL COME TRUE.

REGARDLESS, THEY SEEK *HIS* DEATH NOW, AS JEHOIAKIM SOUGHT URIAH'S.

WHAT HAS OUR NATION COME TO, WHEN WE SEEK TO PUNISH THOSE WHO SPEAK THE TRUTH?

HOW IS IT ANY DIFFERENT THAN BEFORE?

IT HAS HAPPENED MANY TIMES IN OUR PAST.

TRUE, BUT WHENEVER IT DOES HAPPEN, I STILL ...

WHAT'S THIS?

A SPINNING WHEEL, THAT'S WHAT WE ARE ...

... ALWAYS RETURNING TO OUR SINS.

YES, AS MY FATHER SAYS, "LIKE A DOG TO ITS VOMIT."

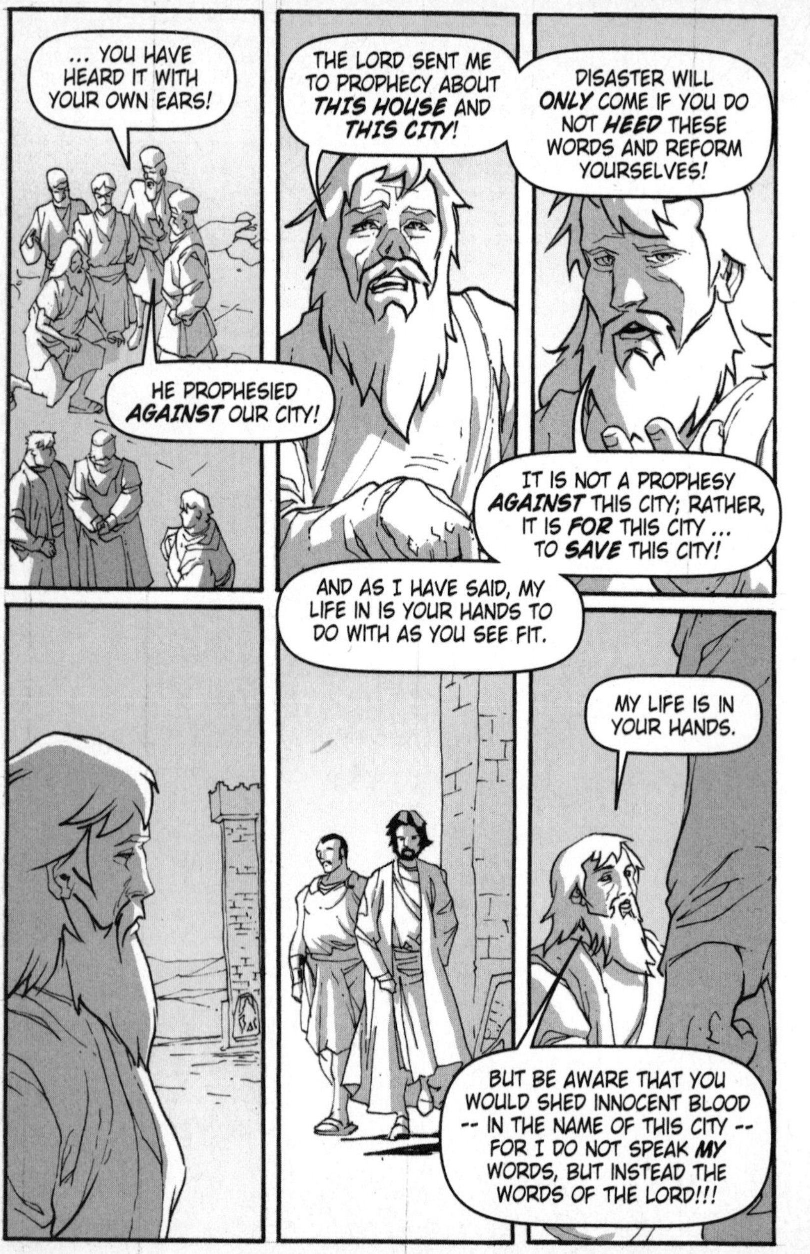
... YOU HAVE HEARD IT WITH YOUR OWN EARS!
HE PROPHESIED *AGAINST* OUR CITY!
THE LORD SENT ME TO PROPHECY ABOUT *THIS HOUSE* AND *THIS CITY*!
DISASTER WILL *ONLY* COME IF YOU DO NOT *HEED* THESE WORDS AND REFORM YOURSELVES!
IT IS NOT A PROPHESY *AGAINST* THIS CITY; RATHER, IT IS *FOR* THIS CITY ... TO *SAVE* THIS CITY!
AND AS I HAVE SAID, MY LIFE IN IS YOUR HANDS TO DO WITH AS YOU SEE FIT.
MY LIFE IS IN YOUR HANDS.
BUT BE AWARE THAT YOU WOULD SHED INNOCENT BLOOD -- IN THE NAME OF THIS CITY -- FOR I DO NOT SPEAK *MY* WORDS, BUT INSTEAD THE WORDS OF THE LORD!!!

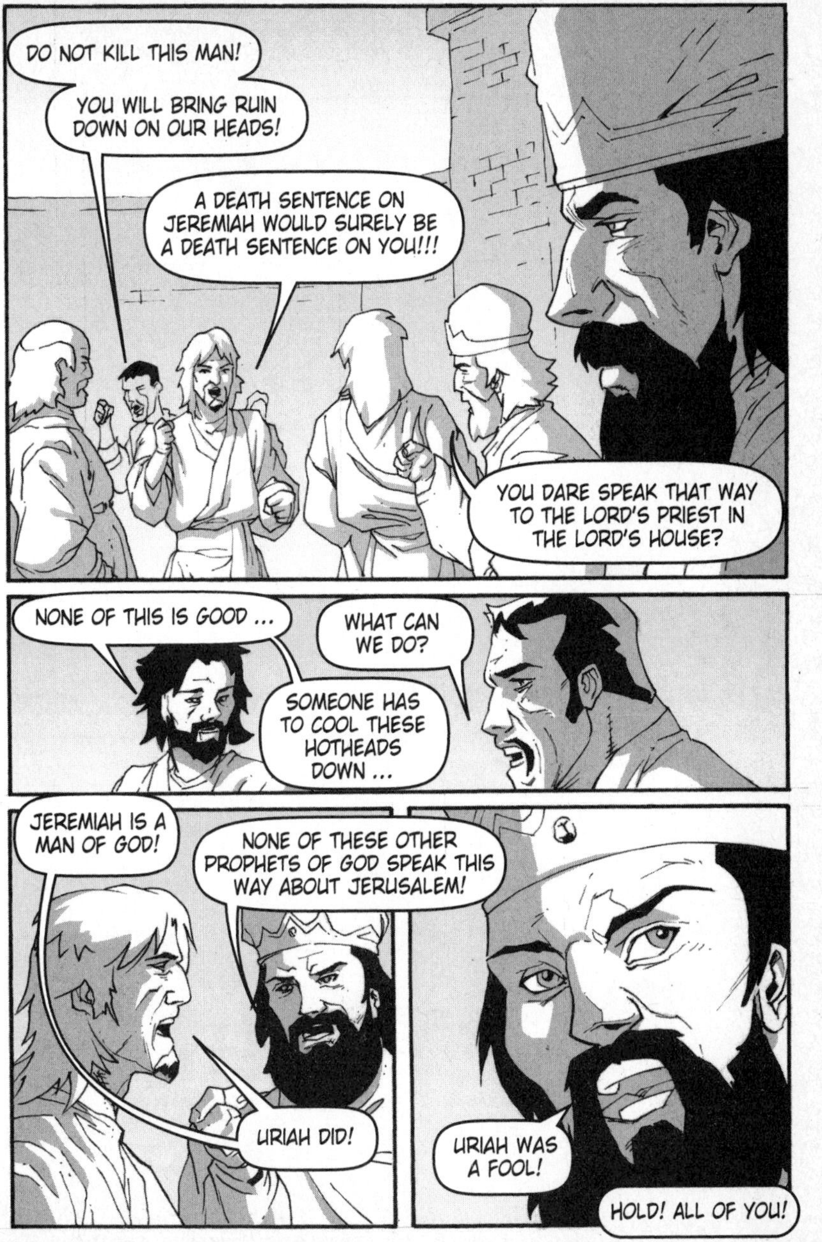
DO NOT KILL THIS MAN!
YOU WILL BRING RUIN DOWN ON OUR HEADS!
A DEATH SENTENCE ON JEREMIAH WOULD SURELY BE A DEATH SENTENCE ON YOU!!!
YOU DARE SPEAK THAT WAY TO THE LORD'S PRIEST IN THE LORD'S HOUSE?
NONE OF THIS IS GOOD ...
SOMEONE HAS TO COOL THESE HOTHEADS DOWN ...
WHAT CAN WE DO?
JEREMIAH IS A MAN OF GOD!
NONE OF THESE OTHER PROPHETS OF GOD SPEAK THIS WAY ABOUT JERUSALEM!
URIAH DID!
URIAH WAS A FOOL!
HOLD! ALL OF YOU!

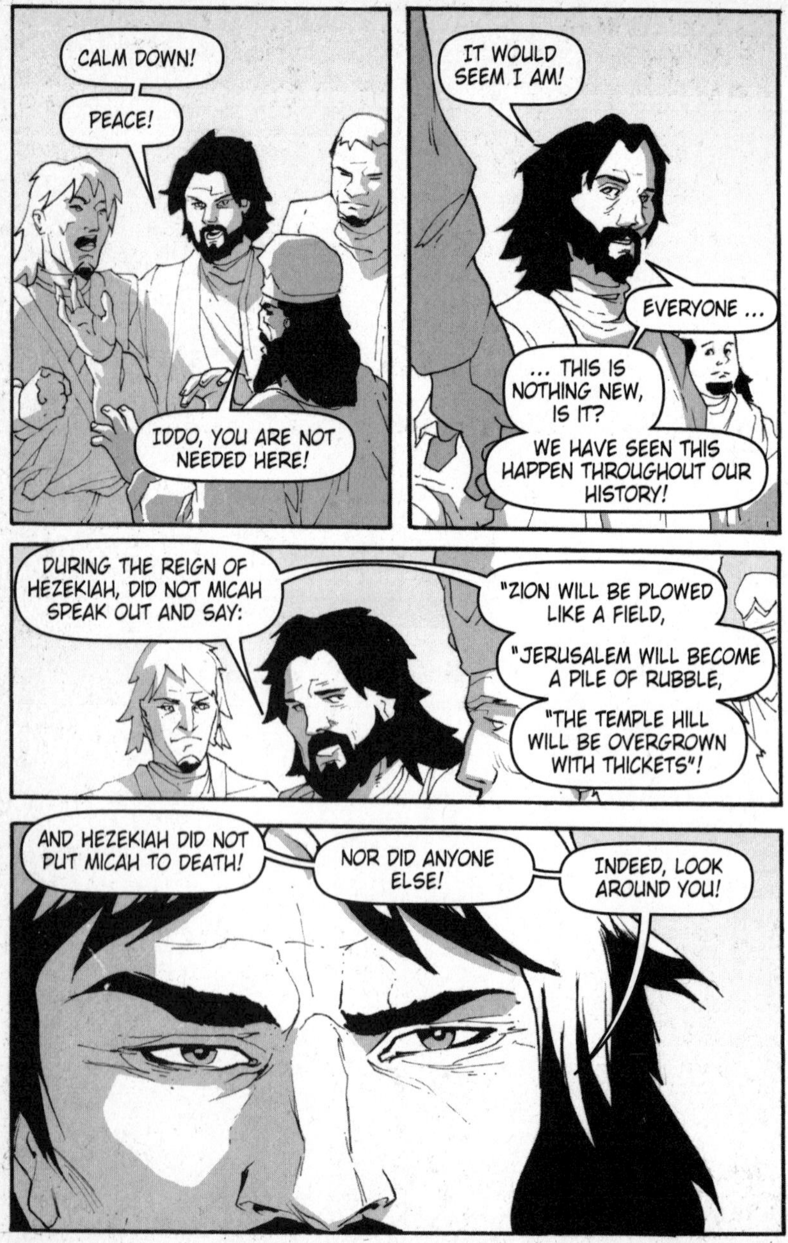
CALM DOWN!
PEACE!
IDDO, YOU ARE NOT NEEDED HERE!
IT WOULD SEEM I AM!
EVERYONE ...
... THIS IS NOTHING NEW, IS IT?
WE HAVE SEEN THIS HAPPEN THROUGHOUT OUR HISTORY!
DURING THE REIGN OF HEZEKIAH, DID NOT MICAH SPEAK OUT AND SAY:
"ZION WILL BE PLOWED LIKE A FIELD,
"JERUSALEM WILL BECOME A PILE OF RUBBLE,
"THE TEMPLE HILL WILL BE OVERGROWN WITH THICKETS"!
AND HEZEKIAH DID NOT PUT MICAH TO DEATH!
NOR DID ANYONE ELSE!
INDEED, LOOK AROUND YOU!

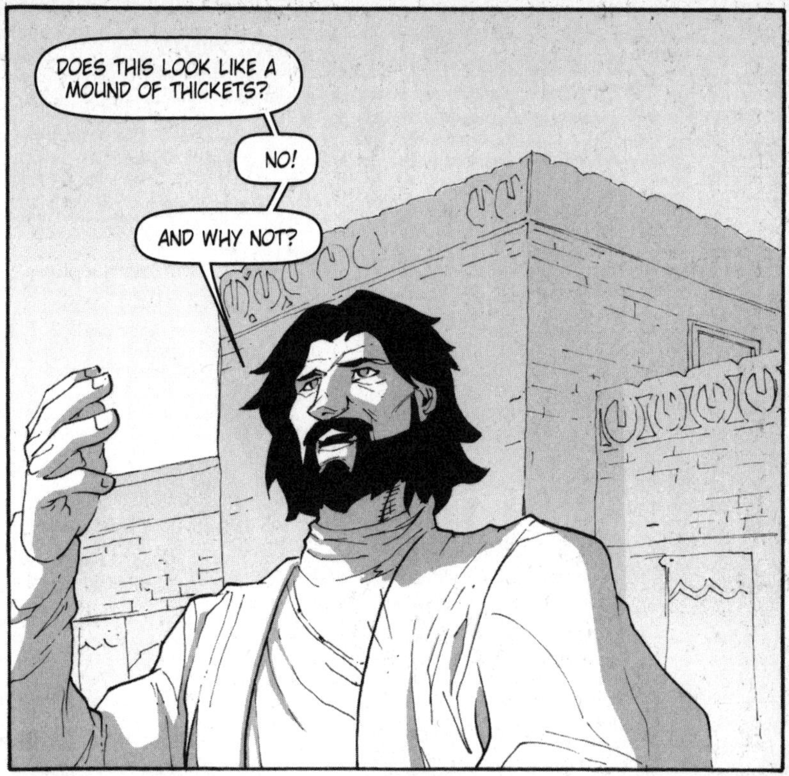
DOES THIS LOOK LIKE A MOUND OF THICKETS?
NO!
AND WHY NOT?

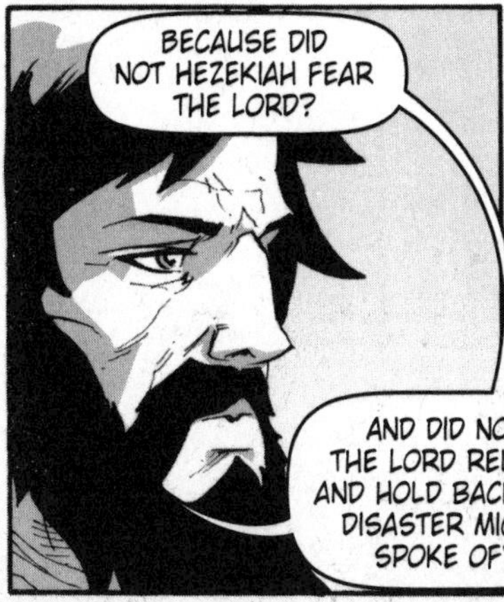
BECAUSE DID NOT HEZEKIAH FEAR THE LORD?
AND DID NOT THE LORD RELENT AND HOLD BACK THE DISASTER MICAH SPOKE OF?

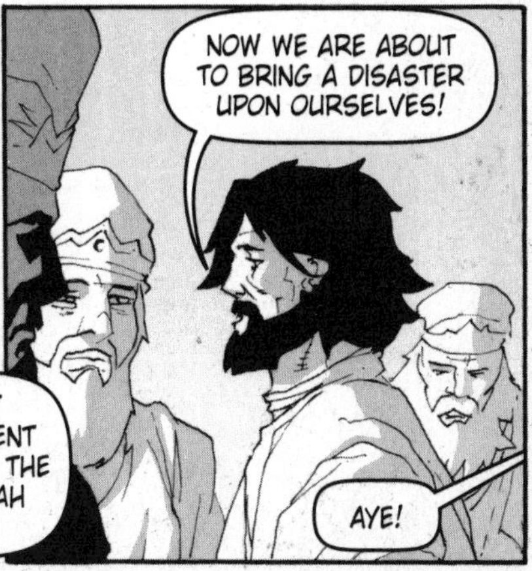
NOW WE ARE ABOUT TO BRING A DISASTER UPON OURSELVES!
AYE!

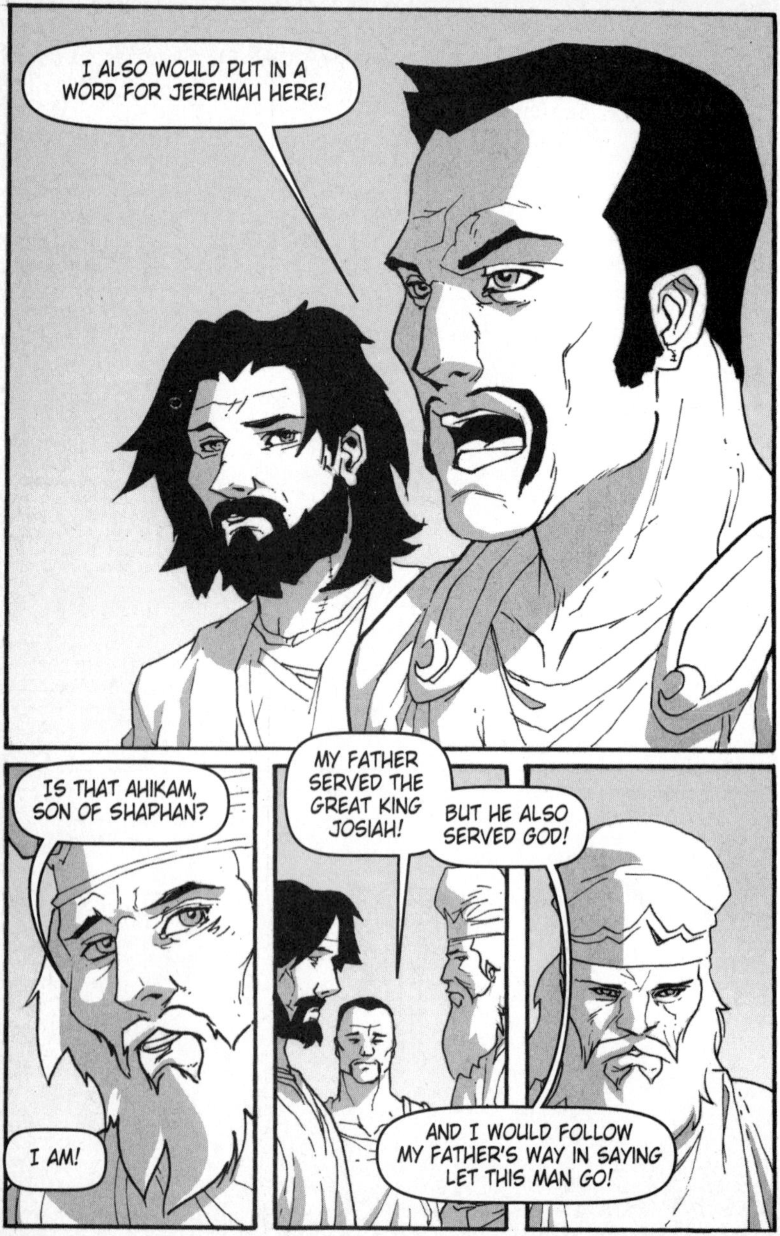
I ALSO WOULD PUT IN A WORD FOR JEREMIAH HERE!
IS THAT AHIKAM, SON OF SHAPHAN?
I AM!
MY FATHER SERVED THE GREAT KING JOSIAH!
BUT HE ALSO SERVED GOD!
AND I WOULD FOLLOW MY FATHER'S WAY IN SAYING LET THIS MAN GO!

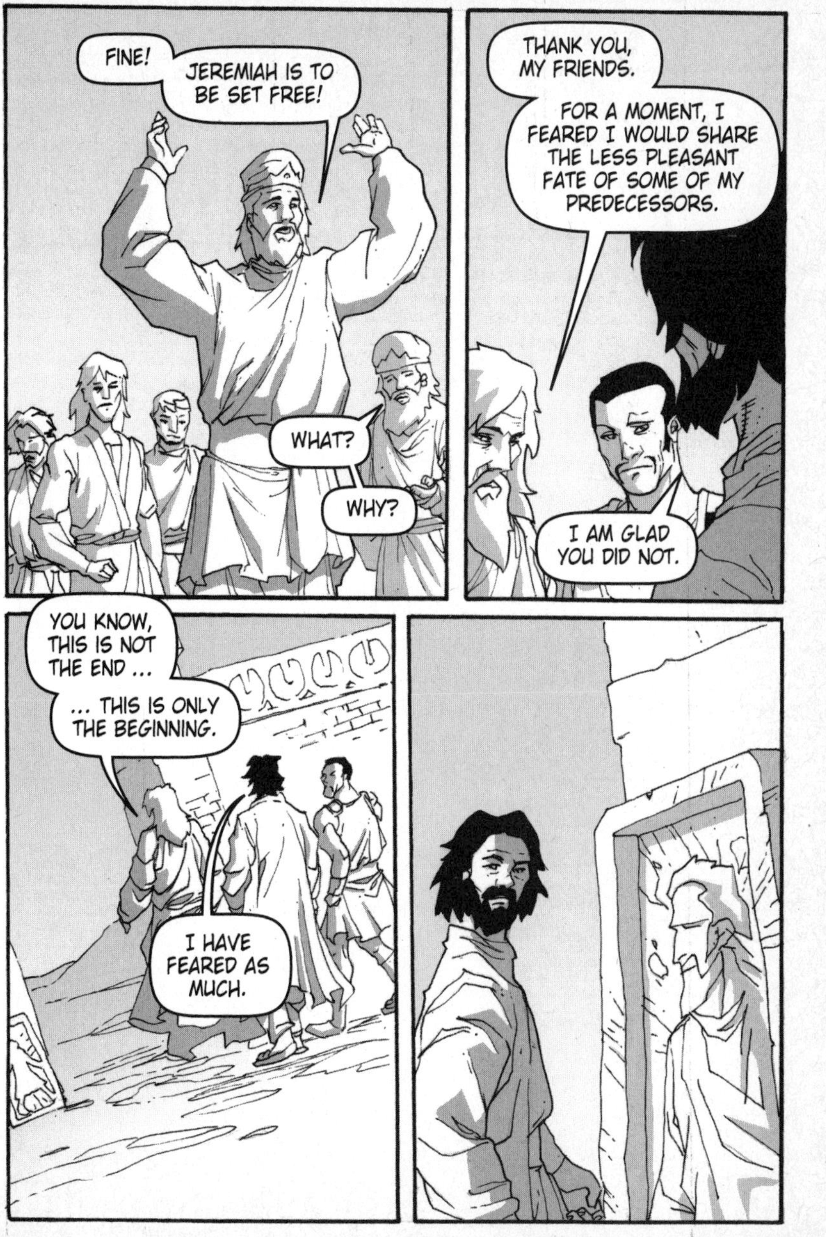
FINE!
JEREMIAH IS TO BE SET FREE!
WHAT?
WHY?
THANK YOU, MY FRIENDS.
FOR A MOMENT, I FEARED I WOULD SHARE THE LESS PLEASANT FATE OF SOME OF MY PREDECESSORS.
I AM GLAD YOU DID NOT.
YOU KNOW, THIS IS NOT THE END ...
... THIS IS ONLY THE BEGINNING.
I HAVE FEARED AS MUCH.

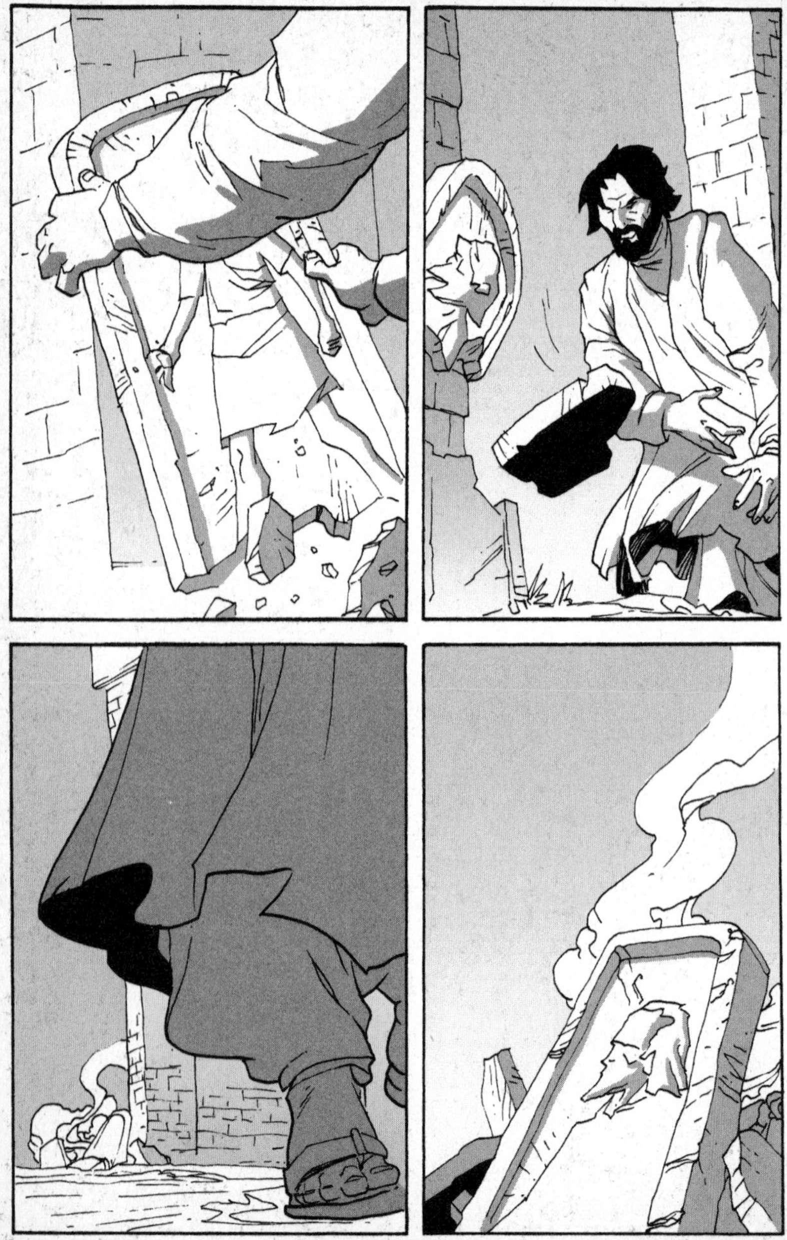

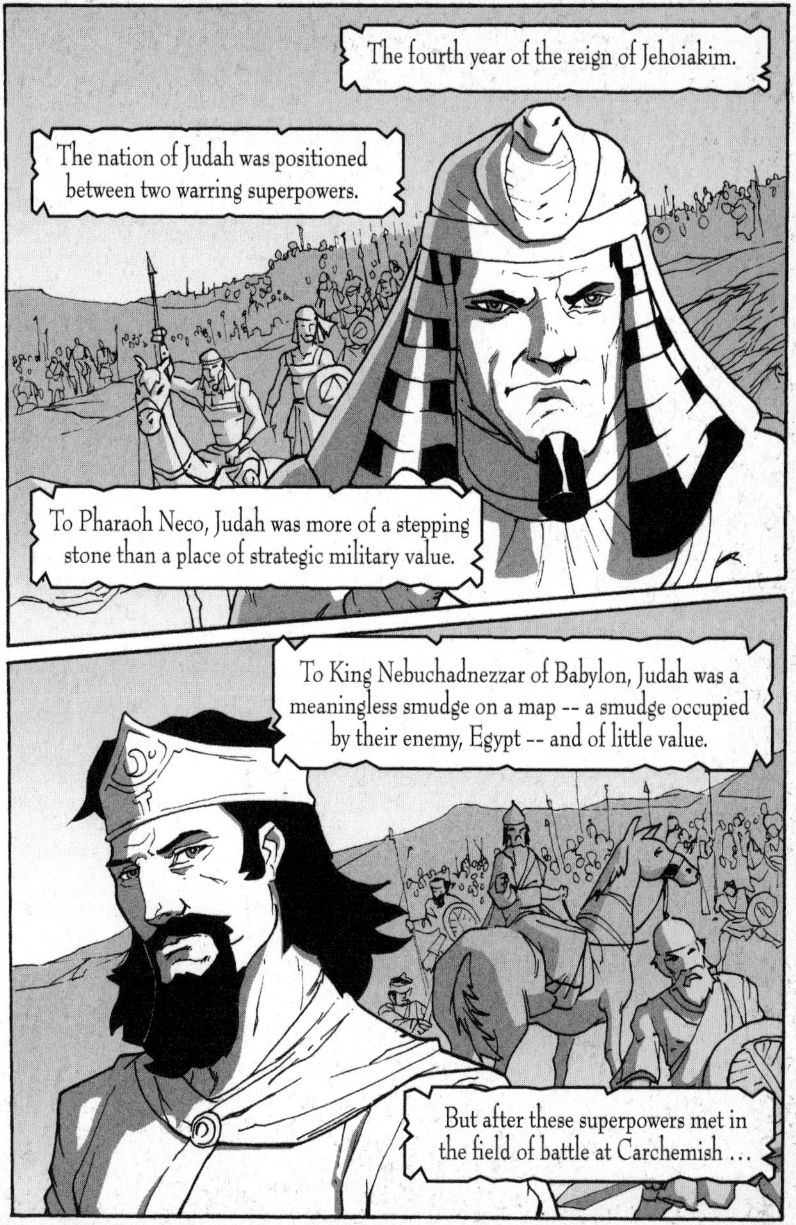
The fourth year of the reign of Jehoiakim.
The nation of Judah was positioned between two warring superpowers.
To Pharaoh Neco, Judah was more of a stepping stone than a place of strategic military value.
To King Nebuchadnezzar of Babylon, Judah was a meaningless smudge on a map -- a smudge occupied by their enemy, Egypt -- and of little value.
But after these superpowers met in the field of battle at Carchemish ...

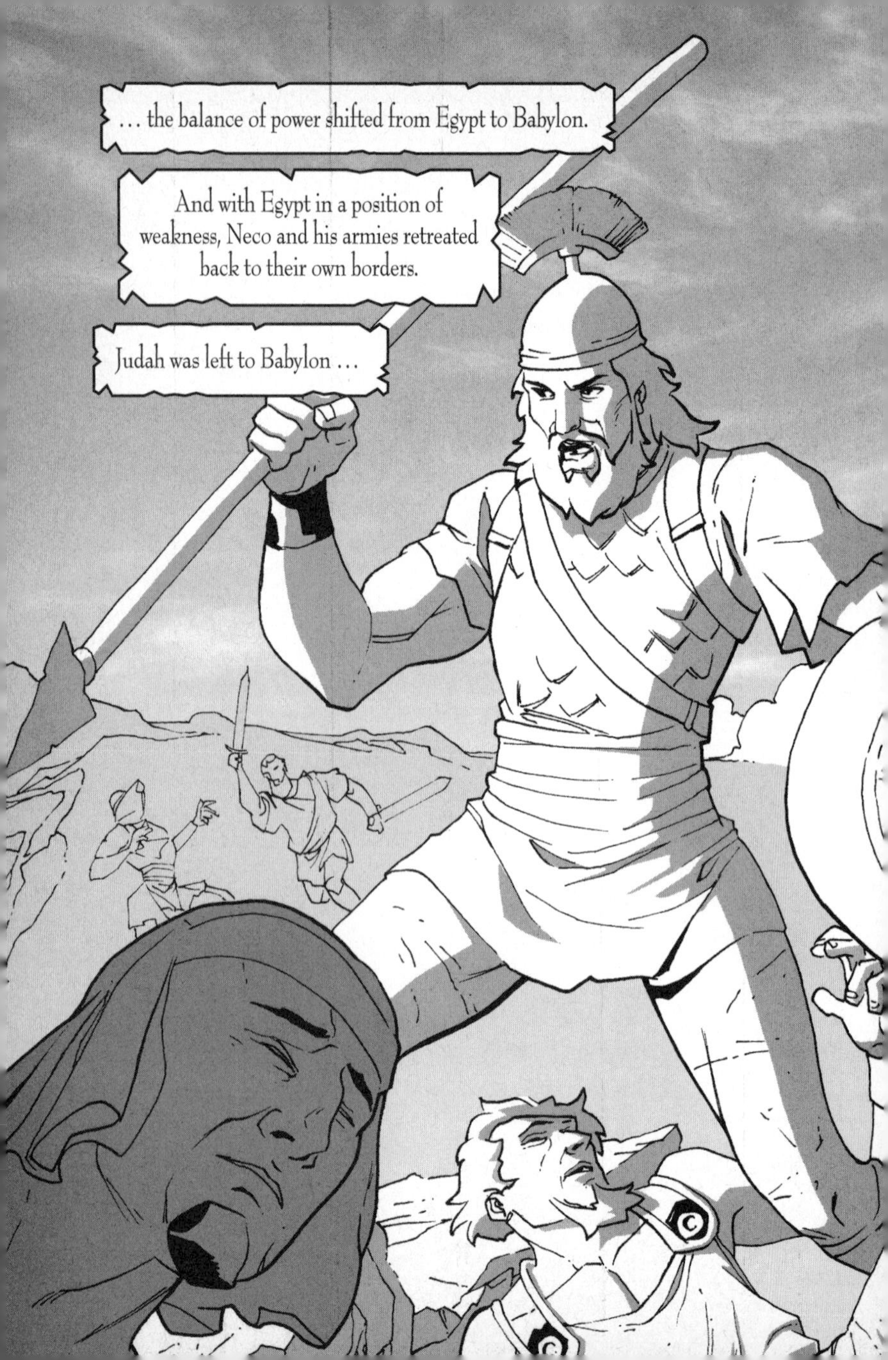
… the balance of power shifted from Egypt to Babylon.
And with Egypt in a position of weakness, Neco and his armies retreated back to their own borders.
Judah was left to Babylon …

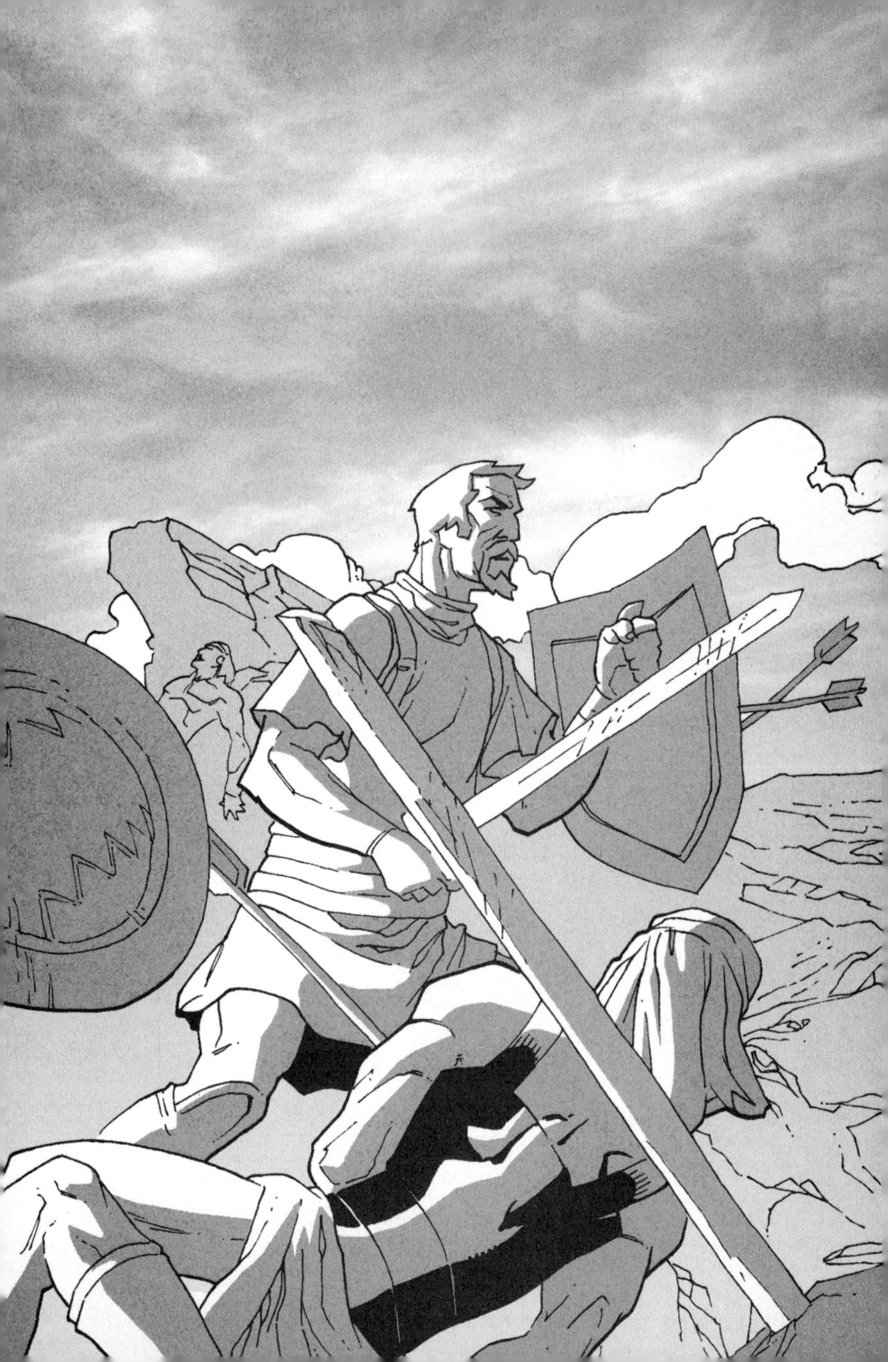

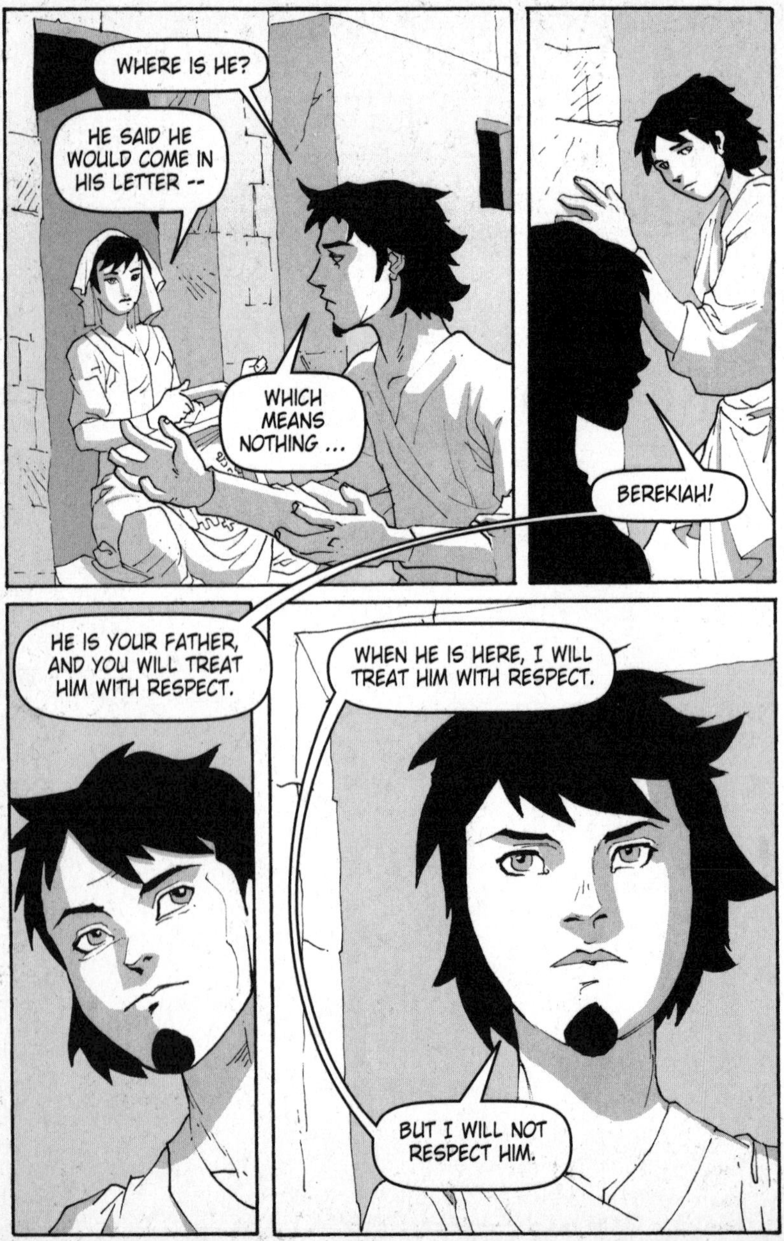
WHERE IS HE?
HE SAID HE WOULD COME IN HIS LETTER --
WHICH MEANS NOTHING ...
BEREKIAH!
HE IS YOUR FATHER, AND YOU WILL TREAT HIM WITH RESPECT.
WHEN HE IS HERE, I WILL TREAT HIM WITH RESPECT.
BUT I WILL NOT RESPECT HIM.

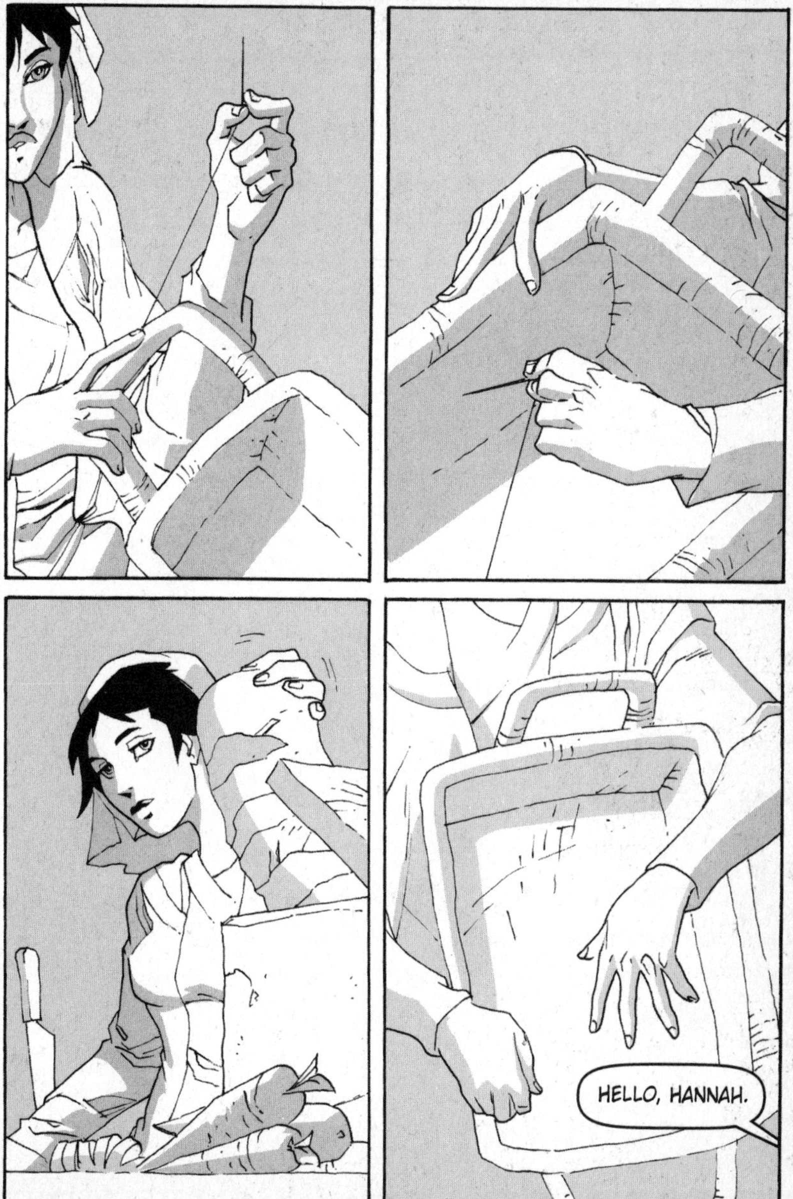
HELLO, HANNAH.

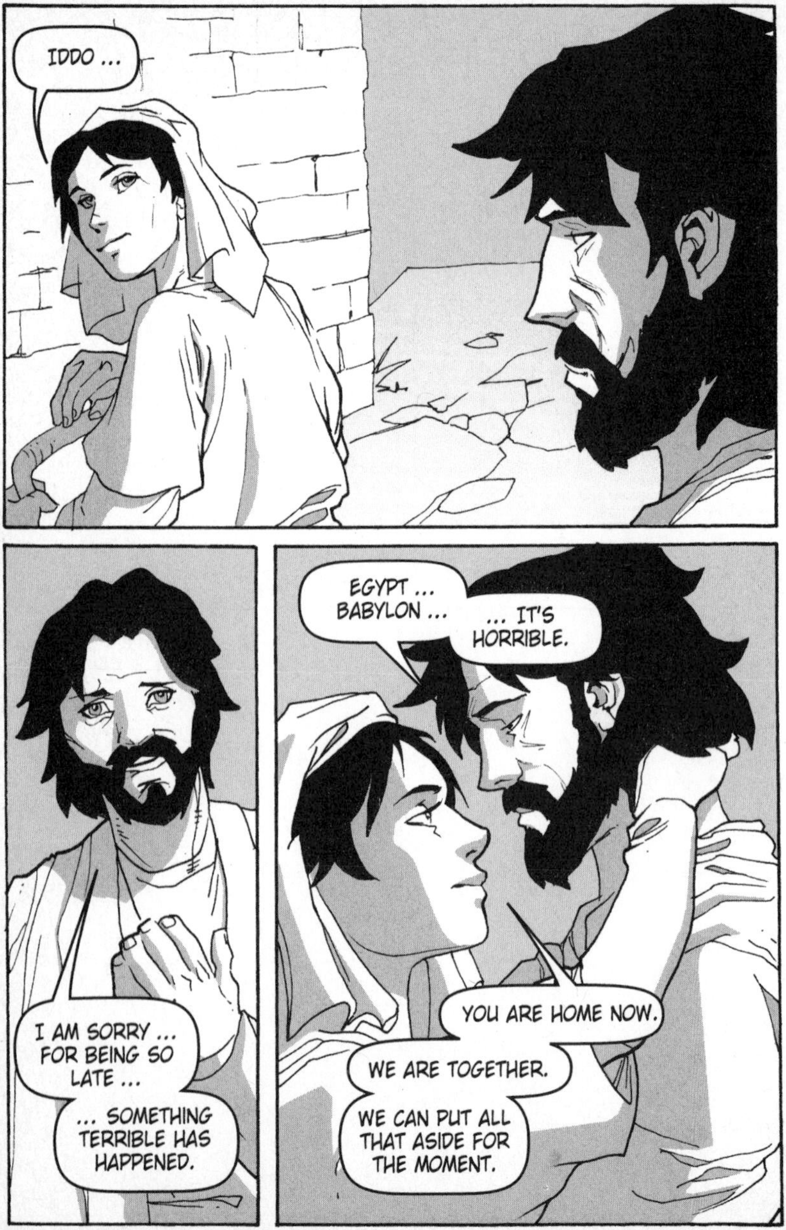
IDDO ...
I AM SORRY ... FOR BEING SO LATE ...
... SOMETHING TERRIBLE HAS HAPPENED.
EGYPT ... BABYLON ...
... IT'S HORRIBLE.
YOU ARE HOME NOW.
WE ARE TOGETHER.
WE CAN PUT ALL THAT ASIDE FOR THE MOMENT.

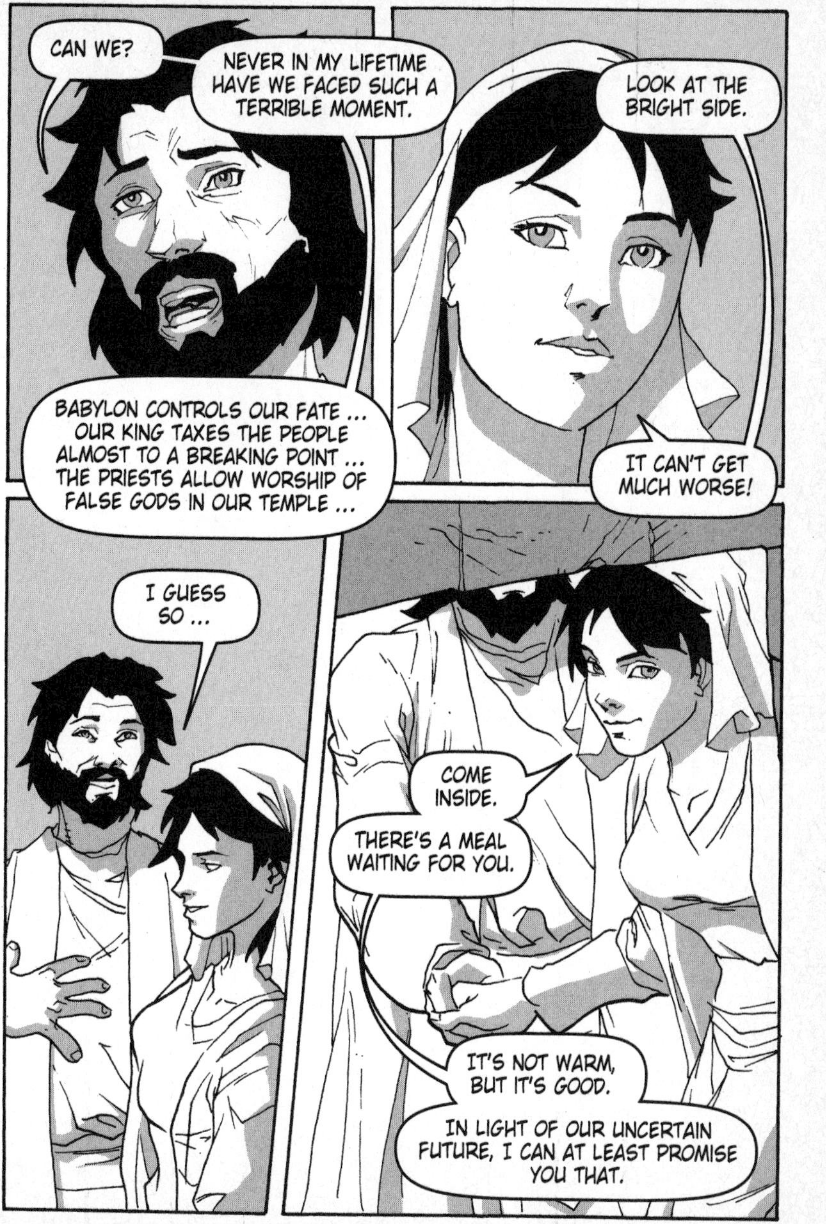
CAN WE?
NEVER IN MY LIFETIME HAVE WE FACED SUCH A TERRIBLE MOMENT.
BABYLON CONTROLS OUR FATE ... OUR KING TAXES THE PEOPLE ALMOST TO A BREAKING POINT ... THE PRIESTS ALLOW WORSHIP OF FALSE GODS IN OUR TEMPLE ...
LOOK AT THE BRIGHT SIDE.
IT CAN'T GET MUCH WORSE!
I GUESS SO ...
COME INSIDE.
THERE'S A MEAL WAITING FOR YOU.
IT'S NOT WARM, BUT IT'S GOOD.
IN LIGHT OF OUR UNCERTAIN FUTURE, I CAN AT LEAST PROMISE YOU THAT.

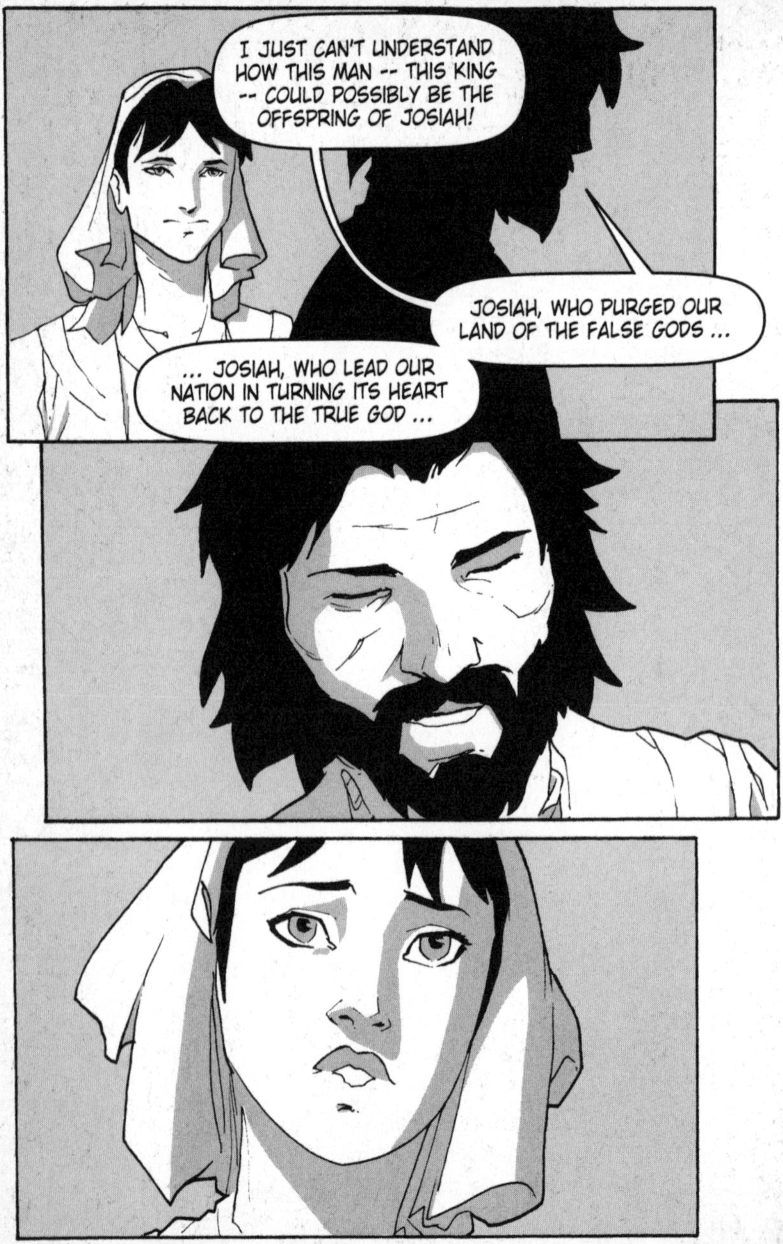
I JUST CAN'T UNDERSTAND HOW THIS MAN -- THIS KING -- COULD POSSIBLY BE THE OFFSPRING OF JOSIAH!
JOSIAH, WHO PURGED OUR LAND OF THE FALSE GODS ...
... JOSIAH, WHO LEAD OUR NATION IN TURNING ITS HEART BACK TO THE TRUE GOD ...

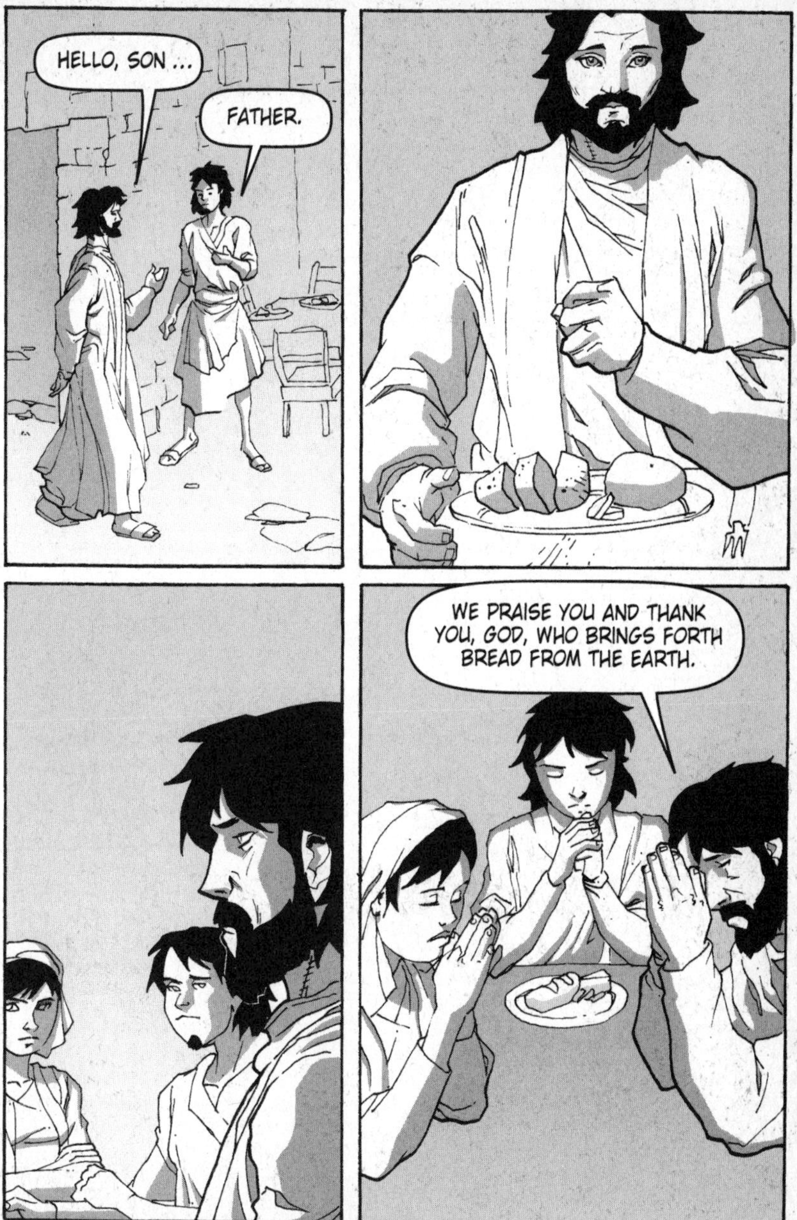
HELLO, SON ...
FATHER.
WE PRAISE YOU AND THANK YOU, GOD, WHO BRINGS FORTH BREAD FROM THE EARTH.

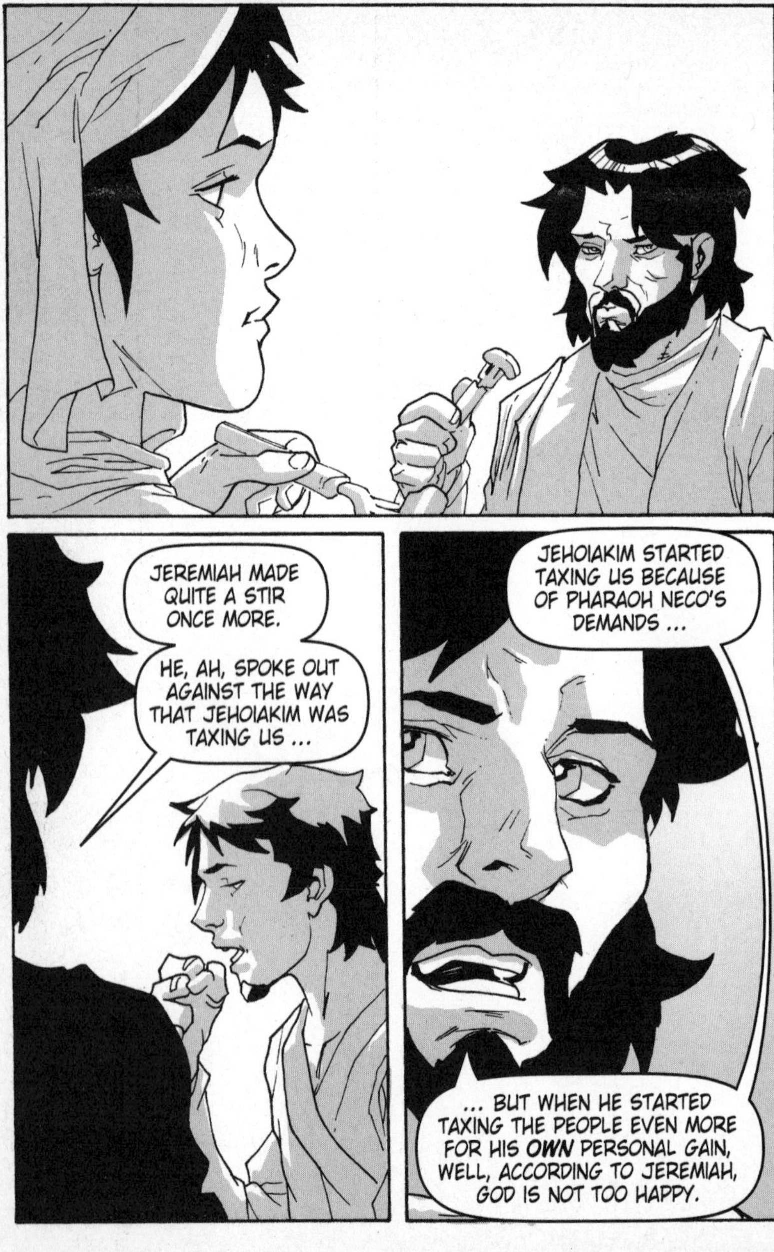
JEREMIAH MADE QUITE A STIR ONCE MORE.
HE, AH, SPOKE OUT AGAINST THE WAY THAT JEHOIAKIM WAS TAXING US ...
JEHOIAKIM STARTED TAXING US BECAUSE OF PHARAOH NECO'S DEMANDS ...
... BUT WHEN HE STARTED TAXING THE PEOPLE EVEN MORE FOR HIS ***OWN*** PERSONAL GAIN, WELL, ACCORDING TO JEREMIAH, GOD IS NOT TOO HAPPY.

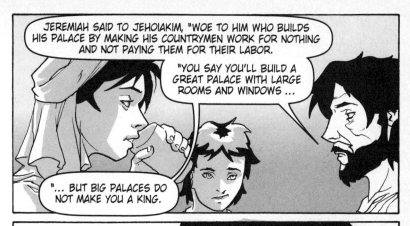

JEREMIAH SAID TO JEHOIAKIM, "WOE TO HIM WHO BUILDS HIS PALACE BY MAKING HIS COUNTRYMEN WORK FOR NOTHING AND NOT PAYING THEM FOR THEIR LABOR.

"YOU SAY YOU'LL BUILD A GREAT PALACE WITH LARGE ROOMS AND WINDOWS ...

"... BUT BIG PALACES DO NOT MAKE YOU A KING.

"YOUR FATHER DID WHAT WAS RIGHT, BUT YOUR EYES ARE SET ONLY ON YOUR *OWN* GAIN.

"YOU WILL DIE AND NO ONE WILL MOURN FOR YOU.

"YOU WILL HAVE THE BURIAL OF A DONKEY, DRAGGED AWAY AND THROWN OUTSIDE THE GATES OF THE CITY."

IT'S TERRIBLE, HOW MANY CHILDREN OF GREAT MEN TURN OUT TO BE HORRIBLE TYRANTS.

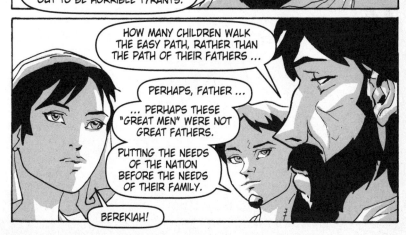

HOW MANY CHILDREN WALK THE EASY PATH, RATHER THAN THE PATH OF THEIR FATHERS ...

PERHAPS, FATHER ...

... PERHAPS THESE "GREAT MEN" WERE NOT GREAT FATHERS.

PUTTING THE NEEDS OF THE NATION BEFORE THE NEEDS OF THEIR FAMILY.

BEREKIAH!

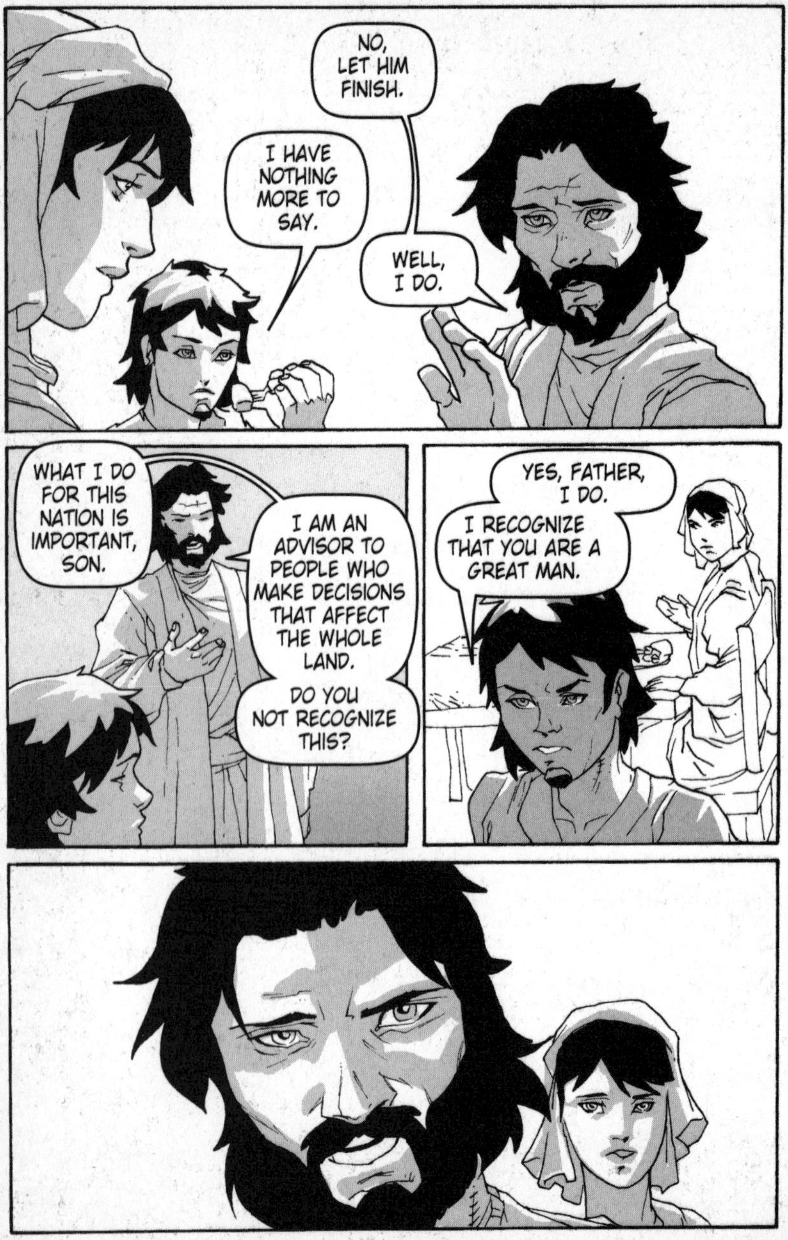
NO, LET HIM FINISH.
I HAVE NOTHING MORE TO SAY.
WELL, I DO.
WHAT I DO FOR THIS NATION IS IMPORTANT, SON.
I AM AN ADVISOR TO PEOPLE WHO MAKE DECISIONS THAT AFFECT THE WHOLE LAND.
DO YOU NOT RECOGNIZE THIS?
YES, FATHER, I DO.
I RECOGNIZE THAT YOU ARE A GREAT MAN.

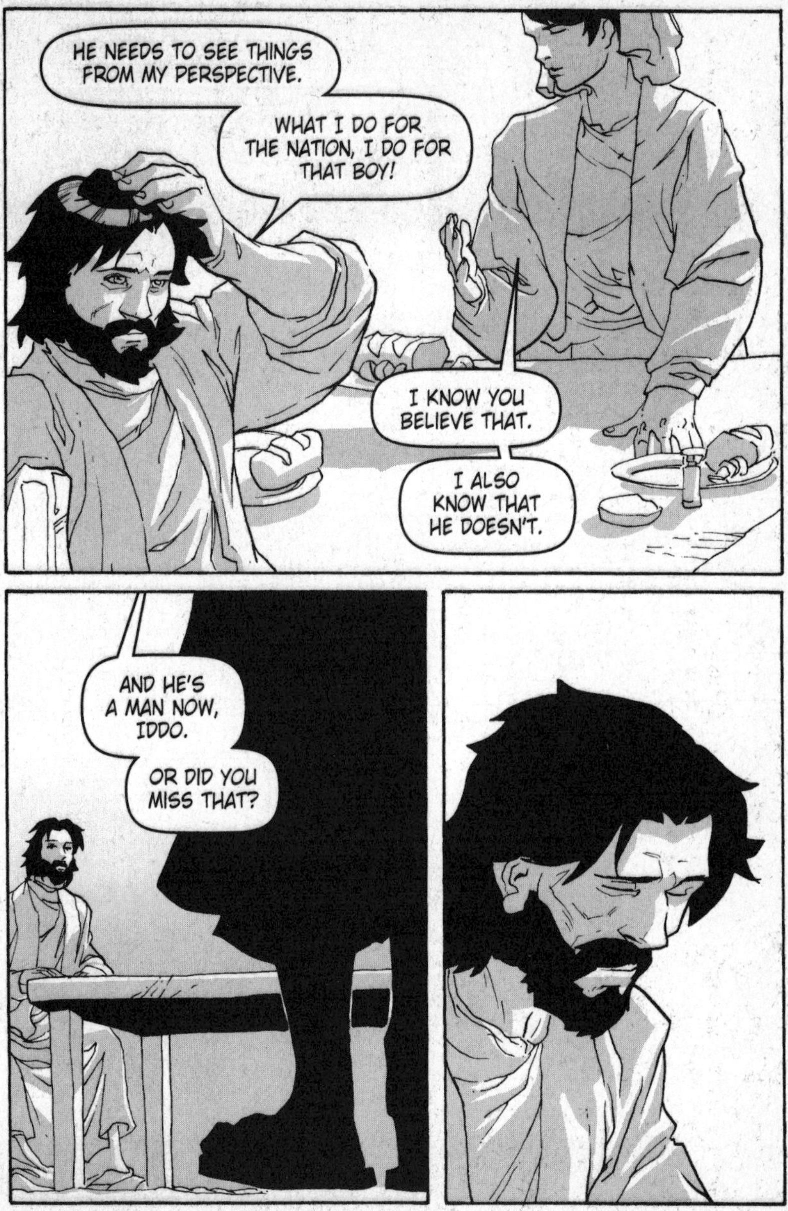
HE NEEDS TO SEE THINGS FROM MY PERSPECTIVE.
WHAT I DO FOR THE NATION, I DO FOR THAT BOY!
I KNOW YOU BELIEVE THAT.
I ALSO KNOW THAT HE DOESN'T.
AND HE'S A MAN NOW, IDDO.
OR DID YOU MISS THAT?

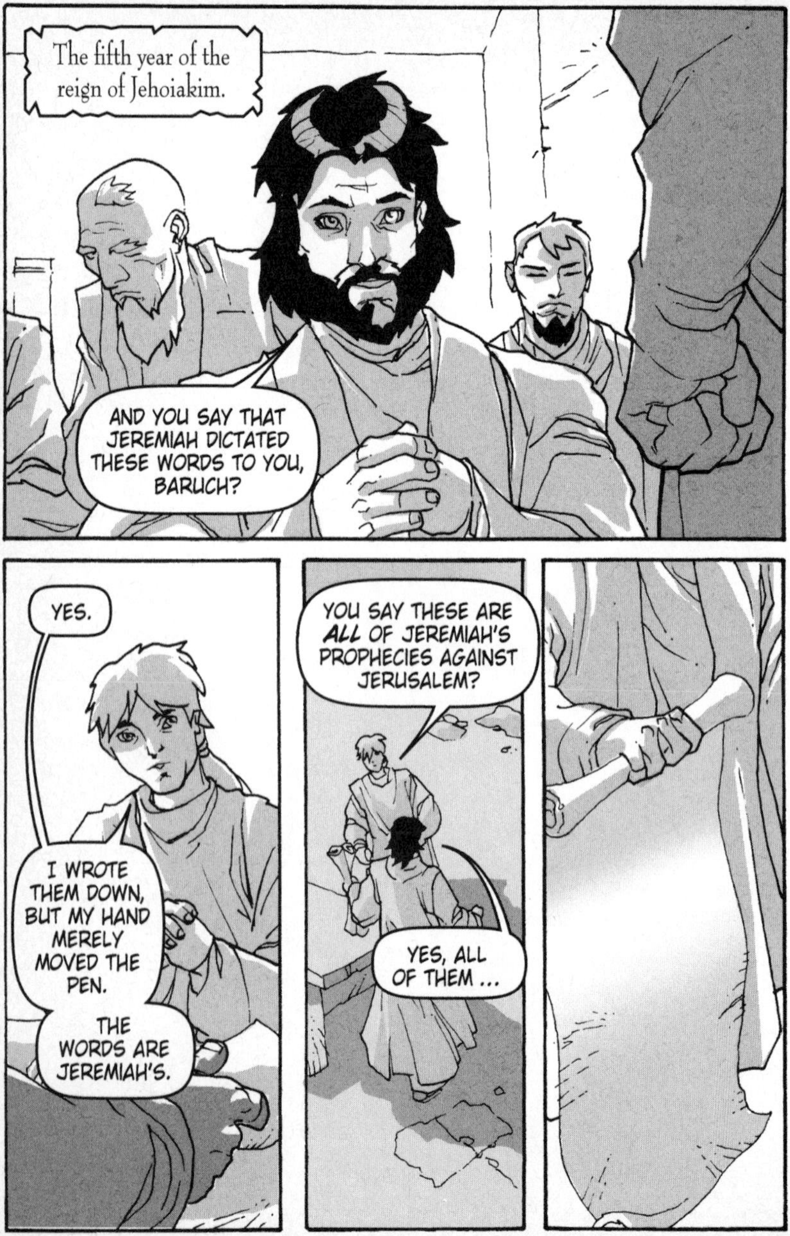
The fifth year of the reign of Jehoiakim.
AND YOU SAY THAT JEREMIAH DICTATED THESE WORDS TO YOU, BARUCH?
YES.
I WROTE THEM DOWN, BUT MY HAND MERELY MOVED THE PEN.
THE WORDS ARE JEREMIAH'S.
YOU SAY THESE ARE *ALL* OF JEREMIAH'S PROPHECIES AGAINST JERUSALEM?
YES, ALL OF THEM ...

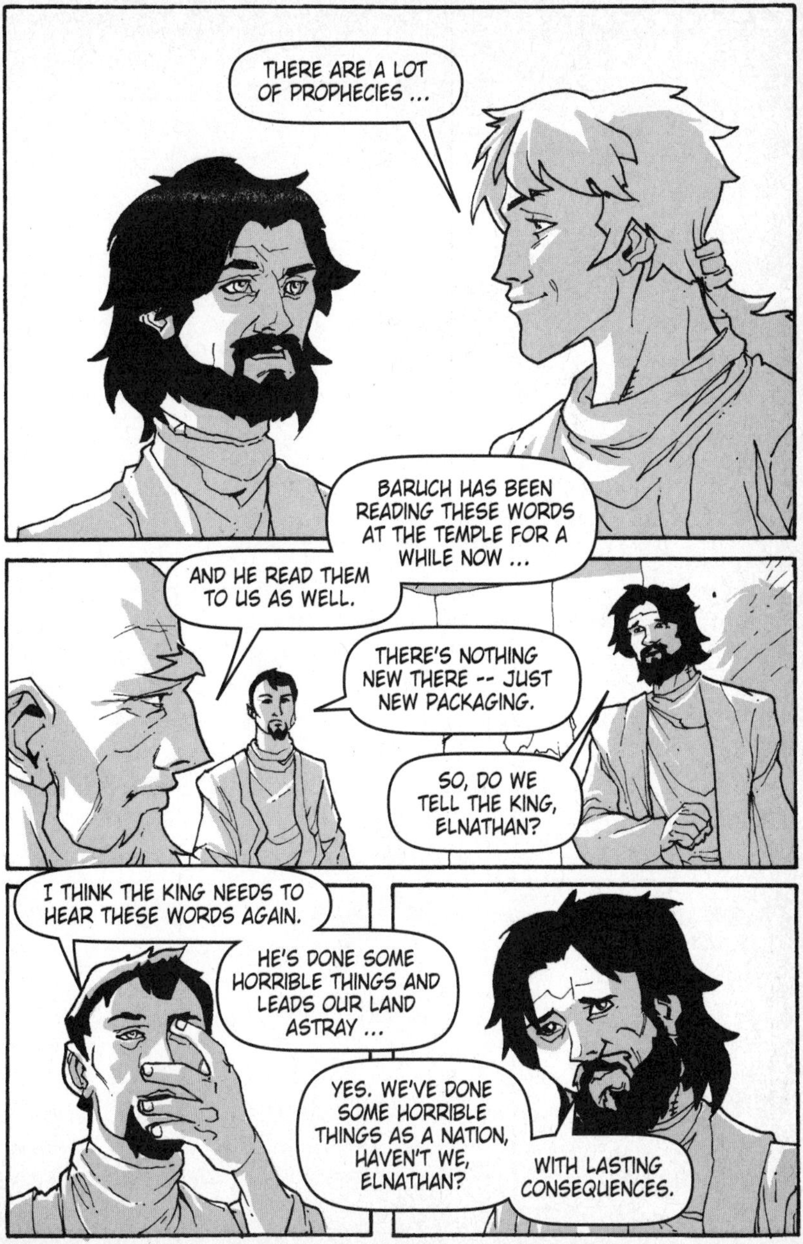
THERE ARE A LOT OF PROPHECIES ...
BARUCH HAS BEEN READING THESE WORDS AT THE TEMPLE FOR A WHILE NOW ...
AND HE READ THEM TO US AS WELL.
THERE'S NOTHING NEW THERE -- JUST NEW PACKAGING.
SO, DO WE TELL THE KING, ELNATHAN?
I THINK THE KING NEEDS TO HEAR THESE WORDS AGAIN.
HE'S DONE SOME HORRIBLE THINGS AND LEADS OUR LAND ASTRAY ...
YES. WE'VE DONE SOME HORRIBLE THINGS AS A NATION, HAVEN'T WE, ELNATHAN?
WITH LASTING CONSEQUENCES.

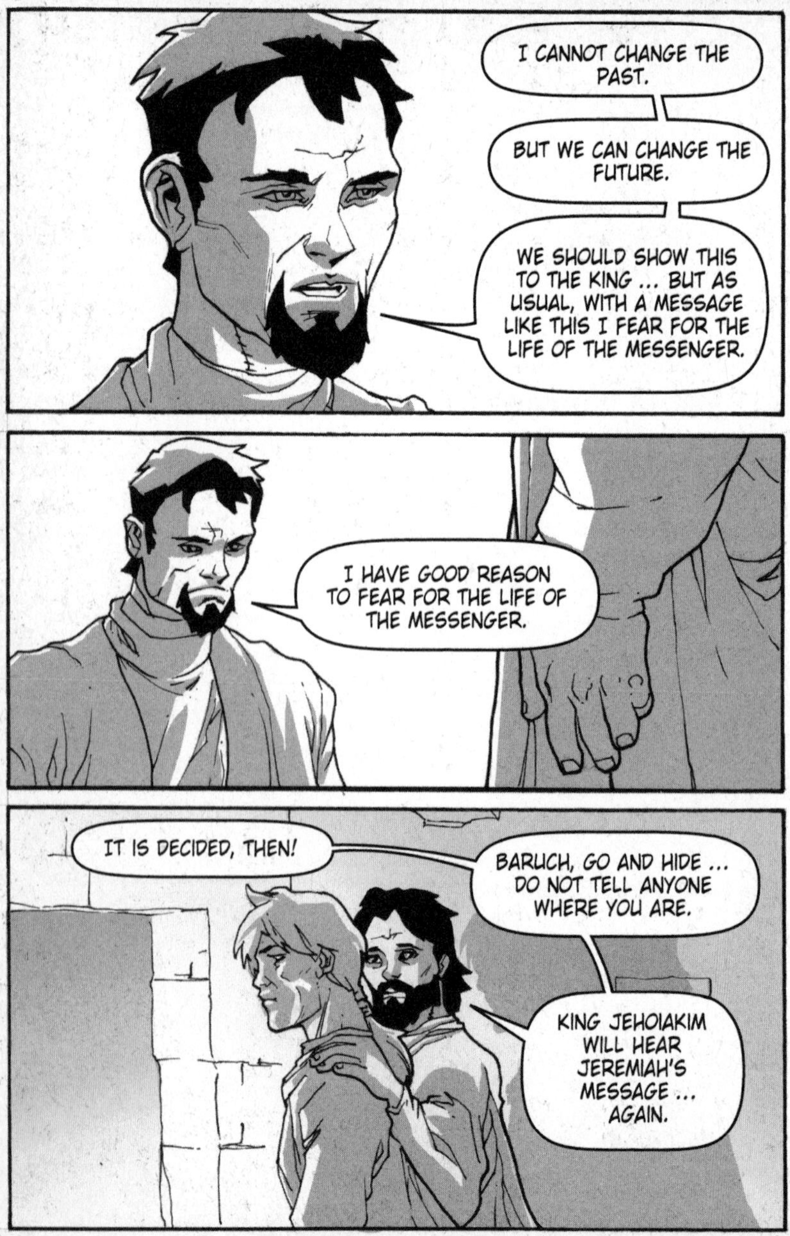
I CANNOT CHANGE THE PAST.
BUT WE CAN CHANGE THE FUTURE.
WE SHOULD SHOW THIS TO THE KING ... BUT AS USUAL, WITH A MESSAGE LIKE THIS I FEAR FOR THE LIFE OF THE MESSENGER.
I HAVE GOOD REASON TO FEAR FOR THE LIFE OF THE MESSENGER.
IT IS DECIDED, THEN!
BARUCH, GO AND HIDE ... DO NOT TELL ANYONE WHERE YOU ARE.
KING JEHOIAKIM WILL HEAR JEREMIAH'S MESSAGE ... AGAIN.

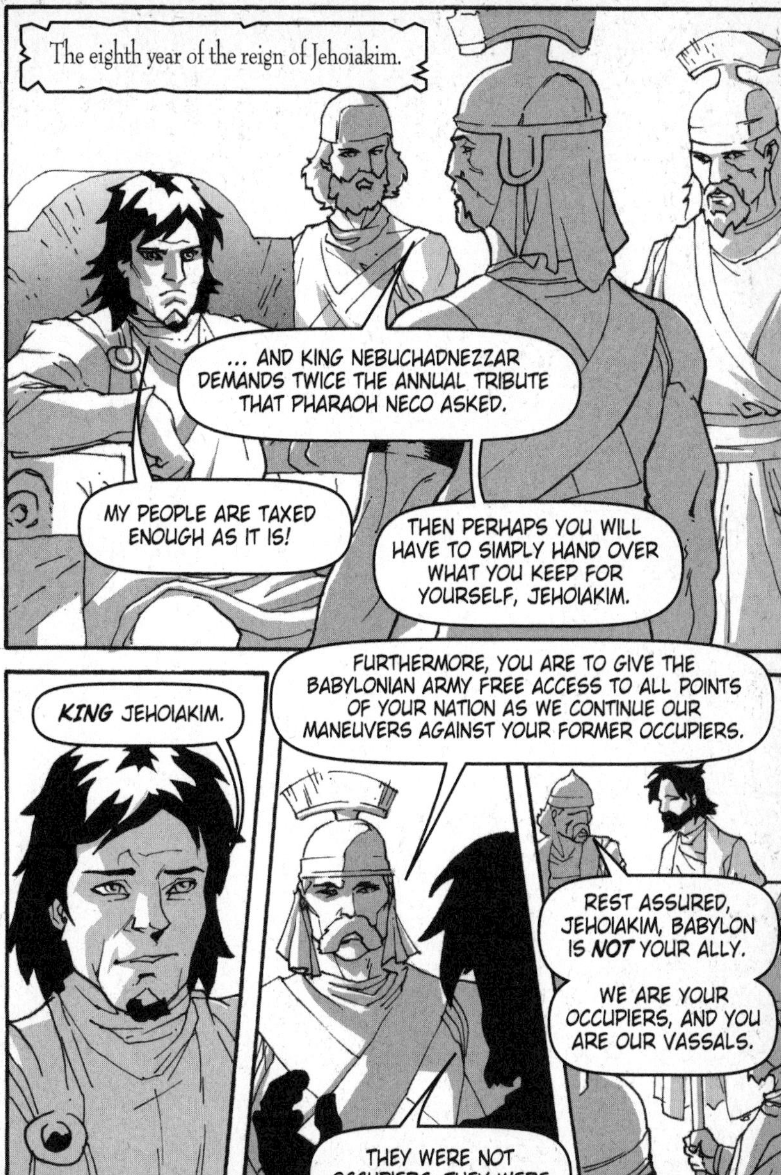
The eighth year of the reign of Jehoiakim.
... AND KING NEBUCHADNEZZAR DEMANDS TWICE THE ANNUAL TRIBUTE THAT PHARAOH NECO ASKED.
MY PEOPLE ARE TAXED ENOUGH AS IT IS!
THEN PERHAPS YOU WILL HAVE TO SIMPLY HAND OVER WHAT YOU KEEP FOR YOURSELF, JEHOIAKIM.
KING JEHOIAKIM.
FURTHERMORE, YOU ARE TO GIVE THE BABYLONIAN ARMY FREE ACCESS TO ALL POINTS OF YOUR NATION AS WE CONTINUE OUR MANEUVERS AGAINST YOUR FORMER OCCUPIERS.
THEY WERE NOT OCCUPIERS; THEY WERE ALLIES.
REST ASSURED, JEHOIAKIM, BABYLON IS *NOT* YOUR ALLY.
WE ARE YOUR OCCUPIERS, AND YOU ARE OUR VASSALS.

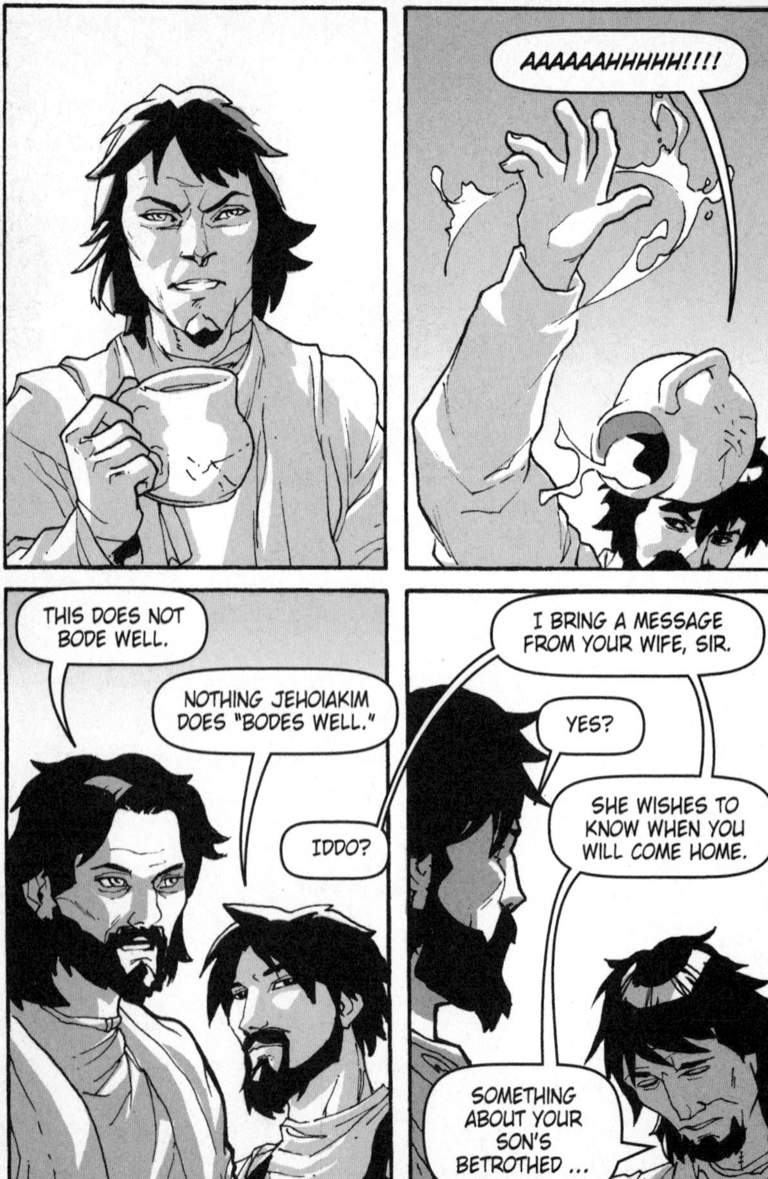
AAAAAAHHHHH!!!!
THIS DOES NOT BODE WELL.
NOTHING JEHOIAKIM DOES "BODES WELL."
IDDO?
I BRING A MESSAGE FROM YOUR WIFE, SIR.
YES?
SHE WISHES TO KNOW WHEN YOU WILL COME HOME.
SOMETHING ABOUT YOUR SON'S BETROTHED ...

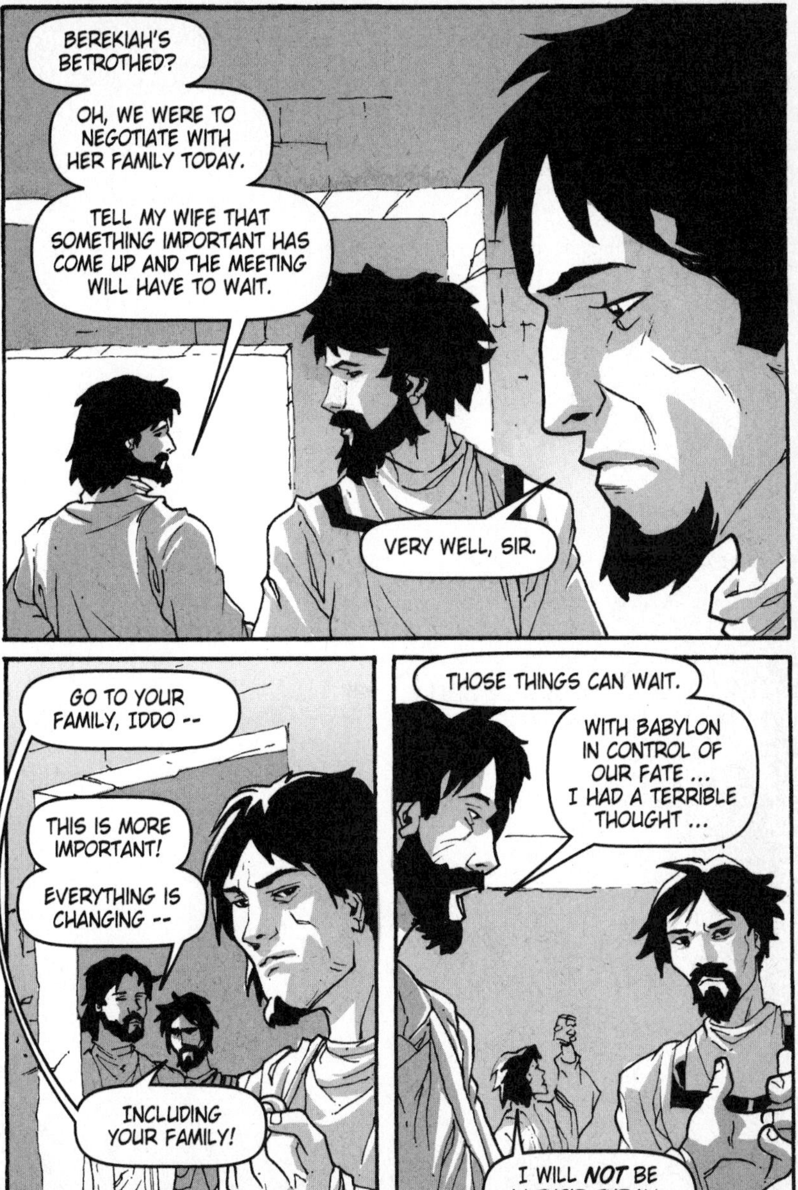
BEREKIAH'S BETROTHED?
OH, WE WERE TO NEGOTIATE WITH HER FAMILY TODAY.
TELL MY WIFE THAT SOMETHING IMPORTANT HAS COME UP AND THE MEETING WILL HAVE TO WAIT.
VERY WELL, SIR.
GO TO YOUR FAMILY, IDDO --
THIS IS MORE IMPORTANT!
EVERYTHING IS CHANGING --
INCLUDING YOUR FAMILY!
THOSE THINGS CAN WAIT.
WITH BABYLON IN CONTROL OF OUR FATE ... I HAD A TERRIBLE THOUGHT ...
I WILL ***NOT*** BE IN THEIR THRALL FOR ***LONG!***

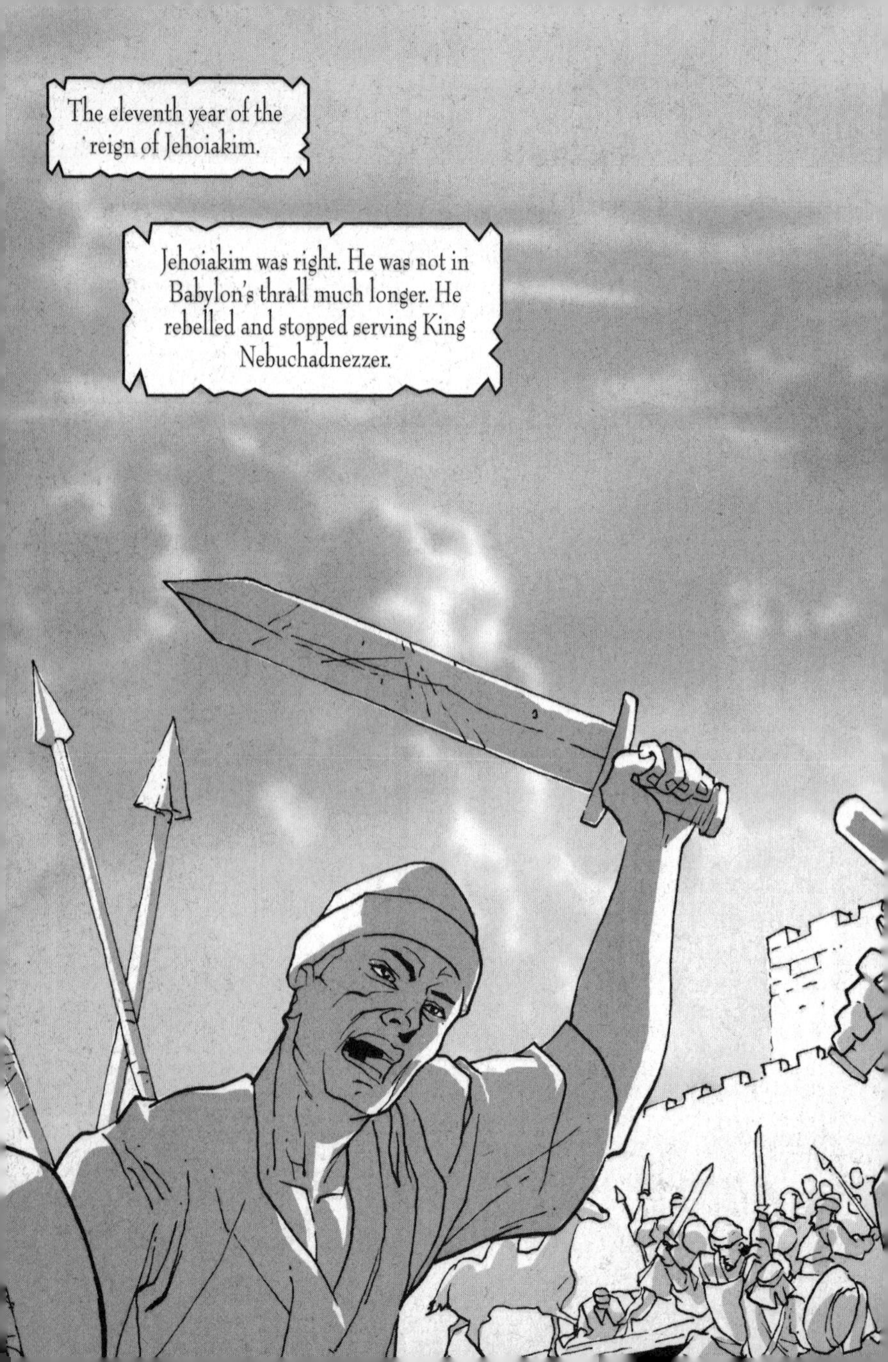
The eleventh year of the reign of Jehoiakim.
Jehoiakim was right. He was not in Babylon's thrall much longer. He rebelled and stopped serving King Nebuchadnezzer.

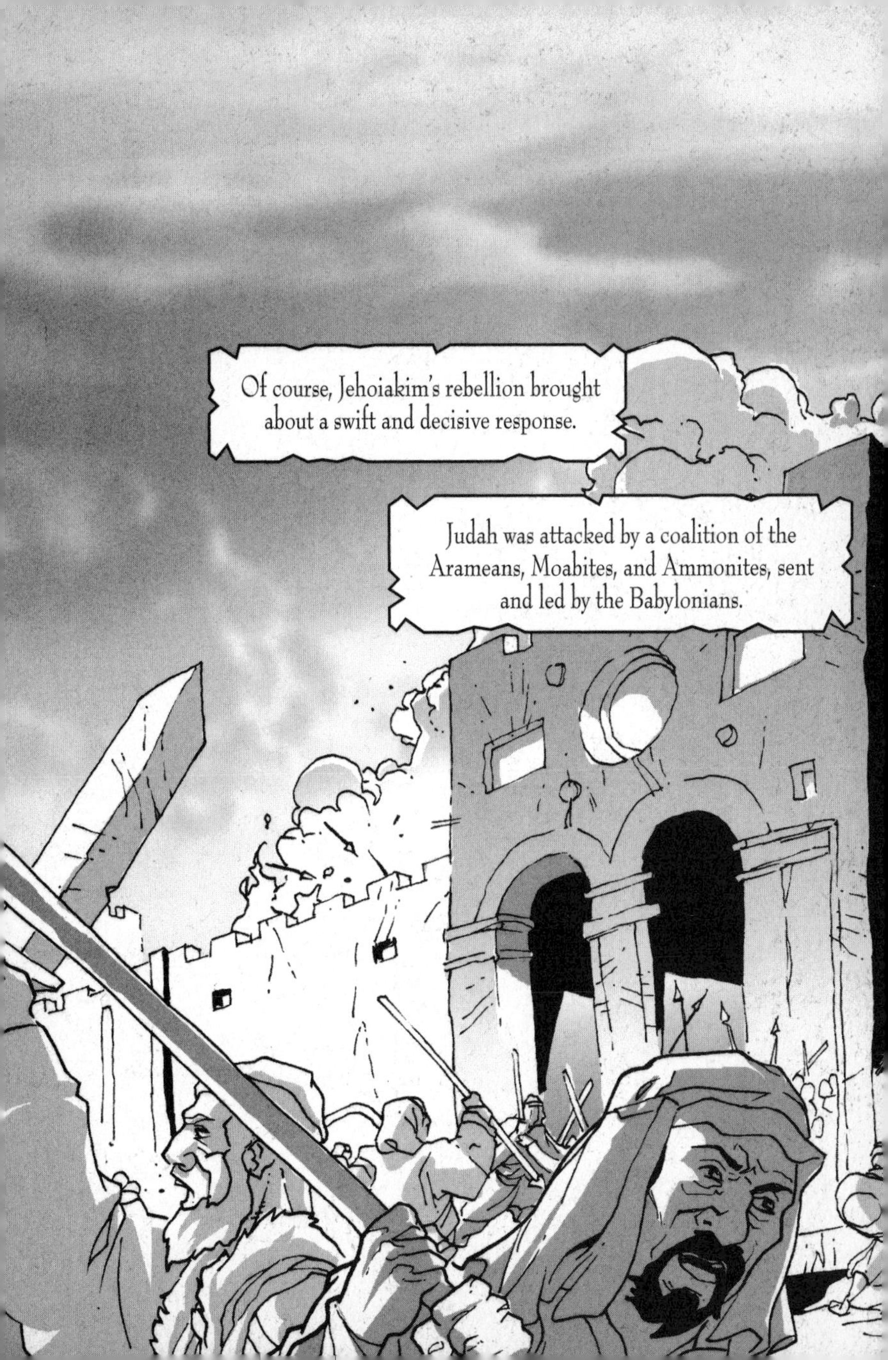
Of course, Jehoiakim's rebellion brought about a swift and decisive response.
Judah was attacked by a coalition of the Arameans, Moabites, and Ammonites, sent and led by the Babylonians.

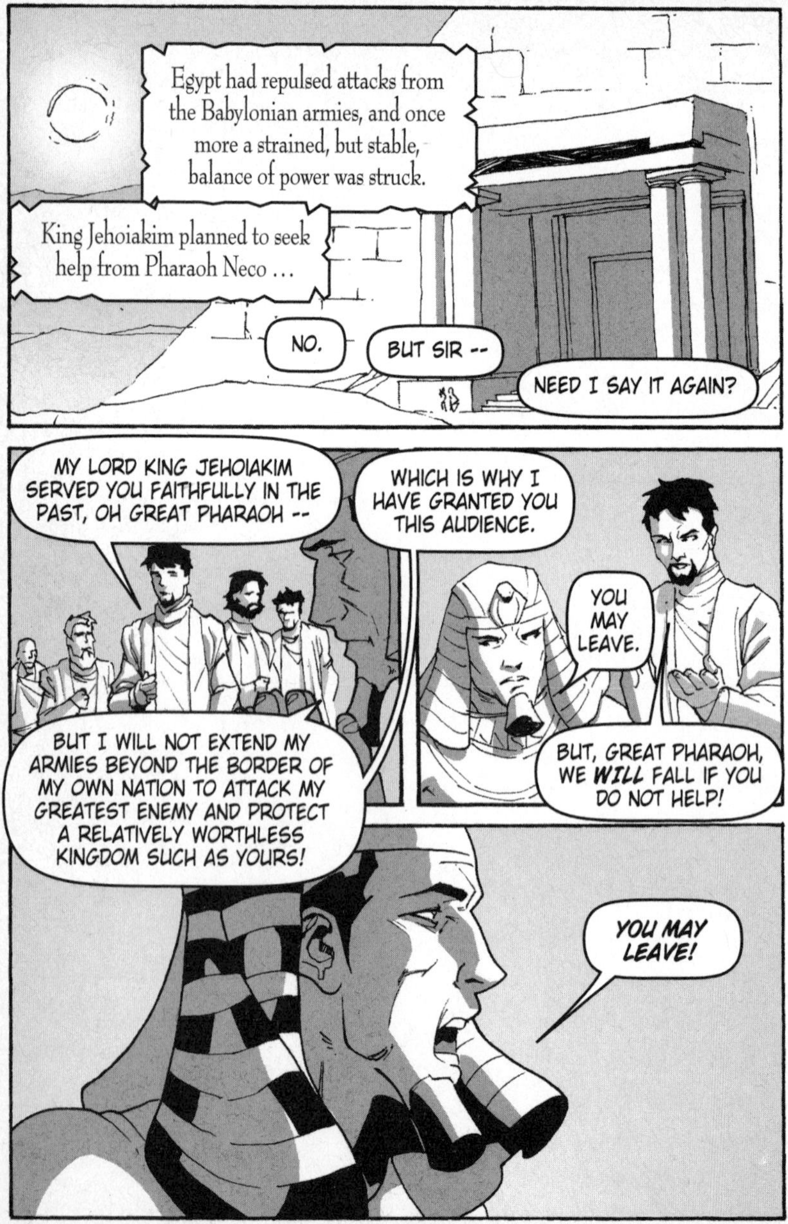
Egypt had repulsed attacks from the Babylonian armies, and once more a strained, but stable, balance of power was struck.
King Jehoiakim planned to seek help from Pharaoh Neco …
NO.
BUT SIR --
NEED I SAY IT AGAIN?
MY LORD KING JEHOIAKIM SERVED YOU FAITHFULLY IN THE PAST, OH GREAT PHARAOH --
WHICH IS WHY I HAVE GRANTED YOU THIS AUDIENCE.
BUT I WILL NOT EXTEND MY ARMIES BEYOND THE BORDER OF MY OWN NATION TO ATTACK MY GREATEST ENEMY AND PROTECT A RELATIVELY WORTHLESS KINGDOM SUCH AS YOURS!
YOU MAY LEAVE.
BUT, GREAT PHARAOH, WE *WILL* FALL IF YOU DO NOT HELP!
YOU MAY LEAVE!

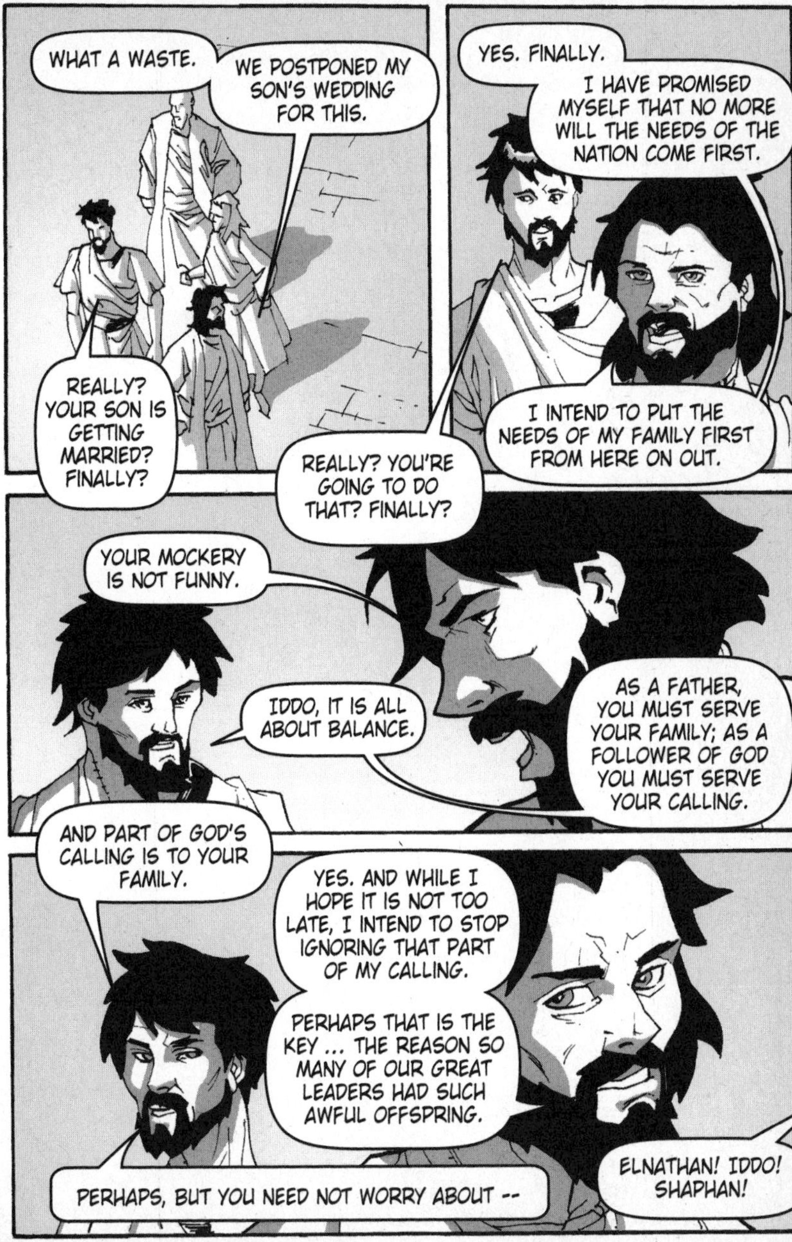
WHAT A WASTE.
WE POSTPONED MY SON'S WEDDING FOR THIS.
REALLY? YOUR SON IS GETTING MARRIED? FINALLY?
YES. FINALLY.
I HAVE PROMISED MYSELF THAT NO MORE WILL THE NEEDS OF THE NATION COME FIRST.
I INTEND TO PUT THE NEEDS OF MY FAMILY FIRST FROM HERE ON OUT.
REALLY? YOU'RE GOING TO DO THAT? FINALLY?
YOUR MOCKERY IS NOT FUNNY.
IDDO, IT IS ALL ABOUT BALANCE.
AS A FATHER, YOU MUST SERVE YOUR FAMILY; AS A FOLLOWER OF GOD YOU MUST SERVE YOUR CALLING.
AND PART OF GOD'S CALLING IS TO YOUR FAMILY.
YES. AND WHILE I HOPE IT IS NOT TOO LATE, I INTEND TO STOP IGNORING THAT PART OF MY CALLING.
PERHAPS THAT IS THE KEY ... THE REASON SO MANY OF OUR GREAT LEADERS HAD SUCH AWFUL OFFSPRING.
PERHAPS, BUT YOU NEED NOT WORRY ABOUT --
ELNATHAN! IDDO! SHAPHAN!

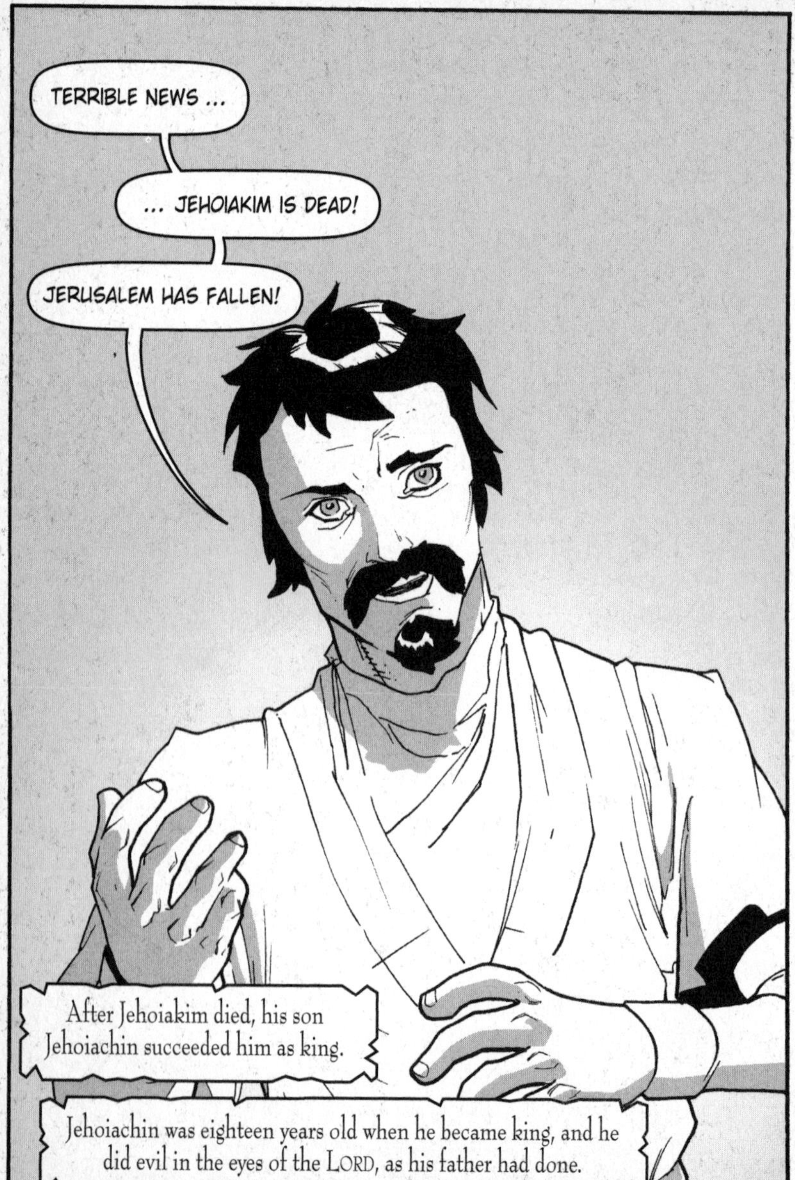
TERRIBLE NEWS ...
... JEHOIAKIM IS DEAD!
JERUSALEM HAS FALLEN!
After Jehoiakim died, his son Jehoiachin succeeded him as king.
Jehoiachin was eighteen years old when he became king, and he did evil in the eyes of the LORD, as his father had done.

CHAPTER THREE
"All the Treasures of Judah"

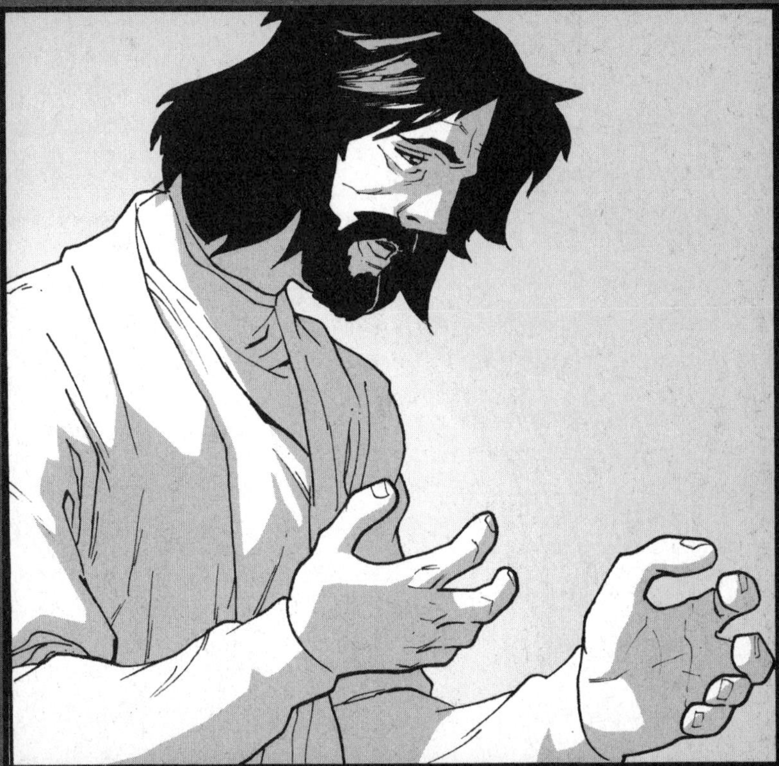

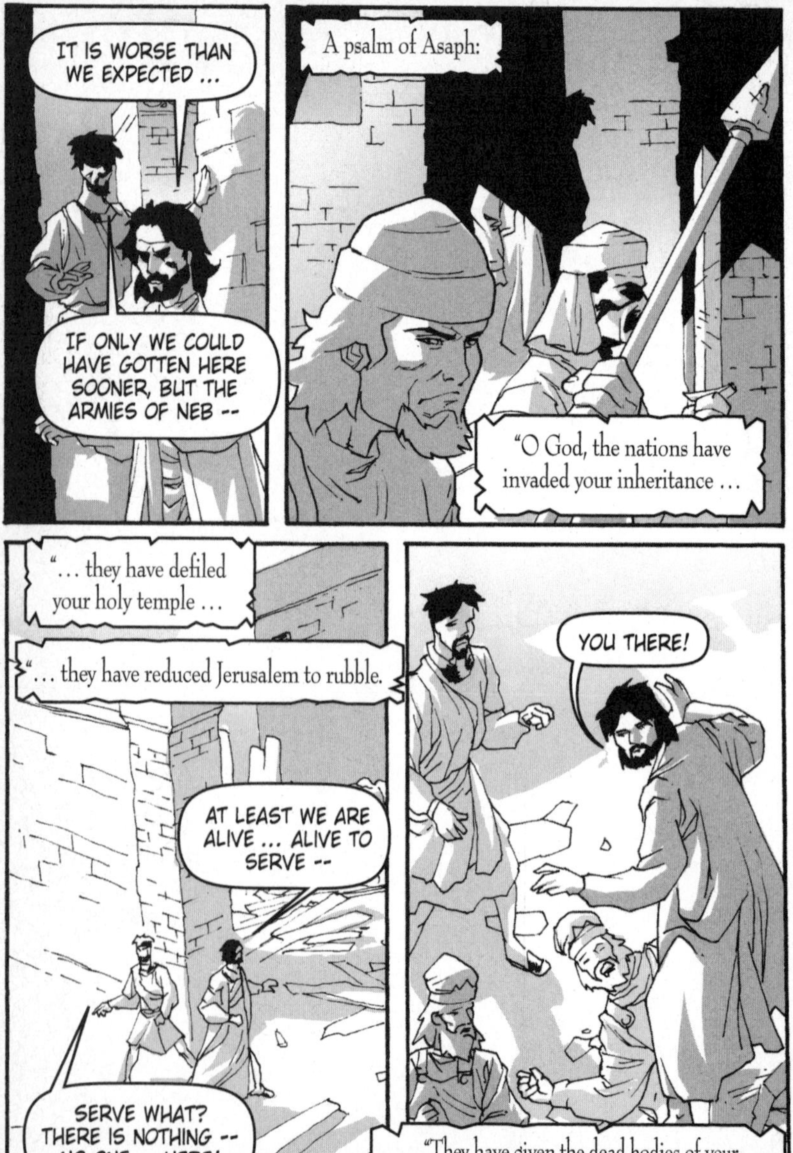
IT IS WORSE THAN WE EXPECTED ...
IF ONLY WE COULD HAVE GOTTEN HERE SOONER, BUT THE ARMIES OF NEB --
A psalm of Asaph:
"O God, the nations have invaded your inheritance ...
"... they have defiled your holy temple ...
"... they have reduced Jerusalem to rubble.
AT LEAST WE ARE ALIVE ... ALIVE TO SERVE --
SERVE WHAT? THERE IS NOTHING -- NO ONE -- HERE!
YOU THERE!
"They have given the dead bodies of your servants as food to the birds of the air, the flesh of your saints to the beasts of the earth.

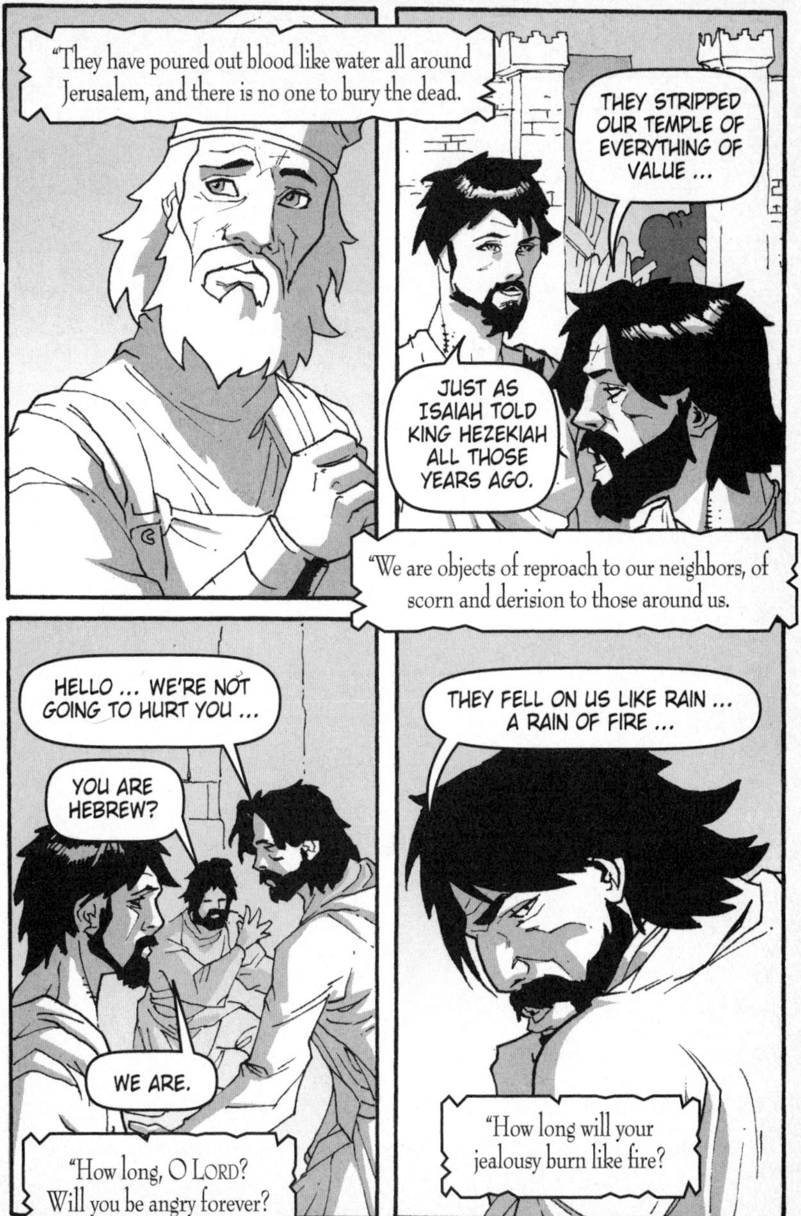
"They have poured out blood like water all around Jerusalem, and there is no one to bury the dead.
THEY STRIPPED OUR TEMPLE OF EVERYTHING OF VALUE ...
JUST AS ISAIAH TOLD KING HEZEKIAH ALL THOSE YEARS AGO.
"We are objects of reproach to our neighbors, of scorn and derision to those around us.
HELLO ... WE'RE NOT GOING TO HURT YOU ...
YOU ARE HEBREW?
WE ARE.
"How long, O LORD? Will you be angry forever?
THEY FELL ON US LIKE RAIN ... A RAIN OF FIRE ...
"How long will your jealousy burn like fire?

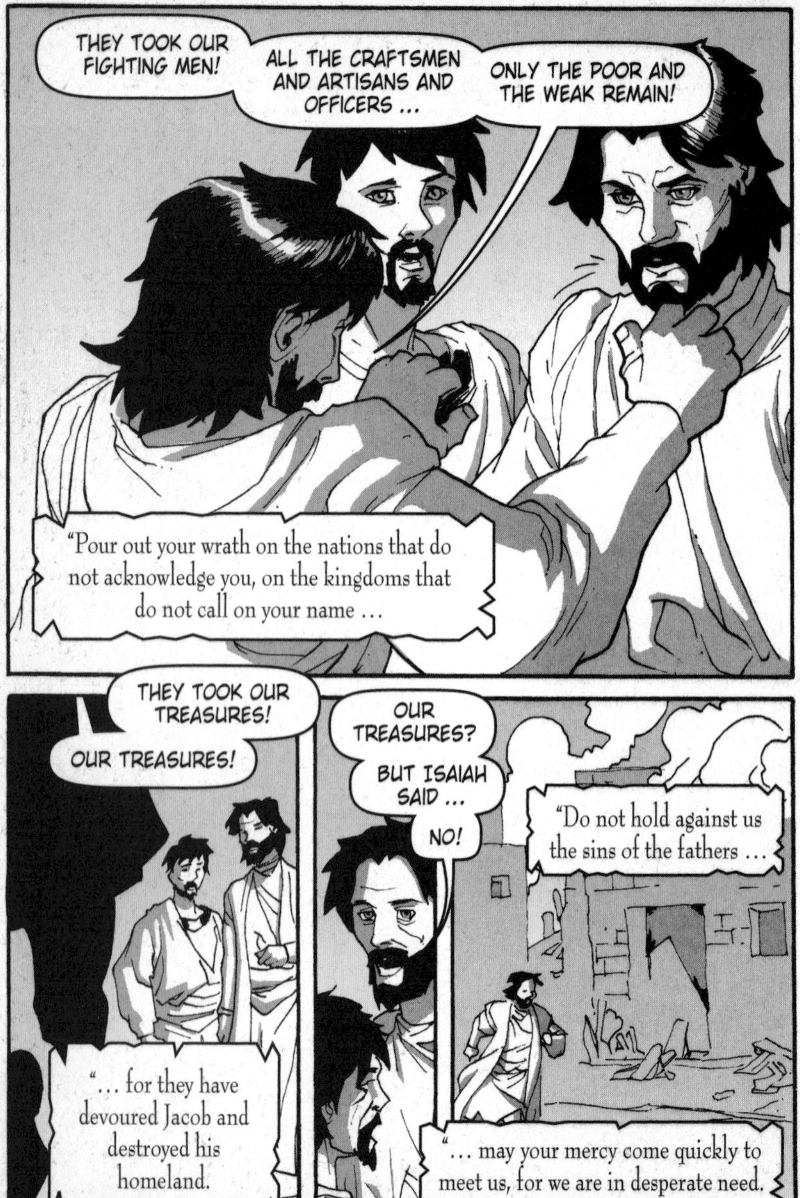
THEY TOOK OUR FIGHTING MEN!
ALL THE CRAFTSMEN AND ARTISANS AND OFFICERS ...
ONLY THE POOR AND THE WEAK REMAIN!
"Pour out your wrath on the nations that do not acknowledge you, on the kingdoms that do not call on your name …
THEY TOOK OUR TREASURES!
OUR TREASURES!
"… for they have devoured Jacob and destroyed his homeland.
OUR TREASURES?
BUT ISAIAH SAID ...
NO!
"Do not hold against us the sins of the fathers …
"… may your mercy come quickly to meet us, for we are in desperate need.

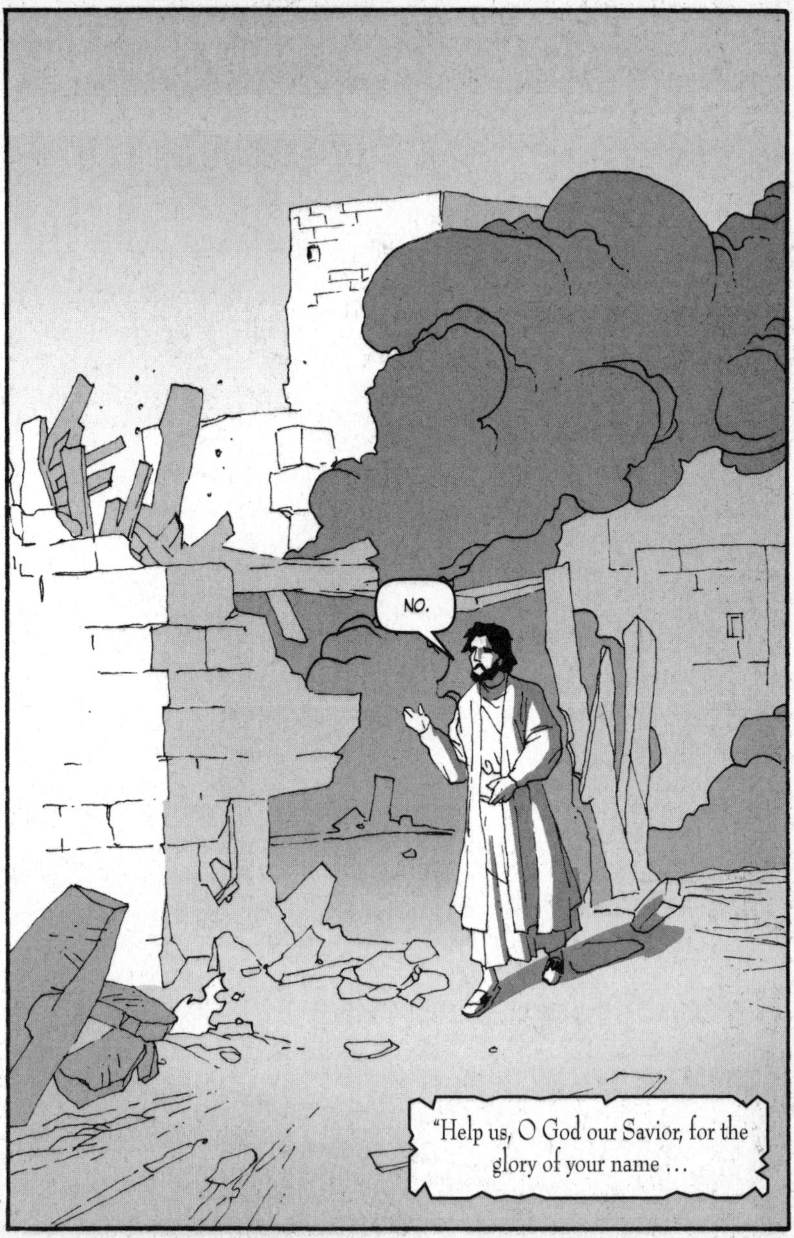
NO.
"Help us, O God our Savior, for the glory of your name …

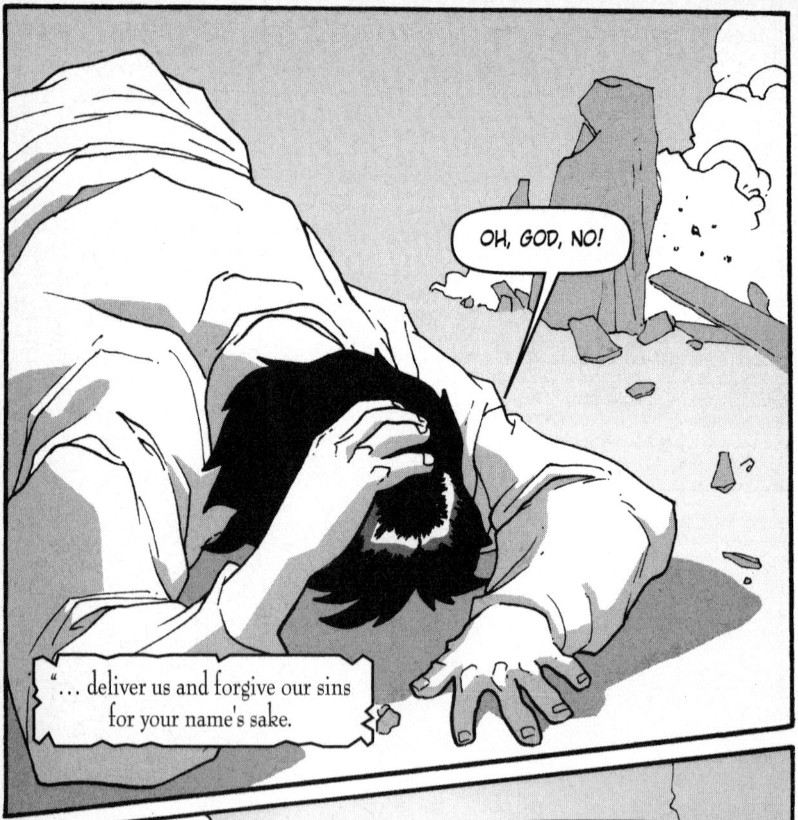
OH, GOD, NO!
"... deliver us and forgive our sins for your name's sake.

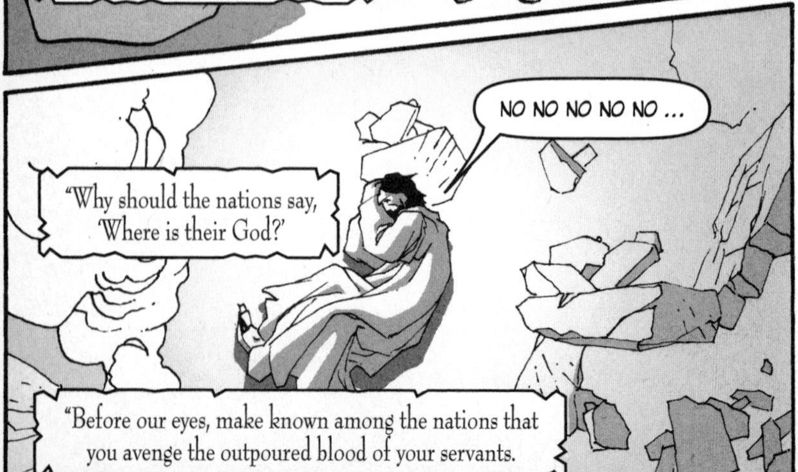
"Why should the nations say, 'Where is their God?'
NO NO NO NO NO ...
"Before our eyes, make known among the nations that you avenge the outpoured blood of your servants.

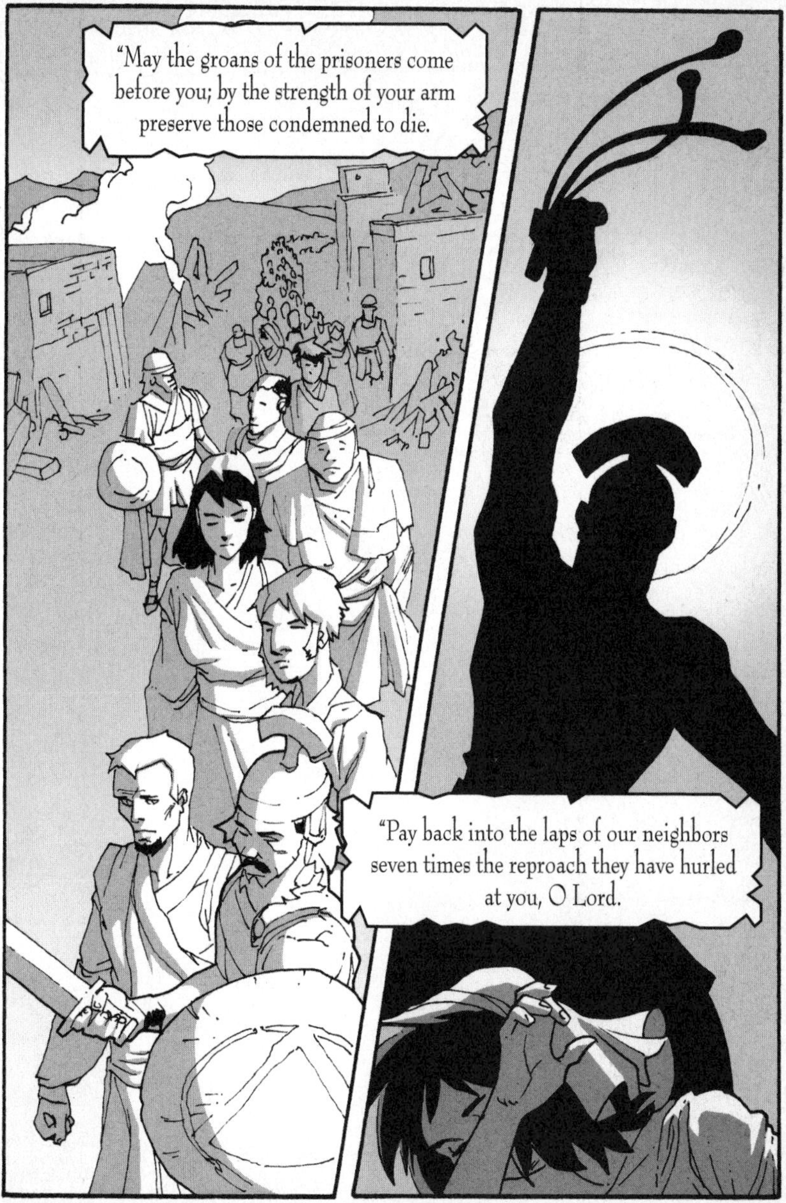
"May the groans of the prisoners come before you; by the strength of your arm preserve those condemned to die.
"Pay back into the laps of our neighbors seven times the reproach they have hurled at you, O Lord.

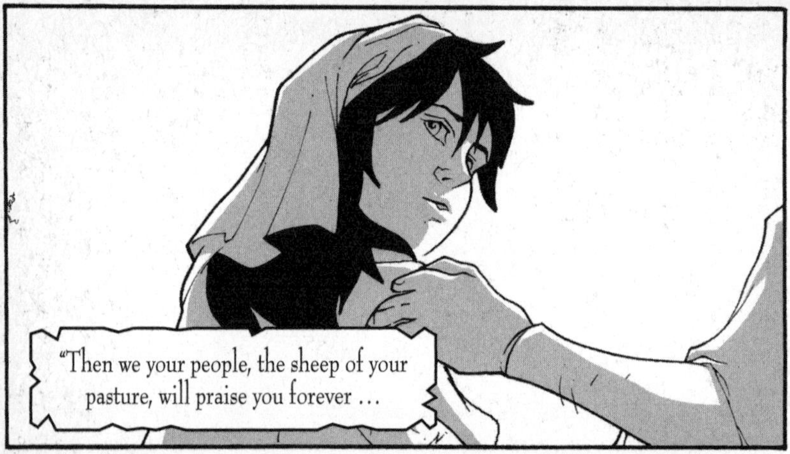
"Then we your people, the sheep of your pasture, will praise you forever …

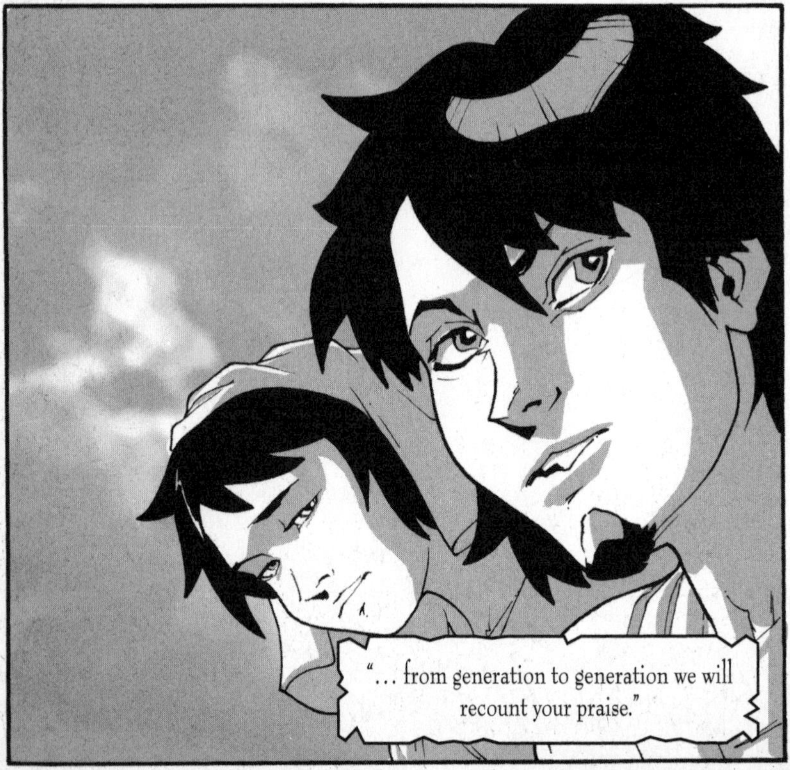
"… from generation to generation we will recount your praise."

FLYING THROUGH TIME TO SAVE THE WORLD!

Pyramid Peril
Available Now!

Turtle Trouble
Available Now!

Berlin Breakout
Available February 2008!

Tunnel Twist-Up
Available May 2008!

AVAILABLE AT YOUR LOCAL BOOKSTORE!

VOLUMES 5-8 COMING SOON!

ZONDERVAN®

We want to hear from you. Please send your comments
about this book to us in care of zreview@zondervan.com. Thank you.

Grand Rapids, MI 49530
www.zonderkidz.com

ZONDERVAN.com/
AUTHORTRACKER
follow your favorite authors

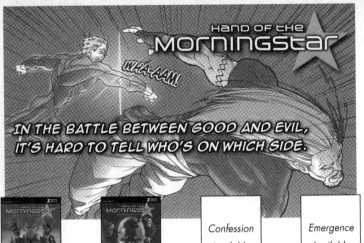

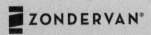